Dangers That Lie Within

Loving Blindly series

Alicia Amberg

3

Is it mommy or daddy issues?
We accept both.

Acknowledgements

First and foremost I want to thank my editor, Sadie, founder of Dot The i Edit, for saving me from failure. If it weren't for you, this book would not be readable.

I would like to thank Melissa Lam who I was lucky to find in the writing community. I learned so much from you and am thankful for all the dedicated time you took to help me grow.

Thank you to all my Alpha, Beta, and ARC readers.

To my Brother Trevor for helping me with a title and Kaziah for helping me with the cover.

Dedication

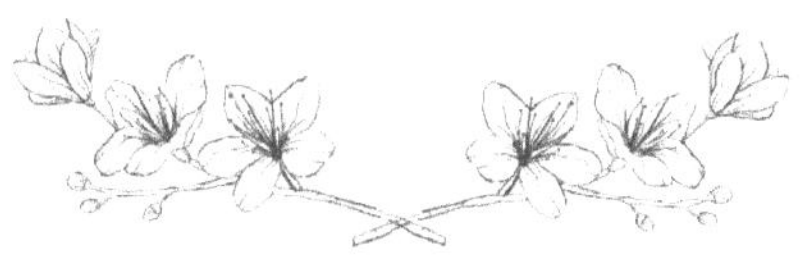

Husband, not only did you contribute to scene inspiration but were forced to listen to the trash draft. I love you. Buckle up for round two.

Trigger Warnings

Graphic sexual scenes, pregnancy Loss, gun violence, death, murder, torture, talk of potential SA, eating disorders, mature language, death of a character, graphic threats, blood, parental death.

*Please be advised, that this book may contain a trigger that is not listed.

Playlist

I Feel Like I'm Drowning - Two Feet

Play With Fire - Sam Tinnesz, Yacht money

Put It on Me - Matt Maeson

Blood // Water - grandson

She Knows - J Cole, Cults, Amber Coffeman

Feel Something - Bea Miller

Go Fuck Yourself - Two Feet

Panic Room - Au/Ra

Don't Blame Me- Taylor Swift

Mount Everest - Labrinth

Shameless - The Weekend

Daddy Issues - The Neighborhood

Like That - Bea Miller

I Fell In Love With The Devil - Avril Lavigne

Do It For Me - Rosenfeld

Bad Drugs - King Kavailer, ChrisLee

Regrets - Stevie Howie

Dollhouse - Melanie Martinez

1

Gwenevere

I thought life would be filled with light and I'd be soaking in its warmth like a sun-kissed flower amongst the beautiful meadow. I may be a flower, but I am not basking in the warm glow of the evening. I am hidden within the trees, looking directly at the light that seeps through the overgrowth, pretending—or maybe begging—it to be all that I can see. The reality is that everything comes with a contrast of light and dark, and frankly, my life has been mostly dark. I was warned of the dangers in the world, but I wasn't warned about the dangers that lie within; the ones deep inside fighting to the surface.

I feel numb watching the gentle pats of rain slide down the window and drown the trees in Mother Nature's sorrows. The steam of my coffee rushes up to hit my face as I inhale the glorious rich scent. I have half an hour until we need to leave for campus, but I refuse to switch out of my cashmere pj's.

"Gwenevere!"

Welp, that is a wake-up call if any. I really don't want to get out of bed and face today. I just want to… well, have a break. The world has thrown one thing after another at me, and I want to slow it down and gain traction.

"Gwen! Coffee!"

I swear it is six-thirty a.m. There is no reason for yelling. I roll my eyes with a huff and carefully slide off the bed so as not to spill my half-drunk cup of coffee. I grab my brush on the dresser when a swoosh of air glides through the room, followed by a stomp on the floor. I look over with my hand still in the drawer and raise a brow at my overly impatient brother. We moved out together when I was sixteen. Alessio was seventeen and the biggest pain in my ass. Now that I'm twenty he still treats me like I am ten.

"Can I help you?" I ask.

"You didn't answer," he says.

"I was about to come out…you know there is such a thing as knocking." I straighten up and shut the drawer before running my brush through the hair lying out of my bandana.

"I did." He glares at me.

Pff "You have one pussy filled knock then," I say under my breath.

"Or you're just Deaf," he scoffs.

I hold my brush to my chest, looking at him as if he told me my fish died. "No. Don't even pretend like I hurt your feelings." He holds a finger at me.

"You're right. But you don't get to use my shitty hearing as an excuse for your lack of strength." I fight back, pointing the brush at him.

"Don't hurt my feelings, *la sorella.* You know these muscles are not for the weak." *Don't hurt my feelings, sister.* He slams his hand into his chest as if I shot a bullet. Lifting his biceps to his lips, he kisses his flexed muscles. While nothing, and I mean nothing, is more disgusting than my brother, his pride and joy is his workout routine, and the man has muscles.

"Take your male ego out of here. Goddess, why are you so gross?" I push on his shoulder and shove him out of my room. He spins with a laugh receding down the hall. I shake my head, keeping a laugh in as I follow him. Alessio can be the most annoying man alive, but he is probably my favorite human. Actually, he might need to fight Sole on that subject.

Alessio has grown a lot since we moved out. Now towering over my five-foot-two frame with his six-foot-three, I feel absolutely tiny. How did our genes end up on opposite sides of the yardstick? I have no clue. He has dark brown hair he keeps generally short and faded, blue eyes, and if you ask him, he'd say he has the most muscular definition in town. *Annoying.*

Alessio continues into the kitchen while I pick up the mail lying on the table. The front door flies open and in strolls Enzo. He has a smirk on his face meaning he's consumed his first cup of coffee and is ready to help jackass number one—making him jackass number two.

I glare at him, already irritated. "You know, usually people knock before they come into, I don't know, rooms, houses, anywhere that is not their space. It's really an amazing concept, you both should really try it," I say.

"We already went over this," Alessio says, pointing between him and me. "I knocked, you're Deaf," Alessio states, as he pours an excessive amount of creamer into his coffee cup.

"Since when do I knock?" Enzo asks.

"Would you even hear it?" Alessio continues.

I glare daggers into his back as he laughs, taking a seat on our renovated emerald green chair I got off the online market. He rests his right leg over his left knee bringing his coffee to his mouth with a smirk.

"Come on, Vee. Lighten up. I'm not gonna rob you." He comes up behind me getting close to my ear. "At least not of anything you would miss," he says for my ears only.

He chuckles, plucking the mail out of my hands, forcing a groan from me. Alessio snickers into his cup pulling out his phone. Enzo plops down on the couch that comes with a matching chair. I stand at the end of the couch with crossed arms giving Enzo a heated glare.

"Well, come on, *Dolcezza.* Would you like my lap?" *Well, come on, kitten.* He glances down at his thigh and then back at me. A not-so-innocent smile plays on his lips.

I huff dramatically, snatching the mail from his hands, and plop down next to him. I swing my legs up and place them gruffly across his. Leaning my head on the arm of the couch, I try to ignore him.

"Grumpy, I see. What has your lips twisted?" He places a hand on my knee with a grin.

I look up past the mail at his hand and then to him with narrowed eyes.

He chuckles again, "*Dolcezza.* Why so tense?" I huff pushing off the couch. I rinse my cold cup of coffee out and place the mug under the coffee machine. I pop out the K-cup from Alessio's coffee and replace it.

"*Dolcezza,* will you make a cup for me?" Enzo asks.

"Do you live here?" I yell back.

"Is your room available? I don't mind sharing." His stupid smirk returns.

"Enzo," Alessio says, giving him a pointed look with a shake of his head.

"Oh, come on. Look at her flustered cheeks. She wouldn't mind at all." He winks deviously.

I drag my hands down my face with a sigh. "Enzo, get up and make your own damn coffee." I add a bit of caramel macchiato creamer into my cup, then head to my bedroom to finish my morning routine.

"Gwen, we leave in ten!" Alessio shouts.

"Can't hide from me, *Dolcezza,*" Enzo says.

I roll my eyes as I make it to the safety of my room. I was hoping to avoid bringing Enzo along but I guess I'm out of luck today. I shoot a text to Sole receiving an instant reply.

Sole: See you soon bitch.

I shake my head with a small laugh. Such a Sole thing to say.

I switch my pj's out for a T-shirt, skirt, and a simple pair of black Converse. I look as if I walked straight out of a 2014 Tumblr post, but let's be real, that was the era of comfortable style. While white shoes would fit this cliché outfit better, I can't justify white shoes. I dirty shoes in a day and somehow can never get the stains out. I can remove blue paint from beige shorts, thanks to Pinterest tips, but not a pair of white shoes. The concoction was genius, until I went to bite my nails; thank you, anxiety. I sat on the phone with poison control for an hour just to find out I would survive... with fewer taste buds.

As I grab my gold chain necklace, I ram my hip into my desk. I drop the necklace bending over with a grip on my hip. I curse, praying the pain subsides. You'd think after I was gifted with a lack of hearing that the Gods would give me a break... *Ha!* Nope, your girl has chronic pain and nerves that truly don't know how to send signals. Feeling like I broke my hip bone, I take several deep breaths.

"VEE, TIME TO GOOO... oh." Enzo clears his throat from the doorway. "I mean if you want me, *Dolcezza,* all you have to do is ask—" He seductively grabs my computer bag, then freezes when he catches me wincing.

"Damn Vee, what did you do?" His hand finds my waist, trading his joking, and very failed pickup lines, for concern.

"I'm... okay... fuuuuck." I wince as a throbbing pain ricochets throughout my body.

"Yup, you look totally fine. Not like you have broken bones at all." Sarcasm drips from his voice.

"I'll... be... fine. Nerves... suck," I groan out, trying to convince myself to forget the pain.

Enzo shakes his head, dropping his hand. Regardless of knowing my condition, Enzo continues to baby me when I'm hurt. Two months after my seventeenth birthday I was given a list of medical diagnoses; fibromyalgia, chronic migraines, and postural orthostatic tachycardia syndrome (POTS) topped the charts. In simpler terms; I am always in pain, my brain is on fire, and I constantly have to stop my body from fainting on the daily.

I know most would be handed their pamphlets and crawl into bed to be consumed by their demons. I, on the other hand, push myself to every limit, probably more than I should. Starting my morning with ricocheting nerve pain, reaching my soul from a simple bump in with my desk, is enough of a push to reconsider my life choices. This might sound melodramatic—and the truth is, I will agree to that statement in about five minutes—but currently, I want to surgically remove my hip.

I take a final deep breath, as the time passes before my vision returns, and the pain subsides to a simple throb. *I'm fine.* I sign.

Both American and Italian sign language has become second nature to me in recent years. My hearing decreases alongside my vision the more frequent my migraines and fainting episodes occur. While I'm not Deaf, I have extremely benefited from being part of the Deaf community. The ability to communicate with my hands when my voice and ears can't work to their full potential has given me back even a little bit of freedom.

Enzo huffs out a slight laugh, but his brows are still furrowed.

"I don't want Alessio thinking I beat you up," he jokes to lighten the mood.

"I don't think you'd make it out alive," I point out, massaging my hip.

"What did you do now, Enzo?" Alessio saunters across the room and inspects me.

"What did I do? I didn't do shit. She was bent over when I walked in. I only assisted in easing the pain."

Alessio ignores Enzo, checking me over like a mother hen.

"I'm fine. Stop being dramatic, the both of you. I thought we had to leave. Man up and get out of my bubble." I straighten my spine and wave them off. I grab my computer bag out of Enzo's hand and pick my necklace up off the floor. Alessio leaves the room with an eye roll.

I move past Enzo to exit the room as well when his hand grabs my arm, gently gliding down to my wrist. His fingers wrap around me, tugging enough to turn my attention back to him. I don't have time to think before his hand brushes a piece of stray hair framing my face to the side. His body holds mine against the wall, our foreheads almost touching.

"I don't like seeing you in pain," he whispers.

I close my eyes, basking in his embrace for a few seconds before looking into his green eyes. Enzo. While I try to deny having any feelings toward him, moments like this make me want to melt into his arms.

Last fall, Alessio went away for a business internship leaving Enzo with me to take care of the house and everything else. I'd say I'm ashamed of what took place that fall but how could I? Staring at this beautiful green-eyed, light-brown haired, muscle man… he takes my breath away with a glance and in the same breath finds a way to irritate me to no end; reminding me that he is in fact my brother's best friend and the most forbidden fruit.

My lungs stutter as I try to look away. He pulls my chin back up with his thumb bringing his lips closer, staying only an inch away from mine. If I only lean in slightly our lips would touch.

"Enzo," I say breathlessly, placing a hand on his chest. "I'm fine. We have to go." I push on his chest but his other hand grips mine, stopping my movements.

"Gwenevere," he begs.

I shake my head looking down and then back into his eyes.

"We can't," I whisper.

"We can." His eyes pleading.

"How? How do you propose that in any world this will work out?" I've thought through our relationship many times. Every time, I come to the same conclusion: Enzo and I need to stay away from each other.

"We can make it work, Vee. I—"

"No. We couldn't make the season work. That's all we are—were." I correct myself. "We were only a season and I need more than just a season, I need… I need love. I need consistency. I need to put myself first. How do you see that working out? You call me naive while you sit here saying we can make a relationship work that we know won't." I sigh heavyheartedly.

"Vee, I can't just forget. Not about us, not about what we have—yes, have. And not about what happened. How can you just dismiss everything? How can you dismiss what happened with our—"

"Don't," I whisper harshly. He stares at me not wanting to leave in defeat. "Enzo, we need to move on. I need to move on. I can't—" My voice breaks, trying to forget the ending of our beautiful fall. A lapse of time that ended in heartbreak and me being broken. Enzo grabs my face in his palm, searching my eyes. His thumb wipes the wetness off my cheek from a tear I didn't notice before. I turn my face away and press my eyes shut.

"Gwenevere, it wasn't your fault. It wasn't anyone's fault but that doesn't mean we have to forget. It doesn't mean that we can't be together. Dammit, Gwen; how do you not want this?"

"Enzo." My voice grows stern.

"NO! You can't shut it out. You can't shut our—"

"STOP!" I push off Enzo completely, rushing out of the room, and shut the bathroom door behind me. I turn the lock and place my back against it. Tears fall in silence while I look at the ceiling. I can't do this right now. Why would he mention it today? Why would he act like this with Alessio lingering in the house? Alessio doesn't know about what happened with us over the fall, and I want to keep it that way. There is no proof of the events between Enzo and me, not anymore, and not that Alessio could just stumble upon.

I inhale looking at myself in the mirror, thankful for waterproof mascara. Not that I wear makeup a lot or care much about it, but I didn't want to alert Alessio that something was wrong. I'm fine. I need to forget and move on.

Today is the first day of summer classes for my junior year in college. Just a little over a year left, four semesters. I'm almost done with my business major and a handful of minors, as I'm the most indecisive person I know. After the fall semester, I am playing catch up. At one point, I almost didn't go back at all. I let myself stumble in the illusion I allowed myself with Enzo. We should have known better, Enzo and I. We should've known better and fate had its funny way of showing me why. I pull myself together before retreating out the door and straight into a muscular wall.

"About damn time, we're gonna be late." Alessio throws his hands in the air.

"No need to be a drama queen," I grumble.

He grabs my face, crushing my cheeks together and giving me a once–over. *Oh shit.* I thought I looked fine. Can he tell?

"Why do you have makeup on? You look like you're trying too hard."

I shove him with a groan.

"You're such an ass." I step into the living room, book bag in hand, without a glance in Enzo's direction. "Come on, we're gonna be late and we haven't even stopped for coffee."

"We had coffee at home." Alessio's forehead scrunches.

"Yeah, but it wasn't Lena's Coffee House coffee, so it doesn't count." I plaster my best smile.

"True." He nods. We all file out of the house to load in the car, but Enzo and I stop in front of the passenger's door. This is usually when we fight over who gets the front seat, but we stare at one another. The rain has stopped now, and the sky is cloudy and glazed over just like the look in Enzo's eyes.

"I'll take the back," I say abruptly, trying to get out of the awkward moment before Alessio notices our tension. Enzo snaps back with no emotion on his face and jumps in the front.

"Enzo, you're getting slow my man." Alessio grips the back of Enzo's seat as he backs the car out of the drive.

"It's the muscles," Enzo says. Alessio throws his head back in laughter while shifting into drive.

"Yeah, keep dreaming my friend."

I stay silent for the rest of the ride trying to reset the day. I can tell this is going to be a long semester the way Enzo is going, and I can't help but be frustrated that he won't let me move on. Forcing myself to focus on school should keep me occupied.

2

Gwenevere

As we pull into the college campus, I play with the end of my skirt waiting to leave the car. Not that the car isn't nice, it's a BMW and Alessio's prized possession, but I need to get away from Enzo. The faster I am inside and away from his grasp, the faster I can relax. My fingers inch toward the handle of the car. The moment Alessio is in the parking spot, I leap out before he has the chance to switch gears.

"Love you, Alessio! Bye!" I slam the door, a slight daze setting upon me but push through. I can sit down once I am far away from Enzo. I slide between the students moving in and out of the building and push through the tight lobby. Taking a sharp right turn down the hall, I skip the first elevator to avoid the crowd of people chatting and slam my hand on the button of the last one. I glance back and forth between the numbers moving over the elevator and down the hall.

"Come on you stupid thing." I groan out, clicking the button several times and chewing the inside of my cheek. *Ding.* The doors open and I scurry inside, not taking my eyes off the hallway. I need to click the close door button as soon as I— *"Oof"*

I hit a wall of warmth and stagger back. The wall of warmth snatches my waist, hoisting me up. I find my footing and fly to the opposite side of the enclosed box.

"I am so sorry, I was looking down the hall not even paying attention to where I was going. I am such a klutz. I am so sorry, thank you for catching me. I can't believe I did that, I've never run into anyone like that," I ramble on, looking at the ceiling when a low chuckle plays to my ears. I bring my eyes down to find the host of the enticing laugh.

He is tall—not as tall as Alessio—maybe six-foot-two? His lips are molded into a bright smile with deep blue eyes contrasting against the golden tones of his skin. Dark hair sweeps back in a messy look. My eyes drop to his white shirt hugging his broad shoulders.

"Well, you had a lot to say and now you're completely silent. What had your interest so keen down the hall you managed to run into someone a foot taller than you?" His eyes sparkle like lights reflecting off waves.

"Um…well." I pause bracing myself against the wall. "My brother. He um…" I keep my attention on the doors as they shut, enclosing me with this man. I take a shallow breath that was meant to be a deep one. *Get it together, Gwen.* I repeat my pathetic excuse of a breathing exercise before continuing. "I um… he dropped me off and ... uh… was." The room sways, or maybe it's me. *God dammit, Gwen!* I shouldn't have gotten out of the car so fast, not to mention my multiple cups of coffee.

"Whoa, you okay?" Mystery man holds my bent elbow in an attempt to steady me. His other hand floats in the air as if to catch me.

"I… um… sorry I—" *Deep breaths, Gwen, come on.* My brain burns as I fight the oncoming darkness. The mystery man's voice becomes distant and jumbled. The tingling that once plagued my skin has dulled, and the darkness has formed in the corner of my vision. I attempt to push through the drowsiness and echoing of my heart, but opening my eyes just makes it worse. I feel myself falling into the familiar deep, dark hole. My heart jumps sporadically in my chest attempting to catch up, but I am far too gone now and my body gives way to the waves.

"Hey, I got you, hold on."

Fluorescent lights blind me as I resurface. I look directly at a white wall or is that a shirt? I inhale deeply, an arm behind my neck is holding my head into the wall of my chest, and another is snaked under my legs. I raise my arms to wrap around his neck. I'm a little relieved it is not my brother, while equally mortified it had to be the cute stranger. He looks down, a line creasing his forehead, but when his blue eyes lock with mine he sighs, smoothing the wrinkles from his face.

"Hey, can you hear me? You had me scared there for a moment." His voice falls to me. I thank him internally as my head throbs, giving him my best nod. He sits me down on a bench at the end of the upper-floor hall. The space is a small, nonofficial study area for students.

"Do you need anything? Water?" he asks.

I nod again with a swift hand movement.

"*Yes, water,*" I sign. His brows fold with an emotion I can't quite place at the moment; confusion, curiosity?

"Hey, can you get us water?" He calls out to a nearby student. They rush off to the water machine and his eyes return to me. *"Parli Italiano?" You speak Italian?*

I raise my brows with a quirk of my head, shocked that he understands my first language, and even more as to understanding the sign. I nod, still not having a grasp on my speech.

"Sei Italiano?" *Are you Italian?* A smile seeps through his voice finding its way through the ringing in my ears.

I shake my head with an attempt at my voice, *"La mia famiglia,"* *My family,* I whisper. My eyes close as I bring in another deep breath, each one returning a piece of clarity.

"Are you okay? Do you need to go see the nurse or go home?" he asks.

I open my eyes, focusing on the water sitting in his palm. He pushes the cup to me and I take it with weak hands. He cups them, subduing the shaking as I take a sip.

"No." My voice comes out gruff.

Maybe I should go home. I don't want to deal with Alessio. Alessio meant Enzo, and I really don't want to talk to Enzo. Much less be in a car or house with him. Seeing Enzo at home with his little drop-ins is enough time spent with him. I hate that he got into the same college Alessio and I did. I chalk it up to bad luck.

"I'm fine, I can get up." I push off the bench and wobble finding my balance. I look like I have sea legs. I am nowhere near stable enough to function yet. Mystery man grasps both my elbows this time with a cautious look.

"You can't stand." He purses his lips. "Usually when people pass out they tend to, I don't know, get checked out?" His sarcasm brings out a genuine laugh from me, causing his brows to relax back into an amused stance.

"Usually people would get checked out, unless they are used to passing out. When you zonk out ten times a week you're not phased as much." A sigh falls from me as the tension in my body dwindles.

He freezes for a fraction of a second. I might not have noticed if his hands weren't still wrapped around me. I look up at his face, the crease returning between his brows.

"*Hmm*, well that's a bunch of bullshit," he says.

"Yeah, you're telling me." I smile warmly. "I'm fine with it now. Or the most I can be. When I was younger I was told I was anemic. Years, several tests, and many doctors later, I was diagnosed with POTS, amongst other things. A simple way of saying my blood doesn't know where it belongs and my heart doesn't know how to rest. One plus three equals me and the floor."

"Are you sure you're okay?" He looks me over once more.

I think about it this time.

"Um, honestly, I don't know yet, I still feel a lot of pressure in my head. I'm not ready for today." I sigh, closing my eyes. The pressure is definitely still evident. Not only will a migraine develop soon but I'm sure another episode. I need salt and a nap.

"Then don't." I laugh, more to myself.

"That's not really an option," I whisper.

"Why not?" he replies. My face scrunches, and I open one eye to peek at him. He shrugs his shoulders without a care in the world.

"Well for starters, it's the first day of the semester, and I could be dismissed from my classes for being a no-show. Secondly, I don't have a car, and I'm not dealing with my brother."

"Don't worry about it, I have some pull with the dean and all the teachers love me. I'll give you a ride."

I open both eyes this time and turn my head to look at the mystery man.

"You realize I don't even know your name?" I say. A deep laugh vibrates from him sending my stomach into a frenzy.

"You're right, probably shouldn't just leave with a random man after fainting when you don't know his name." He reaches his hand out to me. "It's Giovanni, Gio for short."

"Okay, Gio. How can I trust you won't kidnap me or murder me?" I drop my hand back to my lap after shaking his. He shrugs with a smirk.

"You don't, but doesn't that make life much more interesting?" A devious tone plays on his lips. I pause for a moment to think. Seeing my hesitation he continues. "Look, I can call you an Uber, you can go with your brother…. or you can take a risk with a handsome fellow and go with me?"

I know I shouldn't even consider this, but honestly, there is only one option that not only seems practical, but interesting. I let out a steady puff of air as I search the ceiling for an answer.

"Okay." I wave my hand.

"Okay?" His smile returns.

"Okay." I nod. "But, we have to go out the back door so my brother doesn't catch me skipping day one."

He chuckles. I examine the hall checking that the coast is clear. When I'm satisfied, I stand up, inching slowly so as to not let the blood rush from my head too fast. The hall is cleared out now that classes started a few minutes ago. Gio grabs my elbow, steadying me once more, as my shaky legs adjusting to my upright position. A small blush of embarrassment settles on my face. I'm not usually embarrassed by my conditions or the positions they put me in, but in Gio's presence, I feel... silly.

"Thanks." I lean on him for a little support until I'm confident in my standing skills. Gio pushes the button for the elevator with an instant *ding* from the bell. We step in and I lean against the wall, my hand moving to the button. Gio reaches across me brushing against my hand, beating me to it. I look up at him to see his small smirk.

"I'm a gentleman, Love. No doors, no buttons. Not around me," he says.

Blush rises back into my cheeks. I watch as he leans against the elevator wall. My eyes trail down his muscled toned body, his shirt is tucked into a sleek pair of slacks. His hands grasp the pole on either side of him, with prominent veins. Alessio would flip if he knew I was willing to walk out of the school and get a lift home from a stranger, much less this man standing in front of me. I keep my gaze stuck on him until I reach his quirky smile. He's staring at me, watching my assessment of him.

"You like what you see? Do you give everyone such a look down?"

Heat consumes my face, I am definitely red now.

"Sorry, I um… I was thinking how my brother would kill me if he found out that I was leaving school with a man with as much if not more musc…" I trail off. *What the hell Gwen? Pull it together.*

"Go on." The corner of his lips rise.

"Right. He's just protective. Sometimes a little bit too much." I bite my cheek, reminding myself to breathe.

"Mmm, I could probably handle him," he says.

I bend over, wiping tears from my face as I laugh. "Oh that's good, truly, but you don't know my brother." I continue laughing. Gio places his arms across his chest accompanied by a raised brow.

"I think I'm capable of more than your pretty mind can handle," he says in a tone that flips my stomach.

"That's a bold statement." I curse myself for my sudden bold attitude. I'm a little sobered up but intrigued. While I would generally take his statement as cocky, something tells me he might be right. Or at least capable of putting up a good fight.

"I never say anything I can't keep my word on." His voice is daring.

I gulp back the saliva building in my mouth and chew on my cheek. Maybe I should reconsider whether or not I will make it home alive. At the same time, being in his presence blankets me in a sense of ease. As If he'd take on my battles for me, which is insane since I don't even know the man.

The elevator *dings* once more when we reach the ground floor. Gio motions an arm out, letting me go first. My face heats as I oblige. I poke my head out first, clearing the hall before sending Gio a nod that the coast is clear. He turns his head, shoulders shaking as he wipes a hand across his lips. I stay alert but know we have a little while longer before Alessio discovers I went MIA.

"Do you always sneak around your brother's back?" he says.

I huff. "No. He's just a stickler about my schooling." And safety. I'm sure I'll be receiving a grand lecture from him later.

"When we moved out together his overprotectiveness became overbearing. I can't be ungrateful for wanting a shred of privacy." I love how much Alessio cares for me, but sometimes it's a little much. I wish he could just be my older brother instead of a second father.

"Are you always with him?" he asks. I shake my head.

"No. But if he's not, someone he trusts is." I shrug at my reality.

"And who is that?" Gio's questions don't feel invasive, more curious.

"Enzo or some of our old guards…" I pause "I say old but they've been around a lot more lately. Dad has been nonexistent recently."

"You have guards?" His eyes widen, but not to the extreme, shocked expression most have when they hear that bit of information.

"Mm-hmm, but don't think too hard about it. He runs some higher-end businesses and whatnot. Since Alessio and Enzo are here today I've been free of a stalker for the time being." I wonder how much I should reveal to this stranger.

"When you make that kind of money you're bound to enemies I guess." I shrug the statement off hoping to give it less attention than most do.

I know the seriousness of my protection. It's been instilled in my head since I was a child but where my current day trip out of school is concerned, I'm not so worried about my safety in the hands of Gio. Maybe that's naive of me, or maybe the blood hasn't fully circled back to my head yet. One way or another, I am still leaving with mystery man. A part of me needs a minute of fresh air after the morning exchange with Enzo.

"Your dad must be important." He continues in more of a statement. When I think of my dad, all that comes to mind is how much of a stuck-up asshole he is. He cares more about work than his own kids. For fucks sake, he has a whole office in our house. I can't say he isn't important. The man practically has an army of men at his service that answer to him like dogs who obey their owners. Honestly, I assume most would do anything if their pay is good enough.

"Yeah, I guess. I think he more so has his head up his ass," I say.

"You're not easy to please, are you? Strong-willed."

I stop, turning to Gio, he places a hand on the exit door with eyes trained on me. Am I strong? I mean sure I've been through some shit and life's kind of been hell, but I feel like I've gotten through it, not beat it. I gesture towards him, glancing at the muscles that are visible through his shirt.

"Depends on your definition of strong," I say.

Gio nods, pushing the door and letting me out. I hear a slight moaning and turn toward the left to see the source of the noise. Sole is pushed up against the wall with, from what I can tell, a snack of a man devouring her neck. She gasps letting out a small moan again. *Dammit.* I smack my head trying to sneak behind Gio hoping she doesn't see me.

Gio's brows raise. "Scared of a little PDA?"

I shoot him a glare, knowing he just made our existence known to Sole.

"Gwenevere?" Her voice rings in my ears thanks to my growing headache. *You had to skip class right now?*

I clear my throat, poking my head back around Gio. I give a pathetic wave as my face heats.

"Hi," I say sheepishly. "Nothing to see here. I'm heading home. Not feeling too well. Episode."

I try to sound as casual as possible, I am not going to hear the end of this. Will she tell Alessio?

"Looks like a lot to see. Are you okay? Does Alessio know you are skipping? Scratch that I know he doesn't….unless this is your new guard. I know they talked about upping detail but didn't realize they needed so much muscle, and just for classes? Isn't Alessio the class next to yours, and Enzo was supposed to have your first? I don't understand why these men like to be so—"

"ENZO WHAT?" I shout at her. *Oh no.* I have a matter of minutes before there is suspicion about why I'm not in class. Why didn't Enzo or Alessio tell me over Sole? Why the hell is Enzo even in business finance when he took it last year.

"Oh. Enzo didn't say anything? I swear, these men." She looks at Gio again and back to me. "So is he the new guard?"

"Um yeah. This is him and we need to get going. I really just want to go home and lay down ya know? Stupid heart of mine." I pat myself on the chest. "I'll see you later Sole!"

"Not so fast." She pulls my arm and whispers in my ears only. "He's not a guard is he?"

I smile shyly with a little concern for her next reaction. She slaps my arm, eyes bulging out.

"No way! Oh-em-gee. Are you sneaking out of class with a guy? A sexy one at that." She winks, sending Gio a quick little wave.

"Oh my God, Sole. Don't tell Alessio or Enzo. I'm just going home. He offered me a ride after helping me. I truly think I can trust him to drop me off."

"Do you just need a ride home? I can drive you if you want?" she asks, glancing back.

"No. You have your hands tied here. I think I can manage." My lips tug into a smirk. She rolls her eyes, then stares at Gio contemplating her decision.

"You hurt my girl and I will find you, remove your testicles from your body, and shove them so far down your throat you'll be begging for mercy."

Gio raises a brow at her threats.

"Trust me, I wouldn't dream of hurting her," he says, staring at me instead of Sole.

"Can I go now, please?" I ask Sole impatiently while looking at the door. She glances in the same direction, knowing why my patience is dwindling.

"Of course. Go. But text me when you get home and that you're alive so I know if Gio here kidnapped you or not." She stalks up to Gio with her palm up. "ID." His brows furrow at her request.

"ID?" He purses his lips.

"Yes. Are you Deaf, I can sign it for you? *ID* and fast, you have about two minutes before her minions figure out she's skipping and come looking. Your ID is a precaution in case my pretty little friend here doesn't make it home. No chances, so cough it up."

Gio shakes his head but complies, handing her an ID.

"School ID is fine I guess," she sighs, snatching it out of his hand and snapping a picture. When she hands back his school ID she pats his shoulder.

"Take care of her and don't forget." She waves her phone around proudly sending me a smirk.

"Have fun, girly!" she shoots before falling back into the arms of the man who previously had her attention. I waste no time. I grab Gio and drag him into the parking lot.

"She seems friendly." Amusement rings through his voice.

"Oh yeah, she looks friendly when taking down five men at once too. You should try it, I hear it's humbling."

Gio's deep laugh from earlier returns, and so does the feeling in my stomach.

"Oh, I'm sure it is," he says from behind me. "Last I checked I was driving. Where are you going?"

I freeze, completely oblivious that I was dragging him to nowhere. I turn around with a sheepish smile.

"Right. Sorry, I got caught up." I motion to him. "Be my guest or more so the lead."

He grabs my hand and pulls me to a black Escalade. Not creepy, a little gangster-like, but no problem. The Escalade has a tint I'm sure is illegal, much like the one Alessio and I use for outings. Gio opens the passenger door for me, giving me his hand. Surprisingly, the car looks so clean it could be brand new. I expected at least a little mess with him being a college student. I look at the door to see Gio waiting for me…to do what?

"Buckle up." He points to the seat belt.

Oh. I grab the belt and pull it over my shoulder, fastening it in the lock until I hear a click. Gio shuts the door with a nod. I watch him glide around the car. The tint isn't as intense on the inside as I thought it would be, but the vehicle is still quite dark.

Gio slides in, fastening his own seat belt. He does a once-over of the parking lot before pulling out. I don't see any signs of Alessio or Enzo. I still have a few minutes of easy escape. He sits in silence watching the road intently while getting set to leave the parking lot. I clear my throat drawing his attention to me with a raised brow.

"Do you need my address?"

He chuckles under his breath with a sweet smile.

"Yes. Yes, I do. Kinda hard to take you home when I don't have an address." *Right.* "But I was wondering if we could stop for coffee? I didn't get the chance before class."

"You're okay with skipping class to drive a random girl home but not to be a few minutes late for coffee?"

He gives a shrug.

"Better to be early or not show up at all in my opinion. Why sit through a class confused because you missed the entry lecture when I could be sent the lecture notes and pick up in class later?"

Wise. I never thought about it like that. I was worried about the impression I'd give the teacher. Like the impression I am making by skipping my first day.

"Makes sense." I watch the city go by, sneaking glimpses over to Gio once in a while whose focus stays on the road. He is always aware of his surroundings. "So, you're not just using the coffee shop as a way to take me off track and bring me to an abandoned warehouse?" I ask.

"Would you have gotten in the car with me if you had any doubt I would go against my word?"

I shake my head which is returned with a small smile.

"Don't worry. I'm not kidnapping you, and I'm not going to hurt you. You have my word, and Sole has my ID. I think it's safe to say we are just getting coffee."

I nod. A few minutes later we pull into the café, my café.

"Lena's Coffee shop?"

He parks the car, finally turning his focus to me.

"Is this place okay? It's my favorite place in town. Truly hate corporate coffee."

My smile widens.

"This is actually my coffee shop. Well, not mine but my brother and I come here all the time, Sole too. I've never seen you here before."

"I usually come when they first open and in the evenings. I have an assistant to get coffee anytime in between really."

I sit back a little shocked.

"Assistant? *You* have an assistant." How does he have an assistant? Does he work in a higher position or own a business?

"Eh. It's helpful when you have loads of paperwork and get stuck behind a desk."

"So, you have an office job?"

"No. Well yes. At times? It's a complex job." He stops, but I'm not completely convinced. "I'm a business consultant. I went back to school for a master's in finance though. I have to take a few business classes, hence why we were in the same wing on campus."

"A business consultant. That explains the Escalade a little."

"The Escalade?" His lips slide back into a smirk with the question.

"Well by the nice SUV that eats gas and the tint, you have to have some money to get away with one."

"Mm-hmm. So, you noticed my car because of the wealth behind it?"

"Yes, but I more so know it for durability. It's all my dad will drive and my brother jumps between the Escalade and BMW. I prefer how smooth the Escalade drives but I'm a sucker for Jeeps. Not really a reason behind it. I liked the look and have dreamed of having one since," I say.

He laughs under his breath. "You have me best, but a Jeep? If you want one so bad, why don't you get one?"

I tap over my heart a couple of times.

"Can't. Not really. I'm cleared to drive but if I feel like crap I can't, and I feel like crap like seventy percent of the time. It would be pointless to have a car I can only drive thirty percent of the time, and that's *if* my brother will let me drive. I only get a chance when Sole lets me and sometimes Enzo if I annoy him enough."

He nods at the clarification.

"I'd still do it. I would get it and enjoy even two percent of the time that makes me happy," he says. "You already deal with enough, you deserve to have your happiness. Plus you wouldn't have to depend on a man like me to drive you home."

I roll my eyes, giving him a smile. Gio is sincere and not at all what you would assume when looking at him. He hops out of the car and I move my hand to the handle. Gio throws the door open gaze moving to my hand.

"I thought I told you I was a gentleman. No doors, no buttons, not with me." His stern tone returns. I nod my head with an internal eye roll.

"Sorry, I'm excited for coffee."

I suck in a deep breath entering the café. I love the smell of coffee. My focus on bliss is cut short when I hear the little woman's voice.

"My dear, you're already back?" Lena comes to my side eyeing Gio up and down with a light smile. "And you brought a handsome fellow. Does Alessio know? I'm surprised he doesn't have Enzo trialing you. After the last few months, I was sure he'd never leave your side."

My face flusters but I quickly regain my composure. Hoping Gio doesn't see my lapse of emotions, I throw on a smile and hug Lena.

"Hi, Lena, this is Gio, he's... a friend from school. He's driving me home. I had an episode and have a growing migraine."

She nods, not fully convinced but doesn't push further.

"Black or your usual latte?" She grabs a pad and clicks her pen.

My face falls. I forgot how the sugar makes my head throb more.

"Black is fine," I sigh. Gio watches the interaction with a bemused smile.

"And for the lovely fellow?" Lena places her hand on the counter.

"Same please, ma'am."

I'm unsure whether his manners surprise me or not.

"No need to be so formal." She waves him off. "It's on the house for my lovely lady." She grins sweetly between us. Gio places a few bills in the tip jar and drops his hand to the small of my back, leading me to a table. His touch is gentle yet friendly.

Today's going to be a tad more interesting than I thought and the day already started off rocky. Let's just hope Alessio doesn't come slamming through the door. I smile behind my coffee while Gio stares at his phone. Lines form on his forehead as his phone rings. He pinches the bridge of his nose with a huff.

"Give me a moment to step outside. I'll be right back," he says.

I nod and continue to sip my coffee pulling out a book from my bag to fill the time. After a little, I hear the bell ring for the door again. Gio slides into his seat giving me a complex gaze.

"That was my brother, I need to head back. If it wasn't urgent I wouldn't even ask, but I don't have time to bring you back home. Are you up for a detour?"

I think it over for a second. I could stay at the café and call Alessio, or even Sole, but a part of me wants to know what is so important. God, I'm so nosey, and one day I'll get kidnapped, but I highly doubt that day is today.

"Okay." I nod.

"Okay?"

 I nod again.

"Yes. Let's go." I stand and wave at Lena goodbye. She smiles warmly, eyeing Gio again on our way out. I climb into the car contemplating my decisions, but there is no going back now.

I buckle up, and Gio gives a satisfied grin shutting the door. I take a final deep breath as the engine comes to life and watch the scenes go by in silence. This is definitely not where I saw my day going.

3

Gwenevere

I stare out the window for a while, waiting to arrive at our destination. Gio seems frustrated, and I don't want to impose my questions about what changed his mood. I close my eyes, giving myself this moment of peace.

Gio clears his throat, snatching my attention back. "Don't talk to anyone unless they directly talk to you." He glances at me. Shouldn't be a problem. When Alessio brings me along to Dad's office I sit and wait. No talking, no wondering, and no repeating.

"Understood. Alessio preaches the same. I have my book I can read while you take care of business. It usually occupies my time." I give him a soft reassuring smile.

The houses become scarce and larger. Dad's house is in a neighborhood similar to this one on the other side of the city. A large brick home, or more so a mansion, falls through the trees as we pull up to the metal gates.

A man around the size of Gio stands guard, yet the fence towers over him. When his eyes land on Gio's car he nods through him. Deja Vu warps around me, but I can't pinpoint if it is due to the giant house resembling my father's estate or the guards.

The engine dies in the circular drive. I take in the estate for all its glory. The drive is all a beige brick and circles around a beautiful tree with several vehicles surrounding it. A similar brick color coats the walls of the mansion. The window seals are painted, giving the ultimate Italian style home. It's funny to think that another Italian-American family lives just on the opposite side of the city.

Gio opens my door, not letting his gentlemen act down. I take in the trees that line the black fence, keeping out lurking eyes. I suck in the fresh air, an uncommon occurrence in the city. Gio opens the large door letting go of my back and hoovering his lips over my ear.

"Just keep your head down. You're safe here. Give me a few moments and I will be with you." His voice is just above a whisper. He steps in front of me and past some men in formal attire; Gio seems to fit the look while I stand here looking like a high school dweeb. Gio gestures to the living room. "You can sit in here. If you need anything, water, anything, just ask one of the men."

"Okay." Gio stares at me a moment longer. I pull my book out with a wave through the air. "I'll be fine. Go ahead."

With that he turns his back to me, taking the stairs two at a time to the next floor. I let my eyes wander around the living room. There are two large sitting chairs and a sectional couch all of which are black leather.

The coffee table is a large wooden table held up by black metal legs. It looks handmade, maybe custom built for the space? Everything fits so nicely. Vinyl records line the staircase wall that faces the couch. A massive TV is mounted on the wall above the entertainment center.

Everything is precisely clean, much like Gio's car. The plants have to be watered on a strict schedule with how full they are. My eyes land on the men near the staircase. They stare ahead; one at the foray, the other at the staircase. Turning behind me I finally take in the view out the large windows that double as doors. A gorgeous courtyard filled with flowers and a waterfall brings my lips into a smile.

Relaxing onto the couch I dive into my current reality escaping the bounds of paper. I'm not sure how much time passes when a hand taps my knee. I look up to see Gio with a concerned face.

"Did you hear me? Are you going to pass out on me again? I can get you some water. Maybe the coffee was a bad idea?"

"No, I'm fine. *I'm hard of hearing.* When my 'episodes' spiked, my senses went crazy. My hearing and vision were hit the most." I smile while he sits in silence. "I'm okay but if I don't respond just tap me or stomp across the room. If all else fails, yell at me. I'll hear ya if you're in the room for sure."

"Does it affect you when having a normal conversation?"

I shrug. "Yes and no. If they're talking real low or on a bad day it makes things complicated. For the most part, I can read your lips in conversations. It's frustrating when people look the other way, like their voice isn't traveling in the opposite direction and I can't see their lips." My voice rises.

He nods but turns his head to the men making their way down the stairs. I follow his view to find a few men in suits rounding the railing. One man in particular wears the nicest suit. He is tall, six-foot-four maybe? His face is shaped like Gio's but rougher. His hands are calloused and his posture is tense. He speaks to the men ahead who keep their eyes cast down, never quite making eye contact... odd.

All respond with "sir" and "boss." Maybe he's Gio's boss, but where is his brother? He breaks away from the guarding men making his way to us. Wrinkles line his forehead etching in stress and frustration.

He's got the facade of someone who's seen things and knows things. He is the boss and I'm certain he holds more power than what I could simply observe in the few moments I have to asses him. He stops when he sees me. We lock eyes and I can't for the life of me pull my gaze away. He is captivating. My breath hitches as I see his body tense again and stare down at me like he can read my soul from five-feet away.

Seconds are like minutes that feel like hours. My face heats and I'm tempted to break contact, but the depths of his eyes keep me glued. Like I'm looking into the ocean, deep blue irises swarm my vision. Suddenly, a throat clears snapping my attention back to Gio, remembering where I am.

Then I hear his voice, like honey and sweet, sweet molasses.

"Who is this, Gio?" The man's voice demands my attention. Why would he ask Gio when I was sitting right here?

"This is... Gwenevere? I guess I never truly asked you your name or what you want to be called by." Gio quirks a brow.

"Gwen is fine."

"And why is she here?" Annoyance fills the space, yet curiosity sneaks its way through. His eyes never leave mine.

"I *was* taking her home when someone so rudely called and interrupted. She's from campus. She had a medical thing and I was there. She wanted to go home to rest for the day but needed a ride."

The man doesn't respond. Now fully emerged in a staring contest, I bit my cheek as I wait, wondering why I'm still here with this tall man towering above me. Maybe the café wouldn't have been so bad. I would be lying though if I said I didn't enjoy my view.

"Breakfast is ready, have you eaten, Gwenevere?" My name rolls off his tongue, holding me hostage. I'm not a huge fan of my full name but with him, it sounds so angelic.

I shake my head.

"What kind of medical mishap did she have that you couldn't get her breakfast?"

"We stopped for coffee, then you called. I was taking her home before her brothers got concerned about where she was and still is." Gio shrugs out.

"Brothers?" The man finally pulls his gaze away from me to look at Gio with raised brows.

"No."

Both of them snap their heads back to me. I hesitate under their piercing eyes.

"Um… just one brother, Alessio."

"Then who's Enzo?" Gio's forehead scrunches.

"Oh… Enzo?" I blush. "He's just Enzo. Alessio's best friends and previously lived with us." I say picking at one of my nails.

"No one knows where you are right now?" I shake my head.

"I just wanted to go home and rest and not deal with Alessio or Enzo anymore today. After I passed out in the elevator, where Gio helped me, he offered me a ride home." I move my head to point toward Gio.

"Speaking of, we better get you fed and home," Gio says, placing his hand out to me. The man stares down at the hand Gio extended, his face knits into an unreadable expression.

"Gio, we need to talk." He leaves the room without confirmation that Gio is following. Gio sighs, pinching the bridge of his nose and curses under his breath. I bite down on my lip. Gio lifts his head to the other man that had come down the stairs.

"Viktor, can you escort Gwenevere to the kitchen? Don't let her out of your sight and no one bothers her." Viktor approaches us with a smile.

"No problem."

"Go ahead, I'll be just a moment longer and we'll get out of here." Gio motions to Viktor. I press my lips into a brief smile then follow Viktor to the kitchen.

I spot a massive dining table on the right of the wide space. It has to hold at least twenty people, the wood matching the coffee table. I look to the left to see a large L-shaped kitchen and an island nearly the size of the table with matching chairs.

Behind the kitchen, there is an entryway. Past the dining room, a reading nook rests in front of a small breakfast table. I take in the beautiful wine bar last, jealous of the space.

A woman in her mid to late fifties moves through the entryway. A warm smile dances on her face as she lands on me. She adjusts her black dress that sits at knee length. Her natural gray highlights shimmer throughout her hair as she moves through the space. When she arrives in front of me I'm greeted with the smell of sweet lavender and lemons.

"And who might this be?" the woman asks with the soothing voice of a mother. The corner of Viktor's lips rises into a warm smile for the woman.

"Gio brought her. Was taking her home from school when duty called. Can you make her a plate?" The woman nods eagerly, turning back. She reappears moments later with a full plate. I stare at the large amount of food nervously, swallowing back my anxiety.

"Thank you, I'm Gwenevere by the way."

The woman's cheeks rise with her widening smile.

"It's nice to meet you dear, such a beautiful name. Is your family Italian?"

"Yes, my parents are from Italy and moved here when my brother was born. A year later I came along. I've visited but have lived in states my whole life." I reply, taking a small bite of bacon.

"How beautiful. Oh, where are my manners? My name is Malia, but everyone calls me Mila. I'm the lead housekeeper. If you need anything while you're here just let me or one of my girls know." She holds my hand gently. "Now eat before it gets cold. I have to go check on the girls." My mouth is full so I give her a slight nod before she disappears.

I manage to get a few pieces of bacon down followed by some toast. I don't think I can physically accomplish anymore at the moment and frankly, this is a rather large portion of food. Gio enters the kitchen, eyes falling to my plate with a frown.

"Did you not like it?"

"I drank a lot of coffee and my stomach is just unsettled. I truly appreciate the meal. Thank you, for everything." I chew on my lip. His mouth hangs open.

"Are you ready to go home?"

"Yes." I hop off the stool and round the corner out of the kitchen as searing pain fills my head with an immediate migraine.

My body waivers but I try to keep pace with Gio. Gio's form blurs and I hear the world in muffled tones. My muscles grow taut, time slowing down. I try to reach out for support but fail, my legs weakening. I make it fully out of the kitchen when my knees give way and a mild curse finds its way through the tunnel of quieted sounds. A warm wall collides with me as I try to move, but my efforts become useless. I let my body give way, losing myself to the black oblivion and floating away from time.

A blanket of fog that blinds my senses lifts as I slowly flutter my eyes open. *How fucking annoying.* This has to be the most inconvenient day ever. A man slowly comes into view. The man from the living room I can't place a name to. Not for my lack of brain power but because I never received it. The ocean in his eyes bore into me. Mystery man number two. Was he the one to catch me?

Muffled voices return in distant echoes, my skin tingling. I look past Mystery Man, catching a glimpse of Gio and Viktor. I lean my head back trying to find a steady pace of breathing and gather myself.. It is still morning and I am lying in a strange man's arms. I groan, wanting this day to end.

I lift my head to the man holding it. His forehead is etched with concern. Gio comes from behind him giving me water.

I try to focus on his lips as they move but can't make out what he is saying. His face contorts, before lifting his hands to sign.

"Are you okay, do you need water?"

I close my eyes and take a deep breath in. Opening them back up to Gio, I sign back.

"Water."

I try to grab the water, my hands shaking uncontrollably. The man reaches out for the water pulling it away. He turns to Gio who stands and leaves back to the kitchen. Seconds later he appears holding a straw.

I close my eyes again, trying to train my body to work. No matter how often I pass out, it feels like I'm dying, I can't ask for help, and when I come back I'm useless. In a place I don't know, with people I don't know, it makes the experience more traumatizing. Anything could happen to me, and I'd be useless in defending myself. I feel warmth on my cheeks, and I open my eyes to the man wiping the tears that have fallen.

My body shakes with my inhale. He holds the water out to me, this time with the straw. He helps me sit up and puts the straw to my lips. I sip the water but my stomach is unsettled. After a few moments, I can hear the men. I focus on Gio and the man talking—well, yelling. "Giovanni, I don't have patience for your lack of respect. You will stand down. You have a job to do and so help me God if you don't go. She will be fine!"

Gio sighs with frustration pinching his nose again.

"Matteo, you've barely spoken to one another."

"She left a school behind her brothers and guard's backs to sneak home with a stranger. I highly doubt she'll have an issue with me driving her home while you attend to business. That's an order."

His name is Matteo. His voice has changed from stern to sinister. I should be scared at the tone but instead, my body leans closer.

"Gio… I'm… okay." I struggle to find my words. "I'll survive. Go… go… to work." I smile softly. "It'll pass." My body continues to tremble. I lean further into Matteo and hold his jacket while trying to breathe. Matteo tenses holding me tighter. Gio sighs lighter this time.

"Promise?"

"I promise."

Gio's jaw ticks, giving Matteo a glare, before retreating up the stairs. Matteo picks me up,moving us to the couch. I close my eyes grounded in my senses.

Matteo smells like vanilla and teakwood with hints of pepper and honey. Sweet and musky but smooth. I start to drift, not able to fight the exhaustion or maybe I don't want to. I let the darkness take over. Matteo holds me tight in his grasp, and not a single part of me wants to push him away.

4

Gwenevere

I wake to that sweet and musky scent once again flooding my senses. I'm wrapped in soft cotton sheets, my body sinking into the mattress like it's a cloud. Dark curtains drape around the window letting the warm glow of the sun enter the room.

I close my eyes searching for a clue as to where I am. My head is pounding as memories flood my head in scattered pieces. The scent. Matteo.

I snap up but instantly regret the decision. I place a hand on my chest in a poor attempt to calm my heart. I feel movement in the room and direct my attention back to my surroundings. Matteo sits back in a chair, his head resting on the back of the chair, face tilting to the ceiling.

I assess his face. His stress is evident in the tension he carries in his forehead. Matteo's previously worn suit jacket lays across his knee, leaving his

53

broad chest and biceps in view as his dress shirt clings to them. He looks tired. *Does he ever rest?* My heart clenched at the thought but I shake my head.

Letting Matteo relax, I take in the rest of the room. There is a door to the side of the bed, a sink peeking through the small opening. A bench is pushed against the end of the bed and an extra blanket is folded on top.

When my eyes make it back to Matteo, I catch his gaze focused on me. I bite my lip as he watches me and I ponder how long he has been observing me. His lips twitch as he studies my mouth. His eyes return to mine with an unreadable expression on his face.

He glides to the side of the bed lifting my chin.

"You fell asleep. I didn't want to disturb you. You needed rest."

grazing lightly before gently tugging my lip from my teeth. He frowns a little.

"Your lip is bleeding."

I lift my fingers to my lips, feeling the small patch of blood; I bite my lip back, wetting it to wipe the blood away.

"Don't bite your lip."

I pop my bottom lip back out. His lips form in a small smirk, and he steps back.

I snap back, pushing the covers off.

"What time is it?" How could I have fallen asleep? Alessio is sure to kill me now.

"Seven. The sun's almost set."

I wince. *Yep.* Alessio is going to kill me. I scramble out of the bed frantically looking around for my things.

"Oh no. Alessio is going to kill me! He and Enzo probably have the city looking for me." I groan not finding my phone anywhere. Matteo removes all emotion from his face. The man is more closed off than Gio.

"Come on. Your phone is downstairs. I'll give you a ride home."

I bite my lip again. How will Alessio react if I show up in Matteo's car after going MIA for hours? Maybe I should call Sole, but knowing her she'll get lost or take too long.

"Don't bite your lip. Are you ready? If you need a moment I can—"

"No. I'm okay, I just really need to get home."

He opens the door stepping to the side. I rush out before freezing, realizing I have no clue where I am going. Matteo shuts the door and walks with me down the hall.

A guard stands near the staircase completely still until Matteo nods. The man gives a tight nod to Matteo, glances at me, and returns to his composed stance.

We descend the staircase toward the two large wooden doors that sit in the engraved entrance. The guards still stand. Guards still stand at the entrance and in front of the mystery door a few feet from the bottom. Two large wooden doors sit in the engraved entrance.

I spot my phone sitting on the coffee table. I open the phone to thousands of missed calls and messages between Alessio and Enzo. I cringe as I send a text to Alessio.

Me: Be home shortly, don't wait up.

Knowing full well he is going to wait up, I huff, clicking my phone off and returning to Matteo.

"All set?"

"All set."

He holds an arm out at the open door. He ushers me to a black Escalade identical to Gio's. I glide in before he follows suit. A man sits up front keeping his eyes forward. Matteo reaches across my lap, freezing me in place. He grabs onto the seat belt before pulling it over me and clicking it into place.

He retreats his hand with a graze on my outer thigh. I clench my thighs as my lower stomach flops.

"Where to, Boss?"

Matteo raises a brow to me. I crease my forehead in return.

"Gwenevere, address."

I swallow noting how stupid it was to assume he knew where I lived. I'd given Gio my address earlier, not him.

"You will get home a lot quicker if you tell me."

I clear my throat a little.

"376 Olive Drive." My voice falls out barely above a whisper. My cheeks heat watching his lips twitch again. He pats the shoulder of the driver's seat.

"Go on, Bruno." The man nods, shifting the car into gear.

Alessio is going to rip me a new one. That I can foresee from miles away. I puff out some air. Why do I have to walk on eggshells with Alessio? He needs a life. Maybe a girlfriend would help. Another woman to keep his attention, letting me slip onto the sidelines. Maybe, just maybe, then I won't need to sneak around Alessio's back. My heart rate increases not from the lack of blood but from the evening of bullshit I'm about to endure.

Matteo creepily stares at me, but my body doesn't react to him like a creep. I sigh. I hope I can rush out the door before Matteo has a chance to move. If he's anything like Gio, he won't enjoy me opening my own door much less reaching for the handle.

We near my home, houses becoming scarce again. I concentrate on my next movements when the house comes into view. Extra cars fill the drive and I grimace knowing they're here for me. Matteo takes in the cars as well and a shadow falls over his features.

Bruno moves the car to the curb but before he gets to park I unbuckle and turn to Matteo.

"Thank you so much for helping, truly. Please let Gio know I am thankful for him and the coffee. I'll pay him back." I scramble out of the car and run towards the house. I rush inside my home and slam my back against the door. My hand is still holding the knob, eyes closed as I take steady breaths, tilting my head to the ceiling, praying I can make it to my room without a major fight. The thought is laughable.

"Gwenevere." Alessio grits from somewhere in the room. I slowly lower my head down and lift an eye open. I straighten up taking in the room and smile sheepishly. Men surround the table, Alessio standing on the other side, phone in his hand, while Enzo paces behind him.

"She's here you idiot." He slams his phone down glaring at me full force. With a flick of his hand, all the men exit the house. Alessio shoots daggers at me as I step out of the men's way. I glare at Alessio this time.

"Really? I don't need half the city looking for me, Alessio. I'm a grown woman."

He huffs.

"A grown woman? A grown woman doesn't just disappear. I've had our men searching for you for hours. No answer to calls or texts!" He stalks around the table raising his voice. "Last I checked a 'grown woman' wasn't so irresponsible."

Alessio is harsh but it doesn't faze me as much anymore.

"Oh please. A grown woman doesn't need to give her brother a minute-by-minute schedule of her entire existence when she can clearly handle herself. Besides, I was safe and sound and now I'm here." I roll my eyes turning my back to him and grabbing a water from the counter.

"Oh, so you can handle yourself? What happens if you pass out? What happens if you can't fight back, huh? What then Gwenevere? You're willing to risk your life for a day of wondering?" He scoffs. "Very responsible."

This time his words slap me hard. *How inconsiderate and controlling does he need to be?*

"Alessio, I'm not going to argue with you. I'm safe, happy and healthy. I was with Sole anyways and now I'm going to my room." I step past Alessio, a laugh erupting from him. Enzo shakes his head.

"You were with Sole?" he asks, laughing like he made a joke. "You mean the woman who is passed out in your room—you were with her?"

Dammit. Why is Sole here anyway? Obviously, she was not a great cover.

"I don't have time for this, Alessio. I'm not going to sit around and humor you."

I push my door open, Sole is splayed out, computer dangling between her thighs and phone in hand. I hit her foot and plop on the fur chair across from her. She bounces to life, nearly crushing her computer.

"What the hell, Gwen!"

5

Matteo

Work as of late has been slow. Of course we have the occasional kinks but that's to be expected in our line of work. Unfortunately, today was a bust with an actual bust at one of our bars and I need to recuperate our forces. Of course, my second in command is nowhere to be found. *Surprise.*

"Where the fuck is Gio?"

Viktor riffles through the papers on his lap.

"He has classes today."

I groan. Gio taking classes at the local college is great. Not only does he gain practical knowledge to run the business, but it is also a great publicity setup.

I flip through my stack of papers piled on my desk—most of which will be passed to Gio. Not only is he capable but he also tends to do a better job in the office than I do.

"How are we doing with Luciano?"

I rub a hand down my face.

"On the fence."

Luciano is the crime family on the other side of the city. Genovese and Luciano go far back, but in recent decades there has been an alliance between us. We don't get in their way, they don't get in ours. Simple.

The only problem is their chain of command changed. Lavoy retired right before the fall, appointing his son, Alessio, to Don. Alessio is throwing a show. He needs to prove his command is in place which means his alliance with the Genoveses is under review, as are all the other families.

"The kid just needs to get his work around and things will die down." Viktor doesn't look up from the pages, scribbling down notes here and there. "He doesn't want to lose our alliance. To lose us means war, and he won't start with war, especially not over nothing. He might be young but he's Lavoy's kid, he's not stupid. He needs us." Viktor's confidence in his words only confirms my views on the subject.

I lean back in my chair looking at the time. Fuck Gio's classes. I need him to handle this bust. I pull out my phone and speed-dial his cell. I wait a few rings too long for the line to pick up.

"What do you want?"

"You. I need you to come deal with the bust."

"Isn't that your job?"

"*My* job is to do whatever the fuck I want. *Your* job is to also do whatever the fuck I want," I growl at the phone. "You have ten minutes."

I click the line and stare at the stack of papers growing.

"You bicker like children." Viktor chuckles to himself.

"He's the fucking child."

Gio always had his head halfway in the clouds. He didn't have the drilling I did. I didn't want him to, but it left him on the carefree side. Sure he knows when to handle business. He also spends more time in the clubs than I would like of my second.

"Do you hear yourself? Or is it just me?" He raises a brow.

"Just you," I mutter, pulling up our books and comparing numbers with the sheets. Our routine procedure is to ensure everything's running smoothly. One thing goes out of line and the system falls. As I near the end of the page I hear footsteps in the hall.

The door opens and Gio's scowling face walks in. I roll my eyes at his childlike attitude, grabbing the new stack Viktor has set up and plopping it on the desk in front of Gio's seat.

"Nice of you to show up."

"Is this it?" He flips quickly through the papers.

"That and the press." Viktor swirls his pen in the air.

"Fuck the press." Gio leans against the chair, his arms crossed.

"Pretty sure you have; hell if it will get this off my back, fuck 'em again."

He narrows his eyes, swiping the papers off the desk, retreating.

"I'll finish this. You should be free by tomorrow."

"What's got you in a rush?" I am a little amused by his quick come-and-go. Gio tends to come in and lounge around, annoying everyone in the room. I have to force him to leave more times than not. Where does he need to be in such a rush?

"Some of us have lives outside these four walls. Give it a try, you might like it."

"Ain't nothing out there I want."

"Oh right, I forgot you only know how to be a cold stoned bitch."

I clench my fist against the arm of the chair. "I'd like to throw a stone at you."

Gio shakes his head, turns his back to me, and flips me off as he leaves the room. I roll my eyes.

Viktor chuckles rounding his chair. "Like I said, children."

"That's it, I need more coffee." I slap my hands on the desk and stand up.

"Coffee or bourbon?" Viktor snickers

"Both will do."

Viktor and I jog down the stairs and turn the corner. A stop in my tracks. A woman is standing with Gio. She doesn't have the usual club aesthetic he typically brings around. Her curly hair falls from her bandana. A tight blouse paired with a midthigh skirt outlines her curves.

What is Gio doing with someone who looks so innocent? Maybe that's the play, to bring her to the dark. Her eyes sparkle, and if I didn't know better, I wouldn't see the pain she holds in them. She watches as I move towards the room, leaving Viktor talking with the guard. She averts her gaze with a slight blush. Was that for me or something Gio said? My gaze doesn't falter from the woman in front of me as I stop just short of them.

"Who is this, Gio?"

She snaps her head up to look at me. Her doe eyes and rose lips part ever so slightly.

"This is… Gwenevere? I guess I never truly asked you your name or what you want to be called by." Gio smiles warmly at her. A little too warm.

"Gwen is fine." Her voice glides through the air. A sweet melody I didn't want to turn off.

"And why is she here?"

He was to be at the college when I called so why was he trailing Gwen around? Not to mention that he was called here for work. Why would he bring someone along that isn't a part of the *famiglia*? I trail her body searching for something that would jump out to explain her presence.

"I was taking her home when *someone* so rudely called and interrupted. She's from campus and had a medical thing. I was there and thought it was best she'd go home to rest for the day."

I don't respond, still searching her. She pulls at the inside of her cheek with her teeth and twirls the bottom of her shirt in her finger. I give her props for not breaking her gaze from mine since I spoke.

"Breakfast is ready, have you eaten, Gwenevere?"

I know my peak of interest will not pass by Gio and Viktor, but I am intrigued and not ready to break my trance. Her body tenses as her name rolls off my tongue. She pulls at her rosy lips this time, biting on them gently. God her lips are perfect. She shakes her head no in response.

"What kind of medical mishap did she have that you couldn't get her breakfast?"

Gio shrugs from the corner of my view. "We stopped for coffee then you called. I was taking her home before her brothers got concerned about where she was."

"Brothers?" I break away and look at Gio. She's actively sneaking behind her overprotective brother's backs and Gio brings her here. Dear God, he is a child. The last thing I need is some stuck-up asshole with family drama. We have enough of that around here. I glare at him with a promise we'll pick this conversation back up in a minute.

"No." Her voice cuts through our silent exchange. Both Gio and I snap our heads back to her. "Um, just one brother, Alessio."

Perfect. That's just what we needed. Another Alessio parading through our doors. Why did Gio think she had two brothers? I turn to him, his face puzzled with confusion.

"Then who's Enzo?" Gio frowns tilting his head.

"Oh… Enzo." She shrugs. "He's just Enzo. He's best friends with Alessio. And previously lived with us." Enzo? The coincidence doesn't sit well with me, but I push it aside for the time being. She looks young. There's no way she's involved with the Luciano family.

"No one knows where you are right now?"

"I just wanted to go home and rest and not deal with Alessio or Enzo anymore today. After I passed out in the elevator, where Gio helped me, he offered a ride home."

She nods her head to Gio. Passed out?

"Well, we better get you fed and home." Gio places his hand out to help her up. I stare down at the hand Gio extended. I hold my unexplained frustration in at his movements and turn away.

"Gio, we need to talk."

Gio sighs behind me.

"Viktor, can you escort Ms. Gwenevere to the kitchen, she's welcome to anything that we have. No one bothers her, understood?" Viktor nods, passing me with a wide grin.

I don't hear the rest as I move into the entrance of the cellar. Gio follows shortly after.

"Listen, we won't be here long. This wasn't the plan, but you didn't give me any time." I stare at him a moment longer.

"Do we know who she is?"

"Gwen. She literally just told you."

"Right, she gave me a first name and her brother Alessio… and his friend Enzo." I draw out their names. Gio's face scrunches, only proving his idiocy. "You've got to be kidding me. Do you pay attention to anything? Luciano. Ring a bell?"

Gio scoffs. "You really think if Alessio is her brother she'd get away with sneaking away, and secondly, she wouldn't just waltz in here spouting their names off." He crosses his arms with a heavy sigh. "Look, I see whatever interest you've got flowing through your head but she's not it Matteo. She's too innocent. You'll either break her by using her or you'll drag her into a world she doesn't belong in." I wave him off not giving two shits what Gio thinks.

He backs away into the kitchen when Viktor emerges. I motion him over and lean against the wall pulling out my phone briefly.

"I need you to get everything you can about her." His brow raises but he doesn't question.

"Yes, boss."

"This doesn't leave us."

"Of course not." I give him a tight nod, pushing off the wall when I see Gio walk back out from the kitchen, Gwen in tow.

Her body wavers but she keeps pace with Gio. Her face is pale and her eyes flutter as her movements grow sloppy. She slows down, raising her hand to balance on the wall. Gio continues ahead, unaware of her setback in pace. Her body sways and in seconds I'm at her side muttering curses. Gio never said what was wrong with her, and she only mentioned passing out in the elevator. Why is she passing out again? Didn't she go to the kitchen to eat?

Whatever it is, it's not getting better. Her body slides against mine becoming dead weight as she falls into an unconscious state. Seconds feel like minutes as my heart hammers through my chest. I check her pulse, her heart rate matching mine, if not faster, but softer.

"Gio, grab some water."

I don't look away but hear Gio scurry to the kitchen.

After what feels like an eternity, Gwenevere's eyes flutter open. She is still pale and obviously weak as she tries to move, failing miserably. Her eyes slowly gloss as they connects with mine, the exhaustion plaguing hers. Gio comes back in behind me and hands me the water, giving her a warm smile.

"Are you okay?"

She looks at him confused, focusing on his lips. My frustration rises more as I try to navigate what is happening. Gio's face contorts a little in what looks like relaxation after she doesn't respond.

Her hands start to move, and I finally understand. She's signing. What's better? It's Italian.

"What?"

"Are you okay? Do you need water?"

Her chest rises as she takes deep breaths in, signing back.

"Water."

He nods. I watch her as he hands water out to her. She goes to hold the cup with shaky hands. I pull the cup away looking over to Gio.

"Go get a straw."

He jumps back heading into the kitchen, returning seconds later holding a straw. I pop the straw into the water. She closes her eyes, face clearly laced in pain as a tear falls down her pale face.

She is drained, in pain, and freaked. I wipe the tears from her face drawing her light blue eyes back to me. I hold the water back out, adjusting the straw to face her. She takes a few sips and then closes her eyes again.

Turning to Gio, I start my list of commands. "Gio I got this, go work on my bust." He stares at me in disbelief.

"Are you serious?" He scoffs. "You want me to just leave her here like this? I need to take her home and let her rest up. She's had a long day and dealing with your ass is probably the least relaxing thing she can do."

I clench my jaw. "It wasn't a question, Giovanni"

"Matteo, fuck off, the bust can wait a little longer."

"Giovanni, I don't have patience for your lack of respect! You will stand down. You have a job to do and so help me God if you don't. She will be fine."

Gio sighs with frustration, pinching his nose again.

"Matteo, you've barely spoken to one another."

"She left a school behind her brother's and guard's backs to sneak home with a stranger. I highly doubt she'll have an issue with me driving her home while you attend to business. That's an order." I leave my casual tone for Gwenevere, giving him my commands. Gio is stepping out of place, and he knows better.

Gwenevere leans into me slightly. Scaring her isn't going to help the current situation.

"Gio… I'm… okay." She struggles with her words. "I'll survive. Go… go… work." She smiles at him softly. "It'll pass." Her body continues to tremble and she leans further into me for comfort. She grabs onto my jacket taking what I assumed are deep breaths but comes up short.

Gio sighs lighter this time. "Promise?"

"I promise." Her voice shakes, but he nods running up the stairs. I pick her up and bring her to the couch, placing her on my lap. Her lids shut and her body relaxes into me. Her once strangled breathing evens out, sleep taking over her.

How did I go from mob boss to caregiver? I stare down at Gwen, curiosity pulling me into a wavelength of thoughts. What the hell is happening with her? I don't take care of people—at least not in this way. Hell, I barely take care of myself. Yet here I am, holding a sleeping woman I don't even know.

She needs to rest and I need to work. I think she can survive the few hours to sleep. I stand up with her and head up the stairs. I stand outside the guest room before deciding against leaving her in there and continuing down the hallway.

One of my men walks by and I gesture my head towards my door. He instantly stops and opens the door for me. I walk in as he shuts it again, his steps carrying him away from the door.

I move to the bed pulling the duvet back enough to lie her down and then cover her up. I step back satisfied and watch her face. The color is slowly returning to her face, her lips sit slightly open with a rosy tone and freckles speckle her nose and cheeks.

She doesn't belong to the club aesthetic in any sense. She has natural beauty. She doesn't need makeup, or fancy clothes, or lack of, to show it.

She is like a flower, you can carefully admire her but pull her in and the impact will crush her. She doesn't belong in our world. Gio is right about that. The flowers stay in the garden and you gaze from afar. In this world, you have fun and pleasure. A game of catch and release. I could gain my fix with no strings attached, but girls like her attach. They grow vines that tangle around your heart and pierce it.

It takes effort to pull my gaze away and leave the room altogether. I head to my office and sit at my desk. I try to focus on the numbers but my mind keeps wandering to Gwenevere. I growl with frustration and leaving the office. It's a good day to enjoy the view of the garden

Pop

I pour a glass of bourbon, removing my suit jacket. I take a seat in the chair diagonal from the bed placing my jacket across my knee. I feel the burn at the sip of bourbon. Gwenevere's chest rises and falls.

I watch her for some time as the sun falls behind the trees. I don't know if I stare at her because of her beauty or because of the mystery she is. A part of me doesn't want to leave her alone in case something bad happens; but why would I care?

I close my eyes to rest when rustling flows through the room. Gwen's eyes roam the room and then land on my face. Her gaze travels over my chest and lightly bites her lip. Her and that damn lip… all the things I can do with those lips.

She continues around the room before landing back on me. She stills, bringing her lip back in. My lips twitch at the thought of devouring hers. My lips twitch at the thought of devouring hers. I glide over to her, stopping a foot from the bed and gently coax her chin up to me.

"You fell asleep. I didn't want to disturb you. You needed rest." My thumb moves to her bottom lip grazing lightly before gently tugging it free from her teeth's hold. I frown at the small pool of blood coming from the puncture.

"Your lip is bleeding."

She lifts her fingers feeling the blood for herself. She pulls her lip in sucking the blood off. This weird tension flows through my spine at the rebelling thought of my tongue swiping across her lips.

"Don't bite your lip."

She pops her bottom lip back out. She gasps at my demand—a gasp I would've missed had I not been watching her every movement. My lips pull into a smirk. She breaks contact with me, her face pales as she snaps the covers off with speed.

"What time is it?" She flies off the bed.

"Seven. The sun's almost set." I watch her as she frantically looks for her phone and straightens out her clothes.

"Oh no. Alessio is going to kill me! He and Enzo probably have the city looking for me." She groans stopping her search.

"Come on, your phone's downstairs. I'll give you a ride home." She bites her lip again, brows pulling together.

"Don't bite your lip."

Her face reddens as she pops her lip out again.

"Are you ready? If you need a moment I can—"

"No." She places her hand up before resting it back at her side. "I mean, I'm okay I just really need to get home."

I open the door and step to the side for her to pass through. After she passes I shut the door and lead down the hall. I hear her footsteps close behind me as we descended the large staircase.

When we reach the last step she breaks off to the living room retrieving her phone. I look down at mine, shooting a text to Gio and Viktor that I am leaving the estate and another to Bruno for the car.

"All set?" I turn back to her.

"All set."

I hold my arm out motioning for her to move out of the entry. I open the back door of the Escalade allowing her in before following.

I do a once over noticing Gwen still hasn't buckled. I inwardly shake my head, reaching over and pulling the seat belt in place with a click. As I retreat, my hand grazes the side of her thigh. I watch as her body responds to my movements. Goosebumps line her skin while she clenches her thighs. I can see her fighting the urge to bite her lip as she stares at me. I break my gaze turning to our driver.

Bruno waits for my directions through the rearview mirror.

"Where to Boss?" I glance at Gwenevere with a raised brow. Her face scrunches, oblivious that I don't just magically have her address.

"Guinevere, address. You would get home a lot quicker if you just told me."

"376 Olive Drive," she whispers. Her face turns a light blush and her lips part. I chuckle inwardly. *A flower; she is an untouchable flower, Matteo.* I pat Bruno's seat roughly.

"Go on, Bruno." He nods in the mirror and takes off. Gwen stares out the window, as we pull up to her house her features turn tense. I follow her gaze to the line of cars in her driveway.

She chews on her lip as Bruno slows the car down. Gweneveres unbuckles herself and jumps out of the car before I have a chance to move.

"Thank you so much for helping, truly. Please let Gio know I was thankful for him and the coffee. I'll pay him back," she yells through the door and then slams it. She runs to the front of the house and disappears behind the door in seconds.

"Well, that was a new one," Bruno mutters. I glare at him through the mirror, forcing him to clear his throat.

"Sorry, where to?"

"Take us back to the house."

Bruno drives away, my mind stays on Gwenevere. She rushed out as if to avoid me from getting out of the car. I shake my head, running a hand down my face.

She is gone now. Why am I still thinking about her? She is gone. I don't need to see her again. I look down at my phone and pull up my contacts, click on the name, and shoot a text.

I wait a few seconds before the *ding* comes back through, smirking at the return. A little fun is what I need to get my mind off of her. I lean back trying to relax when my phone *dings* again. I read the text.

Victor: Not seeing anything worth much.

My face furrows. There has to be something. Nobody causally has the ambiance I just saw.

6

Gwenevere

"What the hell, Sole," I mock. "You were my cover and you said you were watching out for me."

Sole scrunches her shoulders with a smile.

"Yeah so about that—"

"I can't believe you! Alessio had the whole fucking men in black team looking for me. Not only that but I looked like an idiot when he said your ass was passed out in here."

"Look, it wasn't like that. Your brother knew something was off the minute you got out of the car today and your response? Ditch school with some stranger after passing out and go MIA. You haven't answered any of my calls and honestly, it wasn't just Alessio worried about you." She scowls at me.

"I don't know if this is some new coping thing you do to deal with everything you've been going through, but honestly Gwen, you need to open your eyes and see that everyone's just looking out for you and—"

"No. You don't get to go there and use that on me. I'm a grown fucking woman. How I deal with my shit is no one's concern. I didn't 'disappear' today to cope. I was simply living my life. Everyone around me has done nothing but hold me back and treat me like an incoherent child. I expected a little more from you." I know I am fuming and will regret being so harsh to her, but I need her to know she broke my trust. I made it abundantly clear that I would be okay today. I always suck at answering her calls, and she doesn't have a good enough excuse as to why she'd rat me at Alessio.

"REALLY! Really, right now you want to talk about not acting like a child when you can't even talk to your own damn brother. Have you told him Gwen? Anything? Hell, he doesn't even need to know Enzo was involved. You could have the decency to let people in, and give yourself a chance to fully heal before you run off with some man and go MIA."

I stare at the floor for a moment and process Sole's words. She wasn't wrong but I wasn't ready to admit that and I sure as hell wasn't telling Alessio anything. Sole is my best friend and the one person who can yell at me for my stupid shit but this is different. Losing my baby is not like getting an F in my math class. Losing my baby tore a hole into my heart, Sole can't force it to heal, and Alessio can't sew the pieces together.

Enzo can't fix the empty space. He tried but a part of me didn't want him to. If Enzo fixed the hole in my heart I might forget the piece of heaven that rested within me. I refuse to forget.

"Get the fuck out." My voice comes out so softly I don't know if she even hears me. A few seconds later I bring my head up to find her stare. Emotions wage a war behind her irises, hurt that I would dismiss her like I did.

"I'm not gonna ask again, Sole. Leave." I stare directly at her trying not to break my facade. She puffs out shaking her head and grabs her things. She pauses at the door holding the knob. The seconds burn the flames between us. She slams the door behind her, breaking my locked stance.

I pick a random object from my dresser and throw it across the room with a half-grunt-half growl. I flop backward on the bed, closing my eyes and letting my mind race.

I know Sole has my best interest in mind, but I can't accept her advice this time—that I need to tell Alessio about the baby. If he knew… if he knew it would change everything. It would make it… real? Even if I don't mention Enzo, how could Alessio look at me the same? How could anyone?

I push myself to the mirror, looking at my reflection. I scan my body and fight the tears straining to release. This stupid worthless body. Born broken. The chronic pain I could handle on its own. I wish it was only pain.

I have to live with the embarrassment of not being able to control my own body. Being helpless and incapable. I hate every piece that's been put together to make me.

I am a set of jigsaw pieces that just don't quite fit and in the end, all you have is a fucked up picture with a broken frame.

Tears fall down my cheeks and I brush them away. I lock the door and place my comfort vinyl of the Rolling Stones on. I grab a book and settle on the bed to waste time and clear my mind. I need to get my head out of the dark, even if only a few minutes. I settle into my spot and read.

The Next Day

A whisper of a knock comes on my door. I bend my page for a makeshift bookmark and set it to the side of the bed. Sliding out of bed, I turn the volume down on the vinyl.

Unlocking the door, I brace myself for what's on the other side. Alessio leans against the wall, his gaze on the plush carpet.

"I don't like being that hateful brother. I mean well, Gwen, I truly do, but when you run off like this I don't know what else to do." His tone is full of sympathy but I don't miss the command behind it.

"I know." I concentrate on the limewashed walls not wanting to give him the satisfaction of looking him in the eye.

"Come on, dinner's ready." I nod and step out the door. Enzo is scrolling through his phone at the counter. *Dammit.* I really thought he'd be gone by now. He skims me with a blank face and returns to his phone. I move past him and pick a plate from the cupboard. I fix my dinner and debate my options.

"I'm just gonna eat in my room, I'm tired."

Enzo's head snaps up but before he can speak Alessio chimes in.

"No. Sit."

There is no room for fighting his order. I plop down at the counter and stab a fork into my steak.

"We need to talk, Gwen." Alessio starts what only seems like some type of intervention. "You ran off yesterday and didn't attend your first class. You weren't with Sole and you didn't have a car."

I raise my brows, shoving a piece of meat in my mouth.

"Good observations. Want a gold sticker?" I mumble through chewing. Enzo shakes his head next to me, setting his phone down and leaning back in his chair. His arms are crossed and Alessio glares at me pointedly from across the counter.

"Don't be snarky. It doesn't suit you."

"Being a *dickhead* doesn't really suit you either."

"Gwen."

"Alessio," I snap back. "Are we really going to have this conversation? What was that half-ass apology in the hallway? Or was that just your introduction to your interrogation?"

"I talked to Lena at the café. She said you came back in with a man." Alessio's face no emotion. I refuse to look at Enzo for what he might say. I know he isn't happy. Neither am I but I can't handle Enzo's response right now.

"Oh, so we're going there. Is that it? Am I not allowed to talk to guys either? Why don't you call Dad and tell him you're taking over as daddy of the year? He'd really appreciate it."

"Gwen, cut the shit. You skipped your first day and showed up at the coffee shop with a man no one ever heard about, much less you actively hide information about from us." His voice rises as he continues. "Lena said you left quickly and yet you have hours of time between Lena's and coming home."

"Alessio, I–"

"And apparently you passed out at school? Though maybe that was a part of your lie as you also managed to tell her I cleared your absence?"

"Cleared my absence? Do you even fucking hear yourself, Alessio? I know you're looking out for me, but really you're overstepping your bounds. I am old enough to make my own damn decisions. I don't need another father, the first was disappointing enough."

"You bet your ass I cleared your absence! Why are you so stupid sometimes? Why can't you fucking obey and just listen!"

"Is that what you want, huh? An obedient little girl? Go find some damn whore to fulfill your obsession because I'm not it Alessio!"

"Are you fucking kidding me! Some whore? You have your head so far up your ass!"

"Did anyone ever teach you to mind your own fucking business? You run off for a semester and come back more hot-headed than when you left, and I'm fucking over it, Alessio! You don't own me!"

"You want to talk about changing over the semester, when did you become an insecure bitch who fucks around!"

"Fucks around! Are you serious? You've slept with the whole damn city and then some. I go with a guy for a day and I'm a whore!"

"You're sure as hell denying a lot and pushing off any conversion about it! Who knows what you managed while I was gone!"

"You have no idea what happened while you were gone!"

"Because you keep all your childish-ass secrets!"

"Both of you can stop yelling. Let's just sit down and have a conversation." Enzo tries to de-escalatie. Alessio and I had slowly moved toward each other in our yelling battle.

"Enzo, not now." Alessio lowers his voice a notch but doesn't lose his heated tone.

"What happened when you were gone is not your concern. In fact, none of this is your damn concern, and I'm done sitting here getting scolded." I leave my partially eaten plate on the counter, snatching my purse off the table.

"Where the fuck do you think you're going?" Alessio growls.

"To go sleep around town, Alessio. It's what I'm good at, right?"

"You're not going anywhere," he orders, as if I actually give two shits at this point.

"I'm going wherever the hell I want. Don't wait up." With that, I slam the door. I pull out my phone to the only contact that isn't pissed off at me right now. I hesitate. I have nothing else to lose tonight. I press the phone to my ear listening to the rings on the other side. Just when I think no one will pick up, the line rustles.

"Gwenevere?" The man's voice deposits through the phone with a huskiness.

"Would you be up for another escape?" I ask, worried he'd say no or be annoyed.

"How soon?"

I let out a breathy laugh.

"Now?" I suck back in, biting my lip, and messing with my nail.

"Be there in five."

"See you in five."

The line clicks. A surge of adrenaline kicks in. Fighting against Alessio has always been hard and draining. I never feel this rush but I know it's not because of fighting with Alessio; I'm leaving, back into the mysterious world I stumbled into this morning.

I sit on the curb biting at my nails as I wait for my ride's arrival, looking back cautiously to make sure Alessio or Enzo don't follow me outside. Not moments later, a black Escalade pulls up beside me. The driver's side opens and Gio steps around the car with a smile. He opens the door to the car and ushers me in.

"Someone called for an escape?" He puts on a cheeky grin.

"You're a lifesaver." I smile playfully.

"Let's go before I need a backup plan." I nod as Gio shuts the door. The car is quiet for some time before his voice breaks the silence.

"Do you have a tendency to make escape plans? You didn't seem like the girl who snuck out the windows, your little friend… Sole was it? She definitely snuck out some windows, but you? Your innocence flares through the wind."

I puff a little and cross my arms "Innocence? I doubt you can call me innocent. I can be bad."

"The fact you just said, 'I can be bad,' proves my point." He lets out a soft laugh. "Tell me one thing you've done that's 'bad.'"

"Well… I—I shoplifted last week." I slowly grow confident and send out a smug smile. He raises a brow almost impressed—almost.

"You shoplifted? What did you steal?"

"Paint." I keep my head up. See, not so innocent.

"Paint? Are we talking spray paint or watercolors?"

"It was acrylic paint, thank you very much."

"Okay, so you stole a $2 paint tube?"

"$3 actually." I scrunch my nose feeling less confident.

"Congrats you are the worst criminal. You know what I should turn you in now." I swat his bicep as he chuckles. "See innocent. You're a wimpy criminal, you don't sneak out of windows and I would even bet you're a virgin."

I choke on my spit a little at his last remark, my eyes bulging out. My face instantly heats up.

He howls out a laugh. "I knew it, you're totally a virgin! Innocent."

"I'm definitely not a virgin," I shoot back. "And I'm definitely not innocent." He raises his eyebrows again and hums.

"Yeah, okay. When's the last time you got laid?"

"When's the last time you had a brain? I'm not telling a total stranger when the last time I had sex was," I scoff out. Did he really ask that? My face burns at this point.

"Oh. First off, we aren't strangers anymore, remember? Second, I'm your escape plan tonight which means you wanted me, your friend, to come. So start talking."

"Nope. I'm not telling you the last time I had sex."

"Okay, I'll guess. Six months?"

"Jesus."

"Seven months?"

"You went further out, really?"

He chuckles. I'm glad he's enjoying completely embarrassing me.

"I see then. Five months?" I slam a hand on my face.

"Are you really not going to drop this?" I search his face but amusement is the only emotion present. This is a field day for him.

"I really don't think it's been closer to four months. You're really uptight to have been laid anytime sooner."

"Oh my God. Two months. It's been two months, are you happy?" I rush out just wanting to end this conversation altogether but I only see it getting worse now.

"What about you, huh? When was the last time you got laid? You're surely annoying. I doubt anyone wanted to go to bed with you anytime recently."

"Darling, what do you think I was doing before you called?"

I freeze. *Did he really just say that?*

"Ew." I scrunch my face up as he smiles smugly.

"Don't worry, we were finished and I needed to get out of there. She was too clingy."

"Oh, so you're that type. That explains you a lot more." His shoulders shake with his laugh as he turns down the next road. I had lost track and stopped watching the road, but I honestly don't care where we are going.

"One of those types, huh? So now I'm a man whore?" His question comes out jokingly and I sigh with relief. This is the carefreeness I need today.

"Oh, I never called you a man whore. Wouldn't dare. Slut shaming is not my forte, but apparently, it is my brothers. He accused me of sleeping around with you yesterday." I laugh more to myself. "He can be so damn clueless and hot-headed but calling me a whore? His head is so far up his ass right now."

Gio's smile falls a bit, a line forming down his forehead.

"He called you whore?" His voice tensing at the end.

"Not out-right but he asked why I became such a little bitch who sleeps around since last semester. Which practically implies that he thinks I'm a whore. Little does he know..." I trail off, so Gio won't hear the last part.

"Know what?" I cringe. *Dammit.* I hesitate. Do I lie? I'm so tired of all the lies and secrets.

"I, well the thing is—"

Gio skims me while I stumble over my words, but allows me space to gather them.

"I may have slept with someone he would kill me for even thinking about going near while he was away on a retreat thing, and it didn't end well—"

I drop my eyes to my hands. I haven't been very open about losing the baby, or even Enzo and I, with anyone... I just want to forget it ever happened.

"Did he hurt you?" His knuckles are white against the wheel and his jaw clenched.

"No. No nothing like that. It's just something happened that was out of our control and I just don't know… I couldn't get past it and I realized I shouldn't have even gotten in the mess in the first place. I thought maybe it was a sign, maybe losing the baby was a sign that I was being so, so stupid," I ramble and feel a bit of release from talking to someone.

"Baby?" His voice was a mix of shock and strain. *Shit.* I didn't mean for the whole part to come out. "You were pregnant and lost the baby? And you didn't tell him any of it?" I stumble through my brain to find my next words, my face hot.

"I didn't mean to say it but yes. I lost the baby. I was going to tell Alessio. He was going to be home in a week but when I woke up all I saw was… I just couldn't." I suck in a sharp breath. My chest caves into a giant hole.

"You are stronger than you give yourself credit for. You went through all that, hiding a relationship, a baby, and then ultimately the major trauma of losing a baby, and you still managed to get through your brother's accusations." He peers into my eyes. "It wasn't your fault. And you don't owe anyone anything. But maybe it would feel like less of a load if you told your brother. Even part of it."

I shake my head back and forth, swiping a few tears away.

"I can't tell him. He'll push too much to know who the father was and that will be worse for everyone in the end."

"You can't know that for sure."

But I do. I do know what Alessio would do if he found out it was Enzo. It will change everything between the three of us. A lifelong bond shattered. It wasn't our intention by any means. I had hoped that at least the baby would ease the situation and Alessio would grow to like our family, but I didn't have the chance to confirm.

"You really don't understand how high my brother holds his loyalty. Something like this. This would ruin everything because of me."

Gio nods and pulls his gaze to the neon lights of a little ice cream and burger shop with a handful of checked tables out front.

"How about some ice cream?" The pure joy on his face is comforting.

"Ice cream never hurt." I sigh and check myself in the mirror. My door opens and I slide out following Gio to the counter. I look at the bright sign above—I can not eat anything I want on my own.

"Would you want to share a banana split? I can never finish them by myself, and I don't want to waste it." It sounds stupid for me to share an ice cream and I almost palm myself for the idiocy, but I'm halted from my spiral by his chuckle.

"Sure why not." He shrugs with a slight grin. I lean over the counter where the cashier is waiting. Of course, there is a glass separating us and I groan inwardly. It is already so had to hear with the glass but add the glare coming off it and it's making it even harder to read his lips.

"Hi. Can I get a banana split and a Dr.Pepper?"

"Make that two," Gio says from behind me.

"Actually make that two Dr.Peppers, please." My smile drops as the boy speaks, a remnant of a whisper thrown underwater reaches my ears.

"I'm sorry, could you say that a little louder?" I smile sheepishly. He repeats his previous speech but I swear he said it quieter. I sway side to side picking at my nails. I don't want to inconvenience them, but I honestly don't know what he said. Gio presses against my back, easing my anxiety.

"Extra peanuts, please, and large drinks." He slides his card to the boy and gives me a soft smile. The boy sends back the card and hands us our drink. Gio places a hand on my back leading us to a nearby table.

"Thank you."

"Ice cream is always a great evening snack." He sips his soda.

"Thanks for the ice cream and stepping in." He shrugs with a smirk.

"I could get used to helping you escape." I throw my head back with a laugh.

"I don't make it a ritual, but like you said, ice cream never hurts." I drink my soda and browse the cute parlor. Even though we are near the city, we are far enough away that the parlor feels both scarcely populated and overcrowded at the same time.

Gio leaves to go to the pickup window, coming back with a giant banana split, two spoons, and a massive collection of napkins.

"This looks bomb as hell," I snort.

"Of course, it's a banana split." He hands over a spoon and we devour the treat. We converse in small talk until we are close to finishing.

"Are you gonna eat anymore?"

"I don't think I can handle anymore."

"That's what she said."

I roll my eyes, which he returns with a smirk.

"Really 'that's what she said'. What are you sixteen?"

"Not sixteen but I can confirm that, she said it." He winks. I fake a gag causing him to laugh. His phone rings drawing his attention away. "You want to go home or come back with me?"

"You're not getting another booty call tonight, at least not from me."

"I'm not asking you to come back to my bed, I'm asking if you want to come over and escape your brother longer."

I blush, rubbing the top of my hand.

"Okay. Let's go." Gio scoops up our trash, throwing it away. He opens the door and waits for me to get in and buckle.

His phone buzzes, forcing him to roll his eyes before answering.

"*Cosa?*" *What?* He pauses for the other line. "I'm literally in my car headed to the house."

"I did text you," he groans.

"I'll be there in five." He hangs up the phone and pulls out. "I swear my brother has his panties in a twist every second of the day."

"Your brothers waiting for you?"

"*Pft,* waiting? The man doesn't know what the definition of waiting is. Maybe our brothers should get together for a tea party. You've seen how uptight he is. The business turned him cold but I mean."

"I've seen him?"

Gio's face etches up drawing lines on his forehead.

"Well yeah, he brought you home yesterday."

Matteo is Gio's brother and I'm about to see him again. I clear my throat wiggling in my seat.

"Everything okay?"

"Yeah, no, everything's good. I just didn't know Matteo was your brother." I twirl a piece of my hair then drop my hand in my lap.

"Is that a bad thing? What did he do? I swear he can be a prick sometimes, but if he did anything I will tear into his—"

"No, he didn't do anything I just—I was dazed earlier. He's—"

"Hard-headed? Arrogant? Asshole? I mean the list goes on."

"Something like that."

7

Gwenevere

Stepping out of the car I prepare myself for seeing Matteo. I would see him, right? I mean I'm bound to, it's his house too after all.

We step inside and are greeted by the guards. This time they are more relaxed and sitting playing cards in the foyer. I acknowledge them with a tilt of my head that goes without a response.

The living room is empty and the smell of bleach reaches my nose. We stride to the kitchen but stop at the entry. I stand behind Gio's back not getting a view of the kitchen.

"Nice of you to finally join us." A husky voice that's been locked in my memory falls to my ears.

"Shut the fuck up. Do you have anything else to do besides call me at all hours of the night and day?" Gio grunts.

101

"Of course I do. Unfortunately, your stupid face has to be there for most of it."

Gio grabs his neckline as if clutching pearls.

"Oh I'm blushing. Please buy me some flowers." He moves to the fridge giving me the chance to find Matteo and Viktor sitting at the island. Matteo is seated, relaxing with his arms crossed while Viktor is turned to the side.

My pulse thumps at the sight of Matteo. His jacket is flung behind him on the seat, dress shirt clinging to his biceps. His sleeves are rolled up just below his elbow and the top buttons are open, showing a piece of his chest. I rake over him, drinking in his essence while biting my lip.

"You brought her back?" Matteo scans down my body making me cautious of what I'm wearing. I left the house in what can only be described as pajamas. My off-the-shoulder sweater and a pair of shorts.

Gio shrugs. "We got ice cream."

"Ice cream?" Matteo gives him a pointed look.

"Do you hate ice cream too? You're really a stone-cold bitch." Matteo doesn't respond, fixated on me, his eyes lower to my lips. I pop my lip out from my teeth and swallow. A smirk tugs at his lips and disappears as quickly as it comes.

"Do you need a room?" Viktor brings a glass of bourbon to his face, hiding his smirk. Matteo turns to Viktor giving him a glare. Gio glances between Matteo and me while grabbing an apple from the counter.

"Gio, you have a stack of papers on your desk. I need them revised by the morning." Matteo drops his questioning and my shoulders relax.

"It's literally the middle of the night."

"You '*literally*' ran off for ice cream. That's not my problem. If you start now you'll have it done in no time."

"Jesus." Gio groans and peers at me.

"I can help?" I offer with a shrug of my shoulders as a chuckle escapes Viktor. *Okay...*

"No. Gio, go. We'll keep her company." Gio hesitates but loses his internal battle, sending me a sheepish look before exiting the room. When I focus back on the room I find Matteo locked in on me.

Viktor stands up smacking him on the shoulder and grabbing his own suit jacket. He takes the last swing of his drink and sets the cup in the sink.

"I'm off to my quarters." He passes me with a nod.

Then there were two. I stand still not knowing what to do with myself. This is the last place that I would've been expecting to be tonight. If I knew I would end up in front of Matteo tonight I might have tried to fix my appearance.

"I thought I told you not to bite your lip." My lip pops out again and my skin ignites. "Come sit."

I glide over to the stool. Matteo's eyes follow as I climb into the chair.

"Want a drink?" He points to the fancy bottle of bourbon on the counter. While I really could drink after the last couple of days, I've had an increase of blood loss to the head as of late and think it's best if I don't. But a few sips never hurt anyone, right?

"Small pour, please."

"Over the rocks?"

I shake my head. "Straight." My voice comes out soft. A glimpse of a smile sits on his lips. He hands me the glass and I take a small sip. I don't think I've managed to drink much water today, which is never good. I wipe my lips and glance around the kitchen.

"Ice cream?" he pries, wrapping a hand around his own drink.

I tap my glass, and he follows the movement. He captures every single fluctuation I make. I would even bet he can trace each breath I take and read me like I'm a book for him to study. I clear my throat.

"Um, yeah. Gio had ice cream on his mind I guess." When Matteo doesn't respond right away, I continue, "I got into it with my brother about the whole disappearing thing today, and I just didn't want to hear his bullshit anymore. Gio was my escape planner," I say, babbling probably more than needed. I wiggle in my seat waiting for him to respond.

"You were fighting because you disappeared so you disappeared again." His voice is filled with humor. I pull my lip in a little as I think about it. I really didn't play that too well did I? Alessio is going to be so pissed off when I get home.

"You're bad at listening." I snap my eyes back to meet Matteo's. Did he say something and I didn't hear him? He scoots closer to me and my body pricks. He comes to my face, his thumb brushing against my lip before pulling it out from where I bite it. My breathing quickens and suddenly my whole body is in a rage of heat.

"Are you teasing me?" His brow quirks, but his tone is devious. Was I? The once prickling of my skin is now pure agony. The tension is almost too much to bear.

"What if I am?" I don't think twice as the words flow from my mouth. My body has taken over the rational part of my mind. *Stupid whiskey.*

"You don't want to tease me." The smokey drop in his voice reverbs through me.

"You don't know what I want." Who am I? This is a total stranger. What am I doing? Why does this feel so good? His features grow dark, his thumb still circling my bottom lip.

"I think I do."

Matteo breaks away, throwing back the rest of his drink and slides out of his chair with a palm to me. I don't give myself a chance to think over my actions and grab his hand. Willing to sacrifice myself to wherever he leads. We head up the stairs and back into the room I awoke in yesterday. Matteo opens the door and he pulls me in. I suck in the air, his scent consuming me.

"You must be tired." Matteo's voice dances to me from behind.

"A little." The notion leaves me breathless. I feel Matteo move closer to me. His hand skims the back of my shoulder. He pushes my hair to the side and plays with the button on the back of my sweater. He slips it out of its hold as my skin tingles.

"What do you want?" Matteo half whispers into my hair as he slowly drags his fingers from my shoulder down my arms. His touch leaves a trail of pleasure in such a simple touch. I don't want him to stop.

I close my eyes as his fingers trail ever so slowly back up. He touch feathers along my collarbone until he reaches my chin and turns my face to him. I brace and open my eyes. A wave of heat cascades down my chest only stopping when it reaches my center.

"Do you want this?" His eyes move down to my lips, and I can't help but think of what he wants to do to them.

"Yes."

Matteo crashes his lips on mine. His kiss isn't gentle but I don't mind. I need this. I need this touch. My body pushes greedily against him while our lips fight in a rage of passion. His hand slips behind my head and under my hair where he holds me firmly to devour my lips.

I place my hands on his chest to steady myself, using one hand to grab the fabric of his shirt as if I'm going to be whisked away in the air.

His tongue swipes the bottom of my lip, and I open my mouth eagerly, wanting as much as he will give me. His tongue roams as I embrace every touch. His hand grabs the hem of my sweater, tugging it up. I pull my arms up letting him slip my shirt over my head and discard it.

He dips his gaze over my chest, yet I don't feel an ounce of embarrassment. All I feel is a fire inside me that is pleading to be extinguished—a fire that only he can put out. I reach behind me and remove my bra as Matteo drinks in every inch of me.

I reach my hand to his shirt and unbutton it, placing my lips back on his. He doesn't stop me as I push his shirt off his shoulders. He tosses it and deepens our kiss further.

Matteo's hand glides down my side reaching my shorts. He grips the band and pulls them from my hips, lowering himself to leave rough kisses against my thigh. My hands fly to his belt and I unbuckle them as fast as my fingers will let me. I release the button and slide down the zipper to his pants.

We slowly step back stumbling over our clothes as we move to the bed. By the time we reach it, his pants are discarded and his bulge is stretching his boxers. The notable burn alights between my thighs, aching for him.

Matteo pushes me on the bed. He grasps my hips, tugging me forward. His lips meet mine again, leaving a few kisses before trailing them down my neck. He focuses on the soft spot above my collarbone then moves down, forcing a moan. He stops at my nipple and swirls the bud with his tongue. He takes my nipple between his teeth, licking, sucking, and nibbling. My eyes slam shut as I push my chest into him begging for more. His hand trails my body lower to my aching center.

Matteo's fingers fall to my nub through my panties where he draws small circles. Pressure builds inside me under his double torture. I press against him begging for more friction.

I moan out as his fingers work devilishly on my clit. His pace quickens and I clench my thighs around his arm. His fingers circle a few more times before my body shakes beneath him.

As the sensations simmer, Matteo discards my soaking panties. I sit up the best I can, gripping his boxers. I pull them down allowing cock to spring out. I sit forward and grab his shaft in my hand holding firm. I peer up at him.

His jaw clenches as he watches me with hunger. I open my lips in an O and lower myself to his pulsing cock. I twirl my tongue against his tip savagely tasting the beaded drops of his arousal before lowering and taking him all in. His body tenses under my touch, small groans escape his lips.

I move my mouth along his length meeting the hand I've placed at the base of his cock. I bob my head a couple of times, my movements are cut short as I'm pushed on my back.

Matteo immediately crashes his lips to mine, gripping my hair in his fist deepening the kiss. He presses me into the mattress, grabbing my hips and pulling my center closer to his length.

He looks at me with eyes filled with lust. I nod, giving him the permission he was searching for. With that, he slams into me. I grab the sheets holding on as the intense pleasure mixed with pain fills me.

He stops allowing me to adjust. I breathe deeply to calm my rapid heartbeat. *You're fine. It's fine. Everything's fine.* My hands fist the sheets tight, reeling myself in from my crashing emotions. Matteo pulls out and slams back into me over and over. My body shakes, yet I'm unable to process what is happening until Matteo mutters.

"Shit." His breathless concern snaps my focus back to him. "Fuck did I hurt you?" He scans my face and it's then that I realize that I'm shaking. . . not from the pleasure but I'm crying. I look away but he pulls my face to him.

Tears fall down my face. Of course. I have the sexiest man alive literally inside of me and what do I do? I cry. This is the first time since I lost the baby. I didn't think I would cry, but nobody really knows when the waves of greif will come—no matter the moment.

"I'm sorry," I choke out.

"Why are you sorry?" Matteo's brows are furrowed. "Did someone hurt you?"

"No. No, I—" I pause. Is this really the time? No. I need this. I need to get past this. "Please don't stop."

He studies my face for reassurance. I nod preparing myself for the rough fuck to resume, but instead, he pulls me into him. Matteo places a soft kiss on my lips before slowly pushing inside me. His body moves in a smooth rhythm leaving me raw. His hand grips my hip and the other trails to my hair, holding my head.

He moves against my walls forcing my back to rise off the mattress. I moan into his mouth, his pace picking up. I grind against him as I plead for his mercy. The pressure builds fast; my thighs clench around his waist pulling him flush on me.

My head falls back breaking the kiss as I cry out squeezing my eyes in ecstasy. My body uncontrollably shakes as warmth pools and soaks us. Matteo pumps into me a few more times and grunts as his pace quickens.

"Fuck." He fists the sheets beside my head as he pushes in me a final time. His cock pulses inside of me while he lays sloppy kisses against my swollen lips.

He sets his forehead on mine as our breathing slows and my heart calms. His hand finds my face again, thumb tracing my cheek. A brief tender touch before he pulls away and I'm met with cold air. My nipples harden on impact.

My body is so exhausted I lie there for a second more. Matteo approaches me again with a warm towel. Lowering his hand down to my thigh, he wipes off our sticky mess. He kisses the inside of my thigh then returns to his upright position grabbing my hand to help me up.

I move forward to grab my clothes but Matteo grabs my arm. He pulls back the covers and motions for me to lie down. I debate whether I should but lose the fight within my mind, climbing into the bed and fully relaxing. Matteo steps around the bed and shuffles in as the bed dips behind me.

My brain wants to jump and find every reason to be anxious but I am too tired to indulge. One last inhale of the sheets and I'm falling into a deep sleep.

8

Matteo

I study Gwenevere as she lays peacefully next to me. Once I convinced myself to stay away from her she waltzed back through my door. Everything about her is divine. From her hair to the sway of her hips.

She was just as eager as I was last night. Simple sex.

But things hang in doubt now. How did I allow myself to indulge? I knew what she was, a flower. The moment I pushed inside her I felt the shift. Before I knew it she was crying. Crying. My mind had been running. Did I hurt her? Was this not what she really wanted?

I press the tip of my cock against her pulsing center. Her muscles begging me to invade her. I find her sky-filled eyes, assuring myself that she does in fact want me to corrupt her. One simple nod from her gives me all the permission I need.

I slam into her, fully submerging myself inside her. She clenches around my throbbing member. I settle in, giving her a chance to adjust but only allowing her a few seconds before pulling out and slamming into her again.

"Fuck."

She is fucking divine. I want to burrow inside of her. I thrust a few more times before I'm met with her shaking body. Except this didn't feel like an orgasm. I glance over her distraught features rearing to a stop. Tears fall down her cheeks and she lays as if she's unaware of the action herself.

"Shit." Adrenaline shoots through me. Was I too rough with her?

"Fuck did I hurt you?"

I scan over her as if I can see physical bruises. Her head shakes then turns away from me. Something inside me shifts and yet I can't tell what or why it does. I place a hand on her chin turning her back to me. Tears fall faster and I'm left stumbling along in my own thoughts.

Why is she crying? She was fine right before I entered her. She said I didn't hurt her, but what did to force her to break down in tears?

"I'm sorry." Her words come out hoarse, sending a twinge of emotion through me that I can't define.

"Why are you sorry?" What on earth makes her think she needs to apologize for crying? Did someone abuse her?

"Did someone hurt you?" I swear to God if someone fucking hurt a hair on her head, this night will end in a lot more violence than it began.

"No. No, I—" Her chest rises but stutters as it falls. Her eyes lock with mine, desperation seeping from them. *"Please don't stop."*

I study her, hesitating, wondering if that's exactly what I should do. Stop. But that isn't what she needs right now. She needs me to continue. Whatever flipped inside her, she needs this to heal a piece of what has broken. To my own surprise, I want to be the one to give her just that. Against my better judgment, I take what isn't mine to take and I splinter the flower further; the least I can do is attempt to repair my damage.

I need to give her the attention she needs just as much as she needs it. A Yin for Yang that I didn't know existed—or that I could crave—yet here I am willing to give her just that.

She nods reassuring me once more, but this time I don't slam into her. The rough fuck I had my mind set on at the start of our rendezvous is no longer an option—not for me and definitely not for her.

I grab her hip softly and lower myself to her. Pressing into her with a soft embrace. I leave soft kisses against her lips before easing inside her. A low vibration comes from her throat, a sound made of raw need.

A flush of heat runs down my spine and to my straining erection. A thick desire to pull her closer consumes me. I wrap my fingers in her hair caressing her head in my palm. I seize her hip with my other hand nuzzling as close to her as possible.

Her back arches off the bed as I grind my hips. My once-measured rhythm is at a pace. Our bodies creating a musical of notes between our labored breaths and the audible connection of each thrust.

She lets out a string of whimpers mixed with moans. Her walls clench around my engorged cock as she desperately chases her orgasm; her wet folds drenching us while she chases her releases against my pelvic bone. I'm losing myself within her unadulterated need.

She seizes her thighs around my waist forcing me as close to her as humanly possible. This time she convulses with pure ecstasy. Her walls contract around me and I pump into her with steady thrusts before finding my own high.

"Fuck." I spill my release inside her, tightening my fist in the sheets. I grind to the rhythm of our slowing hearts, giving her every twitching inch with no forgiveness. I connect our swollen lips with disorganized kisses.

I place my forehead to hers matching her labored breaths until they are back to a normal rhythm. I trace her cheek, taking in the Goddess lying before me. Her beauty is enough to bring a man to his knees and weep at a world where it doesn't exist. A Goddess with the heart of a rose and I've just peeled a petal away. I have corrupted the untouchable.

I withdraw from her, rising from the bed, and find myself in the bathroom. Grabbing a couple of towels from the shelf, I dampen them under warm water. I clean myself off and toss that towel into the dirty bin before returning to Gwenevere with the other.

She lays peacefully in the bed, riddled with exhaustion. I remove any trace of our creamy mess and kiss the tender skin of her thigh. I place a hand out lifting her from the bed to remove the top cover and pull back the sheets.

She steps towards her clothes, and I lurch forward clutching her arm. She peeks back with pinched brows. I pull the sheet further as I wave my hand to the bed. I don't want her to leave. I would never let a woman stay over in any other circumstance, but after the events that have played out, I can't bring myself to throw her out.

She gives up the silent argument and climbs into the bed, wrapping the sheets around herself. Reaching my side of the bed I flip the lamp off and dip into the bed beside her.

Her breaths become shallow and the room falls into a peaceful silence.

I snap out of my memory and slide out of the bed. I pick a suit from the closet and dress while my mind wanders. What might have started out casually didn't end casually.

It was slow and raw—too raw. I never asked if she was on the pill. My mind doesn't think straight around her. I wanted quick and fun and now she is sleeping in my bed. The bed I offered her when she initiated her own leave.

I sigh in frustration at myself. I gaze over Gwenevere's peaceful frame. Regardless of my conflicting emotions, I can't deny that I don't mind the sight in front of me. I drag my hand down my face trying to snap my head out of the delusion I'm currently indulging in.

I snatch my phone off the table and step out of the room. A few unimportant texts litter my phone. I jog down to the kitchen desperate for a cup of coffee. I turn the corner to be greeted by Gio and Viktor at the island. I was mildly unprepared for the confrontation from them over my late-night events. Gio glares while Viktor smirks into his paper. I pour myself a cup and lean against the counter, taking my first sip of the pure caffeine needed to jumpstart my day.

Gio huffs, shaking his head. I raise a brow at his boyish attitude.

"Bruno said he had an early night. Gwen didn't leave the estate." His words come with venom. I shrug my shoulder taking another sip.

"She didn't."

"Where did she end up?"

"Don't ask stupid questions."

"Are you fucking serious? Do you ever listen? She's not meant to be in this world. She's sure as hell not meant for you. When did you decide in that big ass head of yours that fucking her was a good idea?"

"I can do whatever the fuck I want. I don't answer to you Gio." I take another sip of my coffee. " Besides, it was casual, don't get your panties in a twist."

"Do you really believe that Matteo? You really believe that woman up there just fucks around?"

"Well she fucked me the day after she met me so I'd say yes." That's not exactly how it went but I'm not going to let Gio know that. The worst part is I know he's right, but that isn't going to change what happened.

"And she stayed the night. In your bed."

My fists clench, I don't need to be scolded by him about my sexual activity or anything else for that matter. Especially before I've managed to drink my coffee.

"Was that your plan?" Gio bites out.

"What if it was?" I responded nonchalantly.

"She's not some whore you can just fuck and discard you idiot," he seethes "You don't even know her." He throws his hands up before dropping them to his side.

"And you do? Since when does it matter who I sleep with?" I bite back harshly.

"I didn't bring her here as a play toy for you to—" The cut of his voice pulls my attention to his line of sight. Gwenevere stands in the entryway looking at Gio and Viktor, avoiding my immediate gaze.

Gio looks between Gwenevere and me then straightens himself with a warm smile. Viktor chuckles to himself shaking his head, and I curse at the clusterfuck dynamic I have single handedly forged.

9

Gwenevere

I shuffle under the soft cover, lifting my head to browse the room in confusion. Images of last night flood my memories, reminding me of what I did and whose room I'm in.

Light seeps into the cold room from the windows. I sit up slightly and look to the side of the bed. The blanket is bundled up, confirming Matteo slept in the bed. My mind dances at the thought of Matteo and his touch.

I shake my head and remove the covers, slipping out of the bed. I find my discarded clothes nicely folded on the bench. I dress and smooth out any wrinkles in the bathroom mirror.

I adjust my bun and examine the room. A giant stand-up tub sits directly behind me with a double shower to the side. A large window sits on the back wall overlooking the trees. I would die for this setup.

I stare at myself, giving myself an internal pep talk. *Yes, you're about to do the walk of shame. It'll be fine. I'm sure no one even cares. I don't really know any of them anyway. Shit. What if Gio's here? What will he think?*

I just met him. It's not like he has much to go off of. So what if I sleep around? Although, our conversation from last night is a sure indicator that the man knows about my sex life. Maybe he'll be happy I got laid… just maybe not by his brother.

I push my shoulders back and hold my head up. I open the door, peering into the hall before stepping out. I head to the staircase and spot a guard at the top. I nod politely but only receive a tight nod back.

"You can find Matteo in the kitchen." The guard's brief comment gives me some hope I can break them down.

"Thank you." I give a smile and patter down the stairs. I greet the guards in the foyer and find myself outside of the kitchen. I stop, listening to the voices arguing just a few feet away.

"Was that your plan?" Gio bites out.

"What if it was?" Matteo counters nonchalantly. I roll my eyes at his stupid smugness.

"She's not some whore you can just fuck and discard you idiot." Gio doesn't sound happy at all. *Is he mad at me?* "You don't even know her."

"And you do? Since when does it matter who I sleep with?" Matteo ends harshly.

"I didn't bring her here as a play toy for you to—"

I am done listening in and don't want to know where this was headed. I round the corner and stop in the doorway, the voices quieting. Gio, Viktor, and Matteo all look at me.

Viktor smirks, shaking his head to himself, and dips into his coffee. Gio gives me a once-over and glances at Matteo.

"Good morning." Gio straightens and smiles at me.

"Morning." I smile back then turn my eyes to Matteo. His eyes trail down my body, devouring me from afar. When his eyes move back to meet mine, a shiver runs down my spine and settles in my lower stomach. Viktor clears his throat breaking my focus.

"Sleep well?" A cocky ass grin is plastered on his face. At this point, I know I'm bright red. Gio throws an apple at Viktor who dodges and breaks out into laughter.

"Are you hungry?" Gio holds up another apple.

"A little. Do you have juice?"

"Orange or apple?"

"Orange, please." I step further in the room attempting to ignore Matteo's gaze. My head spins a little as I reach the chair. I suck in a breath, filling my lungs, and grab onto the end of the counter, shutting my eyes for a second. A hand rests on my back steadying me.

"Sit." Matteo's voice rings in my ear. I follow his directions and sit on the stool nearby, grabbing my head with a groan. One day—I just want one day. Gio sets the orange juice in front of me with a granola bar.

"I'll have the chef cook up some breakfast." Gio stalks out of the room without question.

"Are you okay?" I focus on my surroundings, grounding myself. Matteo is trying to help but he fogs my vision and any sense of rationality.

"Yeah. I just need to eat something." I take a sip of the orange juice and already feel slightly rejuvenated. I lean against the back of the stool and open the granola taking small bites.

A small headache racks my brain but the pressure is more concerning. I'm sure I will develop a migraine. The last place I want to be is at home where Alessio can scowl at me, but I'm not sure I want to be here in all this awkwardness either.

I massage the side of my head as Matteo rounds the counter. He opens the cupboard and pulls out a bottle before replacing it. He returns holding out two pills. I look up and pinch my brows together.

"Tylenol." My face relaxes and I nod. Viktor chuckles to the side and I snap my attention to him confused once more.

"This is going to be fun." He smirks, eyeing Matteo and I. Us? Is he crazy? I'm not stupid. I know exactly what last night was. Sex. Nothing more, nothing less. Yes, I slept in his bed after but it was late and I obviously didn't have a car. Gio was stuck in his office, and it didn't make sense for me to leave and wait somewhere else.

"Viktor." Matteo gives Viktor a glare.

Viktor throws his hands up, gets off his stool with his coffee, and leaves the room. Gio returns accessing the space between Matteo and I, or the lack thereof. I squirm a little in my seat.

He sets a plate of food in front of me and I take a bite of bacon. The tension only grows in the room. Gio clears his throat opening his mouth to speak but I cut him off.

"Um, my brother's probably worried sick about me. I should head home soon." Matteo's expression is blank, but Gio's lip twitches.

"I'm guessing it's not going to be a pleasant homecoming," Gio more so states than questions.

"I'm guessing you're probably right," I grumble. Alessio is going to be pissed. Not only did I run off but I stayed out overnight without informing anyone of my whereabouts. I am in for it and after our last fight, I know it is going to be hell.

"We can leave after you eat." Gio tilts his head towards my plate. I continue to eat my breakfast and Matteo steps back to his coffee.

"I'll be in my office. We have a meeting at noon." Matteo grabs his cup and turns to leave, a tinge of smirk tugs at his lips as he passes me. Once he's gone I relax until I spot Gio's own smirk.

"So my brother." He holds back a laugh as I shoot him a glare.

"Don't." A blush returns to my cheeks.

"I mean I did tell you to get laid. I didn't mean by my douchebag of a brother, although I'm not too surprised."

"Not surprised?"

"Oh no, not you. I knew my brother would see you as some prize to win after I brought you home." I choke on my breakfast, sipping my juice, and fix my gaze back on Gio.

Should I really be shocked? A prize. I mean it's not like I knew the guy. I don't sleep around. Hell, Enzo was my first. Going into that mess I was fully aware of the casual fuck that it was—hit it and move on. And I knew what I was doing last night.

A piece of me just hurts. Hurts because I still feel so empty. Replacing grief and anger with sex only worked in the moment.

"Right." I twirl the rest of the food on the plate.

"Don't get your hopes up with him. He's not the relationship type. He can't and won't give you anything more. My advice? Take last night as a win and move on."

I bite my lip but nod, setting my fork down.

"Can you take me home now?"

"Come on."

I get off the stool and follow him to the foyer. "I'm dropping her off. I'll be back for the meeting, let Matteo know." The guard confirms leaving for the office. I stare off behind the guard. When Gio comes back into sight, I take in his vacant stare.

"Come on," I say with as little emotion as I can muster. This wasn't that big of a deal. I slept with a random guy. That's it. Now it's time to go home and deal with the consequences of pissing off Alessio.

We drive in silence for some time before Gio's voice breaks through the air.

"Don't let him give you too much shit. You're a grown woman."

I laugh an under my breath.

"You don't know Alessio." I stare out the window, twirling my thumbs. I'm prepared for the hell I am sure to endure the moment I walk in the door.

"Hey. If you need anything, call."

"Okay." We pull to my house and I give him a soft smile. "Thank you."

"Anytime." Gio steps out of the car and comes to my door, helping me out. I smile again and leave down the driveway. I hear Gio's door shut and leave.

I open the door, finding Alessio in his chair with raised brows. I turn at the feel of another presence finding Enzo. His eyes are cold as he looks over me.

"Finally decide to come home?" Alessio seethes.

"Finally decide to get your head out of your ass?"

"Was that him?" His jaw clenches.

"Who is *him*?" I say playing dumb. I know what Alessio is implying, and I don't want to get into it with Enzo around or at all for that matter.

"Don't play stupid, Gwenevere," he growls at me. "Is he the reason you've been so different since I came back?" *Oh.* That's not where I saw this going. My stomach drops and Enzo tenses just enough for me to catch it.

"Alessio." I shoot him a warning tone, though, all it seems to do is give him momentum. He jumps from the chair stalking forward.

"Don't 'Alessio' me. You're keeping too many damn secrets, Gwen! Is he the one you've been trailing? I'm not stupid, I know something happened, and you've been shut down since."

"You don't even know what you're talking about! You don't get anything! Why are you so fucking naïve!"

"I'm naive? If he's not the one, then it was someone else. Is that what you've made yourself up to? It's been less than two months since I have been back, and you're already sleeping with someone new and going behind my back again!"

"I'm not going behind your back! I'm just living dammit! I get to live my life the way I want to. I'm a grown woman. I'm not just the little girl you have to save any more!"

"Not a little girl I have to save! Then why are you always crying? You are constantly shattering! Who else is there to pick up the pieces!"

Tears rush down my face, his words stabbing into my ribs. If only he knew how bad it's been. It doesn't give him a right to pull me apart word by word.

"You just keep putting yourself out there to get hurt and pushing me away! Do you even think? Going out fucking around, you're going to get knocked up—or worse!"

"Oh, so that's what would make this worse? Huh? That would be the worst thing in the world wouldn't it? Your whore of a sister getting knocked up and you have to pick up all the pieces! You aren't doing shit but hurting me more. You don't care about picking up any of the pieces, you care about your fucking image and what you can control! You could give two shits about what I've lost as long as it doesn't hinder how you look, but you can't control this Alessio! You can't fucking control this and you sure as hell can't pick up the fucking pieces!" I can feel slivers of my heart breaking off. Tears stream down my face as the pieces of me tremble, waiting to fall.

Enzo steps forward but doesn't touch me. I know what this is doing to him, but this isn't about him right now. This is about Alessio and me. Why Enzo bothered to stay was beyond me. I've told him time and time again—that I can't. Right now, Alessio has all intention of tearing every wall I have down.

"What, Gwen? What can't I control? What can't I fix? What have I not done for you? I put my head on the fucking line for you! What is so bad, huh? What did you lose that you can't even fucking tell me!"

"MY BABY!" I scream, mere feet from Alessio. His movements still, becoming speechless. Enzo's chest rises and falls, fear laced in his eyes. Alessio squeezes his eyes shut, clenching his teeth together.

"Your baby?" His voice cracks as he strains the words out. My tears flow faster as I break, no longer able to hold myself together.

"My baby," I whisper shakily, my voice undoubtedly giving me away. I feel movement before Alessio grabs me, pulling me into his chest. I snap, the final piece falling. All the pieces I've duct-taped together crumble, proving Alessio right. I am broken and I can't put back the pieces, not by myself.

I cry into Alessio's chest my knees buckling. He holds me like this until my tears are scarce. He presses my head into him, his chest rising.

"Who?" One word. One easy answer, but it's one I can't give. Not now. Not ever. I pull away, longing to be able to open up to him but knowing that isn't possible without someone getting hurt.

"Alessio…" Enzo speaks up and I jump out of my skin. No, Enzo can't confess. Alessio can't know.

"Please just don't. I can't do this right now, Alessio. I can't look back. I just want… I want to move on." I look him in the eyes. "Please. Please just let me move on."

I don't expect him to let it go but he won't get anything more from me. If I admit that Enzo was the father, it will never and I *need* this to disappear. Alessio scrunches his face before giving me a tight nod.

"For now."

I let out a sigh as Alessio kisses my forehead and pulls away. I clear my throat and wipe my tears.

"I need to check my emails. My teachers are sending over my material so I'm ready for tomorrow." I bite my lip hoping Alessio won't fight me.

"Okay."

I take that as my chance and dash to my room. Before I get to my door I hear a loud thud and some curses. I listen closely to try and make out the words.

"I didn't even know she was fucking pregnant. How could she not tell me?" His voice sounds pained and angry. "She never mentioned anyone on our calls, much less that she had a whole baby and they lost it. I'm her fucking brother." His voice fades a little. "I was going to be an uncle and I didn't even know." His voice completely breaks off.

My heart clenches hard and I try to reel myself together. I know how much it hurt me—and even Enzo—to lose the baby, but I never imagined how much it would hurt Alessio.

"She's right. I don't know how to pick up the pieces. I can't control this." I can't listen anymore. I step into my room and pull up my computer. I do need to check my emails and maybe the mundane task will give me some relief from the war coursing through my soul.

A couple hours deep into the reading material, I shut my laptop and pick up my phone. I hate how Sole and I left things yesterday. She was right, I should've told Alessio a long time ago. I dial her number and on the second chime, the line connects.

"Hello."

"Sole?"

"Gwen."

"Lena's Coffee Shop?" I hear a little rustle on the other end and then a sigh.

"See you in five?" I sigh in relief.

"See you in five." I grab a simple pair of leggings and a vintage T-shirt I thrifted. It's not that I need to go to the thrift shop, but they have by far the best vintage tees. I change into my outfit and fix my messy hair. I slip into my shoes and swing my bag over my shoulder.

I catch Enzo in the living room on my way to the door. Unsure of where Alessio is and how I can get out the door, I take a survey of the room.

"Vee?"

"I'm meeting Sole at Lena's Coffee Shop. Can you tell Alessio?"

His brows pull together with a grimace and he nods to me. I bite my lip with a turn and leave before he has the chance to say anything else.

I make haste to the café getting there in minutes. I swing open the coffee shop's door. The fresh scent of ground coffee rushes to my nose. Heaven. The steam whistles in the air as I spot Sole in our corner spot. Her eyes focus on her phone until I am above the table.

"Hey."

"Hey."

I slide in the seat across from her taking in her pained look. We don't argue, and never have a reason to.

"I'm sorry. I blamed you when you were just trying to help. I shouldn't have been so hateful."

She gives me a light smile, raising her shoulders.

"It's okay. I get it. I'm just tired of seeing you hurt and I just got protective. I stepped out of line a little." We give each other a brief hug over the table before sitting back down.

"I told Alessio."

She sits back with wide eyes.

"Everything?"

"No, just about the baby." I take a deep breath in an attemptto keep my emotions intact.

"How did he take it?"

"Good, I guess. He wanted to know who the father was but I couldn't tell him. He... let it go. When I left the room I think he punched something. He told Enzo he couldn't believe I didn't tell him he was going to be an uncle or more so that he wasn't anymore." I drop my gaze to the table.

"Wow. Enzo was there?" She pipes a brow up.

"Yeah... well I didn't come home till this morning, and he had the whole crew with him."

"You stayed out last night? Where? With who?" She leans against the table eating the crumbs I've laid out.

"You remember that guy from school? The one who brought me home?"

"You were with him! Did you... you know?" Her brows wiggle suggestively as she leans against the table.

"No. Well not exactly. We went for ice cream and then back to his place. He had to finish some paperwork so he left me with his brother I met the day before. He had driven me home which was nice but..." I struggle to pull the words out, knowing the reaction they will cause. "There was a lot of tension and one thing led to another andifuckedhisbrother." I smash the words together, completely embarrassed at this point.

"WHAT!" Sole shouts on the edge of her seat. The people in the café glare at us. I put my hand up apologetically before giving Sole a glare myself. She mouths, *"sorry,"* with a breathy laugh.

"*Shhh.* Jesus, the whole café doesn't need to know," I whisper to her.

"You slept with his brother? A complete stranger? Just like that. I really didn't think you had it in you."

"I didn't think so either, but Matteo was there and looked like a God. I wanted to melt like putty. He could've taken me right there on the counter and I would have let—"

"Okay, now who's telling the whole café?" She laughs a little, cutting me off. I smile sheepishly.

"I don't know what came over me, I just did it." I knew though, he was the perfect stepping stone for moving on.

"You said you didn't come home till the morning, did you sleep there?"

"Yeah."

"Where?"

"Where? In his bed, where else?" She grabs the table, staring at me with glowing eyes.

"Where did he sleep?" I look at her dumbfounded. You got to be kidding me. Where did she think he slept? Isn't she used to this type of rendezvous?

"In his bed, where else would he sleep?"

"Oh my God. You slept with a man and then literally slept with him. In his bed." She laughs a little bit to herself. "He likes you."

"*Pfft,* likes me? Hah, no. He didn't even walk me to the door. We fucked, slept, then Gio drove me home in the morning."

"His brother drove you home." She deadpans, her lips pressed in a slight grimace.

"Yep. Oddly enough, Gio didn't believe I could do casual either. He told me I was just a prize to win since Gio brought me home. Any other time I might have taken more offense, but honestly, I wasn't much better. I saw this sexy piece of a man, jumped his bones, and left." I shrug as if it were nothing. But a sense of dread rises in my chest for a moment that I can't explain.

"You just fucked and moved on? Why do I think there's something you're not telling me." I bite my lip and tap the table.

"I cried," I sigh.

"You cried? Like when you were leaving?" Her brows scrunch together.

"When we were, you know…"

Sole chokes, patting a napkin on her face with her fist to regain herself.

"I don't know what happened. We were going and then he, you know stuck it in, and before anything took off I started crying."

"And you guys stopped? What did he say?" She was soaking this in like it was her Thursday night soap opera.

"We didn't stop. He just pulled me closer and we finished," I whisper to her as she stares at me speechless. Before she can respond a muscular body approaches the table. I look up to see Gio and my face drops. I glance at Sole, as she drinks the man in once again.

"Good morning, ladies." Gio gives me a cheeky grin. A hint of blush flies to my cheeks as I pray he didn't hear my last comment.

"Funny seeing you again," he continues when I stay silent.

"Did you suddenly go blind?" I tease, to which Sole rolls her eyes.

"Oh, the ladies would love that. I'd get all the girls." He chuckles when my line of sight is drawn to the café entrance. Viktor and the one and only Matteo, step inside.

"We came for coffee after boring ass meetings back to back. Actually, we're headed back to the house, wanna join?"

"Can Sole come? She'll get a kick out of your guy's place."

"Why not? The more the merrier."

Sole winks to him with a flirtatious smile. It's my time to roll my eyes.

Lena rounds the counter, our lattes in hand. Her smile reminds me of Alessio and my nanny from when were kids. A sense of warm love flows over me.

"Here's those coffee ladies." She looks at the men and back to us. "Looks like you got yourself some company." I lower my head with a blush, grabbing my coffee with a soft thank you. We reach the men, receiving a smile from Viktor and a tilt of his head. I smile back then turn my attention to Matteo who is looking directly at me. Goosebumps line my skin, enhancing the flip of my stomach. All of the things I would do to this man. I jump out of my thoughts as Sole elbows me. I break contact and bite my lip.

After the men get their coffees, Gio grabs the door allowing Sole to exit. Viktor ushers me ahead. The moment I'm outside a firm hand presses against my lower back, warm breath lingers on my neck.

"I told you not to bite your lip."

My thighs clench and I suppress a slight moan. What the hell is wrong with me? Matteo pulls back revealing his mischievous grin.

"We will tell the guards to let you in. Just follow us."

I nod to Matteo and pull Sole to our cars. *Which car do we take?*

"Want to take your car just in case?" I look to Sole for confirmation.

"Of course, come on."

The men get in their Escalade and we follow behind in Soles.

10

Gwenevere

"Guards?" Sole exclaims, glancing between me and the road as we follow the men. "They have guards and you casually never mentioned that?"

"I have guards." I give a pointed look.

"They don't count. They're barely around and it's just because of your dad." She waves me off. "What do they do anyways?"

"Gio said something about being a business consultant? I think Matteo's his boss."

"Oh my God!" She grips the steering wheel turning her knuckles white. "I totally forgot! Matteo! Don't think I missed that little whisper." She smirks.

"It's not a big deal."

"Are you serious right now? How much have you seen them in the last forty-eight hours?" She gives me a questing brow. "And how long ago was he 'casually' in your panties?"

"Sole!" I scold her.

Matteo's presence is intoxicating and I can't deny wanting to be around him. This is the rebound I need to get Enzo out of my mind and everything that comes with him. I just want to forget. I want to jump out of my sad depressing life and into the mysterious life of Gio and Matteo.

"I just need the distraction. A rebound if you will. I need to move on even if it's just the simple indulgence of an extremely sexy man who kinda terrifies me."

"I get it. You need a rebound. I'll be your wing girl." She winks. "But promise me you'll be careful? I don't want you getting hurt, and you aren't really the girl who does the whole no feeling attached thing."

"I'll be fine. This is what I need. No feelings attached. A little fun… some pleasure… no hurt feelings."

"God you're in for it. What did you do to my best friend?" She shakes her head with a little smirk. Sole's jaw drops as we pull up to the mansion.

"Oh. My. God." Her eyes bulge out and I laugh at her. "This is where they live! You've got to be kidding me. No wonder you've been spending all your time here." She stares in awe as we park.

She grabs her purse as Gio opens her door. I let out a snort but am startled when my door opens. Matteo holds a hand out to me. I rest my hand on his and step out of the car. I pull my hand back and try to hide my giddiness.

"Always so slow." Viktor tsks from the entrance. Matteo shakes his head letting me go in before him.

"You're just not a ladies man," Gio teases.

We are greeted by the guards in the foyer before landing in the living room. Games line the table and Viktor resembles a kid in a candy shop.

"Monopoly, Charades, or Cards Against Humanity?"

"Monopoly—Cards Against Humanity," a chorus of voices answer in the room. I chuckle a bit at everyone. Matteo relaxes back onto one of the couches, an arm resting on the back. Gio and Sole plop onto the couch and Viktor the chair. My choices are to sit next to Matteo or the empty spot by Gio. I bite my lip and pop it back out sitting next to Matteo who keeps his eyes on me until I'm settled.

"Monopoly isn't allowed." Matteo gives Viktor a stern look.

"You're no fun." Viktor mumbles to himself, placing the box to the side.

Sole studies the room with a laugh. "Why not?"

Gio chuckles resting his arm on the back of the couch behind her. They are awfully comfy. I give her a smug smile which is returned by sticking her tongue out. Mature.

"Because the game ends in black eyes or guns drawn." Gio cracks. Sole's eyes widen and I stifle a laugh. Sounds familiar. Matteo looks at me with a twitch of amusement before it disappears.

"So, Cards Against Humanity?" I say, moving the conversation along.

"Okay. Yeah," voices ring in unison. A cell phone rings and Matteo reaches into his pocket to pull out his phone. His face turns to stone as he puts a finger up and dismisses himself from the room. I can't help feel a bit sad about him leaving. Not that I can't enjoy myself in the presence of these three. I crave his graze and touch and—

"Earth to Gwen." Sole waves in the air. I peel away from the empty space Matteo left behind and focus on the room.

"Sorry, lost in my head, just a bit tired. I did not get enough coffee."

"There's a fresh pot in the kitchen. You are welcome to get a cup." Gio nods to the kitchen.

"I probably should. Thank you." I search the counters of the kitchen for a pot. I spot the tower of coffee cups displayed next to it, grab a cup, and fill it up. I take a sip and close my eyes, relishing in the amazing cup of coffee.

The odd sense of someone in the room washes over me and I turn to see Matteo leaning on the counter, eyes locked on me. I gulp and tap the coffee cup as I clear my throat to break the silence.

"So um… about last night. I wanted you to know that's not my usual, um, behavior. I just don't want you to think I'm like some whore that's sleeping around, and I'm also not gonna

follow you like a lost puppy. I honestly don't even know how I already ended up back here in your kitchen, but I'm here because of Gio. I just don't want you to get the wrong impression because I'm really just—"

"Gwenevere." I snap out of my ramble, my gaze having fallen into my cup. I've been going on like a little girl talking to her crush. I mentally slap myself, chewing on my cheek.

"I don't regret the things I did with you." He steps closer to me and I take a step back bumping into the counter. He inches forward and lifts his hand to my face, brushing his thumb across my bottom lip before pulling it out from my teeth. His eyes devour me like I'm his next meal.

At this moment, I want nothing more than to be just that. For him to take me right here, right now, not caring who walked into the kitchen. My body grows a thousand degrees hotter as I melt under his gaze.

"I never thought you were a whore." He drops his hand and backs away, opening the fridge and grabbing a water. I take in a sharp breath and release with a laugh.

"Well, I'm glad."

"You don't dress like a one and they perform better."

My jaw drops to the floor as I stare at this egotistical man. He did not just say that. His face stays blank as I'm on the brink of throwing my coffee in his face.

"Your body responds differently." He places a finger on my chin, trailing it back to my ear, then down my neck—a reminder of the path his kisses followed last night. He stops at the soft spot on my collarbone, a smirk playing on his face. Matteo leans in and whispers.

"The funny thing is I don't even know who you are and yet I know what makes you scream." He kisses me behind my ear and pulls away, leaving the room completely. My head spins in a daze the pulse of my blood pumps with eagerness.

I calm the full-on ache he has created inside me. I sip my coffee hoping the caffeine will distract me and ease my growing headache from this morning. The medicine Matteo gave me is wearing off, but I don't want to ask him for more. Matteo's nowhere to be seen once I make it back to the living room which allows me to relax. I settle into the couch as the game starts.

After a while of playing cards, way too many sexual jokes, and numerous flirtatious looks from Sole, my head is pulsing and the noise of our chatter sounds more like static now.

I blink my eyes and push my fingers into my temple for the millionth time. Stretching my neck I try to find any type of relief. I turn to Viktor who is shuffling for the next round.

"Where's the bathroom?"

He assesses me, brows furrowing.

"Walk up the staircase, straight down the hallway, it's the last door on the right." I stand with a little waver but regain my balance. "Are you okay?" His voice is hesitant.

"Yeah, I just need to refresh real quick." I walk around the couch and shoot Sole a smile. She returns my smile and goes back to Gio. I ascend the stairs, following Viktor's instructions down the long hall.

When I near the end my head spins a little but I ignore it, grabbing the door handle. I open the door and stumble in. I search for the sink to splash water on my face, in its place I find a desk. My face wrinkles in confusion, eyes landing on Matteo.

"Can I help you?" Matteo mutters. Mrs. Priss is not in a good mood, my bad.

"Um no I… I'm looking for the bathroom." I point around behind me. "I thought this was the door but obviously not."

"Obviously." His annoyed tone irritating me. My head throbs harshly again sending a wave of nausea through me. I grab onto the door handle for support. Seconds later Matteo is at my side balancing me by my arm. I snatch my arm away quickly.

"I'm fine, it's just a headache. Sorry for the inconvenience," I respond with the same annoyance he had given me and turn to leave.

"Gwenevere." I look back at Matteo as he rounds his sleek wooden desk. Opening the drawer he pulls out a bottle and hands me the Motrin and water. I sigh taking them.

"Thank you." I gaze up with half-squinted eyes.

"Go lay down in my room. You can use the bathroom there, they'll be fine without you. You need to rest." I shake my head. While the offer is sweet, I can't go back to his room.

"No, I'm fine. Really. I just needed to freshen up."

"You look like shit. Go lay down before I bring you to the room myself."

I gulp biting my lips nervously. His eyes dart down but he chooses not to say anything. He nods down the hall and I reluctantly head to his room.

Once inside the cold room with nothing but a little light seeping from the windows, I take a big breath in. I am intoxicated with the musky vanilla scent that saves my senses from the harsh cleaning chemicals that cloud the air in the estate.

I splash water on my face in the sink to cool my head down. I return to the room where I pull back the nicely made bed and lay down. I've spent more time in this bed than my own in recent hours.

I slowly drift off thankful for the offer, or more so the demand, to rest. I smile softly as sleep takes over.

I stir awake. My head no longer pounding. I'm in his bed, again. His massive bed might I add. I unravel myself from the covers. I make my way to the bathroom to adjust my bun that has fallen out. I fix it to the best of my ability until I completely give up. Curly hair is not for the weak. I straighten out my clothes and head back into the room.

I screech and throw myself against the wall of the room when I notice a figure on the other side sitting in the chair. My hand slams over my heart when I fully register who it is.

Matteo sits, suit jacket tossed on the small table. His dress shirt is unbuttoned partially and sleeves are folded to his forearms. He gracefully leans back in his chair with a glass of bourbon, watching me.

"Jesus, you scared the shit out of me."

"You like to scream." He suppresses a smirk. My face reddens and I'm taken aback.

"Wouldn't you like to know?" I cross my arms, tossing him a smug look.

He tsks and sets his glass down on the table. His eyes roam down my body from afar.

"Don't you remember last night?"

"Oh, for sure. I just don't remember the whole, I don't know… screaming part?" I twirl my finger through the air. "You must have a vast imagination." I try my hardest not to burst out laughing while I egg him on. His jaw ticks as his hand tightens around the arm of the chair making the veins in his arm pop, and I wish he was holding my hips instead of the chair.

"Stop biting your lip."

I slowly let my lip go, stalking, rounding the bed and leaning against the bedpost closest to him. I pull my lip back in. His features darken with dangerous promises.

"You don't listen well," his voice dips, gaze never leaving my lips.

"I've never been good at obeying orders." My chest rises and a knot forms in my stomach.

"Take your shirt off."

I pause, processing his demand urging me to undress myself in front of him.

"Do I need to repeat myself?"

I swallow in hopes of clearing my suddenly very dry mouth. My body is rigid with warmth and for some crazy reason, I listen. I glide my hand to the hem of my shirt and pull up slowly.

Matteo watches my every move with patience. I discard my shirt on the floor and cover myself with my hands.

"Don't hide. It's nothing I haven't seen." The heat that covers my face flows lower.

"Now your pants."

I swallow hard again, trailing my fingers down my stomach to my leggings. I grip my thumb inside before sliding them down, stepping out, and standing back up with them hanging from my finger. I drop them over my shirt, meeting his eyes.

Matteo studies me like a predator with unwavering attention. The muscles in his jaw flex, and he strides to me, pushing me into the post. My chest presses into him as my desire for his touch radiates through me.

He slides a hand behind my head, gripping my hair with soft control. Matteo turns my head, lowering his face to my neck. He suckles my ear and leaves a trail down my neck revealing the soft spot above my collarbone. A let out a soft gasp as he nips and sucks, sending a tingling sensation into my depths.

The world fades into bliss and I grip on to his biceps. He grips my waist, gliding his finger to my panties. I moan when he touches my clit, playing with me through my panties. I push my chest out further to touch him. He stops his touching and pushes me back against the post. He tilts my head, forcing my eyes to him with a bent finger.

"I'm in charge. You do what I say, and you obey." His eyes are dark and all I can do is squirm. Heat rises and wetness pools between my thighs. "Do you understand?"

I nod.

"I want to hear you." I nod again.

"Your voice *Bella.*" *Your voice Beautiful.*

"Sì," *Yes.* my voice falls out breathless. His muscles tighten on me and I know my Italian turns him on just as much as he did for me. His hand travels down my chest, sliding underneath my panties this time.

"You're soaked."

I moan while his fingers circle my entrance but don't enter. I grip tighter onto his arm.

"I want to hear you, *Bella*." He slides the tip of his finger inside, coaxing me to let out a gasp. I lean my hips up to give him better access.

He watches my face as he pushes his finger further in. I let my eyes shut, accepting his invasion. I let the bliss of his touch take over me.

"Open your eyes."

I snap my eyes open.

"Don't take your eyes off me. I want you to look at me when I make you scream."

I squirm, my heat pulsing begging for touch, for a release.

"Please." My plea comes out far more needy than I expected. His lips tip into a sly smile.

"Say it again." I push my front against his.

"Please, Matteo," I whisper, begging him. With that, he pulls his finger out replacing it with two, before pushing them back in. Repeating the driving force with his fingers he uses the hand in my hair to keep my head straightened, leaving me no choice but to look directly at him. The tension inside me builds with his movements.

He curls his fingers perfectly, hitting my hardening walls just right. I groan, my climax getting near. I hold onto him as my knees buckle. He uses his thumb to rub circles into my clit.

"Don't hide your voice, *Bella*." He pushes into me harder, forcing a moan out with each thrust.

"Sei così bella quando gemi." You are so beautiful when you moan

That's all it takes for my walls to clench around his fingers and drive me into madness. My moans grow louder as I cry out from his tortured pleasure. I tremble as my orgasm barrels through me. Matteo pulls his fingers out of me, bringing them to my lips.

"Suck."

I open my mouth as he slides his fingers in, sucking my release off. He removes them, grasping my jaw in his palm. His other hand stays in my hair and he runs a thumb over my lip.

"Good girl."

He called me a good girl. Like an obedient little dog.

"What was that again about my imagination? You might not obey anyone else but you will obey me."

A knock comes through the door and my heart plummets. Shit, I completely forgot about the rest of the world. Matteo's seductive mood turns cold. Matteo hands me my shirt and I throw it over my head. Another knock sounds at the door.

"What?" Matteo responds. Gio steps through the door looking straight to Matteo.

"Have you seen Gwenevere? She went to the restroom and never came back. Viktor said she didn't look well." I'm unable to see Matteo's face from here but I watch as his hand gestures toward me drawing Gio's gaze over. His face drops momentarily before gaining his composure.

"Right. You definitely *saw* her." Gio presses his lips together.

"Giovanni." Matteo's voice rumbles. Gio raises his hands, backs out of the room, and drags the door shut. I pick my pants off the ground and fully dress.

"Um, I should get back down there." I adjust myself the best I can without a mirror avoiding Matteo's face. When I veer back to him he has his bourbon in hand. He slides over to me, drawing within reach.

"Everyone's going to know what I did to you," he pauses, moving a hair out of my face. "I didn't know hanging out with a friend consisted of fucking his brother." He retreats from the room and I grant myself some time before leaving the room too.

I need to walk out of here like Matteo didn't just make me beg him to finger fuck me. When I gain enough courage I exit his room, finding my way back to the living room. It's late afternoon now and when Sole spot's me she darts up, grabbing me by the arm.

"We'll be right back, just grabbing a drink!" She smiles sweetly at the men while dragging me away. Once in the kitchen, she whirls around with the biggest grin.

"Oh my God, you blissful."

"I mean I think I am in heaven." I fake swoon then give a soft shrug. "Honestly, this is the best sex I have ever had. He is a downright God."

Sole wipes invisible tears away. "I'm so proud."

"Oh my, let's go." I laugh and tug her to the living room where they sit around joking. I clear my throat, bringing their attention to us.

"We should really get going. I told my brother I'd be back soon and I'm pretty sure I've already passed anything considered 'soon'."

Gio cruises up to us. "I'm a phone call away." He smiles warmly and gives me a soft hug.

"Thank you." I smile and Sole bumps into me. We make our way to the door, Sole steps into the evening air, but I'm stopped short by hands grabbing my waist from behind.

"I don't get a goodbye?" His husky voice sends tingles down my spine. A playful smirk forms on my face. I twist into him without reeling my eyes up.

"Didn't think you'd want one." With that, I whirl away and jump in the car.

"What did he say!"

"Just go." I roll my eyes and buckle up. Was Sole right? Could Matteo like me? I mean he isn't hiding his attraction to me, and he wanted a goodbye?

What would that even look like? Matteo and I that is. He's a cold businessman, just like my father. *Last I checked my father didn't make me feel like that. Eww.* Matteo is different though. It's like poker. He hides behind a stone wall so you can't see what's behind it.

But what could Matteo's cards be? He's rich, I know. Some type of business consultant? Or does he run the business? What about women? What was I? Gio obviously sleeps with whoever he wants but what about Matteo? He takes what he wants, but am I what he wants? He wants me physically no doubt but can I be anything more than that?

"Oh no. I know that look." Sole glances at me accusingly.

"What *look*?" I glare back but I know what she means. I'm not going to be the one to say it outright though.

"The *look* you get when you start getting feelings," she says bluntly. I scoff at her accusation.

"I don't have a *look*," I mutter.

"So you admit you have feelings for him?"

"I don't have feelings for him, I'm just curious about him."

Is that so wrong? He has this essence about him; a mysterious puzzle I can't wait to unlock.

"Curiosity killed the cat."

"But satisfaction brought it back." I poke her. "Everyone always forgets that." Would it be so wrong to let my curiosity fly a little? We pull into the parking lot of Lena's.

"You said you were gonna be careful."

"Who said I'm not being careful?" I sigh. "All I'm saying is why can't I have a little fun while cracking open a mystery box? It's a little game and I've seen it played enough times. My heart has nothing to do with it."

"If Alessio finds out…"

"Then he finds out." I shrug. "It's a man, not a drug crime. And it's not Enzo."

She sighs, shaking her head. We both know she won't be able to change my mind.

"You better head home." She pushes my arm.

"Yes, mother. Father is waiting for me. It's like I have a new set of parents sharing their daughter after a divorce." Sole laughs as I step out of the car and return to mine.

Before I know it, I am pulling into my driveway. Alessio smiles up at me from his phone when I enter the house. Setting his phone down he pats his lap inviting me over. I drop my bag on the table and glide over to him, plopping down sideways on his lap. I lean my head on his chest and he plays with my hair.

This is the side of Alessio I needed. I would've had this sooner if I had just told him. It wasn't fair to keep him in the dark.

"I'm sorry." I whisper. His hands stops for a beat of time before he strokes my hair again.

"Why are you sorry?" His voice is taut and riddled with confusion.

"I should've told you." I press my face into his shoulder as a tear falls down my cheeks. "I was going to. I was going to tell you everything as soon as you got home but…" I let out a hiccup. "She didn't make it."

I couldn't tell if it was my heart or his that hammers aloud. His arm tightens around me and he leans down kissing the top of my head.

"I wanted you to meet her, Alessio. I did. I knew you would love her regardless. I knew you'd love me regardless."

"Gwenevere, I will always love you regardless." He lets out a sigh, cradling me tight. "You would've been a great mother. You are still a mother."

The relief that comes from his confirmation is more than I'd ever anticipated. Why have I been so caught up in him being angry with me that I was too afraid to let him in? We have never kept secrets from one another, and I kept a huge part of my life from him.

"Were you happy?" His voice comes out soft. "Did he make you happy?"

My vision blurs with the wet droplets.

"I was beyond happy." My voice breaks as the truth bares more and more.

"Were you in love?"

"I was."

Maybe that is the saddest part. I was in love, but I can't love Enzo anymore. I can't look at him without seeing the pain and loss.

"Gwen? Who's the father?"

My sniffles come to halt. I know he won't drop this until he knows. I lean up to peer at his face.

"Alessio."

"Gwen. It's obvious that losing the baby hurts you." He watches me closely as he says his next words. "But you can't tell me it didn't hurt *him* either."

I can't tell him that because I know. Enzo has told me countless times.

"He lost two people he loved, Gwen. You know I can find out, but you deserve to tell me."

"Alessio, I can't." I whisper, dropping my gaze. It isn't worth the pain it will cause all of us because I can't be with him anymore.

A knock sounds at the door. I swipe my tears and slide off of Alessio. He opens the door and I step into the kitchen to grab some water. When I round back into the living room Enzo is talking to Alessio.

"I'm going to run into the office." Alessio leaves the room and silence elopes us.

I swallow hard, biting my lip. Enzo opens his mouth to say something, but I cut him off.

"Enzo, please."

"You told him about the baby."

I nod but keep my gaze in the distance. "I did."

"What about me?" Enzo's voice is hoarse as he pivots my face to his. "I love you, Gwenevere. I will always love you."

"I can't tell him." I plead.

"I need you, Gwen." His eyes glow with desperation. "I can't lose you too." He leans closer, placing his forehead against mine.

I pull away. "I already lost myself," I whisper, disappearing down the hall. All of this is too much. Alessio; Enzo; the baby. This is what I've been trying to numb.

11

Gwenevere

I sit across from Gio sipping coffee during our usual meet-up time. It's become a ritual to have coffee in the mornings at Lena's. Alessio has been busy, meaning Enzo isn't around. I've taken this as the perfect opportunity to spend more time making connections with the outside world.

I've spent most of my life keeping to myself, only having Sole around to keep me company. Alessio, Beatrice, and I grew up with Enzo. It was the four of us forever. Things changed drastically when I was ten. Beatrice was in a wreck, dying only days later. Dad took Alessio under his wing soon after with Enzo at his side. Mom had always been a loveless bitch, which left just Sole and me. I didn't hate it either; things were simple. I kept my head down, did my work, then spent whatever time I could with Alessio.

Enzo and my love didn't spring from a growing romance that came to bloom—not entirely. It wasn't until we moved into the new house away from our father's estate and in with Enzo. I started to look at him differently. The nicknames, the glances, and the bumping into each other.

When Alessio left for his trip it was our first chance to be truly alone. He was all I knew, and at the time more than enough. Getting pregnant wasn't the plan but it wasn't totally minded—at least not by us. Alessio was another story, but we never got around to that part.

Having Gio as a friend gives me a new perspective of friendship—and Matteo. Matteo awakens things in me that I could have only imagined. It is as if he takes all the air in the room and the only way to breathe is to beg him in every way possible for it back.

Gio clears his throat. He gives me a smile with a wave across my face.

"Hello? Did I lose you to your head again?" I laugh, taking a sip of my coffee.

"Sorry, my head is in the clouds. It's been so quiet around the house lately I've been losing my mind."

"Am I boring you too?"

"Gio, I don't think you could be a bore even if you wanted to." He chuckles leaning back in his chair.

"I'm sure I could. I can do anything I set my mind to, Baby Girl." He winks at me using the nickname he took upon himself to give me. I roll my eyes only causing him to laugh harder.

"Do you want to get breakfast?" He pulls his watch up to look at the time. I hadn't eaten breakfast but I'm not currently in the mood to stuff my face.

"I'm not really hungry." His brows furrow slightly.

"You know I have barely seen you eat since I met you." I shrug my shoulders.

"I only see you for an hour or so a day, Gio. A short walk wouldn't hurt though."

"Then a walk we shall have my lady." He places an arm out for me to lead the way. We make our way down the sidewalk strolling for a little bit at the nearby shops. He lays his arm around my shoulder and we talk amongst ourselves. I grow exhausted, twisting to Gio with a small smile.

"You ready, Baby Girl?" His eyes smile as he chuckles softly.

"Definitely, just not for the boring, lonely day at home," I pout.

"Then why go home? I have the day off, come back to the estate. We can chill and watch movies or whatever you want." I snort and laugh at him.

"You want me to come 'Netflix and Chill'?" Gio rolls his eyes, shoulder-bumping me.

"Just because your nickname is Baby Girl, doesn't mean you are my *Baby Girl*. Besides, you're off limits."

I stop in my tracks merely steps from the car, staring at the back of his head.

"I'm off limits?" I look at him like he's crazy. His brows raise in what can only be translated into *really?*

"Don't look at me like that." I scrunch my face and cross my arms.

"Don't act like the whole estate doesn't know you end up in Matteo's bed every time you two are within a five-mile radius." I roll my eyes again trying not to blush at his remark.

"I don't *always* end up in his bed."

"Oh let me guess you fucked on the chair instead, yeah?" This time my face heats and I'm certain it's bright red.

"We didn't *fuck* on the chair," I mock, pushing past him, not wanting to know the next location he chooses to prove his point.

"Oh, what a gentleman."

"Shut up, Gio." I hit his chest playfully but he only smirks back. He shuts the door, jogging around the car and jumping in. I buckle up as he prepares to drive.

"So are you too ladylike to fuck on the chair or…"

I slap his chest harder invoking laughter to erupt from him.

"GIO! Do you only think about sex?"

He throws a hand up in surrender, keeping the other on the steering wheel.

"Hey, I'm not the one who suggested Netflix and Chill."

"In your dreams."

"Oh, Baby Girl, you know it." He winks and I let out a breathy laugh. I pull my phone out to read my book as we make our way back to the estate.

Once there Gio opens my door. I'm continually amazed by the massive beautiful home. Da ja vu plays and a flash of pleasure soars through me at the memories from my last time here.

I push my hair back to cool down as I follow Gio into the home. He sends me a smirk, but I don't think twice, stepping through the door, when a smack on my ass jolts me up. I squeal loudly flying around to look at Gio's devilish grin.

This little shit.

"You Asshole!" I go to shove him but he moves out of the way sliding past me and taking off out of the foyer. I laugh running after him.

"You are going to get it, Giovanni!" His laughter only grows louder with his quickened pace. I chase him as he flies around the couch, stopping on the other side with a wide grin.

"Oh come on, Baby Girl, you have more than that in you." I lunge at him over the couch as his face registers pure shock just before we collide and fall to the floor, landing with an oomph as we laugh uncontrollably. Gio tickles me causing my giggles to rise in volume until I beg and plead for him to stop.

"Gio." The strong voice that has been playing through my dreams for nights stills our movements and ultimately the tickling torture. Gio helps me stand then turns to Matteo.

"Don't mind us enjoying a boring afternoon." I giggle behind him at his carefree sentiment. Gio is the opposite of Matteo. He is always bright and flirtatious, while Matteo is seductive and dark. A darkness I want to explore. Gio takes a step over, giving me a view of Matteo's glaring eyes.

"You could refrain from running around the living room like animals." Gio's eyes light up as the gears channel is next remark.

"We can be animals right, Baby Girl? Fuck like rabbits during our Netflix and Chill." Gio grabs onto me kissing my cheek making me giggle and I push at him. I look back at Matteo who's eyes pierce into me. I suddenly squirm at Gio's touch.

"Brother relax. It's all games." Gio pulls away but not before whispering in my ear, something that doesn't go unnoticed by Matteo. Though I doubt anything goes unnoticed by him.
"We've made the beast jealous, you're welcome."

I stare at Matteo as he glowers with a clenched fist at his sides.

"Right... There's a lot of sexual tension in the room so I'm going to find a movie and maybe we can simmer the heat between us." Gio snickers down the hall. I stay frozen in Matteo's presence once again.

He steps forward seizing my face in his hand. His aura makes me forget what year it is. The warmth of his hand seeps through my face and I bask in the touch, closing my eyes for a moment before looking into his.

His phone rings, slicing the tension growing fast between us like a knife. I pull back averting my gaze down and fumbling with my bracelet. He scowls down at the phone and retreats completely. I take what feels like my first breath in minutes and make my way to the movie room. Gio smirks from his seat in the theater.

"Let me guess, a quicky on the couch?" I throw the pillow sitting on the end chair at him.

"You are a disgusting specimen," I tease him. He throws his head back with a contagious laugh.

"Oh, but you love me for it." Gio plays the show and we settle down into the chairs. I think over the brief interaction with Matteo. I can't clear my mind of his touch and the heat of his stare. He is thrilling in all the right ways. I try to clear my mind long enough to understand the show but it is a losing battle.

After hours of binge watching our show, my eyes flutter close and I let sleep overtake me knowing Gio won't mind. I feel safe here.

12

Gwenevere

My phone chimes next to my computer. I smile when I see Gio's name across my screen.

Gio: How is my escaper?

Me: Trapped in her Rapunzel tower.

Gio: We can't have that. Lena's?

Me: Give me ten?

Gio: See you in ten.

I shake my head. Alessio is back in town and definitely wouldn't approve, but I never heard him come home last night so I'm going to take that as my all clear. I slide out of bed and into the bathroom.

I take a fast shower then brush my hair and apply a light amount of makeup. I decided to dress myself like a decent human being instead of a couch slum. I skim my jeans searching for the only pair I will actually wear out

173

of the several sets I own. I grab a simple off-the-shoulder blouse and get dressed.

I adjust in the mirror, my lips tugging into a smile feeling accomplished. My skin has a slight glow to it and my eyes have a tad more light in them.

I look at the clock, seeing I have a little time to kill. I head to the kitchen for some water. I need to get some hydration in before I drown in caffeine. Gio and I have been having a routine coffee date together everyday for the last two weeks. I've gotten used to having a friendly face around. Sometimes Sole joins us but really it's just a trip for caffeine and an hour of chatting. I haven't seen Matteo but in passing since our moment in the living room.

I'd be lying if I said my mind doesn't float back to him in my daydreams. I refuse to ask Gio anything regarding him. He doesn't seem too thrilled with the overall idea of his brother and I, though, he doesn't resist teasing me from time to time.

I pull my phone out of my pocket at the ding.

Gio: Here :)

I place my phone back in my pocket, grabbing my bag off the table. I lock the door behind me and meet Gio at the passenger door of his car. He gives me a sweet smile and helps me in.

"My lady, your carriage awaits."

"Oh my, how kind you are, sir." I place a hand over my chest and he shakes his head. When we drive off a thought escapes me.

"Why do you always drive yourself but Matteo has a driver?" It has crossed my mind a few times and I'm genuinely curious.

"It's not really necessary for me. It gives him the ability to work while on the go. I keep my work for the office. At least when I can." While it clears up my car question, Gio's response intrigues me further.

"What *does* Matteo do?" I watch as Gio hesitates. "I mean I know you are a business consultant and if Matteo is your boss then he runs a business, no?"

Gio clears his throat, thumping his fingers on the wheel.

"Well, I suppose he runs a couple of businesses. He runs them simultaneously. I help him make decisions, do the check-ups, and monitor the books."

"What's his biggest business?"

"Casinos." Gio's Adam's apple bobs.

"Casinos?"

He nods, glancing at me. My brows crinkle in confusion.

"I thought all the casinos in the city were run by the crime families?" Gio's hands tighten on the wheel but he doesn't respond as we pull into the coffee shop.

Right as he puts the car in park his phone rings. He looks at the caller ID then places the phone to his ear listening to the other end before pinching the bridge of his nose.

"You got to be fucking kidding me. Right now?" He lets the person talk again. "I haven't even made it into the coffee sh—" he stops and pulls the phone away from his face.

"*Pezzo di merda!* The bastard hung up on me. *Cazzo di stronzo.*" *Piece of shit! The bastard hung up on me. Fucking asshole.*

I raise a brow and he sighs.

"I'm sorry but I've got to go deal with some business. You can come to the house and chill in the movie room." I don't have anything better to do today, why the hell not?

"Fine by me."

Gio sends the car back in motion, driving us to the estate. That had to be Matteo on the phone calling him for business. Does that mean I'm going to see him again?

Thankfully I put more effort into my looks today. Not that I really care that much. Okay, maybe I do. I'm anxious to see Matteo. I feel like an idiot fumbling through my whirlwind of emotions.

"Be careful."

I snap my head over to Gio.

"Matteo's not the kind of guy to bring you to the movies and buy you flowers. He lives for his work, I know you guys have this little *thing* going on," he sighs. "I just don't want you to get hurt by him."

"You sound a lot like Sole."

"Maybe Soles right?"

I look away. The logical side of me knows that she's right. His brother, confirming and actively warning me, should hang a bright red flag in front of my face; but it does the opposite. It only intrigues me. Why does this man only see pleasure from all work and play? What made him distant and so set in stone that nobody would dare to expect anything different from him?

"I know you're going through this whole rebound thing, but that's all it will be with him. That's all he can give, and one day he will wake up bored. I'm not telling you this to be an ass. I don't want you to be surprised later after you fall down the path of broken hearts that Matteo strings along."

"Strings?" I roll my eyes. I mean I know what I am getting into, but I can't imagine him getting close enough to actually break hearts. He chuckles looking back at me momentarily

"You're really oblivious to the lifestyle you're involving yourself in."

"What lifestyle *am* I walking into?" I watch the turmoil bubble on his face as he rolls his shoulders back.

"Depends on how long you stay." He steps out of the car rounding the front and opens my door, extending a hand.

"How long are you staying?" I bite my cheek, receiving a smirk from him. We move inside and pause at the foyer.

"Do you want to head to the movie room? I won't be long."

"Yeah."

"I'm not sure how long it will be. If you get hungry you can visit the kitchen and Mila will fix something up for you." He pauses looking around. "Do you need anything else?"

"Nope." I pop and give him a small smile. He Ascends the stairs and I find the movie room. I snuggle into my spot on the couch and ready myself for some hardcore binge-watching knowing I won't see Gio for a while.

I search the TV until I find my current show. I stare intently at the screen, distracting myself for a few episodes until I can no longer sit still.

It has been a few hours and I am starving. After all, we never made it into the coffee shop and I have not had my caffeine fix or an ounce of nutrition. If I don't have it soon I will feel like crap. I make my way to the kitchen where I see Mila flit about. I clear my throat, gaining her attention. She swivels around with a bright smile.

"Well, hello dear." She places her hands on the counter next to me. "I wasn't expecting to see you again." I blush and Gio's words from earlier ring through my ears. Their company must not make much of an appearance here or they don't stay around for long. I chew my cheek; is that saying something about me and why I'm still around?

Gwenevere. I smack myself internally. I've really got to get ahold of myself. This is just a fling. A rebound to move on from Enzo.

"What can I help with?"

"Coffee and maybe a little something to eat? Gio was taking me for coffee and we didn't make it before business called." I wave my hands through the air. "I'm actively starving and on a caffeine withdrawal. Please help." The dramatic words leave me with a playful tone.

"Let's see what we can do." She starts a new brew on the coffee pot before heading to the fridge and pulling a few ingredients out, getting to work. I slide up onto the stool and watch her dance around the kitchen. You can tell that she loves what she does. Her hums flow as she moves effortlessly from the stove and back to the pot, combining syrups to create a latte.

She places the cup in front of me with a warm smile and continues to the stove. I take a sip and outwardly moan into the cup. The taste of caramel and coconut swirls through my senses with a little bit of salty undernotes.

"Oh my God, this is amazing! My mouth is literally watering."

I'm so focused on my coffee that I don't notice the man connected to the familiar husky voice that suddenly vibrates next to my ear.

"I don't like anyone else making you moan." I freeze midsip, a shiver running down my spine. I don't know if it's the hot coffee or that the man is so close to me, the room spikes a thousand degrees.

I sit the cup down on the counter and swirl on the barstool to the man who's heating up my core temperature. Matteo stares into my eyes with his darkened ones. I bite my lip and look up at him with doe eyes. His eyes follow my lips and his body stretches around me with one hand on the counter and one on the back of my chair. He wears a simple dress shirt clinging to his chest with the first couple of buttons open, exposing a small section of his chest.

"You're dressed up." His voice stays low in a statement.

"You seem to be dressed down," I counter. A smirk rides up on his lips before it disappears and he looks up to Mila. She approaches us and hands me a plate of churro crepes that instantly make my mouth water, I dive in immediately, not caring about Matteo's Gaze fixated on me. My mouth waters and I dive in, not caring about Matteo's fixated gaze. Mila hands him a cup of coffee and he takes a sip.

"Hey, Boss, we have like ten minutes left before he's useless. Want to finish him off?" Viktor's voice rounds the corner. I turn my head with furrowed brows not sure what he's rambling about. He stops in his tracks when his eyes land on me. His hand is paused, rolling up his white sleeve covered in red. Blood.

My heart stops as I stare at him. A heaviness expands in my stomach and upon further assessment, his hands are stained in a red tint along with splatters amongst his shirt. I sit completely still afraid of making a single movement. Blood. Viktor has blood covering him like a butcher in the meat shop.

"Sorry, Boss, I wasn't aware of the company." His eyes dart to me with an apologetic look before returning to Matteo. "What do you want me to do, Sir?" I finally break my gaze to look at Matteo, his face void of any emotion.

"Finish him off and have the cleanup crew come in." Viktor nods, taking another look at me before taking his leave. "Oh, and Viktor?"

Viktor pauses, angling back to give Matteo his attention.

"Send Gio to me when he's all done."

Viktor nods and leaves. Matteo studies my face but doesn't give away anything to account for the scene that just played out in front of me.

"Finish your breakfast." He points to my half-eaten plate. His voice is as untraceable as his face. I stare at my plate unable to pick up the fork. The thought of consuming anything right now makes my stomach churn. How can I continue this casual meal? Viktor was covered in blood. Another man's blood, that they are 'finishing off.' They needed a cleanup crew and Matteo is in charge of it all. Is this why Gio needed to come home so fast? This is his 'business.'

"Gwenevere." His voice is a million miles away as my memories rush in from my earlier conversation with Gio. Matteo runs businesses, mainly Casinos, but I knew they were all owned by the crime families. Crime families. He is in the mafia.

I look back up at Matteo, who is concentrating on me. His brow raises at my lack of response. I stand up, not taking my eyes off him. I glance back to where Viktor stood. My skin crawls. I stare, unable to move. I allowed myself to get comfortable around these men knowing absolutely nothing about them. Another conversation with Gio pops into my mind.

"I think I'm capable of more than your pretty mind can handle."

And another.

"Okay, Gio, how can I trust you won't kidnap me or murder me?"

He shrugs. "You don't, but doesn't that make life much more interesting?"

Is this why Gio avoids talking about anything regarding their work—or Matteo?

"What did I say about your lip?" I crinkle my brows in confusion. The world is spinning and my ears are ringing.

"My lip?"

"Yes."

"You are worried about my lip when I just saw Viktor covered in some man's blood headed to finish the job that *you* ordered. My lip."

He scans over me and then steps forwards. I flinch back pressing myself into the counter. Mila is long gone and I am alone here with a man who can determine if I make it out of this house alive. A man I let have his way with me—command me.

"Your lips concern me." His voice stays low and even. Anger builds in me and I lose any chance of saving myself from him.

"My lips are none of your concern," I growl at him. He takes another step towards me, but I have nowhere left to go. He reaches me, brushing the back of his hand over my chin.

"Do you really think that?" I swallow hard, focusing on my anger. How can he be trying to seduce me right now? Does he think this is a joke? Or is this a threat?

"Are you that insane?" I push his hand away. "Do you think I'll just crawl into bed with you and forget all about what just happened? I'm not some paid whore you can write off. Is that what you thought this was? Because you were far from being right, buddy." I poke his chest holding my frustration the best I can. He raises his eyebrows at me with a smug smile before lowering to my ear.

"You are whatever I want you to be." I laugh at him. A full-blown laugh.

"Do you think you scare me? If that is your tactic you should try another one. I can hold my own ground, Matteo." I don't know where I am pulling my front from. I am a thousand percent terrified, but there is something about the way he is looking at me that makes me determined to fight back.

"Say it again." His voice floats to me. How is he so calm?

"Say what again?"

"Say my name." His thumb caresses over my lips.

"Which one?" He staggers for a moment as his face wrinkles in confusion.

"Which one?"

"You know, which name? Jackass or Egotistical Asshole? Both suit you very well right now." I grimace at him. His hand grips my chin forcefully. I now regret my choice of words and rebellious actions.

"Is that how you want to play?" His tone finally dips, darkening, and my heart hammers in my chest.

"Who said I wanted to play any games with you?" I stare directly into him.

"Matteo!" Gio's voice rings with demand. Matteo doesn't move from glaring at me.

"What the actual fuck, Matteo." Gio booms out over the kitchen, finally pulling Matteo's attention away. He releases my chin but doesn't back away.

"Seems we've got ourselves a situation to take care of." Anger is slashed across Gio's face before dropping into realization.

"Viktor."

Matteo doesn't respond as Gio pulls a hand down his face and looks back at me. "Fuck." As if he uttered his name, Viktor strides back into the kitchen.

"Boss. I need to talk to you. *Now*." He leers to me, vacant of any regret he held when he left.

"What is it, Viktor?" Matteo growls.

"I think we should talk in—"

"Viktor."

Viktor stops on my face. It feels like time falls away.

"I got a hit back on your request."

Matteo's jaw ticks with no response.

"What's your last name?"

I grow puzzled again. My last name? Why does he need to know my last name? To make sure no one cared about me so they could take me out too? They know my brother is protective. They know I'd have people looking for me. I glimpse at Gio with panic. We are friends now... he wouldn't kill me too, would he?

"Viktor, what the hell is going on?" Gio's face tightens, both easing and unnerving me.

"What is your name?" Viktor repeats. All the men look at me and I swallow hard. Whatever Viktor is doing doesn't seem like it will end in my favor.

"Luciano. Gwenevere Luciano." I frown, still unsure why he wanted me to say my name. The men collectively tense and the entire room shifts. The muscles in Matteo's jaw grow tight, anger breaking across his previously unreadable face. Gio stands unmoved, staring at me. An overwhelming pressure lands on my chest from the sudden mood change.

"You are a Luciano?" Hints of betrayal line his voice. My confusion clouds with panic. Why is Matteo so mad about my name? And why does it look like Gio doesn't recognize me?

"Yes. Born and raised. Why does my last name matter?" My brain spins with every possible scenario. "Is this about my dad? His businesses? Did he do something?"

Viktor scans over Gio but his face is stone. Matteo grits his teeth, turning to him as well.

"You brought a Luciano into my house?"

Gio scoffs.

"I knew as much about her as you did. At least that's all I did. You fucking slept with her! I told you not to fucking get involved in the first place. You finally fucked yourself didn't you," Gio snarks back.

"Giovanni, watch your damn mouth!"

"Are you kidding me? Do you realize what this means? You stepped over a boundary and I'm the one who needs to watch myself?"

"I swear to fucking God, Gio!" Matteo stalks closer to Gio.

"How about instead of being pissed at me you figure out how you're gonna fix your own damn mess now that you fucked up the alliance!" Matteo revs up but I need answers.

"What alliance? With my dad? What does any of that have to do with me?"

Matteo's heated gaze stays on Gio but Viktor watches me.

"I don't understand what the fuck is going on. Can one of you for the love of God please tell me what I'm missing!" I growl out, frustrated. Gio studies me for a silent beat.

"She doesn't know."

13

Matteo

"You're right. You're not a whore you a fucking rat." The instant it leaves my mouth her hand slaps me across the face. I close my eyes, breathing in deeply to control the anger raging inside me. Viktor steps forward.

"What the fuck is wrong with you! How am I a fucking rat?" She screams pushing on my chest. "You. Are. A. Low. Life. Stupid. Scum!"

I stand like a brick wall; I can overpower her by tenfold. Viktor takes another step, opening his mouth to chime in, but before he gets a chance I grab her by the throat. Her face lands at the perfect height to look directly into her eyes.

"You're a fucking Luciano." I grit through my teeth. Her face drops and her body slumps. Viktor stands at my side watching the scene unfold. Gio stares at her, a look I can't quite recognize as he continues his nonsense. Nonsense I secretly hope is true.

"She doesn't know. She doesn't fucking know who she is." I keep my stance, keeping a firm hold on her. How can she not know she is part of a major crime family? I knew the names Alessio and Enzo were too much of a coincidence. I should have been on guard from the beginning but I let her slip. I was wrong. She wasn't a fucking flower—she was a rat.

"Of course she knows," I growl, staring at Gwenevere. Gio shakes his head at my side looking between Gwenevere and me.

"No. Think about it. Think about her house. Think about the way she mentioned her family. All she knows is her dad is wealthy and he needs protection. She told me Alessio went away for a business internship, she has no clue what her name stands for."

I loosen my hand but stay in place as she struggles to talk.

"What are you talking about?"

"Matteo, let her go," Gio gripes.

"How can we trust that, Gio? I'm doing her a favor by not bringing her into the cellar." She winces at my tone and blinks back tears.

"I'm. Not. A. Rat," she strains to speak in a hoarse voice. "My brother works for my dad. He's a business consultant, just like you guys. I have no clue what you're talking about. What happened between you has nothing to do with me. If you think he sent me here to do something you are highly mistaken. He doesn't tell me shit."

This time I let go of her but keep my place in front of her. She is clueless. Gio laughs under his breath shaking his head.

"You have no idea," he sighs, running a hand down his face. "Have you looked into your family? Ever hear your name around?"

"Why would I look into my family? While they are assholes, Alessio isn't capable of anything terrible, not that I'd know anything about their work." He sighs again and hands her his phone, gesturing to it.

"Look up the Luciano family." I stay silent, watching the interaction. She opens the phone going to the search bar and types her name in hesitantly. Her eyes swirl with curiosity and confusion.

"Add crime family to the end." Gwenevere freezes but types it in. Her face only reveals her innocence as she scrolls down the list of articles. She reads the headlines sucking in all the air her lungs can hold.

She scrolls down to a family photo she was excluded from, Alessio had to be eight or nine then. She clicks open the article and reads.

"Luciano Crime Boss: A Family Man?"

She leaves the article and scrolls again. Thousands of headlines showcasing her father, Lavoy, and Alessio. Others show Alessio and Enzo. She clicks on the most recent of them. "Alessio *Luciano to Take Over the Crime Family. Enzo Portillo, Second in Command."* I watch her and it's as if I can pinpoint the moment she shatters. Gio was right, she had no idea who she was or the family she belonged to.

"Will Luciano Stay Allied with Genovese?" A photo is displayed below; on the left hand side, Alessio and Enzo stand together. Her face pales when she takes in the men on the right—Gio and I. She looks up to Gio and then to me.

"I—" She stands at a loss for words. She knows what this means. Her eyes display every emotion bubbling behind them. She now understands what it means for her to be standing in front of me right now. Everything that has happened between us and her friendship with... she's beginning to understand.

"I didn't know," her voice breaks.

"How could they never have told her who she is?" Gio presses his lips together before grabbing the back of one of the stools, his knuckles turning white.

"You guys—" She glances between Gio and me. "You're the Genovese crime family," she says mostly to herself. I readjust my jaw and clench my fist. Not only at Gio but at myself. But more than us, I am pissed at the Luciano's. How could they let her go through life freely with so many enemies lingering, and being unaware of the dangers around every corner? Her guards are obviously shit. If Alessio knew she had been involved with us he wouldn't have allowed her into my home much less the frequent visits Gio has with her.

"Our families? We're allies?" her voice rises with her brow.

"For now," Gio grumbles, glaring at me. She looks up at me as her brows scrunch together.

"For now?" Why for now?" This time her voice panicked.

Gio glances between Gwenevere and me when the realization hits. She slaps her hand over her mouth but it doesn't do her justice. She laughs. Full heartedly laughs. Her laughing continues until she files through all the new information and sobers.

"What now? We're allies for now, but if I thought my brother was going to kill you before he sure as hell will now and he'll start a whole damn war while he's at it."

"Let him." I brush the notion off. We both might be strong families but I've had a ring on mine for a while. Alessio just stepped into it. If he starts a war this soon, he will fail and I will gladly watch.

"Matteo. You know there's an easy answer to all this. You just have to—"

"Gio," I growl lowly.

"Oh come on. You're telling me you wouldn't enjoy it in the least? You're already fucking her. It would solve everything."

"GIOVANNI!" I roar, the warning gone.

"What is he talking about?"

I couldn't do that to her. The last thing I need is an arranged marriage. I've always been pushed to have one with different women of course. A family to keep the name—to have an heir with royalty. I will one day, but that day is far from now. Very far.

"Drop it." I say between gritted teeth.

"Arranged marriage." Her eyes widen at Gio's unwanted statement. She wants an arranged marriage as much as I do. That should make me happy but her reaction touches something in me. I don't want this with her, especially not over an alliance... but could a marriage as a business arrangement keep Alessio at bay?

I glare daggers at Gio but he holds his ground. Would that really fix it? An arranged marriage between the families? The sister of a Don, to a Don. It is a perfect assurance of alliance. I'd be a fool to not recognize the benefits. Especially when I've already slept with Alessio's sister. The precious mafia princess hidden from the world corrupted by your one and only. It would cause a war. An arranged marriage would set the balance.

"Arranged marriage? You want me to marry him?" She points to me. I smirk inwardly, almost taking it as a challenge. Gio sighs and then looks at Gwenevere sincerely. I can tell this whole thing is bothering him. Who would've known a random girl he helped would be Luciano? Though the signs were present, no one really knew she existed until now. It wasn't an obvious option but an option we overlooked.

"I know it's not ideal and you're already dealing with a lot, but it can keep peace within the families and keep you safe." I close my eyes, pinching the bridge of my nose.

"This is ridiculous. Alessio won't agree to it, he's possessive and she has never been mentioned," I grit out.

"It's not Alessio you have to worry about," she mutters under her breath, but I pick it up none the less.

"Who should I be worried about?"

She doesn't lift her head to me but her tense posture lets me know she heard me. If not Alessio, then who? Her father? His power is strong in the families but Alessio is in charge now. Sure he still has connections but it is a game of loyalty. Do their loyalties lie with Lavoy or the family?

"Gwenevere, who should I be worried about?" I growl at her. She snaps her head up at the anger coursing through my face. I stare at her as she sits quietly, pleading and regretting the words coming from her mouth moments ago. She is on the verge of breaking but I need her to be strong for this. I need to know everything.

"Who was the father?" Gio's voice cuts like glass through the room. I'm locked in shock but become mortified in seconds. Fucking Luciano's.

"Father! You have a child?" My voice rises but instead of inflicting fear, she matches my irritated tone.

"Really?" she yells at Gio before turning to me. "And you. You don't get to go there. You don't know anything about me. You might know my name and my family, but don't you dare act like you've asked me anything genuine. All you've been is egotistical."

I curse and Gio approaches Gwenevere, proceeding carefully.

"Gwen, if he has anything to do with this we need to know."

"Of course he is! They have a child together!" I fling my hands through the air.

"No, we don't!" Her face reddens and tears brim her eyes.

"Then how is he the father?" The sarcasm drips from my voice. How is this even happening? I swear to God I'm going to kill Gio after this. Her tears slide down her face and she wipes them away. I search her face trying to understand as it slowly clicks. My shoulders drop and I take a calming breath.

"You lost the baby." More tears fall as she stares at me. My anger simmers away at the flashes to our intimate night when she broke down. No one hurt her. "That's why…"

I stumble, trying to find the right words for the delicate situation. One I refuse to disrespect with my own hate that lingers for the Luciano's.

"Gwen. Who was the father... Gwen?"

Her eyes stay on the floor as if she can't fight to lift them.

"Enzo," she whispers in defeat. I turn and throw my glass of bourbon across the room with a crash of the pieces across the floor. I lean against the wall with my closed fist dropping my head. She had been pregnant with Enzo fucking Portillo, Alessio's second. If I thought this was complicated before it just got a whole lot messier. Alessio may be pissed about my connection with Gwen already but with Enzo's influence, this will be war.

"Jesus fuck," I mutter. Gio runs his hand down his face and looks at me.

"You need to propose a deal."

I laugh, shaking my head in disbelief.

"A proposal? A fucking proposal? That's your answer? She was carrying Alessio's second's baby—Enzo Portillo's baby. And you think they'll agree to a proposal? Are you out of your fucking mind, Giovanni?"

Gwen stays quiet, her face numb to emotion. My chest constricts and my control slips.

"Matteo."

"Leave."

The men take their exit and Gwenevere steps forward to follow when I snap my head over to her.

"Not you."

She swallows back looking at me but stays in place. Gio glances at her hesitantly before following suit with Viktor and stalks out of the room leaving us alone.

It is silent for a long time. I want to know what's going through her mind. Her whole life flipped in a moment and everyone around her just became murders to her. Her entire life has been one giant lie. Not only that, she was forced to share a trauma she seems yet to fully heal from. I wonder how the relationship stands but more than anything I need to know how long ago. If Enzo is still clinging to this life with her, nothing will work for her and me.

Is that even what I want, a 'her and me', whatever that means? She stays in her numb-like state, urging me to cross the room to ease her mind. To make her forget like she's been trying to do all along. Except this time she is not only mourning a baby but her life.

"When did you lose the baby?"

Her eyes lift to me but the pain speckles in them. I don't push but keep my eyes trained on her every movement and expression. I'm no longer angry, at least not at her. If anything, I'm angry *with* her.

I have never felt someone else's pain as my own. Our world doesn't allow for many emotions. They are dangerous and will get you killed at any sign of weakness. It is a constant game of poker, and a flower like her doesn't belong in this world, regardless of where she came from. Yet, here she is, and I'm starting to think she won't be leaving anytime soon.

Her voice comes out soft and strained as if it takes everything in her to not only say it but to not break down while she does.

"August."

My brows furrow as I process her statement. August.That was… Jesus, no wonder. This wound is still fresh.

"That was three months ago."

She's lost so much and everything changed in such little time.

"I needed to move on. You made me forget and I wanted so badly to forget, Matteo." Her voice breaks and her lips quiver. This is what I wanted to avoid. I wanted to avoid the emotions—the weakness—but Gwenevere makes me feel weak. I can't watch her break anymore, not without helping her pick up the pieces and protecting her from anything hurting her again. I'm a damn fool for it but I'd be a bigger fool to deny it.

I cross the room and lift her chin with my hand. I search for an answer to how to make it better and make her heartbreak go away. I need to see where she is with everything that has been dumped on her. I need to see how shattered her heart has become.

"What do you want now?"

Her scent is a sweet vanilla mixed with roses, begging me to move closer. I watch her eyes furrow in thought.

"I want you to help me forget."

I hold her face and place my lips softly on hers. For a moment, I forget. I forget who I am and everything in the way; the fear of weakness I've been fought to resist. It's just Gwenevere and I. Her lips are soft and plump from crying, and I want to hold her and embrace her, but refrain from pushing her too far.

My kiss is shorter than in our past transactions. This time it's softer and filled with the need to please her and take away the pain. I rest my forehead on hers waiting patiently for a sign.

"I'm so lost, Matteo. I wanted to forget my life, and now I'm seeing more than I ever have." I listen with a soft hold on her. "Matteo, make me forget."

14

Gwenevere

It's been a week since my entire life flipped. Since the Genoveses told me the truth of who I am. It hurts to know my life has been a complete lie. I'm not sure how my dad or Alessio hid it from me this entire time. How can they hide the things that they've done? Maybe Alessio and I moving out so young made it easier. But now that Alessio has taken over, how is he able to keep it under wraps?

How could Enzo have kept it from me? Sure he is Alessio's second, but our relationship had meant something, right? It had to. He's been willing to risk his friendship and by the looks of it his life. He's been willingly risking it all for me. We were going to have a baby and he never thought to mention that our child would be an heir to a major Crime family?

I don't know whether to mourn my life or to be angry at the ones who kept it from me. I'm not mad at Matteo's reaction. I can see his position, why he thought I was there to hurt him. If I had been aware of my family, I would have known intertwining myself with them would be a threat. Yet I had no clue. What do I do now? I resent Alessio for keeping me in the dark, and I don't want to pull away from Matteo and Gio.

I don't care what that means for the Luciano family. I will keep us in alliance but if I can't do that? If it wasn't for the Genovese's bringing me into the light I would still be oblivious to the web of lies Alessio and Enzo have created.

I've continued my daily coffee runs with Gio. I spent that night with Matteo but he left by the morning and I haven't seen him since. Gio said he is out of town for business and I haven't pushed further. I don't think I want to know what his *business* entails.

I lay in bed staring at the ceiling. I don't want to get out of bed. I know Alessio and Enzo have been home all day, and I am avoiding them like the plague. I haven't spoken to either of them in a week. I can't unless I want to break down and rage. I can't even look at them.

The front door slaps and I open my door a crack, straining my ears to listen for anyone. When I'm confident they have left, I slip out of my room and down the hall. I freeze at the sight of Alessio and Enzo concentrated on separate stacks of papers. Both of them shoot their heads up to me. Alessio sits back in his chair, crossing his arms.

"So you have been avoiding me."

The last thing I want to do is have this conversation with him. I haven't even had my first cup of coffee. I take a deep breath trying to avoid letting my anger get the best of me. I move across the room to the kitchen and start a new coffee. I lean against the counter staring at the ceiling as the machine gets to work.

I get the sense one of them has come into the kitchen but I don't look over. I don't want to talk to either one and making eye contact would give them the impression that I do.

"Is this because you don't want to talk about the baby?"

Of course, that's what Alessio assumes my avoidance is for. He has gotten so comfortable in his web of lies he doesn't suspect I know all his secrets. My coffee beeps indicating the finished brew. I spin around, adding the creamer in.

"Gwen." Alessio steps towards me but I ignore him again and move around him. He grabs my arm, glaring at me.

"Gwenevere."

"Don't," I bite out in warning and a fevered stare.

"Don't what? Worry about you? Do you really think avoiding me would work?"

"Alessio. Let. Go."

"What is going on, Gwenevere?" He stares into me. "What has you all strung up, huh?" Enzo stands in the corner of the entrance watching the scene unfold. I don't need them cornerning me. I don't need their 'concerns'.

"Alessio." I give him my final warning the hate and resentment pounding in my chest, begging to be unleashed.

"No. Don't Alessio me. I'm not playing stupid little games with you anymore. You're not a little girl. Stop acting like one. I have to leave today for our business trip and whatever you have going on needs to be fixed. Now."

"Ha." I move my tongue over my teeth laughing. He blinks rapidly at my change in demeanor. Enzo swallows deeply, maybe he thinks I'm going to expose us. Except it's the exact opposite, I'm exposing them.

"What kind of business trip? Are you murdering someone or running the casino? I mean now that daddies handed over the *famiglia* it's all your dealings now; isn't it?"

Alessio stills at my condescending questions as his Adams apple bobs while he stares at me.

"You really thought you could keep that little secret forever? Do you really think I'm that much of an idiot?" I laugh rhetorically. "You let me walk through my entire life not knowing who I am? The dangers my life is constantly in? How many hits have been on my head, *huh*? Five? Ten? More?"

I look at Enzo, my furry rising. "And Enzo, don't think you get to sit there untouched. Not once did you ever mention it to me. You two truly fucking belong to each other, really. You are perfect for each other."

Enzo steps forward but I raise my hand stopping him in his tracks.

"Don't." I shake my head and move my piercing gaze to Alessio.

"Do you have anything to say?"

He opens his mouth but shuts it several times. I purse my lips and nod to him. "Right. I've got to go."

"You're not going anywhere."

"You can't keep me here. I'm not a little girl anymore; remember? Your words, not mine. You're not my *Don,* Alessio. You're just my pathetic excuse of a brother." I push past him glaring at Enzo. I grab my purse off the table and head to the front door. I'm greeted by Gio leaning against his car, waiting for me with a smile but it drops in seconds, putting him on guard.

"Gwen, do you know who that fucking man is!" Alessio's voice booms out after me. I don't stop, continuing down the drive.

"Of course I fucking know who he is. I've had all the stranger danger lessons, and right now he is less of a stranger than you."

"GWEN!" I swirl back to him with the best glare I can muster to hide the pain burrowing in me.

"What, Alessio? Do you want to talk now or just order me around and lie to my face again? Hell, how can I know anything coming out of your pathetic fucking mouth is true!"

"You think I'm so terrible? He is a hundred times worse. You have no idea what you are doing. Do not get in that car." He steps further down the drive forcing me closer to Gio.

"At least they're honest with me. I can trust the words coming out of their mouths, I can't believe any of yours." My hatred grows as Alessio treats me like a child incapable of understanding the situation at hand. He looks at Gio raising an accusing finger.

"You fucking told her? Is that your play?" Gio steps forward until I put my hand up.

"Of course not. How could it be? No one knew I existed. Fuck, I didn't know I existed. I mean really Alessio, a round of applause, you did a hell of a job. This isn't about whatever cock headed motion of power you have complex in your head. You may be a Mafia Boss now but you're still little Alessio with your head stuck up your ass!"

I glance at Gio before looking back at Alessio. "You want to talk? You set up a meeting with the Genovese's and hope I decide to show up. You know Matteo's number, *sì?*"

Alessio's jaw ticks. He has lost his control and he isn't hiding it well. Enzo gives Gio a piercing glare, fist tightened at his sides. With that I turn back to Gio.

"Don't get in the car, Gwenevere."

I don't stop. Not even a pause as I make my way to Gio.

"Get me the fuck out of here." Gio nods, opening the door for me. He shoots out a message as he rounds the car. Once in he brings his attention to me.

"Are you okay?" *No.*

"Please, just get me out of here." I pull my legs up to my chest and curl into myself. Gio drives off and I let myself fall into my pained thoughts. Tears flow out of the corners of my eyes.

"I'm guessing you told him you know?" Gio asks after some time. I use the sleeve of my sweatshirt to wipe my face. A pathetic sniffle escapes me in the process.

"Do you still want to go to the coffee shop or back to the estate?" His voice is tender as he tiptoes around my fragile state.

"Can we go to the estate?" He nods and he picks up his phone. I zone out and watch the buildings pass by.

"Matteo will meet us there." My head snaps over to Gio. Matteo's in town? Gio chuckles lightly, shaking his head.

"That piqued your interest didn't it." I lift my face up and roll my eyes. It does though, I craved Matteo. I had no idea he was back and right now I want nothing more than to be in his embrace.

We pull into the estate a few minutes later. I am beyond exhausted now. No coffee, a week's worth of crying on our short trip across the city, and I am drained. Gio opens my door and I trudge beside him up to the entrance. He opens the door letting me in and my gaze instantly locks on Matteo.

When he hears us come in he turns; his brows furrow taking me in before glancing at Gio. He gives him a soft nod, inclining his leave. Gio offers a slight squeeze to my shoulder before taking off to the kitchen. Once Gio is out of sight Matteo holds out his hand.

I crush my body into him and break down all over again. Matteo lets me cry, holding me to his chest. He rubs circles in my hair as he holds my back, giving me support as my body trembles with my cries.

Matteo swoops me up and makes his way up the stairs. He carries me to his room and lays me on the soft bed. He shuffles for a moment taking off his suit jacket and shoes before climbing up behind me. He turns me towards him, grasping my head to pull me into him again.

My ear lays on his chest and while the sound is extremely faint, the vibrational rhythm of his heart eases my emotional frustration.

I don't want to be anywhere but in his arms right now. His caress brings me peace and safety. My crying evens to shallow breaths as the exhaustion rolls through me.

"How bad was it?" Matteo finally breaks the silence.

"He's mad. Throwing useless threats."

He stiffens against me but lets me continue. "He's just fuming and trying to wrap his head around me knowing."

"That or he wants war." His tone is clipped but not at me.

I shake my head. I know Alessio, maybe not as well as I thought I did a week ago, but if I know one thing for sure, it's that he won't try to purposely hurt me. He will set up the meeting when he realizes that I am in fact, serious. He'll do anything for me. At least, I really hope so... I don't want him to prove me wrong. Not on this.

"He won't." I draw patterns on his chest but stop when a thought crosses my mind. "Matteo?"

"Yes?"

I lift my head to him chewing on my cheek.

" I um... need a place to stay, just for a little bit until I can figure something out." He doesn't respond right away, sending me into an instant panic. "Sorry. Forget I mentioned it. I can call Sole."

"No. You can stay here."

I give him a warm smile. His hand slides from the back of my head down to my chin before circling my cheek. His eyes glance down to my lips and he leans in, leaving a soft kiss like the time before.

"Farei qualsiasi cosa per te." *I would do anything for you.*

I bite my lip as he stares at me. His thumb glides down, popping my lip out. He crashes his lips on mine. This time with desperate need.

His lips move hard against mine. I don't fight him. Instead, I open my mouth, allowing him to explore. My hand travels to his chest grasping his dress shirt. I pull him into me, pressing myself against him. His hardness presses into my leg and he glides his hand back into my hair. He props himself above me, gripping my hip with this other hand.

"I need you," I plead, matching his hungry eyes filled with lust as he dips his head into my neck. He trails kisses down my neck, tugging my shirt, and pulling it over my head. I'm left in my lace bralette. The thin fabric clinging to my pebbled tips. His mouth lowers down gently sucking through the fabric. He swirls the other under his fingertips.

Matteo goes back and forth between my aching peaks as I push my chest into him, moaning out. His face dips further and his mouth travels down my stomach. I run my hand through his neatly done hair making him even more inviting. His hands find the tops of my sweat shorts and glide them down my legs.

He kisses my ankle then trails up my leg to my inner thigh. I squirm but he holds my hip down while his mouth draws closer to my throbbing core as heat radiates off of me. I throw my head back and arch up, giving him more access. My body hums at his tortuous sucking and nibbling. His hand slides up my leg allowing his fingers to arrive at my clenched opening and he lets out a groan.

"You're dripping for me, *Principessa.*" *You're dripping for me, Princess.*

I hum, biting my lips. His eyes find mine studying me as he thrusts his finger in. I slam my eyes shut moaning. His fingers caress inside of me. He pulls his finger out then thrusts back in with two.

Matteo curls his fingers and sucks my swollen clit. Within seconds, I'm crumbling in a heated mess. My walls clenching around him and I grab him.

"Matteo, please."

He runs his tongue from my opening up, lapping at my juices before taking his thumb across his bottom lip, forcing a groan to vibrate within him.

He holds my face to his and bends down to me. I didn't see him unbuttoning his pants but take note of his exposed throbbing member. He lines himself up to me still tracing my lips with his. He doesn't push in but instead teases me with his tip against my clit. I push my head further into the mattress and pull away from his lips coming up for air.

His eyes meet mine and my chest rises and falls in anticipation. Matteo thrust into me dipping his head back down and sucking on my bottom lip. Pleasure erupts inside me as his thrusts find a steady rhythm. His interchanging grunts and my moans make a euphoric chorus against the walls of the room.

My eyes water in pleasure as he pumps into me and my nails dig into him. I lose my control, meeting his thrust hard, and grinding against him to chase my orgasm. Just as my orgasm flows through me, I feel it rush between us where we are connected.

"Matteo," I exclaim breathlessly.

"Say it again." His voice comes out like honey in between thrusts.

"Matteo," I cry out, gripping onto him as the pressure builds up again. His pace picks up and I lose any ounce of self-preservation.

"Lo sono pazza di te." *I am crazy for you.* His grateful confessions flow to my ears. *"Mi sono perso nei tuoi occhi."* *I've lost myself in your eyes.*

His grunts come quicker as his body slams into mine. I hold onto him, letting him find the pleasure that I'm certain I'll find with him again.

"Gwenevere," he moans, plunging deep into me and holding my body to him.

"Matteo." My words come slurred, letting our releases flow between us. His lips find mine laying sloppy kisses. I'm engulfed in Matteo, and I can't be more content. The outside world is a void. All I can think about is Matteo.

He rolls off the bed, sliding his hand into mine, pulling me into the bathroom on shaky legs. He holds onto me and I take in his deep blue eyes and his post sex afterglow—if he was attractive before, he is absolutely jaw---dropping now. I take him in as the mixture of our cums runs down my thighs.

He pulls me forward, gently leading me to the large bathtub. He adjusts the knobs to create a flow of water and feels for the perfect temperature. When he's content he adds soap, creating bubbles underneath the fall and spreading them throughout the bath.

Matteo slips behind me and my skin prickles from his closeness. He returns in front of me holding a towel before bending down and kissing my innermost thigh. I watch him clean the evidence of our shared intimacy from between my legs before he discards the towel and motions for me to step into the bath.

He helps me in the water which soothes my aching muscles. He sits behind me and turns the water off, resting his legs on either side of me and pulling me to his chest. I lean my head against him. He grabs a fresh towel from the side of the tub, dipping it in the water and lathering it with the soap.

He slides the towel up my arm and around my shoulder. His hand dips down my chest and circles my tender breasts. Matteo continues further brushing past my thighs and back up before letting go of the towel. It slides down my body and he grabs my chin turning me enough to kiss me. When he pulls back I take a moment before opening my eyes at look at him.

"Is this what you want?"

Is this what I want? Do I really know him? I know what he does, kind of. I know his brother. He knows a lot about me—probably more than I know about myself.

With Enzo it was a simple, yes or no. He knew me and I knew him. Or at least I thought I did. With Matteo I know all the worst parts up front. Yet, even though this man has blood on his hands, they caress me tenderly and pick up the pieces that have been strung out by the ones I trusted most.

This may not be what I envisioned but I have the clearest view of what I do want. I want this. I want to repeat every touch Matteo lays on me. He takes all the pain away.

When I found out who I am—what world I really belong to—I couldn't help but hear Gio's voice ringing in my ears, *"Depends on how long you stay; how long do you plan on staying?"* At the time, it felt like a ploy to ease my current anxiety; though now, after recent revelations, I'd find that not to be true.

"What if it is?" What does he want?

"I won't let you go. You won't get to run home when you decide you hate me."

"I don't think I could hate you."

"Did you think you could hate Alessio and Enzo?"

Enzo, potentially, but Alessio? Maybe some brotherly-sister fighting and fake hate but the resentment and anger I hold for him now? No. I never thought I would.

"Stay for a week. If you still want this and don't hate me by the end of the week—" He brushes the hair from my face. "I'll make you mine."

15

Gwenevere

"Have you eaten?" I shake my head as I rest against Matteo, both of us still submerged under the water. I have been so overwhelmed I haven't managed a single cup of coffee.

"Come on, let's grab something." I nod and he stands up, swooshing the water like mini tidal waves in the bath. He quickly dries off, tying the towel around his waist before helping me out and giving me a towel of my own.

We leave the bathroom and I stop in the doorway—I have no clothes. Not a single item for the entire week but I am definitely not going back home. As I'm thinking about how I'll be in my pjs all week, Matteo returns in front of me with some boxers.

"Put these underneath for now. I'll have Mila send something up while we eat and we can get you something for the week afterward."

"You really don't have to."

"What are you going to wear? Your one pair of pajamas for the whole week? We're going. End of discussion." I bite my cheek, nodding before swiping my clothes off the floor and dressing.

"Thank you."

He grips my hips from behind and sinks into my neck. He whispers into my ear sending chills down my spine.

"Non ringraziarmi mai per essermi preso cura di te." Don't ever thank me for taking care of you

"That would be rude."

"Only if I say it is."

"Just because you say something isn't rude doesn't mean it's not." I spin around to gaze at him.

"Whatever I say, is what I say it is."

"With whom?" I laugh playfully.

"Everyone."

"Guess I'm not everyone because I think it's rude."

"No, you certainly are not everyone," he chuckles, shaking his head. I slide my last piece of clothing on and turn to see Matteo in his suit attire except for his jacket that rests on his forearm.

"Ready?" He doesn't look up as he adjusts his shirt.

"Yeah."

He opens the door and I step into the hallway looking around like a teenager who's going to get caught sneaking out with her boyfriend. I hear Matteo laugh behind me.

"Is the coast clear?" He smirks. "It really would be a shame if someone saw us sneaking out of my own room, in my house."

I roll my eyes at his retort.

"It's not like the whole estate hears you screaming my name."

Heat washes over my face and my eyes bulge out. I swivel back to him forgetting about the hallway.

"They heard us?"

"*Principessa*, the walls are not soundproof up here. Everyone will know who you belong to, *Bella*." He tucks a piece of hair behind my ear with amusement.

"Who said I belong to you?"

"You have a week to decide whether or not you stay with me." He steps closer pinning me to the doorway. He trails his finger over my collarbone. "But while you are here, I'm the only one who will touch you—see you. You will be mine for the taking." He backs away, releasing me, and strides into the hall. I smile at the guards at the end of the hall. A mix of small smiles and nods reach me before their attention is drawn back to their conversations.

"That was the first time I got a real reaction," I say, mostly to myself.

"They are aware of you, and they also know you are not a threat while you're on our grounds, but should you make yourself a threat you will be treated as such."

"Right. So they'll actually acknowledge my presence?"

"Yes, but remember they are there to protect and do their jobs. They're not here as your personal buddy system."

"Gotcha. Anything else I should know? Booby traps, rules, women?"

Matteo stops and I run into his shoulder.

"One, don't go into locked doors."

"Makes sense." I shrug.

"Don't be a rat."

"I'm not a rat," I huff, why are we still on this? I clearly have no intention of hurting them.

"You weren't a rat because you didn't even know who you were. Now you know I'm a potential enemy."

"I don't think recent activities upstairs qualify me for the position of an undercover agent."

"You'd be surprised how many women are used for the dirty work."

"I'm not here because Alessio wants me to be here, in fact, he wants the exact opposite. I'm here because I don't want to be there, and the only place I'd rather be is here."

His lips pull into a small smirk.

"You forgot about the women," I tsk playfully. I'd be an idiot to think I'm the only one Matteo has had in his bed. Hell, I'm probably not the only one this week.

"There aren't any women, at least not that I've brought here."

"You didn't bring me here," I point out. Does he think I'll believe he doesn't have women waltzing in and out of here?

"Unlike Gio, I'm a little more classy with my women."

"Ahh, check me off the list." I motion to my current attire of pajamas and his boxers. "I'm the most boring, unclassy one yet."

"Who said you're boring?"

"So you admit it, I'm not classy. It's okay. I mean the whole thing with Enzo, then jumping into bed with you causing all the drama in the first place. Just like Alessio; don't be hypocritical."

"Hypocritical?" He throws his head back with a laugh this time. A wide smile lines his face, one I could get used to.

"I'm a whore for sleeping with more than one guy in my lifetime, but you men… you can have two in one night and that just means you have game. Don't get me wrong, Alessio calling me a whore for going out a few nights a week was a little shocking, seeing as I hadn't even slept with you yet."

"Your brother called you a whore?" His smile drops as quickly as it had come.

"Yeah, it's nothing really, besides I can hold my own. I gave him a real shock to his system."

"And how did you do that?" He raises a brow with a genuine interest in my story.

"I told him my body yeeted my baby. He definitely regretted his bullshit then."

Matteo stills, the frustration that had been growing is completely replaced with softened features; like the day he found out, the room grows quiet. My dark-humored words aren't settling how I expected.

"Sorry, I um, it's okay. I mean it's not and it sucked, and it still sucks, but I'm okay."

I twiddle my thumbs avoiding his direct gaze.

"How far along were you?" I'm surprised at his questions, half expecting him to avoid the conversation.

"*Erm*, I had just turned twenty weeks… it was a girl." I offer up with a tight smile. "She was big enough to hold but not big enough to—" my voice breaks off and I drop my eyes to the ground. Matteo wipes a tear that escapes before lifting my chin to look at him fully.

"I'm sorry." I bite my cheek nervously, closing my eyes briefly.

"She wasn't meant to be here or I would still have her. I'll get my chance again maybe someday, but for now, I'm okay."

He studies me but ultimately nods and we finish our way to the kitchen. Viktor sits on a stool next to Gio as they discuss something work-related. Matteo waltzes to the coffee machine and I linger at the counter. Their conversation flattens at my presence and in turn, we receive smirks from the two.

"Welcome back. We weren't expecting an appearance so soon." Gio snickers as Matteo glares at the back of his head, and my face heats up for the millionth time today.

"Who says they're finished?" Viktor pipes, popping a candy in his mouth.

Matteo passes me a cup of coffee and takes a sip of his own. Sweet notes of caramel hit my nose and I moan into the cup of coffee. My caffeine fix has been greatly deprived. The men laugh at me as Matteo eyes me.

"I swear you'd die without coffee. It's like your body is fueled with caffeine instead of water." Gio tilts against the back of the stool.

"You're probably right." I take a big gulp of the coffee. My constant headache is still a level above where I would like it to be this early in the day, but crying almost always indicates a migraine to be.

"Is there some headache medicine lying around here? I need something to knock this headache out." If I attack it now I might get lucky enough to dodge the migraine. Gio goes to the cabinet Matteo had pulled from last time.

"Caffeine not doing the job?"

"Unfortunately, caffeine isn't strong enough to cure my head of this morning's stress. Lack of food isn't helping either."

Gio raises his brows looking at Matteo.

"With Alessio, Jesus," I mutter. Gio laughs, rummaging through the pills.

"Two hundred milligrams good?" I scrunch my nose. "Okay, not good then. What's your usual?"

"Eight hundred milligrams." Gio purses his lips, looking at the bottle.

"Maybe I should just grab the stronger pills. Is that even safe with the amount of migraines you get?" Gio places the bottle back into the cabinet and turns to me.

"Eh, it'll probably kill my liver, but at least my head won't hurt as much." I take my time sipping my coffee, relishing in the taste. After a moment of no one talking I glance above the cup to see Matteo and Gio exchanging looks with each other.

"You'd think in a room full of people who literally kill men for a living, they would be way less shocked over this little inconvenience."

"For one, you're not a man. Two, you haven't done anything we would need to kill you for. It's not like we just go out and shoot people for fun. And it's not a little inconvenience." Gio sends me a pinched look.

"You get used to it." I shrug while Gio finishes his search through the cabinet.

"I don't have eights down here, let me run to the doc." I stare at Gio's retreating back, confused.

"Doc? You have a doctor in the estate?"

"We can't go to the hospital with bullet holes without questions being asked. If I have a doctor on the premises, we never have to worry about suspicions rising," Matteo clarifies, resting his palms on the counter.

"Right..." I lower onto the stool next to Viktor who goes back and forth typing and reading on his laptop. He probably won't tell me what he is doing but I'm nosey and it's the perfect opportunity to start a conversation. I'd like to know Viktor better, seeing as he's close with Gio and Matteo. I'm still unsure of his position in the *famiglia*.

Viktor is always quiet. I wonder how he discovered who I am. Maybe he is the tech brains in the group? Only one way to find out.

"What are you doing there?" I ask, taking another sip of my coffee. Viktor slows his typing but doesn't look away from his laptop.

"Writing a proposal." My brows raise in surprise. He actually told me. I mean he didn't look at me but it's something.

"What kind of proposal?" He glances at Matteo so briefly I might not have seen it if I wasn't staring right at him.

"A marriage proposal."

"Oh." It's my turn to glance at Matteo. He watches the interaction between us carefully. I look back to Viktor. "My marriage proposal?"

"Yes, more so a potential one." Viktor breaks his eye contact from his laptop and I purse my lips.

"We need to be prepared for all our options should Alessio make a move. We aren't sure how he'll react. If he's anything like his father he'll be hot-headed."

"What *are* the options?"

"Depends on what he knows." Viktor glimpses between Matteo and me. *Oh.* So whether or not I'm sleeping with someone from the Genovese family—more specifically, Matteo. I am, but Alessio doesn't know that and he doesn't need to. Not now at least.

"All he knows about is my friendship with Gio and that I at least know him." I point to Matteo.

"He did accuse you of sleeping around just because you didn't come home one night." Matteo pipes up. He isn't wrong, but I don't think Alessio would assume I'm sleeping with Matteo.

"So, say he doesn't know."

"We continue our negotiations, you go back home and clear the waters, and if he allows it you can come and go freely."

"Allow me? He's not my father."

"No, he's not, but he is your Don."

"He's not my Don either. I get he's my brother. That makes him family by blood but I never once took his stupid little *omerta*. He's not my Don and I don't answer to him. He sure as hell hasn't proven himself to be worthy of my devotion either." I cross my arms with a huff. Like I would let Alessio have that control over me. He already possesses more of my time than I'd like him to. My relationship with Enzo proved that.

"You aren't going to take your role in the family?"

"Who said I have to? Why do I have to choose to take anything from him? Just out of spite I can join the Genovese's. He'd get a kick out of that."

Matteo smirks and Viktor chuckles to himself.

"What? What is so funny?"

Viktor clears his throat with a fist over his mouth. He rubs his forehead before placing his palm on the counter.

"You can't just join another group."

"Why? Because I'm Luciano? That's bullshit."

"No, because you're a woman."

This time I raise a brow crossing my arms.

"You mean to tell me I can't be in another 'group' because instead of having a dick hanging between my legs I have a fucking vagina and set of tits?" I scoff, my inner feminist rising to the occasion.

"Precisely. Women don't take the ranks unless they inherit it, and even then most are not accepted."

"So I wouldn't be able to join a group at all?"

"No, you can, in a way."

"Okay, you've lost me now," I grumble. I'm tired of this riddled guessing game and want to get straight to the point.

"Technically you're a Luciano member. You are, after all, Lavoy's daughter. You didn't inherit the lead as Alessio is the rightful heir to the 'throne.' That being said, you can make an active claim that you are not to be associated with the *famiglia,* but in the majority of the cases, you'll still be seen as a Luciano." Makes sense I guess but their sexist rules are still bullshit.

"Then there is marriage. In most cases, it's families creating alliances. If a woman comes from outside the realms of the crime world, once she is married to one of our men she is under the protection of the *famiglia.*"

"So my options are to accept my place in the Luciano family or create an alliance?" Viktor nods, placing his chin on his intertwined hands as his elbows rest on the counter.

"More or less. You could marry without creating an alliance and disconnect yourself from the Luciano's but you would indefinitely cause war."

"Alessio wouldn't," I puff out in his defense. He wouldn't cause a war. Not that I wanted to cut him out completely. I'm pissed that my whole life was a lie thanks to him but he's my brother. We've been through so much and he's always been right there for me. In a way, I know he hid this life to keep me safe, but in doing so he kept me sheltered. I wish I had known the world I've been living in all along. Instead, I was thrown in head first twenty years later. I am lucky it led me to the Genovese's footsteps or my fate would been a lot worse.

"He'd have to. If he didn't, he'd look weak and unwilling to fight for what he wants. He'd lose business and alliances, being seen as a pushover." I study Viktor, processing everything at hand. I only have two choices: create an alliance between the families or end my friendship with Gio, and well, whatever I have with Matteo.

"This is so stupid," I groan out in frustration, setting my elbows on the counter and covering my face.

"Welcome to the mafia, *Bella.*" Matteo sits to my left, placing his cup down. I rest the side of my head in my hands to look at him.

"It's all up to you, but be prepared to choose because when Alessio comes knocking you have to answer."

"And if I don't?" My heart hammers against my chest staring at Matteo.

"You won't like the repercussions." His voice holds a warning but I am distracted by Gio reentering the room. He holds out some pills and I pop them in my mouth, swallowing them down with my coffee.

"Oh my God, you're my lifesaver," I groan. I drown the rest of my drink and carry myself to the pot for more.

"Always for you, Baby Girl." Matteo glares at Gio's pet name. Gio raises his hands but sends me a wink.

"Don't be such a sour patch kid." He waves off as Viktor and I stifle a laugh. Matteo rolls his eyes when his gaze is drawn to the back entry. Mila walks through with a big smile.

"A full crowd this morning—oh, and my darling, *Bella,* your back!" If Mila's face could brighten anymore, it does when she spots me. She sets her platter down on the table and rushes over placing her hands on either side of my face. She gives me a once-over taking in my attire.

"Oh, I wasn't expecting you this morning, should I be expecting you every morning?"

"I'll be staying for a bit." I smile at her and glance behind her to see Matteo, a smile resides on him.

"Oh, you will now?" Her tone comes out teasingly as she follows my gaze landing on Matteo and the woman shrieks.

"OH MY GOD IT'S HAPPENING! IS IT HAPPENING? OH MY GOD!"

"What? What's happening?" I grow tense with her outburst.

"Is she joining the family? Oh Matteo, I knew you'd find the perfect girl to break that little wall around your heart. Oh, she's perfect, your mother would be so happy, *mi chio.* When's the wedding?" *Oh, she's perfect, your mother would be so happy, my boy.*

"Oh no, I mean um, well we... um," I scramble to find the right words. I mean I'm not, at least I don't think I am. I still have time to think about the whole wedding thing.

"Mila, she's not joining the family." Matteo steps in and I let out a breath, a little deflated at his words.

"Not yet," Gio scoffs out.

"Oh, you just give it time." She turns back to me. "You just need time." She winks before retreating out of the kitchen. I suck my lips trying to hide my embarrassed smile.

"Breakfast looks great," I say, dropping into a seat on the side of the table and diving in.

"She already has a spot at the table and is stealing the food, maybe we should call Mila back in for the wedding preparations," Gio teases, and I shake my head throwing a strawberry at him.

"Feisty. You'll need that around here, someone ought to put Matteo in his place."

"I'm in my place perfectly well, which is putting you in yours, move." Matteo pushes Gio out of the way and sits at the head of the table. We all dive into our food making light talk with jokes flying around the table. Once breakfast comes to a finish, Viktor and Gio check their phones. I drink the last bit of my third coffee of the day.

"Mila should have an outfit set out for you upstairs. Go ahead and change and we'll leave."

"Okay." I smile at the men and take my leave up to the bedroom.

When I enter I spot a small white dress lying on the end of the bed with a pair of light blue slip-ons. I grab the set and slide them on. I grab my purse laying on the chair and find my way back to the steps. Matteo meets me at the bottom now wearing his suit jacket. I drool at the sight of him.

"Ready?" I cling to his arm as we exit the estate. He leads me to a car pulled in front and opens the back door for me to climb in. Once settled, I pull out my phone to read through my messages while he informs Bruno of our plans.

Thirty-three missed calls and forty texts between Alessio and Enzo. I inwardly groan. They don't get it, do they? I don't want to talk right now. Whatever excuses they have mustered up, I could care less for right now. I shut my phone off and throw it in the pocket of my purse.

We pull into a parking garage a few minutes later and pile out of the car. Matteo glares at me as I shut my door. I blink with a raised brow.

"What?" He grabs my wrist in one hand and my chin in the other.

"Be patient."

"Oh," I say with a little clarity.

"Has a man never opened your door?"

"I mean Enzo did sometimes." His jaw ticks. Right probably shouldn't mention Enzo.

"I'm not Enzo." No Matteo, no you're not, in so many ways. He pulls me along the parking garage and into a building. This place is up-scale, though, that's to be expected. Matteo pulls off, speaking to a woman while I scan the aggressively polished store as I wait.

"*Sì*, follow me." I turn to the woman and Matteo motions me to follow her. She guides me to another section of the store, showing me several different collections before sending me into the dressing room with a handful of items. The pile of clothes is all dressy and not at all what I need for this week.

"Matteo? Maybe I should try something less, I don't know, fancy?" I yell over the dressing room door.

"Gwenevere, put it on."

I huff looking at the dresses and picking the first one in front of me. I'm impressed that it fits like a glove since I did not give the sales lady my size. I twirl in the mirror attempting to pull up the zipper. After no luck, I pad to the door and peek out. Matteo sits confidently in his divine power, waiting in the middle of the sitting room. I step through the door with my most confident look. His eyes float to me and fall down my figure. I bite my cheek rubbing the material.

"I can't get the zipper, do you mind?" I point to the back of my dress and Matteo waves a finger to him that I gladly follow. I turn my back to him and pull my hair to the front. He slides a finger down the skin of my back until he reaches the zipper before pulling it up the rest of the way.

I clear my throat stepping toward the full wall mirror. The dress really does fit in all the right places; I had forgotten I have a few curves going for me.

"It's cute but I probably won't wear this at all this week." He swipes his finger across his chin before motioning me to twirl again. I huff, twirling for him.

"Next." I glare but retreat back to the dressing room, staring at the mountain of dresses. I continue trying on endless amounts of clothes and receiving the same response from Matteo each time until I give up.

"Are we done yet?"

The woman steps back from adjusting the back of a cocktail dress that is less fitting for what I came for than the first dress I wore.

"Have you found what you want?" Matteo asks from his comfy spot on the couch. *Bastard.*

I look around at all the items on the racks that I've tried on.

"Um, those over there on that rack are nice." I point to several outfits on the rack that contains a micture of nice sweat sets, jeans and some less fancy dresses.

"That's it?" Matteo seems unimpressed by my chosen collection.

"It's comfortable enough for the week." I shrug my shoulders receiving a head shake from him.

"Let's go." I stagger back for a moment looking at the dressing room.

"Oh, um, let me change out of this." I turn to the dressing room.

"No need, you'll wear it out of here."

"Oh, that's okay, really, Matteo." He stops to glare at me.

"You need to work on listening. You're wearing the dress out." He turns to the associate ending the conversation.

"Can you please collect all the items, Miss Luciano took an interest in and have them dropped off at the estate. Throw it on a tab and we'll take care of it in the books." The woman nods and my mouth drops.

"Do you know how many things I tried on? And how much they are… you can't get all of that."

"I can and I will. Are you planning to argue with me all day?" His voice drops as he peers over.

"No, Mr. Genovese, I'm not."

"Car. Now." His eyes turn dark at my mocking of his name, and his voice tethers. I follow him as the tension between us grows. When we make it back into the parking garage he stays a step behind me and I become self-conscious. I refuse to let go of the fired up energy and sway my hips as I walk. I climb into the car and adjust my dress. Matteo swoops in behind me and looks up to Bruno.

"Back to the estate. Don't open the privacy window. If there's an emergency tap three times."

"Yes, Boss." Matteo shuts the privacy window and swivels to me. His eyes roam over my body causing my skin to prickle.

"That dress looks nice on you, Miss Luciano."

"Thank you, Mr. Genovese." I grin with a heated gaze.

"Too bad you've lost your obedience." His voice is dangerous but body alluring. "Don't mock me."

"Or what?" His jaw clenches with restraint.

"Take them off."

The prickling becomes full-blown waves of intensity across my skin.

"Take off your panties, *Principessa*."

"We are in public," I say shyly, glancing out the tinted windows as we pass through the city.

"Did you not hear me? Take. Them. Off."

I gulp, my internal temperature rising. I run my fingers up my thighs until I reach the lace of my panties and pull them down and out from under my dress. I hold them up by my pinky over his lap and drop them.

"Happy Mr. Genovese?" I mock him again, loving the warm feeling rushing through me.

"Do you like playing with fire, *Principessa*?"

I don't respond but watch him as I move to face him and spread my legs by lifting a leg onto the seat. He has a full view of my sweet center as I glide my fingers back up my thigh. His eyes follow my movements and I let my dress crumple in my lap as my hand draws closer to my heated core.

My fingers graze over my folds leading up to my sensitive clit. I circle a few times and lower between my folds; ever so slightly, I press into my entrance, forcing a moan from my lips.

This is far beyond anything I've ever done but the look of need on Matteo's face fills me with exhilaration. I want to give him a show until he can't help himself anymore—to make him lose his control.

I pop the tip of my finger out and trail my wetness around my clit. I go back and forth until aching tension begs me for more. I press a finger inside my warm lips and bend it, grazing against the top of my walls. The slow pressure builds and I drop my head back.

I pull my finger out and send a second finger in. I close my eyes for a second and when I reopen them I lock on to him. I can tell he is using every ounce of restraint to not touch me.

The hunger in his eyes only makes my need grow. I thrust my fingers in and out and my wetness coats my fingers. I hum at the sensations and the feeling of Matteo's eyes on me, completely entranced in my movement. I teeter on the edge and my motions become jerky, my chest rising and falling with the build-up.

"Stop."

My fingers slow at his demand but I can't stop. I'm too close.

"Gwenevere." He grabs my wrist and my eyes shoot to him. I'm left aching for a release with a pained gaze.

"Matteo."

"Beg me."

"Please, Matteo." I squirm under his orders, unable to resist the need for his touch.

"Please what, *Principessa*?" His voice is husky and on edge. He is trying to hold on just as much as me, restraining himself as my punishment.

"Please touch me."

"And what?"

"Please make me cum. Fuck, Matteo," I mutter to him, pushing my hips forward as his fingers thrust into me in the same shift.

In moments he finds my sweet spot almost sending me over the edge on contact. I moan out, not able to control myself. Matteo slaps his hand over my mouth and continues the raw pulsing against my sensitive walls. I grind against his fingers searching for my climax.

"Don't cum until I say so."

I moan again, his command only pushing me closer. He sets his thumb on my nub while his finger glides inside me making my eyes water in frustration. I can't beg with my mouth so I beg with my hips.

"You want to cum?"

I nod my heavy head unable to give much more.

"Then take it." With that he grinds his fingers, sending a frenzy of sensations through me. Tears slip through my eyes with the intensity of my orgasm wracking through my body. He removes his hand from my mouth, crashing his lips onto mine, not letting my orgasm come down.

"Matteo." I kiss him harder as I lose myself around his fingers. He pulls them out, placing them on my lips. I suck them until he is satisfied.

We pull into the estate as I pull my dress down, and Matteo steps out to help me, tucking my underwear in his suit jacket.

"I have business to attend to. Would you prefer the movie room?" I take a moment to gather my wits and respond.

"No, I think I would like to read. Do you mind if I just sit on the couch or in the room?"

"You want to read?" His interest perks.

"Um yeah, I'm almost finished with my book." I rub my arm. *Am I too much of a nerd?* I'm surrounded by killing machine mafia men and I want to read a book.

"I have the perfect spot for you."

This time my interest perks up as he leads me down the hall where the movie room sits . Instead of turning right, he glides to the door on the left pushing it open and stepping to the side. I enter the room and my jaw falls slack. The last thing I expected was the enchanting sight in front of me.

Bright natural light falls into the room from a large window extending from floor to ceiling. It connects to an overhead dome window making up the entire point. Built-in shelves line the entire room, including the second level, leading to the nook at the large window. I twirl slowly admiring the room.

Matteo leans against the doorframe with a soft expression. I smile and skim over the books on the closest shelf. I could never leave this room. I turn to him, fully raising my arms and waving my hands around.

"This—this is beautiful Matteo." Matteo crosses his arms, clearing his throat.

"Will this do?"

I laugh at him as his face flushes with panic.

"Will this do?" I laugh out in disbelief. "Matteo this is a library of dreams, I'm literally in a personalized heaven right now. Are you kidding me? Look at this place!" I run my finger over a row of books, amazed that of all people, Matteo has a library like this.

"Okay well, I'll be back in a little while for lunch." I spin around, staring at all the books, before looking back to him. I walk up and kiss his cheek.

"Thank you. Trust me, I'm not leaving here until you drag me out."

He chuckles, shaking his head, and leaves the room. I grab my book to finish so I can explore for a new one. I snuggle into the cozy nook and sigh, turning to my saved page.

16

Matteo

Gwenevere's love for the library eases the part of me that worried about letting her use it. I smile as the scene of her gawking at the room replays through my mind while I make my way to my office. When I step into the room I meet Viktor and Gio's knowing gazes. Viktor snickers as Gio out right chuckles, leaning into his chair.

I drop my smile and head to my chair behind my desk. I shuffle through my papers but stop at the unnerving feeling of eyes on me. I peer up at both idiots staring at me with cheeky grins.

"So, how was your date?" Gio chirps in first.

"It wasn't a date. I bought her some clothes, she has nothing for the week." I roll my eyes setting the papers down.

"So you bought her a whole wardrobe for a week?" Viktor asks with an accusing tone.

"I didn't buy her a quarter of what a woman's closet would be in this estate. You're being dramatic, how would you know what she got? We haven't made it to the books yet."

"Because I watched the whole thing being delivered to your closet right after you arrived. What are you doing Matteo?" I roll my eyes again, not wanting to indulge in whatever lecture I'm about to hear from him.

"Only weeks ago she was a stranger Gio brought home, and now you're moving her into your room? Did you forget that she is Luciano? Regardless of where she stands with Alessio right now, she's going to get over it."

"It's not your business, Viktor, " I warn, but ultimately I know Viktor is right. Yet I can't help myself when I am near her. I thought after we fucked a couple of times I'd get over her and move on, but my need for her is far from satisfied.

"What about Enzo? You said she didn't lose the baby all but three months ago. He is not going to let her go easy. They have feelings for each other. What if she comes out of whatever rebound stage she's in and goes back to him, bringing you and the *famiglia* down while she's at it?"

"She's not going to do that." I shake off.

"And why not? Why wouldn't she go back?"

"She loved the idea of him and their little fantasy world. It is all she ever knew. Alessio kept her on such a tight leash, hell she didn't even know who the fuck she was! Do you really think if she found out before I came along that she would go back to him after he lied to her, her whole life? She was carrying his child for fucks sake! She'll be able to forgive Alessio, but on some deep level she will never forgive him."

"He's got a point, Viktor. Do you really think she can forgive him enough to go back to him?" Gio shrugs and Viktor sighs. She could potentially care for him and maybe be his friend, but loving him? Trusting him? She knows where his loyalty stands and I don't think she could ever be happy knowing it's not with her.

"Where is she anyway?"

"The library." I drop back to my papers writing a few numbers out.

Gio practically chokes and Viktor crosses his arms.

"You brought her into your mom's library and left her there?" Viktor stares like I've grown two heads. Gio sits blank, blinking.

"No one has been in the library since Mom."

I pour a glass of bourbon from the bottle next to my computer, shrugging off their interest. I know it is a big deal but making it seem like one would only fuel their energy.

"She wanted to read. I didn't want her lounging on the couch and bottling up in the room wouldn't be much better. It gives me a piece of mind that she's not roaming the house. It's not a big deal." I take a sip of my bourbon, the sharp sting in my throat awakening my mind.

"Not a big deal? You haven't let anyone touch that room."

"Drop it, Gio."

"You know the whole wardrobe thing I could maybe get behind but the library? You don't even know if she will stay past the week." I pull my gun out and set it on the table. Giving Gio a sharp glare. He raises his brow.

"Really? Do you want to shoot me? I'm only pointing out the truth. Not but a month ago you couldn't care to look at another girl twice, and now you've moved her in and pulled her into your little cold heart when she is quite literally a possible enemy. I love Gwen, don't get me wrong, but you are going to get bored of her and move on like you always do."

Viktor tenses a little in my side view as he listens.

"Do you want to keep talking?" I speak calmly.

"You're going to break her heart, Matteo. I'm not sure how much more she can take."

"You think I want to break her heart? Do you think I've let her stay around this long with the intention of discarding her like she's nothing? Does she really seem like she's nothing to me Gio?"

"You don't even know her!"

"Shouldn't I be the judge of that?" Our voices rise with each word. Gwenevere is stirring the house already.

"No! That's why you have us here! For when your head is stuck too far up your ass; we can level you out so you make the right decisions for the business."

"Is she not right for the business?" This time Gio shuts up, grinding his teeth.

"She's fucking perfect, Gio." Viktor pipes up finally. "This might be what we need for a standing alliance."

"So you're going to toss her straight into this world to tear her apart for business?"

"Aren't you supposed to make the best decision for the business?" I push out rhetorically.

"Yes, but I also do it for the *famiglia*. If you marry her she will be *famiglia*. Do you want that, Matteo? You want to bring her into this family, into our world, and let her fall with the blood on your hands? She might be a Luciano but we all know she is the opposite of all of them. She is innocent, Matteo."

The same questions plagued my mind from the moment I laid eyes on her. Can I handle breaking her at the fault of my own hands?

Sure marrying her is great for the business but what about her, her sanity? Does she have what it takes to survive?

I take a big swig of my bourbon leaving the glass empty and dropping it back on the table. I push the chair and grab my gun off the desk.

"Look in the damn mirror, Gio. You already protect her like she's family, you've already risked your life for her, the whole damn *famiglia* has, and you are the one who keeps bringing her through our door. Don't scold me like you don't want her here too." I move through the room throwing the door open with a loud thud.

I jog down to the kitchen, snatching a drink from the fridge and finding the time. I'd been arguing with Gio far longer than I thought, Gwenevere must be starving.

I make my way to the library door that's cracked, light seeping out of it. A light hum flows to my ears and I succumb to the memories.

A woman's voice seeps from under the door humming a sweet melody. I push the wooden door open to reveal my mother. Her hair is swept into a bun and she is on her ladder organizing books. Dad always brings home books for Mom, and anytime she leaves the house she stops at the bookshop.

Mom turns to me with a bright smile, waving me in and climbing down her ladder.

"My sweet, Matteo, what can I do for you, love?" She pulls me into a soft caress before pulling back to look at me.

"Can you read to me?"

She laughs softly, rubbing a hand over my cheek.

"Of course baby, go grab a book and meet me in the nook."

I bustle over to the shelves she keeps stocked for Gio and me to pick out my favorite book and meet her in the nook. I climb in, settling into her arms.

"Of course you choose dragons." She ruffles my hair and then turns the pages of the open book. Her voice trickles down to me with nurture as she

reads to me. I love listening to Mom read. One moment I am heavy and the next I am light.

"He saves the princess and they live in their castle, happily ever after." She finishes and closes the book.

"Mom?"

"Yes, sweetheart?" She smiles down at me, playing with my hair.

"Will I ever find my principessa?"

"Matteo, one day you are going to find the perfect princepessa. She will be like a flower; so unique that she will stick out from all the others in the garden. When you find her, you don't let her go."

I smile, imagining what my principessa will be like and how I'll know I've found her.

"And Matteo?"

"Yes, Mama?"

"Don't squish a single one of her petals. You can't undo the damage to your flower once you've torn it."

"Yes, Mama."

"Promise?"

"I promise."

I snap back to Gwenevere's humming. I push the door open to see Gwenevere rustling through some books on the floor level. She doesn't hear me so I allow myself to observe her for a moment. She runs a finger down the spine of a book before deciding to pick it up and flips through some pages.

She reads a page then shuts it, turning around and catching me. She flies a hand to her chest and her eyes pop.

"I didn't mean to scare you."

She fiddles with her dress and holds the book up.

"I found a new book to read. Took me forever, there are so many great books to choose from." She lowers the book, holding it to her chest and juggles her weight from foot to foot. "Is it okay if I borrow it while I'm here?"

"You can borrow as many books as you like. The library is always open for you."

She smiles, lowering the book to her side and gliding over to me. She glances back to her things and then to me.

"Is it lunchtime already?"

"Indeed it is, are you ready?"

"Yes, let me just grab my bag."

"Don't. You can come back for it later, you live here remember?"

She chews her cheek with a pink blush forming across her cheeks.

"Right."

We head back to the kitchen at the same time Mila walks out with her daughter—her trainee—with lunch in hand.

Gio and Viktor saunter into the kitchen bickering about who knows what. I pull a chair out for Gwenevere and she sits, pulling out her book. I shake my head with a discreet smile and sit down at the head of the table. She dives her nose between the pages reading away as all the men grab their food still bantering.

Once everyone is settled, Viktor looks to Gwenevere with a raised brow; Gio sits back and tilts his head. I shake mine at him but understand the silent exchange.

My mother enjoyed books. She read to Gio and me every night as kids. We'd often find her lost in her books spending any free time she had reading. If she was in the 'good part' or almost finsihed, she'd read through dinner and more. Seeing Gwenevere with her head in her book at the table and enjoying the library reminds me of happier times.

"Earth to Gwenevere." Gio waves to her from across the table. She doesn't make any indication that she hears him though. "She's just like mom."

I watch Gwenevere intently. I'm not the only one to see the warm light that glows around her. She brings the sun into our dark home. I can't fathom how the light hasn't been snuffed out of her. She comes from a world of suffering and yet here she is.

"Gwenevere." I try to grab her attention but when she doesn't respond I grab the book out of her hands, saving the spot, and tossing it on the other side of the table. She sits with a sour scowl, hands still in place from where she held the book.

"Close your mouth and fill your plate." I point to the table full of lunch.

"I was reading that." She looks at the book and then gives me a glare.

"Yes, and? Eat."

"What if I'm not hungry." She crosses her arms, eyes piercing into me. If only she knew what opposing does to me.

"I doubt that. Stop arguing and eat."

"No. I think I'll read, thank you." She snatches her book off the table while the two morons hide their grins at our debate.

"Gwenevere. Sit," I growl. She picks up her water, narrowing her gaze, and exits out of the room. I stare at the entryway where she left. Not only did she not listen, she told me no. She is a force to be reckoned with, and she is more than willing to prove her own power, even if it's against me. Viktor and Gio push my buttons but I have the final say. I am Don. Yet Gwenevere waltzed out of the room against my direct orders without a tinge of regret.

I hear snickering to the side and snap my sneer at them. Gio's laugh rises and I stab my fork on the plate and take a sip of my water.

"I get it now," Gio announces through his fit. I don't engage and eat, contemplating how I'm going to deal with her later.

"You know, this whole 'book nerd who pushes your buttons; you need someone to keep you on your toes' thing you guys have going on, has a whole *Beauty and the Beast* vibe to it."

"Vibe?" My annoyance drips out at his modern slang.

"Of course, you are the beast in the scary mansion as you swoop her away from Gaston."

"I'm not 'swooping' her away and Enzo is not Gaston."

"How is he not?" I roll my eyes at him.

"For one, he hid their entire relationship, much less marrying her?"

If he asked for her hand in marriage he'd have to go through Alessio, and we know he hasn't done that.

"You don't think he will? She carried his baby. I doubt he's letting her go anytime soon." I hate that she has this connection to him. What I hate more is being reminded of the fresh wounds she has in place because of it. Gio repeatedly bringing this up only irritates me further.

"It doesn't matter, she won't."

"Right… Matteo the heartless beast who can never love such a sweet thing like her. Why is she sleeping in your bed? Why does she have access to the library? You're telling me you'll let her go when she decides to leave?"

"She has a week." A week until her fate is sealed with a Genovese stamp.

"You gave her a deadline for what exactly?" He sits back in his chair, arms crossed.

"She either goes home to Alessio and cuts us off or she stays." I ignore their eyes as I take another drink.

"She can't just stay," Gio breathes out, annoyed.

"She marries me." I shrug. I set my glass down once again.

"Is this an agreed-upon arrangement or is it at your command? We see how well she listens to you." I glare daggers at him.

"Do you have something better to do than investigate my life?"

"It's literally my job. Besides, I want to know if I'm going to have a sister-in-law." He jokes, but we both know what that means for the families. There are so many reasons we should and not enough that we shouldn't. Viktor sits forward resting his focus on me.

"We all know she's a right fit for the home. The guards love her and Mila loves her. I see the way you look at her whether you want to admit it now or later, and we both know she's not going anywhere. Don't give her a reason to run back."

Viktor's words cut into me like a knife. 'Don't give her a reason to run back.' That is exactly what I am afraid of. The moment the air clears with her and Alessio, will they ultimately patch up with Enzo?

Will she choose him?

I drop my fork on my plate leaning back with a growl. I run a hand down my face, trying to figure out how I got here. Everything has run smoothly as of late and now I'm talking about my potential love life with a Luciano.

"Matteo, can you sit here and tell me that if Alessio showed up to that door right now and she decided to forgive him and leave, you would honestly let her?"

I don't need to answer him out loud. I throw down the rest of my drink and push my chair out. I grab the bottle of bourbon and a second glass. I find my way to the library in search of Gwenevere, but when I arrive she is not in the room. My brows crease as I think of where she could've gone.

What if she left? Would she? She couldn't leave, not without me knowing. I retreat back down the hall and up the staircase. I open the door to my room to see her curled up in the chair with the book in her hand, just about to fall from her grasp.

She's peaceful in her sleep as if she dozed in the middle of reading. A smile reaches my face and I place the liquor on the table. I glide over to her sliding one arm under to support her head and the other her legs. I scoop her up, bringing her to the bed and settling her under the covers.

She scrunches her face and grabs my hand tugging gently.

"Stay." It isn't a question, but a soft demand. One I would take freely. I shake off my suit coat and toss my dress shoes to the side, sliding into the bed behind her. I grip her waist, pulling her into me.

I run my fingers through her hair and push it behind her ear. She hums peacefully as she nestles into my grasp. Her breathing evens out and it's then I notice she's changed from her dress into the comfy clothes I had delivered.

I made sure to get all of the sweat outfits she liked in every color knowing she'd flock to them. She chose the deep green that contrasts against her pale skin. Her hair is in a loose bun that is falling everywhere except for the ones I moved.

She is perfect like this. She doesn't need makeup, she is beautiful without trying. I have to admit that Alessio was smart for hiding her from our world. Not only to keep the murderous eyes away from her but in doing so it kept her from the corruption.

She isn't a mafia princess who needs the most expensive jewelry or the prettiest dress in the room. Although, I wouldn't mind giving her just that on a silver platter if she asked. She wants a book, some sweats and not to be interrupted while she enjoys them.

She will have all of that. Except for interruptions. I will do as I please and making sure she eats is not negotiable. She is going to push me. She may have been shielded from what her life consisted of but she isn't stupid. She is more than capable of holding her own.

While she is shielded from the world, enemies still lurk, and it won't be hard to connect Alessio with her. I'm surprised we hadn't discovered her with her connection to Enzo. Most eyes have been trained on Alessio's big entrance over the last year, and even he didn't know what was going on in his own house.

I hate the thought of her and Enzo. He isn't getting her anymore. He lost the chance the moment she walked through my door.

I am not making the same mistake. If honesty is what she needs, I'll make her stomach churn with the truth, but I will give her everything she wants. Gwenevere has me wrapped around her finger and I want to know everything about her. I want to see her smile and not be the reason for it falling. I will take down anything that threatens her happiness.

I hold her gently in my arms, burying my face into her hair. An hour won't hurt to lay with her before returning to work.

17

Gwenevere

I pick at the binding of the leather chair in the library and dial on my phone. On the third ring the line picks up and a familiar voice comes through.

"Hello?" Sole rustles on the other end.

"I miss you."

" I miss you too."

"Are you busy?" I bite my cheek, making patterns across the chair.

"Nope. When are you coming over?"

I laughed. Of course, she knows my next question.

"Soon? Would you pick me up? I don't want to bother anyone here."

"Sure, Alessio being a pain in the ass?"

"Something like that."

"Be at your place in say… fifteen."

"Actually… I'm not there."

"Oh. Where are you?"

"Do you remember how to get to the Genovese estate?" There's a short pause in the line and scrunch my face as I wait in silence.

"The Genovese Estate?"

"That's the one." My heart rams in anticipation. I know Sole will voice her opinions and make them loud and clear. I need her advice but most importantly I just need a familiar face.

"Okay. I'll see you soon."

"Okay." The line clicks and I push off the comfy chair, grab my current read from the table, and head to the bedroom to change. I throw on a simple pair of leggings and a Rolling Stones T-shirt with some light gray sneakers. I stop at Matteo's office giving a light tap on the door. The reply is muffled by the door and I can't make out the words. I open the door anyway and pop my head in. Matteo searches through his papers not bothering to look up. I clear my throat drawing his attention.

"I um, wanted to let you know I'm gonna head out for a little bit." He scans me before returning to his papers.

"Take Gio."

"I highly think that's unnecessary." I open the door further and cross my arms with a huff.

"I highly think it wasn't a question."

I exhale roughly through my nose and look at the ceiling.

"Matteo, I'm a grown woman. You are not my father and you sure as hell aren't Alessio." He chuckles lowly and stands, moving around the desk to me.

"How do you figure that?"

I send him a pointed look as he stops just inches from me. His thumb finds my bottom lip, tracing it. I don't answer his question, instead, I gawk at him like an immature teenager. His mouth lowers to my ear as his hot breath flows down my neck, sending tingles across my skin.

"I don't think you'd fuck him like you did me."

My breath catches at his unrefined statement. My phone rings, breaking the tension enough for me to back away and clear my flustered state. I know it is Sole announcing her arrival but I can't break my eye contact.

"I still think it's ridiculous to bring Gio with me. I'll be with a friend and it's not like I'm going somewhere scandalous."

"That doesn't matter. You are now interacting with two of the biggest families in the city. You have more enemies than that pretty little head could comprehend. It's not a choice. You take Gio or you don't go." I growl, swirling out of his office and slamming the door behind me. I hope that bothers him as much as he is bothering me right now.

I send a text to Sole and stop at Gio's office, knocking once before the door opens. His phone is pressed to his ear with a tilt.

"She's right here. Yes, I got it. Okay bye." He hangs up the phone with a large grin.

"God he can be such a princess and you royally pissed him off."

I laughed at his judgment, rolling my eyes and spinning on my heels down the hall.

"Let's go." I wave over my shoulder. Gio chuckles, shutting his office door and jogging up to me.

"Jeez, thanks for the invite." I roll my eyes again looking at him with a raised brow.

"We both know Matteo is forcing you to go."

"I wouldn't say forcing. More like profusely threatening." We move fast down the stairs passing the foyer Guards.

"Miss Luciano," a guard greets me briefly, and my precious smile is restored. He hasn't greeted me before; an introduction.

"Leo." I nod to him as Gio and I step out the door. I survey the drive until I catch a glimpse of Sole leaning against her car. I run up and wrap my arms around her neck.

"God I missed your face." I squeeze her, the familiarity giving me a sense of peace.

"This silly thing?" Gio clears his throat and I retreat, giving her a sheepish smile.

"Right, um… Gio's tagging along. I hope you don't mind."

"I don't mind at all." Sole offers a devious smile and rounds the car but is stopped short.

"Why don't we take the Escalade? There might be more wiggle room and you girls can chill in the back. I can be like your personal chauffeur."

"Fine by me. My car is a bit messy. Gwen?"

"Why not, might as well put you to use." I shrug my shoulders. Gio clasps his chest as if he's offended. I shake my head giggling with Sole as we follow him to his Escalade. Sole and I climb in the back and Gio settles in the driver's seat.

"Seatbelts my ladies." Gio's accent takes a midcentury gentleman twist.

"God, you're so weird."

"That's why you like me." Gio winks through the viewfinder and puts the car into drive.

"So where too?"

I turn to Sole for an answer, we didn't really specify our plans over the phone.

"I haven't eaten lunch, wanna get something?"

"Yes, I'm starving too. Do you know any good places on this side of town?" I glance to Gio who grins widely.

"Of course, sit back and relax. I'll let you know when we're there."

Sole sighs and gives me the look. I sign to her discreetly.

"*Not right now.*"

She nods peering up at Gio and then me.

"So how long have you been at the Genovese Estate?"

I narrow my eyes, that is not the definition of not right now.

"Coming up on a week?" I say, but it comes out more like a question *Wow*. Time has flown by and my week is almost up. She hums observing my outfit but I beat her to the next comment.

"I didn't even notice but your hair looks amazing."

She hums out a thank you. I meant my compliment, her hair is in a complex braid I'd never be able to accomplish on my own. Sole impresses me with all her new updos she's able to pull off.

"I love your new outfit. Where did you get it?" She cocks a brow and I chew on my cheek.

"Um, Matteo, actually. He got me a few things." I know exactly where this is headed and she is being anything but discreet.

"How much is a few things?" She smirks.

"How are your classes?" I try to divert her… again.

"Boring especially since you're not there. I mean I get why you left but it honestly sucks." She pouts this time crossing her legs.

"You dropped out of your classes?" Gio pipes from the front. I play with the seat belt nervously. How is the attention back on me?

"Yeah. It's no big deal. I was all over the place already and I wasn't focused last semester at all. I think I need the semester off to get my head back on." He nods with lightly pursed lips.

I wonder why he is bothered by me not going to school anymore but drop the thought as soon as Sole speaks.

"None of the teachers are hot. It's like they don't want to keep our attention." I roll my eyes, grinning at her.

"I'm pretty sure that's not what they're there for."

"It should be. I never really cared for school anyhow."

"Honestly, me either, but I enjoy getting out of the house where I'm constantly surrounded by men."

"Honestly, I don't know why you ever complain."

"Because it's my brother and his best friend."

"You weren't saying that a few months ago,"she sings. I elbow her in her side, with a glare and she rolls her eyes. I sigh leaning back in my seat. After a short ride, Gio parks at the small diner we came to the first night he helped me escape. He shuts off the car and positions himself to us.

"I hope you like burgers and fries." He smiles widely.

"As long as I get a milkshake to dunk my fries in."

He shakes his head at my response.

"You can have whatever you want, baby girl " He sends me a wink and we all jump out of the car. My mouth waters from the aroma of food as we get closer... I pat my pockets and curse to myself.

"You guys go ahead. I left my phone in the car." They nod continuing to the diner as I jog back to the car. Approaching the Escalade, a burly man rounds the back of the vehicle, eyes locked onto me. My stomach clenches with an eerie feeling.

"Pretty girls like you shouldn't be in a parking lot alone."

My nose wrinkles at his vile voice.

"Good thing I'm a woman and not a girl," I snap to him, stepping closer to the car. He blocks my sight of the Escalade and advances towards me.

"Good, then I don't need to explain what this means." He lifts his jacket to expose a handheld gun. My stomach drops and I scan the parking lot. I am completely bare of anything to help me out of this. I swallow to wet my mouth that's gone dry.

All I want is a fucking milkshake and to talk to my friends. I have no way to get out of this on my own. I can't push my panic button to signal Alessio with my phone stuck in the Escalade five feet away. Yelling isn't an option, Gio's to far away. I wish Matteo hadn't been right about the threat that looms over me.

"I don't know what you want but trust me, I'm not it."

He gives a sinister smirk and grips my chin between his calloused hand.

"I think you're exactly what I'm looking for."

I tug my chin away the best I can but he holds on tighter, pulling my face to him. Bile rises to my throat at his intrusion.

"Don't fight. Or do. I always love a fun game."

I spit on his face and he drops his gaze to the ground. When he lifts his head he wipes the spit away and looks at me.

"You stupid bitch." He grips under my hair causing me to cry out. "Shut your fucking mouth or I will shove this gun down your throat."

"I wouldn't do that if I were you," Gio tsks. I close my eyes in relief but know this isn't over yet.

"This doesn't concern you," the man grits out.

"Actually, I think it does. See that's my friend there and I'm more than welcome to drop you. I'm told I have a pretty good aim."

The man lets go of my hair, shoving me to the car. I stumble but an arm catches my fall. Gio latches on holding me against his chest. I look to the side and see him holding a gun up at the man. I shut my eyes and bury my face into his chest.

"You have five minutes to get as far away from here as possible before I start tracking you down with a piece of your own medicine. The timer starts now." I refuse to look at the man but can safely assume he isn't standing there anymore. Gio leans back and grips my face to catch my eyes.

"Are you okay?" I take a shaky breath and try to find some comfort in him.

"Yeah, I'm fine. I just want to get my milkshake and go home."

"We should probably take it to go."

Terrified faces line the tables from the other side of the parking lot. I nod, placing my arms around myself.

"Are you sure you're okay?" Gio studies me, but I only offer a short nod again. "Okay."

It's not the first time I've had a gun pointed at me and I was wise enough to know it won't be the last. At least this time I understand why it was there, yet not at all. Why do they want me?

Sole hops off the curb with a crease between her brows. She hands Gio the drink carrier filled with milkshakes and the giant bag of food before crashing into me with a hug.

"For fucks sake Gwen, don't scare me like that." I roll my eyes even though she can't see with my face pressed into her collarbone.

"It's not like I asked for it to happen."

"Are you okay?" She pulls back with hands on my shoulders to search for what I suppose is an injury.

"I'm fine. Give me my milkshake."

Gio hands over a Styrofoam cup and I grab it from him, sliding into the back seat. I fish for my phone and place it in my pocket. I sip my milkshake and buckle while the two of them climb into the car.

When we make it back to the estate we disperse out of the car and into the main house. I send my nod to the guards and plop myself onto the couch in the living room.

"I need to make a call. Do you mind if I snatch my burger on the go?" Gio smiles to me.

"No, I'm going to eat your burger and you're going to starve," I tease him. He shakes his head and picks out his burger and fries before taking the stairs.

I relax on the couch with my burger in hand stuffing my face. Sole does the same eyeing me every once in and awhile. When I'm almost done with my burger she lets out a sigh placing hers down.

"Gwen, are you okay?"

"Yeah, I'm fine." My ears heat up and I try to focus on my food.

"None of what happened is fine, so how can you be?"

"I really don't want to talk about it."

"What do you want to talk about then?"

I glance to the foyer where the guards conversate, ensuring no one else is listening.

"I got in a big fight with Alessio. I don't know how I can even trust him anymore, Sole. And Enzo, that man has some audacity. Everything in my life has been a lie and I don't know how to handle it." I wrap my burger back up, the last bite now daunting. "Alessio is pissed that I left with Gio and he has no clue about my thing with Matteo."

"What exactly is your *thing* with Matteo?"

I bite my cheek spinning my straw around my cup.

"Honestly? I don't entirely know. I like him Sole, a lot, but he's so... I don't know, he's so hard to read."

"You're surprised by this? You never just *sleep* with a guy. You are staying in his mansion, he must like you even a little bit."

I groan.

"I don't just sleep here. I sleep with him. Every night, regardless of if we, you know."

"Oh, so he really likes you. I knew you couldn't make it in the casual sex world." She grins with triumph.

"I know but this is different. I couldn't handle being around Alessio, still can't. I needed a break and Matteo said I could stay here. One thing led to another and now I'm sharing a room with him. The man bought me a brand new wardrobe. I think it's bigger than the one I have at home. And the library is to die for. Don't get me started on the food."

"He bought you a whole wardrobe?"

"Everything. I have more outfit options than I can count. Half the shit I'm terrified to wear! I know I'll ruin them."

"Who just casually buys someone a whole wardrobe?"

"Exactly. I mean it's not just that, it's well, he just takes care of me. With guys before, I mean I felt noticed and maybe loved, but I feel seen. It's as if he can see my soul with a glance my way." I shake my head covering my face with both hands.

"Oh my God. I sound absolutely ridiculous. That's it, I'm on the loopy train." I sigh. How could I ever think Matteo has any interest in me other than his immediate pleasure? I am just a fun thing to have around until he has had his share.

"I don't know. By the sounds of it, he definitely has a thing for you too."

That is the last thing I expected to come from Sole.

"You think so?"

"Why don't you just play it out for a little and see how it goes."

That's exactly what I've been doing, but my week is ending and I need to make a decision soon. I can't tell Sole that though. I can't drag her into all of this. Not yet.

Sole's phone chimes pulling our attention away from the conversation. She scans her phone quickly, sending a quick reply and turns back to me.

"Don't hate me, but I've gotta head out." She smiles sheepishly. I give her a pathetic eye roll.

"I could never hate you. Thank you, for the rant session."

"Of course, don't be a stranger anymore." She gives me a tight hug. "I want all the details."

"Of course."

"Are you going to be okay?" She holds me tighter and I don't complain, letting out a soft sigh.

"Yeah, don't worry about me." I squeeze and pull away. "I love you."

"I love you too." She gives a final smile and leaves. I pick up our lunch that remains and grab my now melted shake. I make my way into the kitchen and dump everything.

I ascend the stairs to the bedroom in hopes of crawling into bed for a little nap. A mix of stress and a full stomach is making me tired.

Once in the room I strip down to my underwear and grab one of Matteo's T-shirts for comfort instead of a sweat set. I flop on top of the covers and lay out comfortably. Unfortunately, after some time, I still can't get myself to sleep.

I need a way to relieve some of the stress and I know the quickest way to do it. I roll over, shimmying myself into the perfect position, and glide my hands to my breast through the shirt. I take each bud and roll them between my thumb and pointer finger.

Sensations flow through my body down to my core aching for traction. I slide one hand down my stomach until I reach where my panties lay. I grab the fabric of the T-shirt pulling it up to give myself access to my lower layer.

I dip a finger down gently glazing over my aching mound and breathe out as I make slow circles building the pressure. I lower my finger down to feel my wetness seeping through the cloth and moan.

Raising my hand to the top of my panties, I slide my fingers underneath the fabric reaching down to dipp the tip of my finger into my dripping center and dragging it to my swollen bud.

I rub in patterns gasping against my own movements. Pressure builds more and more as I thrust a finger inside myself moaning out once again.

"Matteo." His name slips past my lips shamefully as I envision him in place of my finger. I grind against my hand, pushing my finger further and rubbing my palm against the top rosebud. I pick up my pace running my other hand under Matteo's shirt, breathing in his scent, when I feel a presence in the room. I snap my eyes open, gasping at the sight of Matteo leaning at the end of the bed with darkened eyes watching me.

I bite my lip, pulling my hand out of my underwear.

"I didn't say to stop." My retreat stops as I look at Matteo. My skin is in flames underneath his hungry gaze, and he licks his bottom lip while his eyes wander over me like they did in his office. Only this time in a much more vulnerable state.

"I want you to show me what you want. Every thrust. Every move." My chest rises with the throbbing inside me. "Don't stop until I tell you to."

I obey his command, drinking in his muscles that stretch out his dress shirt. I lower my hand, caressing my nub once more, and hold my bottom lip between my teeth, taking in every sensation with closed eyes.

"Open your eyes." I snap them open.

"I want to see your eyes as you cum, begging for me to touch you." My wetness pools between my legs as I continue my patterns. A warm knot slowly forms in my stomach.

"Take your panties off so I can see exactly how you want me to fuck you." I clench my jaw in restraint, pulling away from my core. Reaching for the laced cloth I pull them down and remove them from my body completely.

Matteo's hand sweeps down, taking the fabric from me and grabbing it in his fist.

"Go on. Play with that pretty pussy and show me how you want me to fuck you."

I lower my hand, grazing my bud leading down to my warm center. I tease the entrance with my hand causing my legs to tense up in anticipation. My movements against the outer lips create a pucker sound.

I slide my finger in resting my head back. I moan at the feeling as a wave of pleasure flows through my body. I pull my finger out and repeat the motion a few times going deeper. Ready for more, I pull out and slide a second finger in.

"Matteo," I gasp his name, locking eyes with him and thrusting my finger. Pressure builds fast and I curl my fingers up hitting a spot that forces my eyes to close. I rub my fingers against the rising bulge inside my walls. Seconds later I groan out as I cum around my fingers.

"Fuck… Shit." I ride the wave of pleasure running through me. When my head levels enough I find Matteo.

"You didn't keep your eyes open."

My heart patters hard against my chest as he walks around the bed, trained on me.

"You still don't know how to listen." I lay spread open with my flowing juices covering my thighs and fingers. I stare at him, silently begging him to touch me.

He unbuttons the clasp on his wrist and then his shirt before tossing it to the side.

"Come here."

I sit up, crawl to him, and sit on my bottom.

"On your knees." I swallow back and pull my legs under myself, settling on my heels. Matteo pulls the shirt I stole over my head.

"You don't need this anymore." I blush, now completely exposed to Matteo.

He sucks on my neck, a notch below my jaw, and I hum with the tickled pleasure. He sits back and my eyes drop down to his pants.

His large bulge presses against the zipper as if one move will pop it open. I grasp his bulge in my hand. He groans, gazing down with hooded eyes. I unbutton his suit pants and unzip to release his member from restraint.

I push both sides of his pants, lowering them before his boxers. His cock springs out and I grasp it in my hand. I dip my hand to the base, tightening my grip and guiding my hand up and down his shaft.

I lick his tip lightly then take him into my mouth. My throat vibrates against his cock and his tenses. His member pulses under my grasp as I take in more, inch by inch. When I've almost taken him all the way, he pulls away steering my chin to him.

"Are you trying to take my control, *Principessa*?" I gasp in the air with my now empty mouth and look at him through my lashes. He hoists me up by my waist, tossing me further on the bed and slides his pants the rest of the way down.

He climbs up the bed and over me dipping his head down to my tight buds. He sucks hard while messaging the other and I moan at his pleasurable tongue.

"Matteo." I gasp breathlessly, pleading for his touch.

"Tell me what you want."

"You."

"No. Tell me exactly what you want."

I hesitate but give in to his command.

"I want your cock." I squirm under my own vulgar words but my core enlightens.

"Where, *Princepessa*?"

I lower my hand to show him the entrance of my soaking core.

"Your words." His voice trembles through my body and my movements work against my mind as I listen to his every demand.

"Here."

"How do you ask?" He trails a finger across my stomach as my heart pounds against my ribs. The spot between my legs ache for his touch.

"Please, Matteo."

He thrusts into it with relentless force and I scream out in a mix of pain and pleasure. He rocks against me, guiding my hips to match his.

He grinds into my throbbing bud as his lips find mine, capturing them in his. His chest rubs along my pebbled tips, sending me into a frenzy.

I thrust against him at each pulse he sends. My walls wrap perfectly around his thick cock filling me all the way. It's as if the pieces of a puzzle found their perfect match, sliding right into place. I tremble against him as I lose my ability to fight off my impending orgasm.

"Cum for me, *Principessa.*" He rams into me, and I unravel under him. My mind melts holding Matteo close. He continues his pattern of thrusts into my slick center, building a path for my next climax.

"Sei così bella," You are so beautiful. He whispers between grunts. His speed picks up and my second release comes fast. Matteo dives into me deep and I scream against his shoulder cursing out his name.

My eyes roll back from the intensity radiating through every inch of my body. Matteo dips, capturing my lips with his. The kiss lightens and he rests his forehead on mine, catching his breath.

Matteo locks eyes with me and pulls out. I groan at the feeling of his absence before relaxing into the bed. He saunters to the bathroom and starts the bath. I sigh rolling off the mattress as Matteo returns to the room. He holds out a hand and I smile, grabbing it as he pulls me up, kissing my neck. He murmurs into my ear between kisses.

"Mi fai perdere il controllo." You make me lose control.

I whimper in his hold, his lips planting sloppy kisses. He pulls away and I frown. He chuckles, and drags me to the bathroom, leading me to the tub. I get in first sinking under the water as he climbs in behind me. We both sit together while he gently rubs circles on my arm.

"Gwenevere?"

"*Mhmm.*" I don't bother to form a word in my bliss state knowing he'll continue regardless.

"Do you want to talk about what happened at the diner?"

I'd be stupid to think Gio wouldn't tell Matteo. Hell, he probably knew before we left the diner. I'm not oblivious, But I don't want to talk about it in this relaxing state.

"I'd rather not."

Matteo's fingers dance over my shoulder in a rhythmic pattern. We sit there in silence and he doesn't push the topic further.

After what feels like a graceful eternity I step out of the tub. I grab a towel and wrap it around myself, walking to the mirror to rinse my face.

"You didn't need to buy me everything I need to last a century for my short stay."

"Is it short?"

I turn to him with a raised brow. What does he want me to say?

"Do you want me to make it short?"

He rests an elbow on the ledge of the tub. He looks effortlessly cocky.

"You tend to push your limits."

I scoff leaning against the counter in nothing but a towel.

"You tend to wear your ass as a hat."

My comment only seems to make his ego rise with his smirk.

"If I was an ass, I wouldn't have given you everything you desire."

"If? You humble yourself too much." I raise my brows at him in pure amusement. He tsks getting out of the bath, dripping over the bathroom floor as he strides up to me.

"We both know I'm much worse." He puts his back to me giving a full shot of his ass. This man is going to be the death of me.

18

Gwenevere

I rustle around in the bed, refusing to make my current objective to get out of it. Fatigue has completely taken over me and rendered me to the mattress. I scan the time on my phone, noting a new day has begun and I still feel like a cloud hangs behind my eyes. I compel myself out from the covers and pick a lounge set from the closet.

The cool air from the small room slices across my skin as I reach for a gray sweatsuit and make my way into the bathroom. I slide the nozzle on the shower to hot and look at my reflection in the mirror.

"I plead with my reflection to find the energy to function. The bags under my eyes taunt me and I splash cool water into my skin. I lean against the counter with a hand holding my head. I am unexplainably exhausted. I must be coming down with something, maybe it's just the stress catching up to me? The steam from the shower pricks my skin.

I am already defeated by how much energy it takes to wet my lion's mane I call hair. I haven't been this tired in months. Sitting in the shower, I let the water run over me as I attempt to wake my body for the day.

Turning the water off I step out and wrap myself in a towel and brace myself against the counter once more. The last couple of days have been pretty slow. I took a nap, read a book, and played board games with the men. Why am I so drained?

I dry my face and search through the drawers. I apply my daily cleansing routine in hopes of boosting myself when my stomach grumbles, followed by an instant wave of nausea. I throw
a hand over my mouth and pause in hopes it will pass. I haven't eaten much since the day before last, and frankly, I took my sweet time getting out of bed. I'm prone to slight morning nausea before eating from time to time.

I brush it off and dry my hair. When I think I'm in the clear, another round comes, this time sending me flying to the toilet. I dry heave into the toilet due to the lack of contents in my stomach. I plop on the floor and focus on stabilizing my stomach. The realization of how terrible I actually feel washes over me like my previous shower.

I brush myself off and swipe my clothes from the counter, dressing, and lead myself to the kitchen. Maybe a decent meal and some coffee will pull me together. The smell of brunch falls to the staircase and my stomach churns. Once in the kitchen, I discover Gio sitting at the counter finishing his meal.

"Well, good morning sleepy head," he teases with a grin. I roll my eyes with a blush, embarrassed at how long it took me to get out of bed.

"Good morning." I smile back lifting the coffee pot. I make myself a cup and instantly regret it. I try to swallow back my nausea and ditch the cup in the sink settling on the water. I open the fridge and pick up my bottle of choice and shut the door.

"No coffee?" He tilts his head pointing to my discarded cup with his toast. I shake my head and take a sip of the water, my nausea easing. I search the cabinets for some crackers but fail to find any.

"Not really feeling it today." I pick an apple from the platter, taking a couple of bites. My stomach flops again but I'm able to hold my composure.

"You okay?"

I nod to him, wiping my lips with a napkin, and take another small sip of water.

"Um yeah, just an upset stomach, it's probably nothing."

Gio eyes me, ultimately dismissing it.

"Matteo wants to see you in his office. Alessio called."

With that, my stomach flips and I throw myself against the trash bin vomiting what little contents are left in my stomach.

"Shit, Gwen." Gio jumps up holding my hair away from my face "Maybe you should just lay back down, I'll let Matteo know you're not well."

"No, it's fine, just a little nausea. Nothing I can't handle." I wave him off, sending him a little smile that drops when another wave rushes through. I dry heave for a few minutes, my exhaustion rising. When I've finished puking my guts up, I rest against the counter. Gio rubs my back and sets my hair to the side.

"Okay, maybe I will lay down."

Gio shuffles and passes me a napkin and my water.

"Want me to walk you to the room?"

I shake my head, taking a sip big enough to wet my mouth and wipe my lips of any remaining vomit.

"It's okay, I'm going to speak to Mila first, can you let Matteo know? I want to know what Alessio said."

He nods and staggers before walking away. I go around the corner of the back entry to find Mila. The room is larger than the front kitchen with restaurant-grade appliances. Mila is cleaning the space with a couple of other maids when she spots me. A small smile creeps across her lips.

"Gwenevere, do you need something?" As she gets closer her raised brows pinch. "Oh dear, you are pale. Are you feeling well?" She grabs my face, giving me a once-over.

"That's what I wanted to talk about, I need a favor." My heart beats against the ribs in my chest like bars in a cell, as if the bones were the only thing keeping my heart from jumping out my chest and straight onto the table.

"Anything, dear." I look over to the other maids unsure if I should ask Mila right here. Her gaze follows mine and she looks to me in understanding.

"Come on, let's go into the dining room so you can have a seat." I nod thankfully as we head back into the other room. She brings me a plate of crackers but I glance at them in disgust knowing my stomach isn't going to hold anything now. Her brows go back into a furrow as she watches.

"Is everything alright, hun?" I bite my cheek unsure of how to ask what comes next. What would Mila think of the situation? She'd only just met me, hell they all did. Mila has been the one most excited about my presence though.

"Well um... I need someone to help me obtain something." She stills and I'm sure the idea of sneaking around, especially behind Matteo's back, doesn't sit well. She's loyal. Though part of me thinks she will be willing to do this.

"Gwenevere, I don't kn—"

"I need a pregnancy test." I cut her off and her mouth slams shut with wide eyes.

"Oh my god, oh my god, what, do you think you are? Is it? Oh my, of course it is." She stumbles over her questions and glances to the entryway and back to me. I grab her hand to calm her nerves along with my own.

"Please don't say anything. I don't know and I could cause a fuss over nothing. I just I—I was pregnant before and it started out like this. It could simply be my hormones and lack of eating yesterday making me utterly exhausted, and my stomach is a flight risk but I need to be sure. Please, Matteo can't know. Not yet, he well, he's..."

"Difficult. I understand *la dolcezza." I understand sweetheart.* She offers me a warm smile.

"Thank you."

She pulls me into a motherly hug, almost bringing me to tears. Her warmth and love for this family is undeniable. She is more of a mother than mine ever was or will be.

"It will be okay, I'll get you a test and bring it to you. The girls sometimes keep them around for precaution; there might be one somewhere in this house. Now go lay down and rest, you look terrible."

I glare at her and she grins, shooing me along. I take the long staircase, sneak into the room, and flop onto the bed. I take shallow breaths so I don't dry heave again and pull out my book flipping to my most recent page.

A few minutes later the door knob moves and Matteo comes in. He scans me as he glides to the bedside. He presses the back of his hand to my forehead before sliding it down to my chin. I nestle my head into his hand, appreciating the calm fire that comes with his touch

"I'm fine, Matteo. Just a little nausea, it will pass." I smile sweetly through my tired eyes. Another indicator that something is indeed off.

"I'll call the doc in and have him access you, just to be sure."

"Matteo, seriously, I'm fine." I sit up to look more alive and more believable. "Gio said Alessio called."

He steps back, moving to the leather chair on the other side of the room. He doesn't sit but instead grabs the bottle of bourbon off the cart and pours himself a glass. Finally, he sits, taking a sip.

"He wants to meet, your presence is wanted of course." He pauses, brows furring. "We set a meeting for a couple of days out but maybe we should push it with you not feeling well."

Alessio finally set a meeting. Of course. I'm not ready though. I need to know if what I'm suspecting is true. A piece of me knows the answer but another wants the ultimate seal. Even so, if I push the meeting it will be slightly suspicious. Alessio knows I would meet with him even if I'm not feeling up to par. I sigh, shaking my head.

"No, we need to take the meeting, I'll be fine."

"Gwenevere, you need to rest."

"I don't think Alessio will be too keen on you stepping out of the arrangement regardless of the reason when it comes to whether or not he talks to me. You pull back and you initiate a whole other problem."

He nods and takes another sip of his bourbon. He stands at the door and swivels to me.

"Rest. I'll send Mila with some soup and crackers and I'm sending the doc up." He shuts the door leaving no time to debate. I roll my eyes and return to my book.

A small knock chimes at the door after a few pages and I open the door. On the other side is a younger girl, the same one helping Mila bring out food since I arrived. She smiles shyly causing her already peach-colored cheeks to deepen a few shades of pink.

"*Um*, Mila sent me. May I come in?" I look down the hall then drag her in the room by her arm, shutting the door. "Oh, *um* okay... I'm Mila's daughter, Alice."

"Hi Alice, sorry for the whole kidnap move." I smile warmly. "I didn't realize Mila had a daughter or that you worked here too."

"I work under her. I'm in training to take my mom's place when she retires." Alice is the spitting image of Mila and how I didn't see it earlier baffles me—we had even talked in passing. "She sent me with your *request*." She holds out a tray holding a few items and a little baggie. "She put some ginger teas and crackers in as well to ease your stomach."

I gently grab the bag from her and she smiles.

"I know I'm not supposed to say anything but I can see how much everyone around here cares for you. Us ladies definitely love you." She smiles shyly. "I know the whole mafia thing can be a bit much but life here isn't the life they show out there. You are safer in these walls than you are anywhere else." She points to the window. I laugh under my breath at the irony of her statement.

"The mafia part is the least of my worries. It's the Genovese vs. Luciano part."

The wheels turn behind her eyes and a spark lights the moment the gears click.

"You're a Luciano. It makes sense now."

"What makes sense?"

"Well it's obvious, isn't it? You're practically living here yet Mr. Genovese hasn't claimed you as his formally. It's a business deal."

I scratch my head unsure how to go about that statement.

"In a way, I guess, yeah." My brows furrow.

"Um, I should get going." She turns to the door and dread pools in my stomach.

"Wait!"

She tilts her head, peering at me.

"I um… will you please stay? I know you don't know me but I think I need someone to stay for this. I lost a baby a few months ago and I'm not sure I'm ready to go through any of this again. Positive or not." I twirl a finger around the room and sigh in relief when her lips etch into a smile. She grabs my hands in her sweetly, like I'd done with Mila.

"Of course, come on." She leads us into the bathroom and I head for the toilet. She stands near the tub with her back facing me.

My bladder goes shy at the presence of a stranger in the room. I shuffle and purse my lips in the awkward silence. Alice seems to catch my unease and rambles.

"I grew up in this mansion, it's beautiful. My favorite part is the tubs."

My pee releases on the stick as I listen to her confession.

"The tubs?" I finish, placing the cap on the test and sit it on top of the box lying on the counter. I wash my hands and set the timer on my phone, per the box's orders.

"Do you see these things? They are massive and luxurious. The best part of the day."

"Agreed. All clear." I laugh and she turns around sitting on the edge of the tub. I join her and twiddle my thumbs.

"Do you have *luxurious* tubs at the Luciano estate?"

Her question brings something up I hadn't taken into account. Did Alessio and I move out of the estate to keep my reality a secret?

"My dad's mansion has a beautiful bathroom, like a spa. I won't say I don't have a gorgeous setup but nothing like this."

"You don't live in your father's estate?"

I laugh under my breath twirling a finger around a strand of hair.

"No. My brother and I moved into a smaller home with his second." I pause seeing the confusion in her furrowed brows.

"My family hid the *business* from me. I didn't know until the Genovese's. I think it's why they moved me out of the estate."

"Assholes."

"Exactly why I'm here now, partially."

"Partially?"

"At first my friendship with Gio held fair ground, but then Matteo happened and well Matteo is… intoxicating." I smile to myself. "A part of me doesn't want to go back simply so I

can be with Matteo. He steals all the air in the room just so he can give you a breath of fresh air in return."

The timer goes off interrupting my calming daydream and I freeze. Once again he is sucking the air out of my lungs and he isn't even in the room, but a piece of him might be.

"Gwenevere, exhale. It'll be okay, whatever that test says." She points in the direction of the test and stands in front of me. "That test doesn't define you and it doesn't define your future."

I laugh at her remark. Doesn't define my future? Is she crazy? Of course, it does. If that test is positive I have no choice but to be involved with the Genovese's and if it doesn't...

I know in the grand scheme of things it seems silly to hope there's a baby, and hope I have a chance, but I do. I lost my baby. It broke me and this is a chance to start over; this time in a reality I'm aware of. Would I want to leave anyway? It fumbled through my head over and over the last week. I had been tortured by that single thought.

"You're delusional, right? This changes everything."

She shakes her head, holding onto my biceps.

"No, it doesn't. The ball is in your court either way. You hold the control. Put on your poker face and bring out your inner Luciano. You act like you have the control and they will listen. I don't know you, not enough, but if I know one thing, you've already proven how strong you are. You are tougher than you give yourself credit for. So whatever that test says. Use it. You are going to be okay because you'll make it okay."

I must have hit my head because I believe her. I nod and drift to the test.

My heart falters, skipping beats before slamming into my chest. I stare down as my body trembles and I cover my mouth. I pick the test up and tears prick in my eyes. I pass the test to Alice, sitting back on the tub.

"You're pregnant."

I'm pregnant. Not only that but I'm pregnant with Matteo Genovese's baby. I have mixed the families and no one knows to what extent. At least not the ones who will change the judiciary of my life with the knowledge.

Alessio is going to lose it. When I was pregnant with Enzo I knew he would freak but he would eventually come around. With Matteo, I don't know if it will be that easy. He may never come around.

So much for my no-strings-attached game. Once Matteo finds out it's game over. I know what Alice said, and while she has a point, it isn't entirely true. I really like Gio and Matteo.

I'm going to be in this world whether or not I raise this baby in Matteo's house or Alessio's. Why would I make things harder? Especially if I don't need to or want to.

Matteo. Do I want this? Him?

It plays in my mind on a repeat cycle like a broken record never fixed. I've known the answer for longer than I've been able to admit, even to myself. I don't want to leave. As simple as I can put it, I want Matteo and I want this baby. I'll be damned if anyone tries to take that from me.

What if he doesn't want it? What if he just wants sex and to keep an alliance? What if this is more than what he's asking for? Matteo is a *familgia* man, but is he a family man?

I stand up from the bed and slouch into Matteo's frequented chair. I pull a leg up to my chest and lay my head to the side anxiously picking at my pants. I hear a slight knock on the door and turn to see who it is.

In comes an older man who appears to be in his late thirties. He has scruff around his jaw and his attire leans more towards business casual. He pulls a leather suitcase bag behind him and closes the door.

"Miss Luciano?" He smiles warmly at me and sets his arms to his side. "I'm Marco, I'm the estate doctor. Matteo sent me, though, Alice had a curious request."

I fidget with my nails, taking a deep breath.

"I'm pregnant."

"She mentioned something along those lines. Do you mind if I give you a formal check-up? Make sure everything is okay?"

I nod and he motions me to the bed. I shuffle over and prop myself on the pillows. He sets his case down on the end and opens it, picking up his stethoscope. He moves to me and places the cold stethoscope on my chest listening to the thumping of my heart. He grabs a blood pressure monitor, attaches it to my arm and nods at the results.

"How are you feeling?"

Physically? Like absolute shit. Mentally? Also like absolute shit.

"Tired. Nauseous."

"Is this your first pregnancy?" My heart takes a pause with me, I swallow back the emotion that comes with my answer

"No." I stare ahead to keep the welling tears behind my eyes at bay. Begging for them to soak back in.

"How many babies?"

The knife that already lay in my heart turns like a glitch, driving deeper.

"Zero." He nods in understanding but my chest tightens. My wounds are still fresh, stinging with each statement that leaves my dried lips.

"I'm sorry to hear that. How far along were you?"

I can't bring myself to fully look at him. I can't handle the sympathy and I don't want it.

"Twenty weeks." My voice comes hoarse.

"When did you give birth?"

Birth. Such a funny thing to call a moment like that. I know I gave birth but how do you handle holding your breathless child? Instead of the wailing screams of happiness, there were only silent sobs.

Holding her was like holding a lifelike doll, except I didn't get to see her beautiful eyes. I didn't get to see into the depths of her soul. I didn't get to know her, hell I only had a few hours with her. I should be grateful for what I had, but instead, I'm enraged and pained at the time I lost.

"Four months ago."

His movements falter but he regains his composure. The knife clicks deeper into my chest.

"My condolences, truly." He observes my stomach and gestures. "May I?"

I give him permission as I lift my shirt. He presses on my lower stomach for further assessment. My anxious energy returns and I twirl my finger in my shirt.

"Have you had any cramping or bleeding?" He pushes and probes uncomfortably on my stomach and a part of me cringes at the motions. I am fully aware they cause no harm to the baby but a sliver of panic seeps through at the possibility it might this time.

"No." I shake my head with my whispered answer.

"Any pain or discomfort?"

"Nothing besides tired and nauseous."

He hums in response. I stare at the ceiling, praying for the assessment to finish.

"About how long ago was your last period?"

"My last one was around five weeks ago."

He nods again before placing his items back in his case. I let the air escape my lungs in relief knowing the evaluation is almost over and pull my shirt down.

"It's too early to hear the heartbeat. I will need to order some equipment to fully assess you. Because of your recent loss, I want to monitor you closely until you are in viability. I don't believe we need to worry but keeping your mind at ease will lower your stress levels. I should have them in a few days, if you need anything before then you know how to find me."

"Okay. Thank you." He turns with his bag to leave and I shoot up in bed.

"Marco."

He looks back at me patiently.

"Yes?"

"Don't tell Matteo yet. I need to be the one to tell him, please."

He's hesitant while pursing his lips.

"I will do my best." I figure that is the best I can get from him and sigh. My stomach grumbles and I scrunch my face with bubbling disgust.

"If your nausea gets unmanageable let me know, and I want you to stay hydrated."

"Thank you." I send him a soft smile and he shuts the door as he exits. Exhaustion rolls over me and my eyes flutter close. I sense someone enter the room but sleep engulfs me, refusing to let me see who or why.

19

Gwenevere

I'm unsure of how long I've been resting. I glance out the window at the warm glow. I pick up my phone.

6:00 pm

I've slept through dinner and the thought of food makes my stomach rumble. My morning sickness has transitioned into starving nausea. I throw myself off the bed, not bothering with my appearance. I stumble my way to the kitchen through the quiet house, past the guards that stand post throughout.

Once in the kitchen, I raid the cabinet in search of my perfect combination. I set all my ingredients out before wrinkling my forehead. *Where are all the pots and pans?*

I peek into the back kitchen in hopes of seeing Mila but the space is empty. Maybe they're done for the day? I sigh and rustle through the cabinets until I've landed the jackpot. I then rummage through the fridge for some thawed chicken.

I might be messing up the kitchen's meal plans but I am desperate and know it's an easy fix. I bread the chicken and wait for the pan to heat. Grabbing the jar of pickles I placed out I open it and take a bite.

When the pan is ready, I toss the chicken in, letting it simmer while I eat my pickle and grab a pitcher of orange juice from the fridge. Orange juice has my heart and soul, well next to coffee I guess, but the baby seems to tolerate the liquid gold more.

Once the chicken is golden I grab the peanut butter and melted butter and take a seat. Picking up a piece of chicken, I split it in half with a delicious little crunch from the fried breading. I dip the piece in my butter before spreading the peanut butter on.

I shove the whole half-piece in my mouth, moaning in pure contentment. Halfway through chewing I turn to see Gio's brows raised. Looking back I see the disaster I left in the kitchen and wince at how messy I look.

"I promise to clean it up. I just got really hungry and desperate."

Gio chuckles and assesses my plate, his face screws up in disgust.

"That's absolutely disgusting. How did you go from puking in the trash can to eating *that* concoction."

I shrug my shoulders knowing exactly how but refusing to let that information slip yet. I take a sip of my orange juice as he rounds the counter. He catches sight of the jar of pickles picks them up and examines it as if I am eating bug eyes.

"Pickles too?" His nose scrunches.

 I roll my eyes moving to the next piece of chicken.

"Pickles, chicken, peanut butter and orange juice. What are you pregnant?" He laughs, but I freeze—damn you, Gio. Swallowing what's left in my mouth, I take a sip of my juice and ignore his gaze. He stares at me when he stills with me.

"Are you pregnant, Gwen?" The tone in his voice is unreadable. My lips move but nothing comes out, I move my gaze up locking eyes with him.

"Oh my god. You're pregnant. Is it Matteo's?" This time I throw a piece of chicken at him. He ducks, barely missing it before glaring at me.

"What the fuck was that?"

"Is it Matteo's?" Of course it's fucking Matteo's you fucking douchebag. Do you really think I'd just be sitting here raiding his kitchen if it

wasn't? God your such a dick." When I'm finished yelling at him I sit on the stool again dunking my next piece of chicken. "Now you've made me waste a good piece of chicken," I grumble, while stuffing my face.

Gio raises his hands in surrender.

"Gwen, I didn't mean it like that." He moves around the counter closer to me. "Have you told him?"

I snicker. Have I told Matteo I'm pregnant? Hmm, let me see, is the house in flames yet?

"What do you think?"

He presses his lips together scanning over my features.

"Gwen, he's going to find out."

"Yes Gio, I know. I just need a second to actually process that I have another baby growing inside of me who's on the verge of being an enemy to my now-known crime family," I puff out.

"Are you okay?" he sighs.

I don't know if it is the tone of his voice or because it's just him, but his simple yet raw question takes me from angry and irritated to downright emotional. The tears I haven't yet shed from the start of all of this roll down my cheeks. I shake my head and my shoulders drop like the tears from my chin.

The pent-up emotions flow through me all at once, breaking my composure and throwing me into a whirlwind of pitiful cries. Gio holds me gently against him and I let go of my reins hoping to rid myself of some pain while in his embrace.

"I can't, Gio. Everyone is going to hate me—hate the baby— I can't do this. Matteo and I... there isn't a Matteo and I. This wasn't supposed to happen this way." I let out a pathetic hiccup between my words.

"Alessio... Enzo... I've been hiding here trying to make a major decision affecting everyone and now?" I look to the floor letting the tears fall into my lap as he holds on to me. He gives me a moment before pulling back.

"Gwenevere. No one is going to hate you. No one. Will everyone be super ecstatic at first? I can't promise you that, but it's not about them. It's about you, and you need to pick you, Gwenevere. Alessio will come around. Regardless, you have me and I can't hate you."

"What about Matteo?"

The wrinkles by his eyes deepen while a smile pulls at his lips.

"If you think for one moment that he won't treat you and this baby like his whole world, you are in for an awakening. You might be in whatever situation-ship you're in right now but he's been working nonstop to find a way for you to be happy with any outcome. He wants you here with him. That makes you a part of our family, simply because he doesn't want to let you go. You Gwen. You being pregnant with his baby is only going to fuel that fire. He wants you. Don't let yourself get talked into anything but that truth."

I trust Gio with everything in me and I can only hope that he isn't just bullshitting me to stop my breakdown. Could Matteo really want me as much as he says?

"You think so?"

"Baby Girl, I know." Gio smiles, wiping my tears. He looks back around the kitchen and winces slightly. "You're not cleaning this."

"It's my mess, I destroyed the kitchen. I don't want to put more work onto Mila."

"You're too kind for your own heart, Gwen. She's more than well compensated. Although, this is more of a pass-off job for the training maids. Mila isn't just a maid, she's *famiglia*." I sigh and turn back to my food. I lift the chicken to my lips, eating the last piece on the plate before gulping the rest of my orange juice down. I place my glass in the sink and peer over to Gio.

He finishes his email, setting his phone back into his pocket. I cover my mouth with the back of my hand as a yawn escapes my lips.

"You should go to bed."

I go to argue but Gio puts a hand up stopping me.

"Gwen, you need rest. You're yawning and barely keeping your eyes open." He scans my face then lets out a soft sigh. "Listen, I won't tell Matteo but you need to talk to him soon. You have a meeting with Alessio coming up and this is important. Okay?"

I chew on my inner cheek listening to him. I know he's right, hell everyone has said the same thing. If I didn't tell him he was going to find out. A part of me feels terrible that I've told so many people before I have had the courage to tell him. He will be the next one to know. A promise I silently make to myself.

I stand but stop parallel to him. He looks up to me with furrowed brows, I don't give him a chance to speak and crash my body into him, embracing him in another hug.

"A month ago I wanted a friend and to put all my shitty feelings to the side. Now I'm living in this estate, carelessly pregnant again and I'm going to hurt them."

"Gwenevere, you're not hurting anyone. You deserve to take care of yourself right now. You always do. You've done nothing but put on a brave face while everyone walked all over you. It's your turn to take that power back."

"What if Alessio doesn't come around? What if he hates me?"

He pulls me in tight, squeezing my shoulders with ease.

"Then we'll be right here, Gwen. We're not going anywhere."

A wave of relief flows through me. Hearing the statement again in full clarity is promising. I hope Alessio won't hate me but in the chance that he does, I don't think I can do this on my own. My head throbs from crying and my emotional rollercoaster of today. I take a step back wiping the mix of wet and dry tears from my cheeks, twisting my face from the discomfort growing in my head

"Are you okay?"

"I have a bit of a headache, might be a migraine." Gio's lips fall.

"I'll have doc send up some meds that are safe for you. Go rest." He nods to the door. I smile softly and oblige.

I cross into the bedroom as the sun sets and lay down. It's not but minutes later a small knock sounds at the door. I sit up turning the lamp on as the figure walks in. Alice glides to the side of the bed sitting on the edge with pills and water.

"Here, doc sent me with pain meds for your headache."

I pop the pills in my mouth and drown them down before setting the glass on the side table.

"Thank you, Alice. How was the rest of your day?"

Her face lights at my question and I can't help but wonder if she has many friends.

"It was good. Dinner was easy flowing and the house stayed pretty quiet. Mom was really excited when I told her about the baby. Good luck with her, it's like she's getting her own grandbaby."

I laugh with her, rubbing my neck.

"Your mom is so precious. You must have had a wonderful childhood." I've daydreamed of what having a mother like Mila would've been like. My mom was so distant growing up. She was never around and I resent her for it.

I won't be that mother. She taught me everything I shouldn't do. I only hope Mila can shine a light on the better parts of motherhood. Teach me her ways if you will. Alice is kind and beautiful, she went right somewhere.

"It had its moments, but she's the best mom I could ever ask for. All she's ever done is look out for me and love me the best she can. What is your mom like?"

"The opposite. I haven't spoken to her in a couple of years. If I'm being honest I really don't want to speak to her. She wouldn't have anything nice to say anyways."

"Her loss. I can't imagine not wanting to be around your glow."

"I think you're seeing the glow of the pregnancy, although I don't feel like I'm glowing at all. I feel like shit." We laugh together and then fall into a comfortable silence.

"Have you told Matteo?" I shake my head. I haven't seen him since our talk about Alessio earlier. He must be busy with work or letting me rest out of my 'sickness.'

"I haven't seen him since earlier and I honestly haven't been in the right mind yet. I'm just trying to grasp the fact that I'm pregnant. Not that my stomach is letting me forget with the constant nausea." She nods, looking around the darkened room, only illuminated by the moon and a soft lamp on the side of the bed.

"Can I do anything for you before I leave?" I think about it, my mind instantly going to food as I smile at her sheepishly.

"Do we have strawberries?" My voice rises as I draw out my question. She giggles pushing off the bed.

"Of course. I'll be back in a moment." She leaves the room and I saunter off to the bathroom. My body is sore and aching and I'm desperate for a nice warm bath.

I examine the bottles lining the tub, choosing the bubble bath soap and pouring a little in the tub. Next, I scour the bath bombs, compliments of Matteo, and pluck a plain white one with a simple vanilla scent. I turn the nozzle and let the tub fill. Heading over to the counter, I wash my face in the sink and let my hair fall down my back.

I hear a soft noise from the room and peek out. Sliced strawberries sit at the end of the bed and I snatch them up. I peel my clothes off and place them in the laundry basket before feeling the water in the half-filled tub. Satisfied, I place the delectable strawberries on the small marble table beside me and glide down into the tub, resting against the edge. I pop a berry into my mouth, humming.

Before I know it the tub is filled to the perfect height and I shut off the water, submerging myself up to my shoulders. The water climbs up the bottom half of my hair, the warmth near my head bringing me some relief. I slide under the water and then return to the surface as I wipe my eyes of water, push any hairs out of my face, and rest my head on the tub.

A hand grasps my chin and his lips touch mine. I suck in the deep musky scent of vanilla as my lips move along his. He pulls away and my eyes flutter open to Matteo. A smile tugs at my lips. Matteo's eyes travel over me and my skin prickles under the intensity of his gaze.

"May I join?"

I blush, hiding my face as he strips his suit off, throwing it to the bin without confirmation. I try to look away but fail miserably as I watch him effortlessly slide his shirt down his arms, reaching for his pants. I catch his eyes watching mine and my face heats, turning away.

"You don't have to stop watching."

I suck my lip in glancing back at him as he teases pulling his pants all the way down along with his boxers. My breath hitches at his slight arousal.

I move up in the bath to allow him behind me. In a quick swoop, Matteo lowers himself in the tub wrapping his arms around me and pulling me into him. He picks up the loofah and applies soap running it up my shoulder.

"How are you feeling?"

I tense, unsure if this is the right time to tell him.

"Okay, my head is pounding and I'm tired." I slide down resting my head on his chest. He plays with my hair, placing strands behind my ears.

"Did you eat?" I hum my answer.

Between the nice warm bath and the soothing strokes from Matteo, I might fall asleep right here.

"How was your day?" My voice comes out quiet as I try to open him up.

"Busy." By his one-word response, I figured that is all the answers I'll receive from him.

"We've been marking up proposals for Alessio. I'm not sure how well he'll take it if you decide to stay."

He spent the day writing proposals.

"Who says I've made my decision to stay?" I poke, wanting to understand what he wants from his own words, not just the one Gio promised me.

"Are you leaving?"

I don't answer. Not because I don't know my answer but because I'm not ready for him to know it.

"Alessio might not take the proposal." Matteo continues, filling the silence. Alessio will take the proposal; if not to simply keep the families from fighting through and alliance, he'd definitely do it for the family I'm creating now.

"I don't think Alessio will deny it."

"You seem awfully confident. I doubt your brother will be happy I'm sleeping with his sister. I'll be lucky if he doesn't try to shoot me on the spot," he scoffs.

"He won't shoot you. I won't let him." My causal toned response doesn't satisfy him though.

"I don't think there's much you can do or say that will keep Alessio in his cool." I smile internally, he underestimates my pull with my brother, regardless of my newfound pregnancy or not.

"No, probably not. He's gonna flip but he will take the proposal."

"If he says no I can't fight him without repercussions."

My chest constricts as the worry sets in. Would Matteo not want to fight for me? If it was just me, would he still put the same amount of effort into keeping me here?

"Would you?"

"Do you want me to?"

I pause again. I don't want him to start a war over me but I do want him to fight for me. But he's already doing that, in fact, that's what he spent his entire day doing. Deep down I know Alessio will eventually agree if he has all the pieces in front of him.

Matteo should have all the pieces in front of him too.

"You won't have to." I trace my fingers over his arm concentrating my nerves into something other than my voice.

"Why are you so sure he will accept us?" His voice rises in curiosity and the overwhelming pulse of my heart pounds to my ears. What if it comes to announcing I'm pregnant with a Genovese baby? I have to tell him because I want to, because he deserves to know.

"Gwen?"

"I'm Pregnant."

The world moves in slow motion—his body, his breath—in this moment I feel every emotion possible at once. Does he hate me? Does he not want this? Should I have said anything? Oh my God, he doesn't want it, he doesn't want me. *He hates me.*

My thoughts flow like crazy as I contemplate getting out of the tub and leaving when his hand reaches for my shoulder and nudges me to him. I turn, avoiding his eyes, but he guides my chin up, eyes searching mine as if looking for any clue I am lying.

"You're pregnant?"

I swallow back, is he mad, in shock?

"I only found out this morning. I've been sick and tired and I've been off the last couple of days and my period was off."

His gaze dips to my stomach and I continue.

"I had Mila get me a test and when it came out positive I had Alice intercept Marco. He agreed to let me be the one to tell you. I wanted to wrap my head around it too, you know, I mean I don't know if I've wrapped my head around it, but I can't let you walk into that room blind."

He grasps my face, running a thumb across my cheek. I wait impatiently for him to speak. *What is he thinking right now?*

"You're carrying my baby?"

"Yes, Matteo. I'm carrying your baby," I huff. Is he slow? His face relaxes and his eyes carry a new shine within them. For the first time, his lips tug into a soft smile.

"Non sei mai stato così Bella" You have never been more beautiful. He leans down, kissing my lips, and for a moment, the world stops. The emotions that have plagued me are replaced with the pure happiness flowing between us. He rests his forehead on mine as we sit in each other's arms in the warmth of the tub.

"We are going to have a baby." His voice is gentle.

"We are." I smile in our bubble until my thoughts come racing back, twisting my heart in the process. "Matteo. I just lost a baby. I… I don't know if this one will... It's so early. I just need you to know that we could—"

"No."

I stop at his interjection, looking up.

"We won't lose this baby."

"Matteo… I didn't think I was going to lose my baby, but I did. I can't promise this." My tears fall at the thought of losing this baby too. Of my heart shattering again after putting everyone through so much.

Things fell out with Enzo. I couldn't be with him anymore. If I lost this baby? Could I still marry Matteo? My heart throbs at the possibility of my life crumbling again. Matteo lifts my chin staring deep into my eyes.

"I will do everything I can to make sure you and this baby are happy and healthy, Gwenevere. I know I can't prevent anything but that doesn't mean I won't try."

My lips quiver as I cry harder. My heart, breaking and fixing itself all at once. The hormones making their appearance known.

"I want to stay, Matteo." My tears drip into the water from my chin. I can't leave anymore. Not with this baby in mind and not with my heart in mind.

Not only can I not do it but I won't. If not for Matteo and the baby then for Gio, Alice, and Mila. Over my time spent here, I have made friends that feel like family. They feel like fresh air after a storm of chaos. They are my family even if they don't have the Luciano name, and leaving means shutting them out.

Leaving means not being with Matteo. I am realizing I knew this was more than a hookup way before this morning. I want Matteo and not just for the sex and the fun. I can't and won't leave, even if I'm begged to, I want this. Matteo watches over me as my mind swirls.

"Voglio essere una famiglia." I want to be family. I whisper to him.

"Sei una famiglia." You are family.

I close my eyes, locking this memory of us in. I don't want to leave this moment in time; the feeling of being safe and content. The feeling of being chosen and cared for.

Time passes us by as we lay together. My body shivering from the now cool water.

"You're shaking, come on." He pushes me forward enough to slip out of the cold tub and grab a towel. He dries himself off and he wraps it around his waist before grabbing another and helping me out.

He wraps the towel around me kissing my nose. I giggle at his cute gesture and follow him through the bedroom until he disappears into the closet. He returns with two pairs of boxers and a shirt. I raise my brow at him for his choice of items.

"You always choose my clothes." He places a pair of boxers and a shirt in my hands before slipping his own on. I throw the clothes on and climb into bed, covering myself for warmth. The covers are cool and I shiver.

Matteo turns off the bathroom light and carries my bowl of strawberries out. I forgot all about them and sit up with my arms out for my night snack.

"Strawberries. You're that easy to please?" He chuckles with a shake of his head.

I roll my eyes, snatching the bowl, but he pulls it away. I huff giving him a pointed look. He rolls his eyes and pops a berry into his mouth. He picks another strawberry up, this time bringing it to my lips.

I lock my eyes with Matteo's and open my mouth. He holds the berry and I let my teeth graze before biting it. He watches as I chew, a smirk rises to his lips with satisfaction, and he hands me the bowl. I take it, scarfing down the rest of the strawberries.

He climbs into his side of the bed, laying on his side towards me. He props himself up and steals another strawberry. I smack his hand, grabbing the last one and throwing it in my mouth. He places the bowl on the side table and turns back to me. I graze over his chest, a large tattoo swirling across it leading into a sleeve. Italian and Roman numerals are embedded with the patterns and designs.

I run my hands along the ink admiring the work. He leans me back against the pillow. His body hovering above me. He captures my lips in his, soft but possessive as they claim mine. He runs his hand further, dipping until his head is resting on my stomach. My heart flutters at his soft actions.

This is the side of Matteo I truly crave and hope for more. Would this be life with him? Could this ever be our normal? My dad couldn't handle the business and home. He paid us no mind and my mother turned into a shell because of it. Will that be what becomes of us? My chest sinks with worry.

"Matteo." He hums in response. I want to stay frozen in this happily ever after world, but I don't want to be stupid by letting my heart love blindly only to find out down the road that's all it will ever be. A fictional happily ever after.

"How will this work?" Matteo's brows furrow and I play with his shirt to calm the anxious tingling blazing through my veins.

"You know with this. You and me." I motioned between us, sighing. "It's just you have the business. How can you go out and do what you do and come home to this?" I gesture to my stomach.

I could have chosen any guy in the city and I picked a mafia king to sleep with. Not that Enzo was a wise choice either, but I only knew half the story.

"You mean how do I go kill someone and come home to you with blood on my hands?" His voice is tense matching the muscles in his arms. I still at the shift in his demeanor. He huffs rising from the bed.

My blood rushes viciously. I've ruined this brief passage of pure tenderness. I reminded him of the war he called his life, of the ruthless killer he could be.

"Matteo..."

"This life is not meant for a woman like you. You are going to hate and resent me and there is nothing you can do about it. You're going to loathe the moment you met me and want nothing but to run the other way. I have had blood on my hands and will continue to."

I swallow hard, wanting to do exactly what he says. Run the other way. Alessio did everything he could to keep this life separate, and so did

Enzo. But I hated him for that. Keeping my life a lie. Never knowing when I was in danger. Being oblivious to his actions. How many lies did he conjure just about his day?

"Is that all you'll let yourself be?" He laughs demonically, throwing on his tossed pants.

"Is that all you see of me? I am exactly that, Gwenevere, and if that's all you want to see, so be it." He grabs his shirt, slides it on, and shakes his head. He scoffs, turning back to me.

"I will make this place hell for you if that's how you want it. I am a Don regardless of your unrequited feelings, and you're fucked regardless. That baby in you? That sealed you to me." He points to my stomach as he growls out at me.

"This baby? This baby doesn't mean a goddamn thing, Matteo. It sure as fuck doesn't mean I have to stay here. One word and I'm back at home with Alessio and Enzo and you don't even get to know this baby." I regret the words leaving my mouth knowing it's not what I actually want. But the audacity of him to blow up in the first place eggs me on. In a flash, Matteo has me pinned. My stomach drops at the realization that I threatened the most dangerous man on the estate; and maybe that I've ever met.

"You so much as threaten me again and I will lock you in the goddamn cellar until my baby is born, and I'll deliver your body back to Alessio."

"Matteo." Gio's voice reaches my ears as I stare into Matteo's not letting my act down. But it's exactly that, an act. I am terrified to my bones but deep within I'm not scared of him. As if his threats have no backing, as if he can't hurt me.

"Go," Gio cuts to him. Matteo's jaw clenches as he stares at me with murderous eyes, planning my unworldly ending.

"Matteo, leave."

This time Matteo's fist clenches but pushes off of me and leaves. Gio stays put while he exits before turning his gaze to me. He rubs a hand down his face resting his chin in his hand.

"I didn't get much of it, but what I do know is this isn't going to work if you don't try and give him a chance. You have to understand the life we grew up in. He was raised a king. You've been raised as a sheltered, princess. This—" his hand waves around the room "—this life, this baby, you need to learn how to be the queen. It's not going to be easy, Gwenevere. We learned how to shoot a gun at seven. This is all we've known. You both will have to learn how to make this work. But you need to at least be on each other's team to get there."

He looks to the door and back to me with a sigh.

"Look I'm going to go deal with him and make sure he doesn't hurt someone. Get some rest and don't threaten anyone else, okay?" I look off to the wall with the urge to rage.

"Gwen? I know this isn't the life you expected for yourself or how you wanted to bring a baby into the world, but we're here now. Try and make the best of it. If it doesn't work out, okay. But just try."

I sigh this time peering at him. I nod my head and he lets out a breath. He retreats from the room and I wrap myself back under the covers.

This is such a mess. How can I do this? Matteo's unpredictable and rash. I want to make this work. Didn't I prove that by asking to stay? I told him I wanted to be *famiglia* and he said I was, then he turned around threatening to lock me up, take my baby and send my dead body to my brother.

How will he handle being a father or a husband? My frustration rises until I go over Gio's words. Is Matteo trying? Trying to find the balance? This week he's been kind. He might have been uptight but every second he's spent with me has been genuine.

I climb into bed continuing pondering my thoughts. My eyes grow heavy from my life-changing day. All I want to do is close my eyes and wake to a new day. I fall into sleep hoping

for a chance. The chance to prove I can be the queen. I need time, but now the time has a deadline.

20

Matteo

I slam my hands against the liquor counter dropping my head between my arms. I thought for a moment that Gwenevere could handle this world—could handle me. When she said she was pregnant, the world froze on its axis as if begging for this to be my chance to truly be happy.

Settling had never been in my view and I didn't expect it to be anytime soon. All Gwenevere had to do was waltz into my living room to change the entire timeline. I am fully aware we were being reckless. I assumed she was on the pill but didn't bother to confirm and didn't entirely care.

To be honest, I didn't mind being reckless with her. Her being pregnant makes the whole fucked up situation simpler in regards to her merging with the Genovese family. I will admit, she never truly had the option not to. Not after she came here looking for a place to hide out for a while.

On the other hand, this is bound to make things more interesting with Alessio. I know he is already livid with Gwenevere residing here during their dispute. He made that abundantly clear when setting up a meeting, per Gwenevere's request. I admire her stand against him.

I, however, don't appreciate her stand against me. She knew who, and what, I was before she stepped back through my door. She was given an option and yet she ran right back into my arms with enough force to nearly knock me down. I'd be lying if I said I wouldn't get on my knees for her if she asked.

She chose to come here. Gwenevere thought she was running somewhere to be safe and secure as she processed her entire life being a lie, but instead, she ran straight into the devil's arms. Now she is carrying my baby.

The Genovese house is going to have its first baby in this generation and it starts with me. On one end it has me doused in pride and the other, doubled in laughter. I was foolish, and a fucking idiot.

I've known Gwenevere for merely a month. I let my guard down and fucked her before I even knew who she was. The best part? By the time her identity came to the surface, she had already grown onto Gio.

No matter how hard I try, I can't pin the blame all on Gio. I wasn't ready to let her walk away. Gwenevere has sliced her way through and left a slash through everyone in the estate.

Gwenevere has me waiting for the next time she walks into the room. My mind is unable to stop from wondering about her. Her presence leaves me rendered to her every need and the desire to see her crumble beneath me.

Now I'm here with a bottle of bourbon contemplating my last couple hours with her. She's having my baby and all she can see is a ruthless killer unable to care for either of them. The moment I laid my eyes on her, I knew the kind of person she was. I knew she couldn't handle this world regardless of where she comes from, and yet I willingly let her rip her way through.

I can't go back anymore. I won't let her walk away. We sealed our futures with restless nights and careless minds. I'm not pissed at myself for indulging with a Luciano. I am furious that I allowed it to be with her.

Gwenevere isn't another Mob princess. She isn't built to understand this world. It was one thing to be the sister of a Don, but another to be under one, to be a partner. She was sheltered
from her own world and now she is being thrown in head first after tripping right into the biggest evil.

This is a dangerous life. Not just for the men participating but the women who wait at home, the ones who become the targets—become your weakness. Gwenevere turned herself into my weakness, whether consciously or not, the world is going to know. If not now, they surely will after the Lucaino's receive the wind shift.

I grab the bourbon and pour myself a tall glass, throwing it back as Gio strides into the room. His face is a clear glass window to his rage and seething, a telltale sign I won't care for his upcoming attack.

I know threatening her like that, or at all, wouldn't settle with him. It doesn't settle well within me either. Gio grew fond of Gwenevere over the last couple of months. A weird chorus friendship. They act as if they are long-lost friends meeting once more and never separating.

I will admit I'm a tad jealous of their bond. Gio became protective of her quickly, even against me. She opened up to him early on about her recent loss, and he helped alongside me to wrap her mind around her brother's betrayal. The last couple weeks have been the hardest for her, and yet she sits upstairs holding the hardest part of the battle inside her.

"What the fuck was that, Matteo?"

I ignore him, refilling my glass and taking a spot at the large window in my office. I avoid his angry scowl staring with void at the garden. I take note of the courtyard's appearance; the plants look pathetic and desperate for a facelift. I'll talk to the ladies that cover the garden in the morning.

"You can't just threaten her like that."

"I can do whatever the fuck I want, Giovanni." I snap at him but he doesn't shut up. I don't see him backing down, not anytime soon. He grits his teeth and continues as if he has to spell everything out for me.

"Matteo, you need to give her time. She has to learn. She's only known this world for a couple of weeks and has barely had a glimpse. She doesn't know what this life means for her."

I keep silent, letting him blow his steam until he gives in and leaves. There is no use in arguing with him, not tonight.

"Do you know what she grew up with? Her dad was so involved in the business he paid no mind to his family and drove her mother mad. All she has seen is the business tearing her family apart and them lying to her. Her. Entire. Life. You don't think she'll have questions?"

I lean against the window ledge feeling the cool air radiate from the glass. I raise my glass to my lips and take a small sip of the brown liquid leaving a burn down my throat. I clench the glass tightly to match the sensation in my chest.

"She's pregnant."

Gio purses his lips at my statement. I wait patiently in the silence for the spur of words that will follow. The words that have already played in my head a million and one times since the notion left her lips.

"I know." He must have heard me yelling at her, driving him into the room in the first place. "She was in the kitchen making fried chicken and peanut butter while eating a pickle. Put two and two together until I called her out. I mean I also held her hair back at breakfast as she vomited into the trash. The late-night craving just confirmed my suspicion with a cherry on top."

I raise my brows at him a tad amused at his confession. She didn't do well in hiding, I just didn't notice. Maybe she isn't wrong for questioning me. She isn't worried about who I am but how this world will affect my life with her. What she will get of me. What did I do in return? Threaten her.

"How did I not notice?" I put a hand up covering my face and rubbing my temples in frustration with myself. Gio sighs across the room.

"Why would you, Matteo? You're not exactly the relationship-type guy. You have spent your entire life leading up to taking over the business and running it as your only priority. Dad has never been shy about putting the business first. Mom didn't sit in her library for days on end because she didn't want to be with him. Dad put the business first. He put the *famiglia* above his wife and kids. You were raised not to notice."

"I want to notice. I don't want her to be a mom." Even the thought tears into me like a fierce and unrelenting fire. I want to preserve Gwenevere. I want her pure, light heart to radiate throughout the halls, shunning out any evil that dares to face her. She is my opposite, but she is a drug running in my veins, and I'm an addict craving my next dose of her.

"Then don't let her. Show up and put her first. She's carrying your baby Matteo. Her last pregnancy didn't end with rainbows and sunshine. This one isn't promised to run any differently. If you want this—her, the baby—you need to show her. She won't stay around for anything less than that, Matteo."

I fight my own mind but know Gio is right. A life with Gwenevere would be new to me but you'd have to kill me to let it out of my grasp.

"I fucked up."

Gio lets out a breathy laugh slapping my shoulder roughly.

"You definitely don't qualify for boyfriend of the year."

I scrunch my nose at his label of my relationship with Gwenevere, giving him a glare. I take another sip of the bourbon as the distaste settles in my stomach.

"Boyfriend doesn't sound right."

Gio laughs harder making himself his own glass of burning liquid before leaning against the window where I have been.

"That's because you've never been one. I think it's safe to assume you two are in your 'dating' phase."

I scoff at him, rolling my eyes.

"That will change after this meeting," I say gruffly, loud enough to reach his ears. He toasts his glass towards me, smirking, then sips his drink.

Fiancé. We will have to wed in order for her protection to be placed by the Genovese's. Well, officially speaking. Now that a part of me is living inside of her, the *famiglia* will protect her regardless. However, I don't think that would have been an issue even without it.

The minute Gwenevere lingered at the estate, every soul in sight fell in love with her. They see the light in her that no one is willing to let loose. She belonged here before I knew it myself.

The pregnancy however does not help with the alliance. The only way to keep the Cosa Nostras at peace and not damage her reputation is to marry her. It will be all in or nothing and I am not choosing nothing.

"How do you think Alessio is going to react?" I move to my chair resting back against the leather.

"Not sure. He was furious when she got in the car with me. He was pissed she knew me. I think what got him the most is that we burst his little secret." He sits on the couch diagonal from me, reclining back as well. "She told him she could trust us more than him. Looked like she struck a chord."

I raise my brow in surprise. While I've been purely under the impression Gwenevere was originally here simply to get back at Alessio, I didn't know how strongly she held her trust in us. In me.

Something in me soars at the thought but plummets into fear of losing that trust. I have seen myself only as the bigger evil not knowing I am one of the few people that has ever been truly honest with her. Having fear terrifies me. Fear can and will be my downfall. She will be my downfall. I have foolishly fallen for her and there is no way of denying it.

Alessio seems to be reasonable since he's stepped into the light but we haven't seen him defend her. He held a tight grasp on Gwenevere and I'm not sure how. He's protected her far better than I could expect in this life and yet he did it.

He has managed to keep her hidden from view so well I hadn't known she existed. Sure I'd seen her in pictures when she was a kid. Then she just disappeared. No one knew her name and no one cared to ask, as if her existence was wiped from the earth and she was just an orphan charity girl that had been in their presence.

My issue lies more with Enzo's influence. He won't simply lose interest. I wouldn't in his position. That being said, she cut him off before I was in the picture and now he has no choice but to move on. Though, I would be an even bigger fool if I thought he has.

Could she? I was the rebound. We both knew it and that's what made our rendezvous perfect. Is she able to move on from him? I'm not expecting all her feelings to crumble to the floor, but I can't help but feel this tightness in my chest when I think of their connection.

It infuriates me that he had that with her. That he's touched her and had his fetus inside her where mine now lays. If I could erase his every touch, I would. I would erase all the pain that it caused her leading up to the moment her blue eyes found mine. If only I could do that, I could erase the pain that she's feeling now as she holds fear for the life of our unborn baby.

"What about Enzo?"

Gio's lips tighten as he looks at me. His eyes fill with dread and I grasp at the vision of removing him from this earth.

"Matteo, I'd be lying if I said he isn't going to be an issue in more ways than one."

I contemplate grabbing a handful of my men and solving that issue right now. I wouldn't be solving anything though. Gwenevere would reconcile all her trust in me and in turn, loathe me. I don't think she can forgive me for shooting her first... was it love? Or an idea of love because it was all she ever knew?

How could she have known what she wanted when all she ever had was a single option and one filled with nothing but deceit? She had a whole world of options thrown at her in an instant and she chose me.

"What if he pulls some shit?"

Gio sighs, swooshing his bourbon against the ice in his glass.

"Then we deal with it the best we can. Don't get carried away. The connection he has with Gwen is understandable. It's not like he did something to royally fuck it up." He takes a drink then places his glass on the coffee table and sets his forearms on his knees.

"I wouldn't be worried about if she'd go back to him. Maybe he will try to pull her back but that girl only sees you. She's carrying *your* baby now and she's scared shitless of losing it. She wants the baby, and she wants you."

I take a deep breath and a shot of my drink.

"She asked me to be *famiglia*." I don't look at him like I can hide the emotion bubbling inside me that he is sure to scoop out.

"You thought she wouldn't? After all this, she just wants books, fried chicken and you. She genuinely wants to be here, even with you threatening to send her body to the Luciano estate."

He takes a small crack at me jokingly. He is right though. After this rollercoaster of a month she's experienced, she still wants to be here, and I want her here.

I want her in my kitchen, my bed, my library, my bath. Her on me, me in her, I want her in every way she is willing to give. I want to breathe in Gwenevere. My pull to her is strong and toxic but my addiction to her can't be subdued no matter how hard I try, and I am done trying.

"Matteo, go to sleep. I'll worry about the paperwork. Viktor has everything else ready for the meeting. You just need your head on right."

I contemplate whether I should listen to his advice or not. Deciding I am in fact tired and I need to be leveled-headed for our meeting, I toss the rest of my drink down and nod to Gio. I retreat down the hall finding my room.

The space has now been taken over by Gwenevere. I have myself to blame. I may have gone overboard on the amount of items she needed, but I knew even before the announcement of her pregnancy that she would be staying much longer than a week.

I didn't mind her taking up the space. I've been aching to go back to the room, not to sleep, but to be in her presence. I usually love my quiet nights but lately, they've been filled with Gwenevere's book plots and day-to-day activities.

She gets so excited and rambles for hours. Eventually, she'll get tired and fall asleep. We meet in the shower or tub and then sleep in almost nonexistent clothing, wrapped in each other. When I'm with her I forget who or what I am. The world is just Gwenevere, and I want of nothing more.

I reach the door and enter to see Gwenevere passed out with swollen eyes. Her hands hold her stomach. My heart sinks into my own stomach at how shitty I had been to her.

I shut the door behind me and strip to my boxers, turning the lamps off, and climbing into bed behind her. She relaxes into me while I wrap my hand around her, resting my palm over hers. A strange sensation flows through me and I can't help the small smile that creeps up my face.

She is strong. Probably stronger than she can fathom herself to be. I will talk to Marco in the morning. I need to know what I can do for her and the baby. I can't let her break again. Not only for her but for me. Now that I have them, I don't want to lose either of them.

With that final thought, I sink my head down into her hair pulling her close. I spend the rest of my evening like this with her. This is her home now. It isn't my room, it's ours, and I am not going to let there be any more doubt around any of it.

I blink as my eyes adjust to the soft glowing light seeping into the room from the morning sun. I run a hand down my face, cleaning my eyes. I glance over at Gwenevere. She is still sound asleep. Her face is relaxed and puffed. Her lips stay parted as pieces of her hair fall on her face.

I smile at her beauty. Not only does she hold beauty on the inside but also outwardly. She is my kind of beautiful. Her carrying my baby only intensifies my attraction to her. I can only hope our baby has her beauty and her heart. I fear the day this world's darkness scuffs the light in her. I will try my damndest to prevent it. I want her to be the light to my dark without diminishing her glow.

I sweep out of the bed so as to not disturb her. I fix my hair in the bathroom before picking out a gray suit and dressing. I head to the drawer behind me and grab a belt, pulling it through the loops in the suit.

Today's business is all about the meeting. Everything is set, now is the waiting game until Alessio arrives. Viktor and Gio have pushed me away to relax. Being worked up with my head in papers won't do me any good once we make it to the meeting.

I am more likely not to blow their heads off if I'm in a better state of mind than where I had landed last night. My reaction to Gwenevere proves that.

I leave the bedroom and start my descent down the staircase and into the kitchen. Gio and Viktor sit at the counter reviewing paperwork and sipping coffee. We spend our early morning gathered in the kitchen. Being locked in the office that early in the day is dreadful. Our routine hasn't been thrown off by Gwenevere as she is nowhere near an early riser.

I grab a cup off the rack and fill it with black coffee. I can drink the sweet creams but prefer the rude awakening of bitter black coffee. I lean against the counter and point my view at the men.

"How's it looking?"

While I'm not trying to involve myself too much, I need to know the updates and ensure that everything will run smoothly.

"The extra line of guards will be here in an hour. The meeting itself is the same. Our best bet is to start with the proposal and move from there. If he gets his panties in a twist we have our backup routes." Viktor spits facts as always and continues through his papers. Gio rests back in his chair with a face I know too well. I wave my hand at him to speak his mind.

"Matteo, I think the best thing is to hold off on the baby announcement. If you can, that is. With Enzo strung high and it being their first in face meeting with you, telling them you're taking his sister and that she's already knocked up might set the tension higher then we need. I think the best play is to set out the proposal and see what he takes. If he doesn't and it comes down to it, announce, but I think your odds for peaceful negation with him will go smoother without telling him right now."

I ponder his opposition while sipping my coffee. Viktor seems to agree as well but could care less. I want him to know that she's mine. Regardless of what Alessio thinks or wants, she isn't leaving this estate without me.

"I'm not negotiating anything. She's a Genovese whether he likes it or not." Gio sighs in frustration and Viktor looks up to participate in the conversation.

"Agreed, but we still need to play the cards right. She's not leaving but that doesn't mean an alliance will form. You piss him off enough, he might just start a war with you."

I scoff at him, setting my coffee down.

"Let him start a war, we have twice the manpower and all the cards. Even if he starts a war, Gwenevere is not going anywhere, and he will fall."

Gio's patience dwindles with me but he keeps his cool, glaring at me.

"Again, agreed, but why start a war when we may lose half our men too? What about the *famiglia*?"

I clench my jaw. I know he's right and while I want to demolish everything for her, I still have a *famigila* to run with their best interest in mind.

"I'm going to talk to the doctor," I grumble and pick my coffee up swinging around.

"Congratulations, Matteo." Viktor stands grabbing my hand and pulling me in with a pat on my back. "A baby around here might just be what everyone needs." He smirks at me as I shake my head.

"How is she doing?" Gio's voice travels over. I sigh looking in the direction of our room.

"She seemed well last night."

"You haven't talked to her since the fight?" Gio sighs at my expression. I know I need to talk to her before the meeting but I will wait till she is awake. She needs to rest.

"I will. Let her sleep for now." He nods and I take my leave.

I'm most sure how I feel about the baby. I am happy but I also know this wasn't in anyone's plans, or at least not mine, but I won't deny that Gwenevere's fear of losing the baby puts me on edge. I make my way down the hall, passing the library, and take a left down the corridor before exiting the back.

I stalk through the courtyard leading to the back house that holds some of our staff housing. I step inside and through the hall to the left until I reach three doors down.

I knock roughly and wait only seconds before knocking again. This time the door opens and my knuckle lands on it. The middle-aged Italian man stands half asleep in the doorway. He is dressed but based on the full cup of coffee in his hands and his lack of eagerness, I can tell he hasn't adjusted to the morning.

"Mr. Genovese, is everything okay?" He pauses. I didn't get the chance to speak before his eyes widened.

"Is it the baby? Is Miss Luciano okay?" he stammers out.

"Do you think I would've left her side if she wasn't?"

"Sorry, Mr. Genovese, what can I do for you?"

I scratch the back of my head pondering how I should ask. Marco's face furrows before sighing.

"Matteo, would you like to come inside and talk?"

I nod and Marco moves to the side as I step into his loft.

With Marco being the estate doctor he stays onsite nighty-nine percent of the time. He doesn't have family so the loft is perfect. He has a little clinic inside along with his own amenities. Kitchen, bedroom, bathroom, and living room. It also holds a spare room and a cozy home office. For nonemergency or less severe injuries, Marco takes patients in his home.

He leads me to the kitchen, pouring a cup of coffee and handing it to me.

"Cream?"

I shake my head and he comes back around the counter, motioning for me to sit in the living room. I take a spot on the loveseat and wait as he leaves the room, heading to his office.

A few moments later he appears holding two folders. He hands me on, pointing for me to open it. I skim through the files to find Gwenvere's medical files. I don't quite understand what they were saying but it isn't anything I don't already know.

"She's going to be okay. Some pregnancies just don't stick. It was unfortunate how far she was when losing her previous baby. It doesn't mean she will lose this one. What's important is that you lower the amount of stress she endures and make sure she's making healthy choices. She needs healthy food options and to rest." He hands me the second folder and I skim the pages.

"That is helpful information on what to expect and what to do for her. If you're stressed about the baby, imagine how she feels."

I sigh, rubbing my forehead and stare at the file before glancing over at Marco.

"You had all this just sitting around?"

"I had a feeling once hearing her previous history and well, just knowing you; it would be best to have something on hand." I nod, closing the file and tucking it in my jacket. I hand him the medical records and stand.

"Thank you."

I head out of the loft and back to the main house. On my way back to the office, I catch Mila. She dismisses herself from the maids she's instructing, coming to me.

"Matteo." She waits for my commands as I pull out the file. I pick up the packet on healthy dietary meals and hand it to her.

A smirk forms on her lips as she takes it and glances over the pages with a small glow in her eyes before she closes the packet. She sets it on the counter behind her, smiling at me.

"It's already being oriented in the meals."

I knew this was probably the case. Mila is a mama bear and she looks out for us more than one would think. I should've known having Gwenvere here, and now pregnant, would put her in full force.

"Thank you." I kiss her cheek and turn to walk out of the back room.

"How is she?" By the tone of her voice, I know this is bound to be a scolding. I wince and turn back to her with a smile.

"She's good, resting." Her eyebrow raises letting me know she is in fact not accepting that as my answer, I sigh.

"We had an argument."

She gives me a pointed look.

"I know I messed up, I'll fix it."

"You better. If your mother was here she would've dragged you by your ear to apologize already." I let out a breathy laugh, nodding. She is right. If mom was here I wouldn't have had the chance to mess it up.

She releases me and I finish my ascent to the office. I stop outside the bedroom, it's quiet and I check my watch. It is nine now, she will be waking up soon. I want to be there when she wakes but focusing the last bit of my time on the meeting ahead of us will keep Gwenevere away from the stress of it.

In my office I take a seat behind the desk, running through emails to find one boring email after another I glance at the stack of papers and then out the office window to the side garden where the white detailed gazebo sits.

I can see Gwenevere sitting out there to read, she would love the space. She spends most of her time in the library. Fresh air would be good for her. Mother had loved the gazebo and her afternoons consisted of lounging across the grass.

The gazebo is surrounded by the grass with no path. I will need to change that for when the baby is here and we need an easy path to it. I laugh under my breath to myself.

I'm planning landscape modifications for a baby. My baby. I shake my head going to the computer and pulling the proposal for tonight's meeting up. While Alessio doesn't get a say in whether she stays or not anymore, I needed to play the negotiations right to protect the *famiglia* and not instigate war.

A knock sounds at the door, stopping my train of thought.

"Come in."

The door opens and Gio moves in. He leans against the frame with his arms crossed.

"Can I help you?"

"Gwen refused breakfast. She doesn't look well either. Though you would know that because you talked to her today, right?" I hop out of my chair and move around the desk.

"What do you mean she doesn't look well?"

He scoffs, shaking his head at me. I glare at him, warning him to refrain from his unsolicited advice right now.

"Why don't you go ask her yourself?"

I glance to the hall, I should've talked to her already. I know that I don't know what to say, but I want to make things right.

"Matteo, she is going through enough right now. She at least needs you at her side." He gives me a tight grin, swooshing off the frame and to his office. I sigh, following out to the bedroom.

I don't bother to knock, finding the lights off. The only light being the glow flowing from behind the black curtains. I don't see Gwenevere but a lump of blankets covering her.

The clock on the wall reads noon and the time is ticking until the meeting. Yet she still lays under the covers. I rest on her side, pulling the covers enough to see her face. She scrunches her eyes together and her hands hold the sides of her head in the fetal position.

Her eyes squint open before scrunching closed again. My brows furrow and my chest clutches

"Gwenevere?" I speak just above a whisper so as to not bother her more.

"Mmmhm,"s groans out, keeping her eyes shut.

"*Bella*, what's wrong?" My voice comes out soft and hopefully soothing. She doesn't answer right away so I push a little further.

"Do you want me to get Marco?" She rustles and opens her eyes with a sigh lowering her hands.

"Migraine." She winces at the loudness of her own voice. I almost forgot about her migraines. She's had headaches here and there over the week but nothing strong like the times before.

"Do you want me to see if he can get you anything?" She nods and I ring up Marco. The phone rings once and the line picks up.

"Mr. Genovese?"

"Marco, Gwenevere has a migraine, can you bring something to the room that will help?"

"Of course, I'll be right there."

I click the phone off and push the hair from Gwenevere's face. Her once-scrunched features are now relaxed. I step into the bathroom turning the tub on. I light a few candles and toss a handful of lavender in.

I return to Gwenevere and remove the blankets fully.

"Gwenevere, come take a bath." She hums and follows me. She smiles sweetly, trying to take off her clothes. She stumbles when she makes it to her pants. I catch her arm to stabilize her then help her in the water.

She closes her eyes as she sinks into the water and I hear a knock at the bedroom door. I open to see Marco holding a bottle of medicine and a couple of oils.

"This should help. If the pain gets unbearable or doesn't go away soon, bring her to the clinic."

"Thank you." I take the items from him and close the door. I grab a water bottle from the cabinet and return to the bath. I read the bottle and pop the right amount of pills into my hand before handing the pair to her.

"Here, *Bella,* take this." She opens her palm and scoops the pills in her mouth.

"Why do you call me that?" Her voice is quiet but sweet. I can't help but touch her with gentle strokes along her cheek.

"Bella?"

She hums and I lift her chin to me, her puffy eyes straining.

"Because you are beautiful. I don't want you to forget that."

She smiles, her beauty only shining brighter. The words I couldn't seem to find all morning are now front in center in my mind.

"I didn't mean what I said last night. I'm not used to this." I motion between us with a sigh.

"I'm not used to your life either." A small smile plays on my lips with a light chuckle.

"Voglio imparare per te." I want to learn for you.

She matches my smile through tired eyes. She relaxes under the water while I continue massaging her head.

"You should rest, don't worry about the meeting."

Her eyes snap open.

"No. I need to be there. I'll be fine."

"Gwenevere, you can barely—"

"I said no. I'm going, Matteo."

I pinch the bridge of my nose. Trying to keep my calm with her. She needs the least amount of stress possible and going into that meeting is doing the opposite.

"Gwenevere, will you jus—"

"Matteo."

I glare at her for interrupting again, sliding my hand down to grab her chin.

"You need to rest," my voice rumbles low.

"And I said I'm fine."

"No, you're not." She huffs out a laugh raising her brows to me.

"Or what?" I grip her throat with enough ease not to hurt her or restrain her breathing. Lowering my lips to her ear.

"Or I will drag your ass back to this room and remind you who is in charge." Her face lights up as her lips part with a gasp. I let go and move to the doorway.

"Rest, Gwenevere." With that I leave to prepare myself for the night ahead.

21

Gwenevere

My migraine eases after a few hours but refuses to fully leave. That doesn't matter though as I dress myself in comfy leggings and a T-shirt. I didn't bother with my hair, an updo will only heighten my migraine.

Matteo warned me, well more like ordered me not to come to the meeting. What he doesn't realize is that I don't care what he has to say on the matter. This meeting is about me. I am the middle ground and the only one to keep their hardheaded sides at bay.

I'm not in the best of conditions to do so with my head throbbing beyond belief but this is far more important than my regularly scheduled migraine. I check the time, I am late but I will be there.

Gio had shown me the meeting room previously so I follow the path from my memory and end up down a hallway that's parallel to the one that holds the library. I come close to the open door when I hear voices. I listen in and see where the men are at.

"You really think I'm going to hand her off to you?" Alessio's voice scoffs. I could only imagine Matteo's face right now.

"I don't see a reason not to. This arrangement benefits both the *famiglias* and keeps her safe. She'd be both a Genovese and Luciano. All while serving for the alliance in the Costa Nostra." Matteo's tone is throaty, his voice can capture the attention of anyone in the room and make them question their own thoughts.

"Who says she wants to be a Genovese?" Enzo's voice shoots through the room and chairs screech. That is my cue.

I push the door open drawing all attention to me as I wince from the bright light. Alessio flies to my side, grabbing my face and looking over me like a mother hen.

"What did that bastard do to you?" he growls out, scrunching his face at my attire.

"He didn't *do* anything and for fucks sake lower your voice. I have a damn migraine." I push Alessio back a little. Enzo moves behind him, eyes searching mine. At first, his face laces with worry until he takes me in and makes eye contact. Something flashes in his eyes before becoming a blank slate.

I clench my jaw and move past Alessio and onto the Genovese side of the conference table. Looking at Matteo my stomach drops. His eyes shoot daggers into me, making me almost regret my decision to come. Almost.

To the side I see Gio smirking, shaking his head. Viktor sits on the other side of Gio, sending me a small smile.

I look back to Alessio who is failing miserably at hiding how pissed off he is. I slouch into the chair, rolling my eyes and motioning for them to continue. No one moves and the room stays silent. I sigh, glancing around the room at all the men with astonishment at the current ratio of heads up one's ass.

"Listen, I'm sure none of us wants to do this all night and my head is absolutely killing me. Where are we at?"

Gio clears his throat while Matteo's glare stays present on me.

"We presented a wedding proposal that creates an alliance between the *familgilas*. Alessio isn't fond of it." When Gio finishes, Alessio scoffs.

"Fond? I'm more than not *fond of it;* it's not happening." His voice comes out bewildered as he stares down Gio. Viktor leans forward to talk.

"It's a great proposal with both parties in mind, and everyone wins."

"Everyone wins? Gwenevere would be in your hands!" Alessio throws his hand out with his insult.

"Alessio, the proposal is good. Take it."

He follows suit with Matteo's glare giving me a similar one. From across the table, I can see the furry rising in him. He's losing his patience and things are going to escalate. I give him a pointed look in return, warning him to back down.

"Are you looking to start a war?"

"I'd prefer not to," Matteo reiterates.

"Gwen, be reasonable, you barely know this man." Enzo gestures to Matteo. "You're not thinking straight. You won't be happy here."

Matteo's fists clench and I can feel the shift of anger in him as well. I place my hand on my side, touching the outer side of his thigh. I hope the little bit of contact offers some relief.

"I know him enough. You don't get a say in this."

"The fuck I don't. You can't possibly love him." Enzo's voice seethes to me but he stares at Matteo with heated fury. Matteo's jaw ticks as he bites his tongue.

"But you love me, right? Is that what you're saying? Go ahead and say what you really mean."

The coldness sweeps through the room upon the words leaving my mouth. Alessio's brows furrow, lost at my change of direction. I hold as much information over Enzo as he does me. But if we are telling the truth, the truth is

Enzo doesn't know what I want, he can't when I've only had the chance to find

out myself after escaping from under their thumbs.

"Gwen." Enzo shoots a warning, glancing at Alessio before snapping

back. He mouths out, *don't.* That's the thing, I'm not backing down on behalf

of him anymore. I will do what I need to for me. If he wants to drag this out, so

be it.

"Don't '*Gwen*' me."

"Let's just review the proposal one more time and discuss it. I am sure

we can come to some kind of agreement." Gio's voice slides over to smooth

the growing tension. An attempt to close the lid on the can of worms I am

about to release. Matteo's gaze leaves me and lands on Enzo this time. The two

lock eyes.

"I'm done negotiating. Gwen stays. That's it." No sign of emotion lies

in Matteo's voice making my skin prick. He is pissed and his command does

anything but de-escalate the situation.

"Gwen is not staying. She is a Luciano. She is under our protection

and doesn't belong around whore hungry men. You don't get to mess around

with her until she's no longer fun to play with and you discard her. All you

Genovese are cold-blooded and I can't trust you with her." This time Matteo laughs. Not a good one though. The kind that reminds you of when the maniacal serial killer breaks out into a crazed laugh after murdering the town's local village.

"You don't trust me? What about your second who thinks he's in love with her?" This time my heart skips. My palms become sweaty as I watch the scene unfold. Enzo jumps back up, Matteo meeting his movements.

"You can't honestly be serious about this!" Enzo yells at me. "You will never be happy. You won't ever be able to."

"Why not Enzo? Why won't I be happy!"

"Can't you see all he wants to do is fuck you? All for his fucking ego." I scoff glancing to Matteo; my face reddening before bringing my gaze to Enzo. His face swirls in realization.

"Oh my God, you already fucked him!" Enzo yells at me.

"What if I did?" I yell back.

"Are you fucking serious Gwen? Was all of it nothing to you? How can you be such a fucking whore!"

"A whore? I fuck you and move on and you call me a whore!" My mind can't move fast enough as I watch Enzo's head fly to the side. Alessio lowers his fist shaking out his hand.

"Alessio!" I yell at him.

"You fucking slept with my sister?" His voice is leveled and scarier than usual.

"Alessio, I can explain later I—" Enzo attempts to stammer out.

"Explain what? Explain how you accidentally slid your dick inside her? Jesus, Enzo."

"It wasn't like that, Alessio. I love—" he tries to speak but is cut off again.

"I swear to fucking God if you finish that sentence—" Alessio stills, his eyes move between Enzo and I, dropping in seconds. He takes a step back resting his hands on the back of his chair. "When."

No one answers and my heart throbs. Enzo fixates on me, all our suffering lurking in his eyes. Alessio knows.

"Gwenevere." My chest pounds as a sickening feeling pools in my stomach.

"Over the fall," Enzo answers for me. Alessio drops his head, sighing out heavily. I can't move and part of me wants to stop breathing as Alessio raises his head, making eye contact with me. My eyes water and my chest caves in.

"Enzo was the father." A tear slips down, followed by another. No one bothers to move as I sit there in my own pile of agony. My lips quiver and I swipe my face.

"It doesn't matter anymore. What matters is this alliance so can you please sit down." I motion to the table.

"I think we need some time to talk, Gwenevere." His voice is cold, but there are cracks in his cover that show bits of pain and betrayal.

All this time I've been mad at Alessio for betraying me when I have done the same to him. I slept with his best friend, behind his back, lost a baby, and never told him. I can see the sting pass behind his stone mask.

"Alessio. You need to accept this proposal."

"Gwenevere, we need to discuss this."

"I'm pregnant."

"You fucking son of a bitch!" The room breaks into chaos starting with Enzo flying over the table at Matteo, fists fly and soon enough Gio and Alessio join. Viktor tries to split up the mess but his attempts are void.

"Alessio! Matteo! Enzo! Gio!" I try yelling at them but no one skips a beat. My head pounds harder and my emotions are strung high. I slide my hand under the table and grip the gun latched to the bottom. I climb onto the table take a deep breath, switch the safety off and point the gun to the ceiling.

I shoot the ceiling twice sending loud bangs through the room. The commotion stops and everyone turns to me. Matteo comes to my feet at the table, glowering at me.

"All of you sit the fuck down," I seethe through gritted teeth. No one moves, irritating me further.

"Sit the fuck down!" I snap the men out of their daze and they retreat to their seats. I step to Matteo and he helps me off the table, trying to hide a small smirk.

"Now that everyone is listening. We are signing the damn proposal, today. Regardless of my current condition, I want this alliance. This is my choice. Gio is my friend as well as Matteo." Scoffs flock from the Luciano side and I rest the gun on the table in front of me. Both men stiffen and I clear my throat

"As I was saying. The Genoveses are family. This pregnancy just confirms where I need to be. I don't care how you feel, Matteo is the father and I need to be here." As I finish, my stomach flips. It takes me all but seconds to realize it's not from the anxiety of the meeting when I throw myself to the side, grabbing the trash bin.

I empty the couple of crackers and pills I managed to get down today. A hand removes my hair from my face while another rubs my back. I dry heave it into the bin until my body can no longer take it.

"Are you okay?" Matteo's voice is soothing but I don't answer only plopping down to catch my breath.

"You should've stayed in the room." I glare at him and he sighs. He grabs his handkerchief and hands it to me to wipe my face.

"You need to go back and lie down." I shake my head, pushing myself up. He assists me holding my elbow.

"I'm okay now. Let's finish this and I will lay in bed the rest of the week. Okay?" Matteo's hesitant but nods, leading me to the chairs. Enzo's jaw clenches matching his fist.

"You have to contact me at least once a week and you don't get to shut me out." Alessio glances between Matteo and me. My jaw grows slack before I slam it shut. Enzo leers to the side, blazing.

"I can do that."

"And I get to be there when the baby is born."

I laugh this time.

"That's obvious, just not in the room."

Alessio scrunches his face but accepts. He turns to Matteo with a disheveled sigh.

"You better not fuck this up. You even look in her direction with the thought of hurting her."

"I wouldn't dream of hurting her."

"Be lucky I'm not starting a war."

"I would start a thousand wars for her." Matteo's confession changes the gurgling in my stomach into sweet flutters.

"Very well. We will hash out the details of the alliance later. I need to talk to Gwenevere." Matteo eyes Enzo and Alessio nods. "Alone."

Matteo tilts his head and everyone disperses from the room except Alessio and I.

"I'm sorry."

Out of everything that just happened, Alessio is apologizing to me. I stare at him trying to understand.

"I'm sorry, I shut you out. Maybe in a way that made you feel like you had to hide all of this." He glances to the door taking in a deep breath.

"I wish you would've told me. I would've been there for you, but I understand why you didn't. Don't hide from me this time. I want to be there for you whether or not Matteo's a part of it. I'm not sure what exactly is happening between you two, but I can see he cares for you."

I smile through my tears, that's all I want. I want to share everything I can with Alessio and still have this life I've ventured into. I haven't known the Genovese's long but I know I am not ready to let them go. The baby brewing inside me puts a stamp on us being a family. The thought of leaving sounds impossible.

I throw myself into his arms, letting my tears fall.

"You can always come home, Gwen, but for your sake, I hope this works the way you hope." He pulls back, moving the hair out of my face.

"How are you really?"

"Sick. It's taking everything out of me. Matteo's trying though. Everyone has to eat the overly healthy meals the doctor listed, Gio's not as big of a fan of that." I laugh, holding my stomach instinctively. Alessio follows my hand down with an unreadable expression.

"I love you, Gwen." My tears come back with a quiver of my bottom lip.

"I love you, Alessio." I go in for another hug as he holds my head to him. We stand there for a while not wanting to let go. Eventually, Alessio peels away with a soft smile.

"I better head out before Enzo starts some shit." I give a tight grin at the mention of Enzo.

"I'm sorry, Alessio. I should've told you sooner. You should've known. We wanted to wait until you were home but it was too late and everything just fell apart. I had loved him. All I see when I look at him is lies and heartbreak. I see what could have been, not what's going to be. Being here, with Matteo, it just feels right, Alessio. I can't explain it, but I need you to know I'm not doing this to hurt anyone."

Alessio's Adam's apple bobs. He kisses my forehead and holds me there.

"Right now you need to be here. I'll deal with Enzo, just promise me you'll keep me in the loop."

"I promise." He kisses my forehead again and leaves the room. I slouch onto the chair burying my head. My tears flow hard as both weights are lifted, yet my chest crashes in one big swoop. Alessio found out about Enzo and me while handing me over to Matteo.

A little over a month ago I was curled up battling through the heartbreak in hiding. Now I'm on the other side of the city, wrapped up in a mafia king with his baby on the way.

The stress of the days leading up to this moment, crash away like waves fleeing from the cliffs. I sob harder, my body clenching. I feel hands on either side of me and I look up to see Matteo. His eyes search mine. He swoops me into his arms and sits with me on his lap.

My tears die down after some time. His musky vanilla scent fills my senses with ease. I lay my head on his chest feeling the beat of his heart vibrate.

"Don't let me go."

"Non me lo sognerei" Wouldn't dream of it.

I love when he speaks in our native tongue. It brings sweet memories and remind me that I can be exactly myself and be understood. I love that in the world of darkness Matteo lives in, he still cares for me.

My stomach rumbles out with the need for food. Matteo chuckles lightly moving to capture my eyes.

"Are you hungry?" I bite my lip nodding. My stomach rumbles again and I get a little wave of nausea. I'm pretty sure that is the baby's way of telling me to get the hell up and eat.

"Actually, starving."

"We can't have that." He sets me down gently. We head down the corridor making our way to the kitchen. The delicious aromas of fried chicken flow through the living space. My legs carry me swiftly as I it towards the food.

Matteo grumbles behind me but I ignore him spotting Mila finishing up in the dining room, humming away. She is like having a warm and inviting mother around. I turn to see Gio and Viktor at the table chatting away.

"This is definitely not on the approved menu," Matteo's grumbles behind me. I roll my eyes at his notion and Gio stands to the rescue.

"It's not, but it is one of our sweet girl's pregnancy cravings and after the day she had, I think we can make an exception."

Matteo glares at Gio before waving him off. I squeal and flop into the seat at the table, waiting very impatiently for dinner to be served. Gio grabs the peanut butter from the cupboard and a spoon placing them in front of me.

Viktor looks at me with a scrunched nose. Matteo sets the jar of pickles down next and I waste no time drenching the pickles in peanut butter.

"That looks absolutely disgusting," Viktor finally speaks up, eyeing my creation. I butter up my next pickle, bringing it to my lips and take a bite.

"Don't knock it till you try it." I wipe the peanut butter from my lips.

"Go on, Viktor, why don't you take a bite?" Gio teases him with a playful glint in his eyes.

"Fuck that," Viktor retorts. This time I get in on the teasing.

"Come one you might like it." I lather up a pickle pushing it to Viktor.

"Who knows maybe the baby is onto something."

Viktor glares at Matteo and I give him the biggest puppy eyes I can until he sighs.

"Okay fine, one bite." Viktor takes the pickle from me and stares at it as if he were eating an insect, then takes a small bite. He shoots out of his chair spitting the remnants into the trash.

"Oh my God, how are you enjoying that?" He wipes his tongue on one of the towels nearby, earning a swat from Mila as she enters the room. He gives an apologetic smile and Matteo and Gio belly over in laughter. Viktor grabs a bottle of bourbon, pouring himself a shot and dosing it back. I take another big bite of my pickle, shaking my head.

"You are such a baby."

Viktor glares at Matteo and we all break out into a chorus of laughter.

22

Gwenevere

I lay across the padded nook in the library, gazing out to the garden. The maids have been working on it all day. I'm not the best gardener. In fact, the longest I've kept a plant alive was a year. It was a succulent.

That being said, I love digging my hands into the soil and connecting myself outside of the regular city ways. I place my book down, marking my spot in the process. I go down the short steps in the library and find my way out the back door.

I take a deep breath in. I love the smell of the flowers Matteo had ordered. Although I highly doubted he actually did it. I patter over to Mila and Alice who hold big smiles upon my arrival.

"Gwenevere, hun, how are you?" Mila steps away from her spot covered in dirt. She places her wrist on my shoulder giving me a kiss on each cheek.

"How's our sweet little baby?" She looks at my belly which is nothing but bloat at this point.

"Our sweet little baby is making my stomach be anything but sweet." I try to keep positive around Matteo. I can tell he's still worried even after Marco assured him, and me, the chances of losing this baby are not high.

Even though I want to believe him, I still carry dread in my bones. I want this to run smoothly. Matteo's eyes light up every time the baby is mentioned and Mila is already making arrangements.

She says and I quote, 'It's never too much when a baby is involved,' I don't disagree, I am just scared of all the sudden movements, as if we will jinx it.

"Would you like for me to make you some of my ginger tea?"

"Oh, you're busy Mila don't worry about it."

"Nonsense, it will only take me a moment." She waves me off removing her apron and gardening gloves. She bustles away to the house as I shake my head in adoration. I wished my mother had been like Mila. My mother doesn't even know about the baby and frankly, I want to keep it that way, for a while.

I know how disapproving she'd be and honestly, I'm not prepared for her dismay. I also don't want her to be involved. It's not like she's genuinely interested anyway.

"Mind if I help?" I turn to Alice who raises her brows.

"You know how to garden?"

I shake my head with pursed lips.

"No idea, but I love to play in the soil and pretend I know what I'm doing."

She grins passing me a handheld shovel.

"Have at it." She gestures to an open place of dirt. A few of the flowers sit next to the garden ready to be placed in the ground. I find a comfortable position on the brick path and get to work pushing the dirt around.

The weather is perfect for once and I enjoy the sun on my skin. With my nausea, I've been kept in my room or the library trying to keep my head out of the bin. It has been a month since the fiasco with Alessio. Sure enough, he calls at the minimum once a week. I've avoided the house though. From what I've gathered Enzo isn't taking the news very well.

I don't exactly blame him. In fact, I don't blame him at all. His heart has been shattered and I dug my heel in twisting the pieces further apart. I felt ruthless and all the while enraged.

Enzo had every right to be mad but not to call me a whore. It revolted me that a man who I'd loved, and loved me back, could stoop so low. It wasn't as if we were happily together and I tore our relationship apart with this thing between Matteo and I.

We were moving on; I was moving on. Just because he didn't want to accept that doesn't mean he gets to rip me apart on his way out. As if he'd ever be fully out. I could hide here all I wanted, but Alessio was home. I'd have to eventually move my things. Mostly, I can't not visit Alessio. He is my brother.

I refused to let a stupid guy hinder my bond any further with him. Even if it is his second in command. Fate really screwed me on this one.

I frustratingly beat the soil making room for the flowers. I am mad at how everything has played out. It doesn't mean I'm not happy where I'm at now, but things may be easier and less stressful if everything had gone as I had hoped.

Sleeping around and having some fun till I met the guy of my dreams who wouldn't hide our relationship from Alessio was all I wanted. I can't say I didn't find that man. Matteo is not shy with Alessio. Though, this isn't exactly what I had in mind.

Shoving the dirt more, I let out timid breaths. I feel a hand on my shoulder and Alice looks at me with a smirk.

"I think you beat the soil enough. If any of these men just saw what I did they'd either be terrified or want to hire you." She puts a hand out to me to help me up. I sigh, patting my hands off my pants, and take hers.

I follow her to the bench. My body already aching from what little work I've done, but I'm not ready to let Alice know that. I don't want more special treatment than what Matteo has already enforced.

"What's going on?" She leans against the bench.

"Nothing." I pull on a smile not really wanting to go on about the same thing I have for over a month.

"Look, Gwen, I know not all of this is ideal but you'll learn to love it. Hell, I could learn to love it just by going to the library." I laugh with her through breaths.

"I just didn't expect this, ya know? It's not that I don't like it here, in fact, it's grown on me enough to say I love it here." I pause looking at my hand between my knees.

"I miss Alessio."

She hugs me from the side, resting her head on my shoulder and I lay my head on hers.

"And what about Enzo?" I sigh and she lifts her head to give me a small smile.

"I miss him in ways I can't describe but I'm angry. It's different with him. Enzo and Matteo have many things in common yet so many things are different at the same time. I wish there was a different storyline."

"I don't think you'd be here if there were."

Her words strike me with assurance.

"You're probably right."

We see Mila strolling down the path with a tray in hand. She hands me a glass and I take a small sip.

"Thank you, Mila." She smiles at me warmly as if she is a sun ray herself.

"Of course dear." I peer behind her and Matteo stands in the doorway watching me. I send a quick goodbye to the girls. As I approach, he steps out of the door frame letting me in. I follow him through the house until we reach the stairwell where he stops.

"How are you feeling?"

"Good." He examines my hands covered in dirt as well as my pants. His lips curl lightly.

"You like to garden?" I shrug my shoulders leaning against the railing.

"A little, I'm terrible at it though."

A low chuckle comes from him, I mix of woozy eagerness fills me at the sound.

"You can't be that bad."

"I've killed every plant I've owned. I'm a plant murderer."

"You really are a Luciano." My stomach curls. I know what that implies but for a second I was happy to have forgotten that my brother is a skilled killer.

"Right." I drop my eyes and rub my finger along the stem of my mug. Matteo clears his throat drawing my eyes back up.

"Go get cleaned up. We leave in ten."

"Where are we going?" I push off the rail in interest.

"It's a surprise."

I groan, giving him a glare only to receive a pointed one in return.

"I think I've had enough surprises for a lifetime," I bargain.

"I think you'll survive. Nine minutes now." He taps his watch and turns away. I whip around and head up the stairs to get cleaned up.

In the bedroom, I find a dress sitting out for me. It is a cocktail type dress. A little bit on the fancy side with a long V-neck. Small strings cross elegantly in the back.

I turn the shower on and strip, jumping in to rid myself of the dirt coating my body. I wet my hair enough to detangle and turn off the water. Getting out of the shower I pat my hair dry and wrap my body in a towel.

I throw some cream in my hair and pull it in a ponytail knowing I'll regret it later but not having much choice. I put a small layer of mascara on and walk back into the room. Deciding the neckline is too low for a bra, I ditch one altogether.

I throw on a pair of black lace underwear that go with the dress before sliding it over my head. The dress clings to my lack of curves perfectly making the illusion that I have some. My cleavage shows more than I would insist on but I don't hate it.

I strap on simple black heels and lay on the chest at the end of the bed. There's a knock at the door but I don't bother to look up.

"One minute, Gwenevere." Matteo's voice seeps through the door. I roll my eyes at his impatience. I wonder where we are going. I'm not dressed casually but also not super fancy. Matteo doesn't usually mind my relaxed attire when going out. We never really go anywhere besides the coffee shop, diner, and 'errands' that Gio drags us on random shopping sprees.

I stand up straightening my outfit out. My stomach sways and I grab my phone. I make my way down the empty hallway to the staircase. Matteo leans against the post at the bottom of the stairs on his phone.

He wears a new, and what looks to be a nicer, suit. One that doesn't do much to hide his sharpened muscles that lie beneath. I descend the stairs, heels clicking on the tiled steps. Matteo's head lifts, scanning me.

"Fuck me."

His eyes drink me in, halting my movements. The tension rising forces me to straighten my shoulders. His jaw clenches as he pushes off the rail and crosses the last bit of distance on the stairs to me.

"Do you like it?" I look down, averting my gaze from his darkened ones.

"I fucking love it." His hand travels down the length of the dress. "I won't be the only one with eyes on you."

"I can find a different dress…"

"Let them look. You'll be on my arm and I will be more than welcome to show them who you belong to." He smirks, putting a hand around my waist and dipping his head down to my ear.

"Sei bellissima" You look beautiful. I blush hiding my face into his shoulder. He raises his head again holding my chin.

"You ready?" His deep blue eyes entrap me and I bite my lip nodding to him.

"Don't make me remind you." My brows furrow; remind me? Remind me of what? He draws his thumb to my bottom lip tugging it down before releasing it.

"Don't bite your lip or I'll remind you how to listen." My face heats and his hand drops, catching my hand in the process. I accompany him down the stairs meeting the other two. Gio smirks as we land at the end of the staircase.

"That blush on your face complements the dress well." I smack his chest, and Matteo shakes his head continuing out the door.

We all climb into the back of a stretched Cadillac. Bruno sets us on our journey and I glance around at all the men. Their suits all seem dressier than usual. Knowing I won't get much of an answer as to where we are going I pull my phone out texting Sole.

I haven't had the chance to talk with her about the baby. She will kill me for not telling her already but I've been so caught up with the whole mafia proposal and everything else in between. I send her a message to meet for coffee soon and I can utterly blow her mind with the latest news.

I place my phone on my lap and mess with the fabric holding my chest together. I would be lying if I said I am not afraid to flash someone. Whoever picked out this dress either wanted to see my tits or didn't realize how low this dress would lay on me.

I hear a throat clear and look up midadjustment to see Gio grinning with amusement. To the side, Matteo studies my chest before reaching my eyes again.

His features are primal and not at all as upscale as he is dressed. He pulls at the tie around his neck and I want to remove the tie together.

We pull into a rather large hotel and by large I mean massive. The walls are lined with well-kept vines and beautiful flowers throughout, and a grand entrance with its stone staircase further romanticizes the building before me.

The vehicle pulls to the front valet where Matteo steps out and straightens his suit jacket. I lick my lips as he swivels to me, placing a handout.

I attempt to leave the car gracefully but to my dismay, I do anything but that. I stumble trying to catch my balance in the rather tall heels. I was clumpy before but somehow being all but two months pregnant has taken my balance completely.

Matteo's arm catches my waist, hoisting me up against him. I peek to him with a sheepish smile only to be met with his eyes staring deeply into me.

"Thank you." My voice comes out breathlessly as I try to recover and reposition my weight on my heels.

"I told you never to thank me for taking care of you." My heart quickens and I meet his gaze. I hold onto his arms losing track of time and my surroundings.

"I don't want to be rude." His lips quirk up in a smile and he leans down against my neck kissing below my ear and wracking shivers through my body.

"You can be as rude as you want, as long as you can accept the punishment." My stomach knots and heat pools below. He pulls his face back to look at me with a glimpse of a smirk.

Viktor clears his throat to the side, snapping us both back into reality and reminding me we are surrounded by people flowing into the hotel. Gio chuckles, slapping Matteo on the shoulder.

"Oh, this is going to be one hell of a night."

Everyone is very dressed up; the women are decked in beautiful gowns and jewelry, and the men in full suit attire.

"What are we doing tonight?" I keep my eyes on the crowd feeling slightly naked with the lack of jewelry. I didn't think to put anything on. I honestly wasn't expecting a group outing to a high-end event.

"Why a ball of course."

23

Gwenevere

Gio's words induce my jaw to drop, snapping my head back to the men. A ball?

"You mean to tell me you gave me no warning to put on some makeup or do my hair or even put on some jewelry to go to a ball!" I try to slick my hair back but know it won't make a difference until I make it to a sink with water. My anxiety picks up and I would give anything to have a drink right now. Instead, I am as sober as I can possibly be and suddenly very nauseous.

"You looked fine to me."

Fine! 'I looked fine for a ball?' I Growl.

"Matteo. This isn't 'fine.' I'm a mess and I'm going to be surrounded by rich snobby bitches all night where I will be the talk because I had the audacity to look like a homeless person at a BALL."

Gio doubles over in laughter and Viktor watches on in slight amusement. I glare between them before turning it on Matteo. I groan again

390

and glance at the dimly lit sky. The sun is setting at this point. He steps closer to me and lowers his voice.

"Put on a pretty smile and act like a lady." I scoff and roll my eyes.

"A lady? You know I'm Luciano right?" My glare at him heats as I send my silent threat.

"Not for long."

"I will always be a Luciano." I step around him not making it past his shoulder as he grabs above my elbow. I stop with slight resistance, not daring to look at him. His voice travels down to me.

"You'd do real well to listen tonight." My eyes glide up to meet his.

"You'd do real well to remember who I am." He puffs out a laugh looking to the parking lot momentarily and swiping his chin.

"*Bellá*, you don't know *who* I am. Don't test me."

The tension rises higher but I'm not willing to back down quite yet, both annoyed and thrilled.

"Or what?"

He stares at me, jaw clenched but not uttering a word back. The silence leaves me more on edge than any threatening words. I lick my dry lips again and swallow.

Matteo turns wrapping my hand around his lower arm and we keep moving.

"You're playing with fire, *Princepessa.*"

I keep quiet as we make it to the glass doors. Two men dressed in work attire stand at either side of the doors. Both nod briefly to Matteo. We head into the large lobby where a massive chandelier dangles above our heads, capturing my attention. There must be a million crystals in the bottom layer alone.

"Gwenevere." My eyes lower to Matteo, still in a bit of a daze from the astonishing surroundings. We stare at each other for a lapse in time before my trance is broken.

"I think we'd all prefer if you two stared at each other once we actually got to our destination." Gio's words slice between us.

Matteo straightens and I drop my eyes. He guides us down the hall until we reach an elevator. It is secluded and private.

Matteo pulls his arm forward, allowing me to step in first. The three men joined me and we stand in silence. We head up two floors when the elevator dings. I step out first, immediately being pulled into Matteo's side.

"Stay by me, we're making a quick stop before heading up." I nod holding on to his arm as he leads me through a wide Casino room. Bright lights flash through the room with loud chatter. My head throbs with the mix and my already tense head from my hair.

I push the pain aside and focus ahead. A large bar with a black glass countertop sits in the middle of the floor. A beautifully lit back bar holds medium to high-end liquors that look dreamy. Matteo chats to the bartender as I scan the crowd.

"Gwenevere, would you like some water?"

I'm not in a water mood and if I want to keep my head on I need something with sugar.

"Can I have orange juice?"

"Orange Juice? I don't think the bar has it but maybe the café?" Matteo raises his brow.

I look to the bartender who's preparing the men's drinks.

"Can I get a virgin Madras, easy with the cranberries?" The man nods, placing the bourbons on the counter and heading back to the coolers. Matteo turns to me, lips raised into an amused smirk.

"Bars are always stored with juice. Not everyone drinks hard liquor."

Matteo shakes his head, taking a sip from his glass. A few seconds later the man sets down my glass and I take a sip in bliss.

"Ah, Matteo, how are you?" A new voice emerges from behind me.

"Never better." I turn to see an older gentleman.

"And who might this younger lady be?" The gentleman turns to me with a curious smile. Matteo wraps an arm around my waist pulling me in.

"This is my fiancé, Gwenevere." The man's brows shoot up, his lips turning into a wide smile.

"*Fiancé.* I never thought I'd see the day Matteo Genovese is engaged." The man lifts a hand to me and I hesitantly take it.

"How rude of me, I didn't introduce myself. I'm Alonzo." Matteo's head lowers to my ear.

"He's *famiglia.*" I nod in understanding and reach my hand out to Alonzo's extended one. He lifts my hand gently to his mouth kissing it. A simple gesture to some.

"Welcome."

I smile sweetly at him. My head is still spinning from my surroundings but I manage to keep an even composure. He lowers my hand before dropping it all together and standing up straight.

"Matteo." Alonzo gives a brief nod before sending one last smile and turning away. My face relaxes as I lean against the bar rubbing my temple.

"What's wrong?" I look up to him, concern etched in the wrinkles of his forehead that you'd only notice if you look close enough.

"Just a little headache, the machines are loud and flashy."

He puts his arm out for me and I wrap my hand around it once again following him.

"Come on."

We backtrack through the casino to the private elevator. The fancy metal box dings and the doors open to a beautiful rooftop filled with high-class men and women indulging in conversation and drinks.

Instead of concrete, the roof is covered in large white tiles. A few marble tables line the open floor with a small bar to the side. Lights shine all around, bouncing off the glass railing. I glance over the edge to the city.

It is gorgeous. The city is lit up and the view is far. I've never seen the city like this. I am always the one looking up and never the one looking down. In Matteo's world, I'd feel like I am on top. Right now I practically am.

"Do you like the view?" Matteo's voice draws my attention.

"Like? Matteo, this place is beautiful." He smiles briefly. A boy dressed in waiter attire walks to us with a tray of champagne.

"Would you like a drink?" I shake my head and Matteo's voice comes out gruff.

"No, do not offer her alcohol again tonight."

I roll my eyes, giving Matteo a playful yet pointed look.

"You didn't have to be so rude." He looks over the crowd, assessing the room.

"I wasn't, I was simply giving orders."

"You could have said please." This time he turns to me with a pointed look. I look past Matteo spotting Gio and Viktor across the room talking to some men. I gesture there, drawing Matteo's gaze to them.

"There's Gio and Viktor."

Gio smiles brightly at me as Vitkor turns to welcome us to the tall table where they have gathered. I glance across to see the men they are corresponding with ogling me curiously. That seems to be the theme tonight.

Everyone is trying to figure out who the mysterious woman accompanying the one and only, Matteo Genovese, is. They are more discreet than Alonzo, thankfully their attention ultimately stays on Matteo. I'm sure it's purely out of courtesy.

"Matteo." The man in the middle glances at me.

"Antonio, please let me introduce my fiancé, Gwenevere."

"Fiancé." Antonio raises his brow, his voice going up in surprise. "You're engaged?" Matteo nods studying Antonio. He raises his bourbon to his lips taking a sip before answering.

"Sì."

Antonio looks between the Genovese men and then me. He holds a hand out just as Alonzo had. I raise my hand with a polite smile.

"I'm Antonio, it's nice to meet you, Gwenevere." He kisses the back of my hand and I slowly lower my arm back to my waist.

"You as well."

"Gwenevere?"

My heart drops as Alessio's voice cuts through clear as day. I swirl around to him. He is dressed nicely matching the aesthetic of the night. Next to him stands a tense Enzo. Alessio looks to Matteo giving him a brief nod which he returns.

I step forward, giving him a small hug. This is the first time I've seen him since our meeting at the Genovese Estate. I miss Alessio more than I am willing to say out loud. I step back glancing to Enzo with a tight smile before returning to Matteo's side. Gio steps forward to stand on the other side of Matteo.

"You know each other?" Antonio steps around gesturing between Alessio and I. Alessio looks at me briefly but his gaze lands on Matteo with a smirk.

"Of course. She's a Luciano." Matteo's grip tightens around my waist and Alessio brings his drink to his lips, smirking as if he is clever. Men and their stupid games.

"Luciano? Is she a cousin you've been hiding?" Antonio jokes.

"Sister," Alessio responds.

Antonio's jaw slacks, this time fully assessing me.

"Alessio Luciano has a sister we know nothing about." Antonio looks to Matteo. "And somehow she ended up in Genovese hands."

"If Alessio had his way I'd still be in hiding," I chime.

"Is that so?"

Enzo's fist clenches as he stands like a rock next to Alessio. My brother stands with a cocky smile. I'm sure the pure satisfaction of fooling every man in this room for so long and finally getting to see their shocked faces is a thrill for him.

I turn my gaze back to Matteo, Alessio isn't getting all the fun.

"I guess secretly sleeping with the rivalry doesn't bode well in the *famiglias*."

This time Antonio's jaw completely drops before he collects himself into a devious smile, laughing.

"I like her, you should have let her out of the tower a long time ago."

Alessio glares at me and Matteo digs his fingers into my hip.

"I need to use the ladies' room." I smile sweetly at Matteo. I scan the room trying to find any indication of a bathroom.

"I need a refill. I'll show you where the powder room is." Gio offers his arm in place of Matteo's. They exchange looks that carry unspoken words. I grab Gio's arm and excuse myself from the men. Once we are far enough away, Gio shakes his head.

"I wouldn't play too many games tonight."

"Don't ruin my fun."

He laughs lightly but I can tell he isn't fully in it.

"Listen, this Is the epitome of a Costa Nostra gathering. These men? They are the definition of evil—they are businessmen. Tonight is about you. All eyes are going to be on you. It's not only the discovery of the mysterious Mafia Princess that's been in hiding but the announcement of your engagement tying the two families together. You're putting on a show tonight, and not for Alessio and Matteo, but for the men you plan to gain respect from as the new queen of the Genovese *famiglia*." I roll my eyes in annoyance. Even Gio wants me to 'behave' tonight.

"So tonight's business and I need to play my part?" I scoff out, growing more frustrated by the second.

"So to say."

Of course, I'd just be a piece to their chest play. Why would I think any different? This is about business and frankly, it has been from the start.

"That's bullshit. I didn't even know about this and now I have to come up with a pretty picture for everyone when I still have whiplash from it myself?"

What did they expect of me? To be the pretty little *principessa* everyone can gawk at?

"You're right, that was unfair. Matteo should have told you about tonight instead of springing it on you. I'm sorry about this but can you save the sly comments until the car ride home?"

I let out a gruntled sigh. I know Gio is looking out for me and genuinely cares about how this night is making me feel. I nod pressing my lips in a tight grin.

"Fine." Gio's shoulders relax and he lifts a finger making a slight tsk sound in the process.

"You know, if you could save the whole ass chewing until we get to the estate that would be even better. These things give me killer headaches."

"I'll consider it, what do I get out of it?"

"I will sneak you ice cream later."

I ponder for a moment.

"Make it sugar-coated strawberries with whipped cream and we can talk."

"Deal." We laugh together as we arrive at the bathroom. "Here you are, my lady."

I roll my eyes and curtsying to him.

"Why, thank you, kind sir." I push his chest and he walks away chuckling. I relieve myself and check my appearance. I don't look as bad as I thought but still wish I had done something more. The dress should've been some indicator to do my makeup and hair a tad fancier.

I wash my hands and double check that the ladies are still in postion.

I skim the area but don't catch a glimpse of Gio. I decide to backtrack in hopes of running into Matteo. Before I can get far I'm pulled back down the hall, and by the time I regain my control a door shuts and I'm now in a room.

I turn to my kidnapper; Enzo. He still holds my arm and I tug it from him glaring.

"Are you serious? You just dragged me into a room without so much as a word. You are lucky I don't start screaming now. What the hell, Enzo!"

"Jesus, Vee, stop being so dramatic. We need to talk and this seems to be the only way I can get your attention." I huff, crossing my arms.

"Well, go on. You have ten seconds to tell me what the hell you want."

"Vee, it's not that simple." He moves closer to me and I take a step back, keeping my harsh gaze on him.

"Now you have nine seconds." His face falters and my chest tightens. I can't be doing this with him. I know what he is going to say, but I can't hear it. It won't change anything.

"Vee, I love you. I always have. If you come back we can make this work, okay? We can raise the baby and we fix everything. You don't have to go through with this. I know we have a lot to figure out but at least it'd be us, and you'd be home."

"Enzo..." Before I can get further he steps closer.

"Gwen, you don't even know him. I know you. You know me. You can stay with me and you can be around Alessio all the time. We can forget all of this ever happened."

"Enzo, stop." At this point, Enzo's hands hold my waist. The pain beneath his eyes is clear from this distance. I know he is breaking. I know this is killing him but I can't.

"Gwen. Just think of everything we could have together. Think of what we did have together. I—"

"Enzo. I can't."

"What is so great about Matteo, huh? He doesn't love you how I love you, Gwen, he never will. He was made for running the *famiglia*. Cold and ruthless. Nothing more. He can give you a baby but he will never love you how I love you."

"I love him." The world seems to stop as the words slip out of my mouth. The door opens and a frantic Gio looks between Enzo and me. His eyes flash before all emotion leaves his face. Seconds later Matteo steps behind him just as frantically as Gio had arrived. He stops as his eyes fall on us. Having a moment to process, I push Enzo away and walk to him.

"Matteo, it's not what it looks like. He pulled me in here trying to convince me to go back and I said no. Please, believe me." Matteo pushes past me landing a fist into Enzo.

Gio is to Matteo instantly to dismantle the fight when Alessio storms through the room grabbing Enzo. The men are pulled apart as curses and threats fly through the air in our native tongue.

"Jesus. How naive are you!" I look at Enzo, heat radiating off of me. I am far beyond worked up. I jab a finger towards him.

"I've made my decision. I'm a grown woman and I know what I want and what I'm doing. I moved on. For the love of God, Enzo, please do the same." I look at Alessio sighing.

"I'm picking up my things tomorrow. Keep him out of the way." I point to Enzo without steering my eyes away from my brother. "I love you."

Alessio nods to me in understanding. I turn my gaze to Enzo once more.

"I'm sorry." At that, Matteo storms out of the room, and I race after him this time pushing past Gio.

"Matteo!"

His steps don't falter as I continue to chase after him. He opens the door to the stairwell starting his descent and I follow in after.

"Matteo, stop, please!"

He doesn't stop though. My heels cause every step to pierce my feet in pain. I push forward until he's in arm's reach. I grab him, turning him to look at me.

"Fuck, Matteo."

He stops this time.

"Nothing was going to happen."

He scoffs

"Matteo. He pulled me into a room. I didn't even know who it was at first. He wanted me to come back. I told him no."

"Am I supposed to believe that bullshit, Gwenevere? He was touching you and you let him. You want to be with him."

"I told him I love you."

Matteo freezes and my pulse stops.

"Matteo, I told him I love you." I sigh looking down at my aching feet. "I don't want to go with him. I didn't before, I don't now. I want you. I choose to be with you. I chose this." I motion between him and me.

"I don't want him. I want you."

Matteo pushes me against the wall softly. His hand gliding up behind my head.

"Matteo, I only want you."

With that, he kisses me hard. Heat rises through my aching body, no longer from discomfort but in need. I hungrily kiss Matteo back as I pull him into me by his suit jacket.

"Matteo," I moan out as he grabs my waist pushing my hips into his.

"Fuck," he groans. He pulls back, putting his forehead to mine. "Not in the stairwell."

I let out a breathy laugh.

"You don't want to put on a show? Be risky?"

He chuckles, shaking his head.

"I want you all to myself tonight." His husky voice leaves my skin tingling in desire. I nod as he takes my hand. We continue down the stairs making it three levels below the roof. He pulls out a key to open the door to the floor. We step into a hallway where the doors are scarce. This must be the penthouse rooms.

We slip down the hall to the end room. A keypad with a code lock sits on the wall outside the door. Matteo enters the number and swipes the key, unlocking the door. Stepping into the room my suspicions are confirmed. The space is huge.

He pulls me in shutting the door. Before I get the chance to wonder, Matteo pushes me up against the wall, capturing my lips again. I moan into the kiss reveling in his touch. His hands travels down my dress gripping my hips tightly.

His lips leave mine as his possessive tone flows to my ears.

"I want to fuck him out of you. I want to erase every touch. Every moan. Every moment. I want you to only think, feel, and hear me. Your lips only say my name. You will only be mine."

I suck on my bottom lip. The heat inside me increased to dangerous temperatures. I want exactly that. I want to be immersed in Matteo. To be his and only his. He pulls my chin up to him.

"I don't just want to fuck you, Gwenevere. I want to make love to you. I want you, Gwenevere. I love you." I stare into his eyes as if I am captivated by his soul. My heart pounds in my chest praying this isn't a fantasy dream my mind has created.

"*Ti amo*, Gwenevere." *I love you, Gwenevere.*

"*Ti amo*, Matteo." Matteo's lips crash into mine. Our lips move in sync as we devour each other with need. A need far more fierce than before. Our bodies and minds crave the other.

Matteo turns me around, pushing the hair falling from my ponytail aside. His lips meet my neck as he grabs the zipper to the top of the dress. He slides it down stopping at my lower back. He glides one side down off my shoulder and then the other causing the dress to drop to the floor. My buds harden at the sudden cold air.

He turns me back to him, capturing every inch available to him. I am almost completely exposed standing in nothing but my black lace underwear.

"Amore mio, Sei Bellissima" My love, you are beautiful.

His lips meet mine again as his hand grips my hip. His other hand caresses my tender breast and pulls me deeper into his hypnotizing touch. I push at his suit jacket encouraging him to remove it.

Matteo discards the jacket and returns his lips to mine. I move slowly to the bed unbuttoning his shirt to the best of my abilities before ultimately giving up. Matteo chuckles and in one swift move, he pops the buttons apart, flying them across the room.

He swiftly takes his pants off before his lips find mine again. The back of my legs hit the bed and I lose my balance falling onto the bed. A second of cool air hits me before Matteo's head rests between my knees drawing a line of light kisses up my thigh. The sensation sends pleasure to my core, making my stomach twist in all the right ways. He hooks his finger into the base of my panties that cover my most sensitive spot. Pulling the cloth to the side he lowers his lips, kissing softly. I moan out in utter bliss of from his touch.

"Hai il sapore del dolce miele." You taste like sweet honey.

I bite my lip glancing down at him, my face bound to be a lovely shade of red. He is intoxicating.

"You are soaking, *la mia rosa." My rose.* I squirm under him as he laps away at my throbbing center. I throw my head back gripping his head. It is as if Matteo knows my body better than I do. My chest rises in anticipation of my soon-to-be release. His tongue swirling and thrusting against me.

My moans come out shallow but often as I fight for air within the pleasure. Matteo slides a finger inside my wet core igniting my high.

"Fuck, Matteo," I whimper as I rest down on my elbows. My body quivers with the pleasure radiating through me. Even so, I'm not finished with our venture and by the looks of it, Matteo is just getting started.

Matteo grabs my waist, throwing me further on the bed. He tosses his briefs before climbing up the bed. Before he gets far, I grab his hardened member firmly in my hand. He freezes, giving me a dark gape.

"Be careful, *amore*. You don't know what you're in for."

I stroke him, studying each and every reaction.

"I know exactly what I'm in for." I lower my head down to his velvet tip. Small pearly beads rise as I massage his thick shaft. I open my lips, placing them over his swollen member. I take him slowly, coating him with my wet tongue before I take him in fully.

I glide my head in repetitive motions causing Matteo to groan and push into me. His hand travels up and grips my hair forcing me to take him in further and harder. I loved the simple torture and open my jaw to allow for his size. Matteo's grunts quicken as my mouth bounces around him. He pulls my head back grabbing my chin and lifting me up.

"I'm not cumming in your mouth, I'm cumming inside your pussy and owning you." I force myself to nod my head, my body responding to me at his vulgar words.

"Get on your hands and knees." I nod again doing as he says. The moment I'm in position Matteo's hand connects to my ass check with a smack. I jump a little out of surprise, leaning back and pressing my ass closer to him.

"You like that, *Princpessa*?" Before I can respond, his hand meets my ass again. I gasp out at the slight sting but only crave Matteo more.

"I'm going to make you forget any man's touch besides my own." With that Matteo thrusts into me jolting me forward. His hands find both my hips pressing me firmly against him. He pulls back before slamming into me again, pulling me against him at the same time. My mind melts into putty from the immense pleasure of his slick thrust.

His movements are firm and demanding. Matteo's arms sneak under me grabbing my breast. I lean back and press my back against his front. One of his hands holds my stomach softly as another lays over my chest, fingers wrapping perfectly around my neck. Matteo's grunts fall to my ear, and my skin lights up with each contact.

"I want you in every way, all the time. I want you, Gwenevere."

I gasp as he releases me. His hands find my hips again. He pulls out long enough to flip me over. I move to his lap pressing my chest against his.

I glide my soaking center around his pulsing member creating friction again. His thrusts hit me perfectly as pressure builds once more.

"Shit," I moan, grinding against him while holding onto his neck for support. Matteo's arms hold me tightly as he picks up pace. A hand finds my hair holding my head as his lips find mine once more. Our kisses are rough as we race for our finish.

"Matteo," I plead for his movements to bring me to my climax, the sensation overwhelmingly strong.

"Gwenevere." His husky groan throws me over the edge. Matteo slams into me as I scream out. My walls clamp down on his twitching shaft, both holding onto each other with tight grips, riding out our highs together.

Our movements come to an end as I sit in Matteo's lap. His hand circles in my hair as he leaves sweet kisses behind my ear.

"Promise it will always be me."

"It will always be you, Matteo."

24

Gwenevere

I turn in the bed, my body sore and nauseated. A mix of cravings fills my senses at the same time. Pushing myself to the edge of the bed, I glance at the room. Matteo has already left. I step into the bathroom finding a note taped to the mirror.

~ I'll be back around noon. Call for room service if you get hungry.~

Sighing, I lay the note back down and continue my wash up. Fixing my hair I throw on my wrinkled dress from the night before. When I finish I make my way back to the main room and sit on the bed. I try turning on the TV but nothing captures my attention. My stomach growls and my nausea intensifies.

Grabbing the menu off the table I scan my food options, all bleak and unappealing. Matteo mentioned a café last night and that sounds right up my alley. I need a good cup of coffee and savory pastries. His need to imprison me in the room is being overtaken by the fetus he helped create wanting for the right nourishment.

I head out the door with excitement in my step. The elevator ride takes less time than it felt like last night. Blush rises to my checks in remembrance of my midnight intertwinement. I find a service desk and approach the young woman.

"Hi. I um... I'm looking for the café. Could you point me in the right direction?"

Her smile widens as she responds with her best customer service voice that I'm sure has been engraved into her.

"Of course, take the elevator to the next floor. There will be a few shops, keep walking straight until you see the large dining space."

"Thank you so much."

I follow her directions humming as I weave through the light bustle of people in the obnoxiously large hotel. I am still in awe that Matteo owns this place. His taste is immaculate if he has any influence. I take in all the small details of the paintings along the way.

When I make it to the next floor I glance around at the small shops mixed with entertainment. I browse through the open doorways until I come upon a layout of tables and chairs and a rather large café bar area.

I admire the view from the large windows stretching across the back wall showing a gorgeous view of the garden. A small feeling of familiarity from the library view at home. My home. I'm startled at the sound of a throat being cleared next to me. I snap my head over to see a young man in a nice outfit and menu in hand.

"Sorry, ma'am, I didn't mean to startle you." I keep my hand over my chest for a moment with a small smile to reassure the waiter.

"No it's okay, I was captured by the view."

He looks out at the windows with a little bit of a relieved face. His face brightens back to a kind smile.

"It's quite beautiful. Would you like to sit near the windows?".

"I would love that."

He nods, gesturing forward, bringing me to a small table near the window.

"May I get you a drink to start out with?"

"Coffee, please." He nods, turning to leave.

"Oh, do you have pastries?"

"Yes, we have muffins, cinnamon rolls, and Danishes."

"Cheese Danish?" He nods again.

"One of those please, oh and bacon?"

He chuckles a little.

"Of course, I'll be right out."

"Thank you." I smile at him once more before he makes his exit. I sigh in contentment about my soon-to-be breakfast. I push my hair behind my ears, leaning back in my chair. I let myself daydream, everything feeling like a fever dream.

I told Matteo I loved him, and he said it back. Matteo loves me. My chest swells and I bite my lip as I recall all the beautiful words exchanged between us last night, at least from the ones that were said. My blush returns, heating my cheeks to my ears.

Everything is moving so fast but perfectly all at the same time. Maybe it is an addiction, but I feel more than that. I believe it is driven by something more than the lust we have for one another. Everything about him ignites something in me that was veiled, only bursting with any piece of him I can seize.

His breath left condensation across my skin as he left a trail of sloppy but sweet kisses. The tips of his fingers brushed along every inch of me. His gravelly mutters in my ear, and the sweet, sweet smell of vanilla overpowered the entirety of my senses.

"You didn't stay in the room." His voice interrupts, my face heating further as I clench my legs, hoping my thoughts can't be seen. I peer up to catch Matteo's devious eyes. He is dressed nicely, but the idea of him never looking delectable is humorous.

"No, I didn't. I was starving." His brows raise.

"I left a note, you could order room service." I sigh with a roll of my eyes.

"You did. Except room service doesn't have what I am craving and baby cravings trump the note." Before I can see his reaction Gio and Viktor catch my eye walking into the café. My smile brightens and I wave them over. I stand up giving Gio a small hug and a warm smile to Viktor.

"Good morning, Baby Girl." Gio swoops into the table followed by Viktor.

"Gio," Matteo grumbles, but in typical Gio fashion, he ignores him, their facetious quarrel.

"How was your sleep?" He mischievously wiggles his brows and I roll my eyes in return.

"I'm sure better than yours." Matteo laughs and Gio sits back in defeat. The waiter returns to the table in a more composed stature. He sets down my coffee and pastries.

"Your bacon will be out shortly." He smiles briefly at me before moving his gaze to Matteo. "Mr. Genovese, can I start you out with a coffee this morning?"

"Yes, coffee's all around, and more pastries please."

"Of course." The waiter retreats and I sip my steaming coffee. My stomach has been iffy with the beverage lately and I'm thankful today is a tolerable day with coffee.

"Seems you've planned a breakfast of champions." Gio's voice travels in a small chuckle to me.

"Baby cravings," I let out nonchalantly as Matteo shakes his head. The waiter returns with the coffee and my bacon. I grab the bacon quickly and devour it. Only there aren't many pieces.

"Can I please get a few more orders of bacon, preferably a plate full?" The waiter nods and leaves again. Matteo's lips curled into a small admirable smile.

"That's a lot of bacon."

"It's just so damn good and four pieces is not breakfast. I'm feeding two, I might even eat more than you." His Adam's apple rises gently with his small chuckle. I get a better look at him and my earlier thoughts on obsession are distorted. My body grows aware of his as I clench my thighs together, stuffing the rest of the bacon in my face. I listen as the men talk about some business that really isn't interesting.

"Gwenevere, I have some work to attend to today, I will have the driver take you back to the estate and I will see you back there around dinner."

"It's okay, I have some errands to run."

 Matteo brings his full attention to me.

"I'm sure you can have one of the maids run them for you."

I readjust myself on the chair taking a sip.

"Um no, I uh..." I hesitate realizing he forgot about last night's conversation with Alessio. I suddenly wish I didn't say anything at all. "I told Alessio I would pick my things up today."

"No." He turns away, giving me nothing more than his harsh demands.

"I wasn't asking Matteo. I need my things." He slams his cup down on the table.

"You're not going."

I scoff, crossing my arms.

"I am going. He is my brother and I need my things. You can't keep me from there. I have to go at some point and I'm going today."

"You are not going by yourself."

"Who said I'm going by myself and what if I did, huh? It's not like I'm an enemy, he is my brother. He's not going to hurt me."

"Gwenevere."

"Don't fucking 'Gwenevere' me." I push off the table, raising my voice. Matteo isn't going to sit there and be insecure messing with my time and needs. I need to see Alessio and pick my things up, it has been too long already.

"I already talked to Alessio about it last night and if it's Enzo that you're worried about he won't be there, not that you should worry about that. I thought I made that crystal fucking clear." Matteo grabs my wrist tugging me toward him, breaking some of my much-needed space.

"Don't act like a damn fool."

"Are you serious right now, Matteo?" I snatch my wrist back and stomp out of the café. Gio says something to Matteo that I can't make out before following in step with me.

"Gwen."

"Not now." I blow out a frustrated breath but keep my pace.

"Matteo's right, you shouldn't go alone. I know that has been your home but that doesn't mean you should go unaccompanied. You are accounted for now and you're intertwined with both families which puts you at a bigger target. Regardless, you will not be picking up a single damn box." I sigh, slowing down. As annoyed as I am about being demanded around on what I can and can't do, Gio has a point. I'm no longer thinking about just me. If I get hurt, the baby gets hurt.

"Matteo is only trying to keep you safe. He cares about you, Gwen, let him."

I give him a pointed glare and come to a stop. I bite my cheek pondering how to compromise.

"Come on, your plate of bacon is at the table."

Ugh, why is food so tempting?

"Fine, but I'm going today."

Gio chuckles, throwing his hands up.

"Can't take that one up with me."

I move past Gio heading back to the table. Matteo raises a brow at my return, his cockiness making me want to throw his hot coffee right in his face.

"I'm going today. Pick someone to go with me."

Matteo's jaw ticks, as he rubs a hand across it.

"No."

I click my tongue holding my stance.

"I didn't ask."

If his gaze could slice a dagger through me he'd have killed me now. His eyes hold mine for an intense battle, though, I refused to back down and show any sign of compliance. I lean over the table letting my next words flow with as much power I can muster to push my chances.

"Either you pick someone to go with me or I go by myself. I. am. going."

His eyes flicker then move to Gio and Viktor before making their way back to me.

"Gio will take you. No Enzo. Right back to the estate. Take it or leave it, that's your only option."

I push off the table, grab my bacon in a napkin and take my exit from the table.

"And Gwenevere, change your clothes."

I scoff, continuing with Gio on my tail.

"Of course, Mr. Genovese."

I know saying his name formally will get me in trouble later but it comes with a sense of power and a thrill. I make my way to the front lobby and open the front door taking in the sun against my skin. I close my eyes letting the warm wind lift my hair.

"You better enjoy the day because I have a feeling your night is gonna be nothing like it." I roll my eyes and give him a push, moving down the steps. I stop at the valet, having no idea how to call for the car. Gio glides up to the man at the booth exchanging some words and handing him cash. He returns to me knocking into my shoulder.

"This is so bougie waiting for someone to retrieve our car."

He chuckles, adjusting his suit jacket and then his watch.

"Our car? Have you accepted your fate as a Genovese?" I throw him a glare, moving the hair that presses along my face from the light wind.

"I thought that was obvious when I forced my brother to accept the proposal." I laugh, watching the car pull up to the curb.

"You may have decided to stay but that doesn't mean you accepted yourself as a Genovese. You simply agreed to a business deal." He opens the passenger door holding a hand out for me.

"A business deal. You're telling me this little bean is just a business deal?" Something flashes across Gio's face too quickly to recognize as his hand grips the door. I slide into the car, sitting comfortably in the seat. Gio braces his other hand on the roof of the car, closing off the light with his body.

"You were never just a business deal." He reaches down grabbing my seat belt and pulling it across my body, latching it, much like that first day we met. I swallow his words down letting them sink in.

I know I wasn't a business deal at the start, none of us knew who I was for it to be. Gio's words seem to have a different meaning behind them but I'm not sure what.

I shake the thought from my mind as we pull onto the main roads. After a few minutes, Gio turns for the Genovese Estate.

"Gio, why are we heading back home?" He glances over to me with merriment before returning his eyes back to the road.

"You don't really want to wear that dress to pack, do you?" I contemplate it in my head. On the one hand, I really want to stay in these clothes to push Matteo's buttons but on the other hand, I feel kind of like shit and want to be comfortable for the packing process.

"I guess not," I mumble, pulling out my phone to shoot Alessio a text that I will be coming by shortly and to ensure Enzo will not be around. I wouldn't have minded before his stunt last night. I can't trust him to keep his hands to himself, and in return, Gio and Matteo's to themselves. He was far too close to kissing me after his hands had been placed on my hips.

I've confirmed, even to myself, where my heart lies now; it's with Matteo. Call me crazy for skipping months worth of time of 'falling in love.' Matteo manages to change the rhythm of the blood pumping through my body with even a thought of his existence. He rewrote a future for me in a matter of months and I could be nothing but content in the waking of it.

I can be completely insane or maybe this can be our fate. I've read millions of love stories and somehow the only one I want to experience time and time again is the one I'm living right now.

We pull into the estate bringing me back to the present and I unbuckle, jumping out of the car. The minute I land on the ground a sharp pain slices through my lower stomach, practically knocking me to the pavement. Gio's arms reach out grabbing ahold of my elbows and stabilizing me. Another sharp stab soars through me forcing me to grab ahold of my lower abdomen and crunch over.

"Gwenevere, what's happening?" Gio's voice is laced with panic over the whooshing sounds of my own anxiety rising to the surface.

"Gio. Gio, something's wrong. It hurts."

Gio throws an arm under my legs, lifting me into the air and into his arms. My body jolts as he runs towards the estate. He yells commands, demanding for the doctor. I groan out in pain twisting in Gio's arms.

"It's okay, Baby Girl, I got you."

I push my face into Gio trying to ground myself from the movement in hopes of reducing any pain. My heart rate increases as whimpers escape my lips.

"Gio, Matteo."

I try to tell Gio to call Matteo but words seem to be hard to find within the sea of pain and rushed yelling around me. I doubt my voice even carries to his ears.

"He's on his way."

I try to get anything out to say thank you but instead, my voice only lets out soft whines. My back is cradled by a soft mattress as Gio's arms retract away from me. I grasp onto his wrist as hard as I can, my vision blurring, casting two visions of the man in front of me.

"Please don't leave me," I hiccup, unable to say more. Loud hustling echoes through the room and I hold onto him with everything in me.

"I'm not going anywhere, Baby Girl, I need to scoot over for the doctor to have room."

The room sways as I try to focus on Gio. Everything slowly becomes more and more distorted. Marco's voice shouts orders through the room as he reaches the bedside. Another sharp stab courses through me as he pushes on my stomach. A harsh burn rushes from my head to my toes. I moan out clarifying my distress but the attempt is useless as the world tunnels into darkness.

"No, Gwenevere, stay awake, look at me."

I toss my head trying to force myself awake and resist the force of my eyes shutting. The more I try, the harder it gets to keep my control. I drift and drift as fear ricochets through my body, causing the last words that leave my lips before darkness completely takes over me.

"My baby," I sob in a whisper.

25

Matteo

"Fuck." I slam the door open to the hotel with a hurried descent down the grand stairs. I shout to the valet in urgency from the top of the stairs and by the time I'm at the bottom, my car comes screeching to the curbside. Viktor is hot on my trail. He only heard part of my phone call but did not waver in urgency to follow me. I tore straight out of the meeting without so much as an explanation.

Something is wrong with Gwenevere. all I could hear was the shouting of my men and the car bleeding cries of Gwenevere in the background. Nicolas, one of my high-ranking men, called to inform me Gwenevere is being rushed into the estate by Gio. She was moaning in agony.

The call came in the middle of a meeting with some of our head suppliers. I wasted no time informing them of things that don't concern them, racing out the door. Nicolas didn't have any useful answers, only that Marco was already on his way to meet her.

She was just here. She was fine but her screams were indication that she is no longer in the fierce demanding state she was. A feeling courses through me that I don't recognize. I am terrified.

I knew Gwenevere would become my weakness, but at this moment, I could care less about what that means for me. I will bring myself down if it means saving her.

"The estate now! Floor it." I throw my demand at Bruno as Viktor jumps in the back. Bruno doesn't hesitate to confirm sending the pedal into the floor of the car, screeching the tires.

I pick my phone up to see if anyone is calling back yet, knowing there would be nothing. I send a message to Gio and another to Nicolas before deciding to send another one to Marco.

I glance in the mirror at Viktor, the fear evident in my gaze. Viktor flashes a look of angst swallowing it back. While we usually keep a calm exterior in times of panic this is an entirely new scenario.

"Gwenevere is—" I can't find the words. My throat hardens, closing up and my body fills with emotions I don't know how to navigate. "Something's wrong."

Understanding passes through Viktor's eyes, his protective demeanor doesn't falter but hardens. We all care for Gwenevere in our own ways and for our own reasons.

Regardless of an instituted paper, Gwenevere is family, she has been a Genovese for a while. My men have begun choosing her side in arguments and games. Mila has threatened *me* not to hurt *her* as if she hasn't stepped in to protect me since I was a boy.

No one including me is willing to lose her—not now, not ever. I am not losing either one of them. Thousands of scenarios wrack their way through my mind as I try to uncover what little details I received. I need to know what happened, like if I know then I can solve it.

Is she losing the baby? Did she fall? Did someone hurt her? My chest constricts and my fist clutches the door as I think of all the possibilities—all the what-ifs—and none of which I have a solution of divinity insuring her well-being. Anger; I'm good at solving anger. If someone hurt her I could think of eighty-nine ways to torture them to death and seventy-five would look like a misfortune.

As we make it onto the highway, Bruno weaves through the cars, looking cautiously in the rearview on alert. I follow his gaze, noticing a car on our tail. The black Mercedes Benz weaves through the cars catching up with us.

"Boss, we have company."

The furry rising in me brings back my mental clarity.

"Lose them."

Bruno jerks the car as he speeds up just barely making the next exit. We fly underneath the freeway and he takes a sharp left as I pop my seat belt off. I turn with my hand on the shoulder of his seat to look out the back window fully.

We continue speeding down the backroads when the car reappears gaining traction by the second. I scan our surroundings, we are still five minutes out from the house, even at this speed. This is the last thing I want to be dealing with. Is it a coincidence?

"Guns," I shout back to Viktor. He pulls two semiautomatics from under the seats sending one up to me. I reach down, feeling underneath the console for the button, pressing it to send off the precautionary alarms to my top men that our car is in distress before flicking off the safety and readying my weapon.

Bruno veers through the roads as the city becomes more and more scarce. We are minutes from the estate now and no way am I leading these assholes there.

"Don't lead them straight to the estate."

The last thing I want is Gwenevere in the chaos of crossfire. If anything more happens to her, these idiotic fucks behind us will be begging me to put a bullet in their fucking heads.

"Yes, boss." Bruno takes a sharp left, curving away from my path to Gwenevere. I don't have time to be frustrated as the following car becomes parallel with the back end of ours. I aim the gun shooting endless bullets until I empty my magazine. I pull my body back in, grabbing a new set from the console as Viktor empties his rounds. We switch again, piercing the Mercedes until it twists off the road sliding into a ditch. I pull the gun back in, tucking it to the side of the seat and turning forward in my seat.

Before I can fully sit down my body jerks, slamming my head into the side window and cracking the glass. Splintering screeches create a melody with the ringing in my ears as we plummet into a spiral. Seconds pass as the dark consumes me. I can care less about the state I will be in, I can only think about one thing. Gwenevere.

26

Gwenevere

My eyes flutter open, light finding its way through my lashes. I groan out softly as the subtle pain clarifies that I'm in fact not dead. I blink my eyes a few times adjusting my pupils to the newfound brightness. I look around the room, to my right there is a machine with hanging liquid in bags and IVs flowing to my wrist.

The memories of stepping out of the car earlier play through my mind. The searing pain and the drowsiness. I move my hand slowly to lie across my lower stomach. My heart rate picks up through the monitor and I scan the space finding Gio resting in the leather chair. The wrinkles on his face are deeper than before with a hand on his forehead holding it up.

I look further to see Alessio's back to me as he stares out the window. My brows furrow; why is Alessio here? I open my mouth but nothing comes out. Swallowing, I try to wet my dry throat and hold it while clearing it. Both the men in the room snap their heads at me.

Alessio pushes off the window, while Gio rushes to the door shouting out for Marco. Gio disappears into the bathroom as I bring my attention back to Alessio. He grabs my hand and brushes my cheek with the other.

"Ci hai spaventato" You scared us. His voice is taut and quiet but I can't tell if it's just due to my hearing. I don't have it in me to voice my concerns, lifting my arms to sign to him.

"Baby?"

His lips pull into a smile instantly settling the fear that has been sinking inside me.

"The baby is okay. You're okay, but you need to rest."

I close my eyes, taking in a breath and letting it out slowly. We're okay, but my body aches. Everything from head to toe is sore. I raise my hands again.

"What happened?"

My mind is a fog, but even before, the pain had come on so suddenly. Alessio looks at me hesitantly. Gio returns taking Alessio's attention away from me. He is avoiding the question, is it that bad? I hit the mattress beside me in frustration drawing him back.

"Alessio, what happened?"

He sets a fist over his lips, contemplating within himself before responding.

"You were poisoned, Gwenevere."

My eyes shoot out as I fling myself into a sitting position. I regret it when pain flames through me. I wince while sliding my feet up.

"Don't move, Gwen. You need to rest, not just for you. You are okay but it was close. You need to relax."

My chest heaves up and down as I process the information. I snap to Gio who comes to Alessio's side and sits on the edge of the bed with a wet towel and some water. He places the towel against my head making me aware of the heat radiating off my skin.

Gio lifts the water to me, placing the straw in my mouth. I huff at the childlike treatment but am grateful I don't have to do the action myself. He removes the water and hands it to Alessio to sit on the bedside table. Moving the towel down my face and onto my neck, he feels my head.

"She's still pretty hot."

Alessio frowns glancing at his watch and then the door.

"Where is Marco?"

Gio keeps his focus on me and I lean my head on Gio's shoulder, forcing him to switch the towel to the other side of my neck.

"He should be here any minute. Want to meet and update?"

Alessio nods and leaves, shutting the door behind him. I find Gio with puzzlement. Why is Alessio here? Where is Matteo? Gio said he was on his way before I passed out.

"Gio." My voice comes out strained as I try to use it. He shuffles a little trying to see my face better.

"Yes, Baby Girl."

"Where's Matteo?"

Gio pauses, bringing back the fear that had escaped. What happened to Matteo? Is he poisoned too? Was it worse? Oh my God, what if he is dead? No.

"Gio, where is Matteo?"

"He's on his way now. There was an accident, he's okay." I raise my head off his shoulder, and an overwhelming sensation of dread fills me.

"He was in an accident! What do you mean he's okay? How did Alessio get here before him?"

Gio Soberly skims over me as if he is calculating. I think of the worst-case scenarios and all leave me sick.

"He has a couple of injuries but he'll be okay, he will come see you as soon as he gets here, but you need to rest."

I pull away completely, pushing myself off the bed. I take the IV needle out covering the wound.

"Gwenevere, lay back down."

I ignore him and rush out the door and down the hall passing the high ratio of guards lining throughout. None of which know what to do about my current panicked state.

"Gwenevere, he isn't here and you are going to hurt yourself or the baby, you need to lay down!"

I push harder as I make it to the stairs only pausing for a moment. A loud bang of the front door flying open ricochets through the foyer. Pounding steps falter forward as Matteo rushes into view.

His body is beaten, blood running from a slash on his head. His hair is completely ruffled and his clothes are torn in a few places. He turns to me, exhaustion evident on his face, but his eyes search me in a frenzy.

I waste no time rushing down the stairs taking steps two at a time until I reach the bottom where his arms hold out for me. I push myself up to his arms but that doesn't satisfy him as he reaches down cupping my ass and pulling me up on him. I wrap my arms tightly around his neck refusing to let go. His hand fists in my hair, holding my head into him.

"Fuck I thought I was going to lose you."

I wince at his croaky voice. Holding him impossibly tighter.

"Not yet," I whisper into his neck. I pull my head back looking into his eyes as his hand travels to my face. He's rougher than he appeared from afar. This wasn't a little accident. His brows furrow as he feels the warmth against my head.

"You're burning."

I bite my lip. I forgot for a moment that I am not in great shape either.

"Marco is on his way."

Matteo looks past me to Gio.

"He's here. Come on, let me bring you back to the room."

I slide my hands down to his chest to push off only receiving a tightening grasp.

"You're not going anywhere."

I huff but don't argue. The rundown to him was more draining than I thought it would be. I lay my head back down against his shoulder, thankful that he is here now.

When we make it back into the bedroom he lays me down in my spot frowning again at the IVs that lay with blood splatter on the floor next to the bed. I smile sheepishly to him shimmying up into a comfy spot. He shakes his head as Marco moves past him and up to the machine. He takes note of the plucked needle with a shake in disappointment before pulling out new IVs.

Matteo rests against the bedpost. His lip is busted and bleeding along with smeared blood under his nose. Dirt and blood cover every part of him, and yet, he stands there watching the doctor hook me back up.

"I'm fine, help him."

"No. You need to listen to the doctor and lie down. Let him work, Gwenevere," Matteo gripes from his post.

"I'm nowhere near the condition you are in."

"I've been in a lot worse and you are pregnant."

I swallow back not being able to argue against that. I brace myself on the pillow, appreciating the softness before a prick draws at my wrist.

I look behind Matteo where Gio and Alessio talk in the doorway too quiet for me to hear. I am still confused as to why Alessio is here, in the Genovese Estate.

"Why is Alessio here?" At the sound of his name, he turns to me, pausing his conversation. Matteo and Alessio nod to each other as Alessio reaches my other side.

"Gio called him when I set off the alarm in the car, he came as a backup to protect you." Now I'm even more confused, to protect me? I am more than well protected even without him here.

"And you were poisoned of course," Alessio adds in.

"Wait, protect me? Gio was here and all the guards, not that I don't mind your company." The room stays silent as the men have a quiet conversation. Clearly, everyone thinks I'm unable to handle whatever it is they can't seem to say out loud.

"What am I missing, Matteo." I stare at him head-on. I know I won't get anything out of Alessio but I at least have a chance with Matteo. His jaw clenches as he grips the side post.

"It was a double attack, they poisoned you and hit me."

My jaw slacks as bile rises in my throat.

"Who is trying to kill us, why us, I don't—what the fuck is going on." My voice rises along with the beating of my heart that plays through the monitor again. Matteo's eyes dart to the machine before closing the distance between us.

"Gwen, calm down, it's okay. We're okay, you're safe now. We doubled the guards and we've thoroughly checked everything. You are the safest you could be right now, just breathe." His hands hold either side of my face, forcing me to focus only on him. I take a deep breath, concentrating. He's right, sending myself into a hysteria is not a good option right now and is not necessary. I am surrounded by some of the most trusted men I will ever be around.

"Are you okay?" I ask in a whisper. Gio told me he was but he appears to be anything but that.

"Never better."

I scowl at him, fully aware he is lying, but arguing about it won't get me anywhere. Alessio clears his throat causing me to blush with embarrassment at the intimate moment. I had almost completely forgotten he was there.

"Can I have a minute alone with her?"

Matteo hesitates, resisting the urge to say no. The war ends with a nod. He places a tender kiss on my lips before checking me for confirmation. I reassure him, giving his final motive to let go and retreat out of the room with Gio.

Alessio watches as he leaves before lying down next to me on the bed. I lean back and roll into him, hiding my face in his chest.

"This is what I tried to avoid."

My hand grips my pillow as I listen to his confession.

"I wanted to keep you out of view from this world. There are terrible men in the underworld and I don't want you to have to face them. I knew if you were in the picture there wasn't a damn thing I could do to prevent you from eventually getting hurt one way or another."

"I'm okay, Alessio."

"You almost died."

I stay quiet for a pause. I understand where Alessio stands and why he did what he did, partially.

"But I didn't. I'm stronger than I look."

"You shouldn't have to prove how strong you are. You are supposed to just be you."

"What if this is me? What if this whole time the Luciano blood pumped through me just as strongly as you, except I lived in a sheltered lie and you knew who you were the entire time."

"Of course, Luciano blood pumps through you. You will always be a Luciano at heart. I just wanted what's best for you, Gwen."

"Maybe it was, Alessio, but it wasn't fair. I would've understood, hell, it would've made a lot of things make more sense. Did you not think I would wonder about all the training and mysterious calls? I didn't question you because I trusted you."

"Can you still trust me?"

I fumble for an answer. Do I trust him? When I wanted to know the truth earlier, I didn't look to Alessio, I looked to Matteo. I trusted Matteo for information over Alessio. His face falters as I peer up to him.

"I really want to."

Alessio closes his eyes briefly, the wrinkles in his forehead scrunching in pain. I hate the way I am making him feel but I can't lie to him and tell him everything is okay. It won't help us figure this out between us. Alessio opens his eyes again.

"I will never lie to you again. You can always come to me, and ask me anything. I will be nothing but open and honest with you. I promise you,

Gwenevere." The desperation in his voice kills me. I can't resist the tear that slips out. He wipes my tears away, kissing my forehead lightly.

"I love you, Vee." I close my eyes, leaning my head back down.

"I love you too, Les."

Alessio pulls away fully this time, pushing off the bed. I roll back to my back as he stops at the end.

"He loves you, Gwenevere. I trust him with you more than I've trusted anyone with you in their possession." He chuckles looking down to the ground and back at the door. A smile plays on my lips from his words.

"I've never seen a man do a third of what that man did for you today." Alessio looks back at me again with a doleful look. My mind races at all the things he has done.

"I will send your things over, it's not safe for you to travel between the estates right now. I'll visit okay? Don't worry about anything but getting better, I'm excited to be an uncle."

I smile sweetly and with that, he walks out the door leaving me alone.

I'm not alone for long as Matteo moves quickly back into the room. Gio is on his trail and Marco is close behind. There is an argument between Matteo and Marco as Gio rolls his eyes gliding over to me, checking my forehead again. He seems a little more satisfied by the temperature but retreats to the bathroom anyway for another damp towel. I zone in on the heated conversation in front of me.

"I don't need to be assessed right now, I have better things to do Marco, I'm standing, I'm fine."

"You could have a concussion or worse, internal bleeding. You were just in a roll-on collision and could have serious unnoticeable injuries. It will take you all but five minutes. She is okay."

"Marco, I'm not fucking arguing with you."

"Beats me," he grumbles.

"Matteo, sit down and let him check you. I'm not going to do this all on my own if you bleed out because of your fucking overreacting, stubborn ass," I demand. Matteo's head snaps back to me with a clear irritation. He growls out before plopping into the leather chair and removing his ripped shirt.

I watch as the useless black fabric falls from his body onto the floor. His toned dirty muscles flex with each movement. He leans back in the chair, and I try to see from over the doctor's shoulder, scanning for any and all wounds. I spot a bullet hole on his upper shoulder that is seeping blood.

I gasp, sitting up straight again, nearly pulling out the IVs once more. Matteo whips his head back to me with a warning.

"Don't you dare get off that fucking bed or I will kick Marco out."

I take a shaky breath.

"You have a bullet hole in your shoulder," I state plainly.

"Must be why there's blood."

How is he so calm right now? He was shot and he acts like it is a scratch from running into the doorway. I stare at him dumbfounded as Marco cleans and assesses the wounds fully.

"It went all the way through."

Matteo hums out in approval, closing his eyes while Marco sews it up. My stomach grows queasy forcing me to look away. Gio sits on the bed with the damp towel in hand. Pressing the towel to my forehead and pushing me back into the mattress.

"How hot is she?" Marco asks monotone over Matteo's shoulder.

"She's still pretty warm to the touch," Gio responds, and Matteo's attention comes back to the room. He attempts to sit up but Marco confirms his grip on his arm.

"Grab the thermometer off the table and check her temperature please," Marco responds gruffly, staring down Matteo. Gio does as asked, grabbing the thermometer and placing it under my tongue. We wait patiently until the little machine begins to signify its finish.

"102," Gio informs him. Marco sighs as he finishes the last stitch on Matteo's shoulder.

"She's been too high for too long. She needs a cool bath, can you help her Gio." Matteo pushes Marco off completely this time.

"Everyone out."

His voice is commanding and spine-tickling. Glances are exchanged but nonetheless, Gio exits with Marco faltering at the doorway.

"She needs a cool bath and medicine. A bottle is on the table. I need her under one hundred soon. Lots of water and rest. Don't overdo it." The last instruction sounds more for both of us. With that, Marco shuts the door behind him.

And then it was two. The last time we were alone was much more enjoyable than this. Matteo stalks over to me clipping the IV and removing it leaving only the tube in my wrist. He scoops me up in his arms just like he had laid me down.

I nuzzle my nose into his chest as he carries me into the bathroom, placing me gently on the counter. He crosses the room to the tub, turning it on. As the water fills he glides his hands down my stomach to my hips, lifting me up and placing my feet on the ground. He pulls the dress down before latching onto the top of my underwear and dragging them down my thighs to the floor to lay with the dress.

His hand moves back to my chin, holding it lightly and leaning in for a soft kiss. His hand falls back down, grabs my hand and leads me to the tub. He shuts the water off and helps me into the tub.

The coolness gives me a shock. The radiating heat is now apparent with the soothing water touching my skin. I close my eyes, resting my head along the back of the tub and give myself a brief spell to catch my bearings.

When I open my eyes Matteo is observing me intently. I lift my hand rubbing his dirty face with mixed emotions.

"You need to clean up, Matteo. I can't bear to see you like this."

My voice haunts the room with sorrowful agony. He places his hand over mine giving me a once over before nodding. He steps away, turning on the shower and stripping himself.

Once fully nude he opens the door to the steamy water and finally takes care of himself. He washes all the blood and dirt away. The shower floor is a whirl of black and red and I'm reminded of what he had experienced as well today. Is this all because of me? My heart hurts in ways I wish I didn't know.

When Matteo is all done, he turns the shower off, returning to me. I scoot forward against the smooth bottom of the tub allowing room for him to slip in. His body presses against mine and I avoid the shoulder that was just repaired. His hand finds my hair and I hum, caving into the feeling.

"I'm sorry, Matteo, it's all my fault."

"Don't ever say that again. This is not your fault."

"I didn't know, Matteo, I'm sorry. I wouldn't have left the room."

I feel Matteo's head shake behind me.

"Bella, prenderei un milione di proiettili per assicurarmi che tu sia felice." Beautiful, I would take a million bullets to make sure you are happy.

My heart flutters at his words, unable to keep myself contained. Tears threaten against my lids.

"I love you, Matteo," I whisper loud enough for him.

"Il mio cuore ti appartiene amore mio." My heart belongs to you, my love.

27

Giovanni

I sit at Gwenevere's bedside, watching as she lays peacefully. IVs and monitors are attached to each arm. She is safe. The baby is safe.

I file through the last couple of days in my mind. There has been no time for me to process each event. I don't have a choice but to get my shit together and throw on the best mask I have. I have to. For Gwenevere, the baby, the *Famiglia*.

It's all up to me now.

Matteo is dead. The attack came from nowhere. We were so focused on aligning the families we fell short of securing our safety. Gwen and Matteo were hit in one swoop. She was the only one to make it out—her and the baby. Pure luck was on her side, whether for the simple fact, I was there in time or not.

My brother, my Don, did not hold her luck. Bruno and Viktor managed to escape with their lives, but Matteo died on impact. I've been locked in this room with Gwen, refusing to leave her side. She has yet to become fully conscious muttering random bits here and there as if her mind can't process that Matteo is in fact gone.

Viktor has stepped up to keep security high, reviewing surveillance with any hopes of finding anything that looks off. I am involved as well, but my focus lies with Gwenevere. Alessio has spent a lot of time at the estate checking in and keeping an eye on her, long enough for me to get some shut-eye and a lick of food. He insists on her returning 'home' but the Luciano estate is no longer her home. This is her home, I am her home. She decided long before, whether merely for the baby or Matteo. I believe I am as big of a factor as them.

Her words ring through my ears as I stare at her paled face. *"The Genoveses have become family."*

I am her family and she is mine. I trace my fingers along her hand, thanking the stars that I at least have her. I know it's selfish and the last thing I should be thinking about and I curse myself for it—from the moment I laid eyes on her in that elevator, I've been obsessed with her. Her plush lips and doe eyes. She is captivating with a need to wrap her in my arms and take all the pain and all the bullshit off of her.

I can't decide if I was angry or simply disappointed when Matteo caught her gaze. As if she was hypnotized, but to ever stand against Matteo? I crushed my obsession deep down, hiding it to the best of my ability. Longing for her in all our moments. I hate—and love—her need to confide in me, as if I am the only one she is truly comfortable to embrace all her true feelings with.

What did I do? I helped their relationship grow, while only leaving soft warnings to her that Matteo wasn't meant to give her what she needed. To give her what she truly wants. Maybe it was her recent trauma that pulled her into Matteo's grasp. But fuck me if I didn't hate him for ever laying eyes on her. I curse the phone call he made to me that day in the coffee shop. If he had never called, she would've chosen me instead.

I hate myself for wishing it at all; he's dead. I should be reflecting on all our proud memories I have but I can't help but wonder if now Gwenevere is mine. She Is, and the fucking bastards that put her here better hope they can hide. The moment she wakes and is back to my healthy Baby Girl, I will search every corner of the earth to destroy them. I'll make sure their existence is erased through a slow, sweet burn.

There will be revenge for her, the baby, and for my brother.

About The Author

Even as a young child Alicia would conjure up stories in her imagination, sharing them with anyone who would listen. She developed her storytelling since then, but the thrill of language and creation since she first discovered it as a child has never gone away.

Alicia has been writing professionally since 2021 and has no intention of slowing down anytime soon.

Lets Get Social

Facebook: Alicia Amberg Auhtor

Instagram: @aliciaambergauhtor

TIkTok: @aliciaambergauthor

aliciaambergauthor@gmail.com

457

In honor of my Aunt Beatrice (Aunt Bea) and giving me my love for books. You would've loved this book.